*Book 5
of the
Cornish Chronicles Series*

The Glittering Sea

Ann E Brockbank

Copyright © The Glittering Sea

by Ann E Brockbank

First published in Great Britain as a paperback in 2018

Copyright © 2018 Ann E Brockbank

The moral right of Ann E Brockbank to be identified as the author of this work has been asserted in accordance with the Copyright, Designs and Patents Act 1988

All rights reserved. No part of this publication may be reproduced, stored in a retrieval system or transmitted in any form or by any means, (electronic, mechanical, photocopying, recording or otherwise) without the prior written permission of the publisher. Any person who does any unauthorised act in relation to the publication may be liable to criminal prosecution and civil claims for damages.

The Glittering Sea is a work of fiction. Names, characters, businesses, places, events or incidents are either a product of the author's imagination or are used fictitiously. Any resemblance to actual persons, living or dead, events or locales is purely coincidental.

Front cover by © R W Floyd, from an original oil painting

All rights reserved.

ISBN-13: 978-1720646815
ISBN-10: 1720646813

The Glittering Sea

To Kate,

a very special friend

By Ann E Brockbank

Cornish Chronicles Series

1. A Gift from the Sea – 1901 - 1902
2. Waiting for the Harvest Moon - 1907-1908
3. My Song of the Sea -1911 -1912
4. The Path We Take – 1912
5. The Glittering Sea – 1912 – 1919

Historical Novels

Mr de Sousa's Legacy – 1939 – 1960

Contemporary Novels

The Blue Bay Café
On a Distant Shore

ACKNOWLEDGEMENTS

Researching this book has taken many hours and has been both harrowing and humbling. My gratitude goes to the national archives and the BBC - I learnt a great deal from these sites.

As always, I couldn't have written this book without the help and support of some very special people. To Cathy, who not only puts the commas in the right places, but also reins in my creative spelling. To Wendy, for always being the first person to read the finished manuscript and to Roger for answering random queries about apostrophes. I am enormously grateful to you all. Your sensitive editorial suggestions have improved the book enormously.

To my beloved partner Rob - your love and encouragement has kept me writing, and your beautiful artwork always adds a special quality to my novels.

To the amazing staff at Poldhu Café, Mullion, for supporting me by selling my books locally.

To my darling late husband Peter. You were there at the start of my writing journey, and you always believed in me. You are in my heart forever.

To my special friend Kate, although you are four hundred miles away, we are never far from each other. This novel about friendship is dedicated to you.

Most importantly, I'd like to thank every single reader who selected my story to read. If you enjoyed this book, I would be enormously grateful if you could leave a review on Amazon. This helps other readers find me.

Last but not least, my gratitude is extended to all those brave men and women who gave their lives in WW1 so that we can live in relative peace.

'We will remember them.'

ABOUT THE AUTHOR

Ann E Brockbank was born in Yorkshire, but has lived in Cornwall for many years. The Glittering Sea is Ann's fourth novel. Her first novel, Mr de Sousa's Legacy, was published in July 2013. The Blue Bay Café, was published in May 2015. On a Distant Shore was published October 2016. Her inspiration comes from holidays and retreats in stunning locations in Greece, Italy, Portugal, France and Cornwall. When she's not travelling, Ann lives with her artist partner on the beautiful banks of the Helford River in Cornwall, which has been an integral setting for all of her novels. Ann is currently writing her fifth novel.

Ann loves to chat with her readers so please visit her Facebook Author page and follow her on Twitter and Instagram

Facebook: Ann E Brockbank.Author
Twitter: @AnnEBrockbank1
Instagram: annebrockbank

The Glittering Sea

Prologue

Sunday 8th December 1912

The cottages of Gweek were lit by the amber light of the late afternoon sunset, but in the shadows a frill of frost formed on the piles of dry chestnut leaves accumulating by the river bridge.

It was a peaceful scene - high tide lapped the river bank, boats stilled, due to lack of breeze, and the good people of Gweek stood chatting, enjoying the last embers of sunshine.

Jory Trevone's cottage was situated at the bottom of Chapel Hill, near the centre of the village. Inside was beamed, whitewashed and scrupulously clean. A Dundee marmalade jar stood centre place on the scrubbed pine table, displaying the very last of the fragrant red roses. Although a good fire roared in the grate, Jory shivered uncontrollably as his unexpected visitor glowered down at him.

'You'll do it tonight!' George Blewett slammed his hand on the kitchen table, upsetting the jar of roses.

The tiny room seemed to crackle with tension, as Jory felt Blewett's threat pulsate through his body.

'I'll hear no more of your bloody excuses. You'll do it tonight, Jory. All right?' Blewett's piggy eyes flashed furiously.

Dodging the mucus which sprayed from Blewett's flared nostrils and deeply aware of an alarming movement within his bowels, Jory swiftly nodded.

Blewett straightened up, sneering at the smell of Jory's fear. He smoothed his waistcoat over his ample stomach and adjusted his bowler hat. 'Tonight... otherwise you know what will happen!'

As the front door slammed in Blewett's wake, quietness ensued but for the tick of the clock and the spit of the fire. Reaching out, he up-righted the marmalade jar, leaving the damaged roses without water. *Oh my god, what have I done?*

Feeling his throat thicken, he clawed his fingers down his cheeks, as a wave of nausea sent him staggering to the stone sink to be violently sick.

1
Four months earlier

The port of Gweek was located at the head of the Helford River, the furthest navigable point on this tidal river. Settled in a deep sheltered valley, Gweek's rich, arable, fertile land yielded fine crops of barley, corn and wheat. The harbour itself thrived, exporting tin and copper from the mines in nearby Wendron, and barges of coal and timber sailed up the river to run these mines. Today the bridge at the centre of Gweek was crowded with noisy well-wishers, dressed in their Sunday best, waiting in the hot August sunshine to send the newly-weds off to their new life, thirty miles away in Charlestown.

Taking shade under a great chestnut tree, Jenna Trevone hugged her good friends Kate and Stephen, before they climbed aboard the wedding wagon festooned with flowers and ribbons. Happy and sad in equal measure, tears bubbled into her throat, fearing she would never see Kate again.

'Don't cry, Jen,' Kate smiled reassuringly. 'I'll write to you. Just as soon as we're settled, I promise.'

With one last tearful embrace, Jenna reluctantly released her hold on Kate. 'You take care of each other now.'

Settling themselves on the wagon, the happy couple turned and waved amid a chorus of cheers.

'It'll be your turn next, Jen. Here, catch,' Kate said, throwing her posy of flowers to her.

Through a veil of tears, Jenna held the posy to her chest, waving enthusiastically until the wagon was out of sight.

Aware of a peal of laughter from the crowd behind her, Jenna turned and shuffled back a step, shocked to find four young village lads knelt on one knee, gazing at her hopefully.

'Take your pick maid, you've got them all swooning

over you,' Charlie Williams shouted, his arm clasped around his sweetheart, Lizzy Pike.

Knowing the lads well, having all grown up together, didn't stop the blush rising on Jenna's cheeks, or the nervous embarrassment simmering in her stomach as the first of them addressed her.

Clasping his hands hopefully to his chest the lad pleaded, 'Oh, Jenna, sweet Jenna, let it be me.'

The crowd, fuelled with ale, whooped with laughter.

'No, Jenna,' said another, shoving the first lad into the dust. 'You must marry me, for you are my heart's desire.'

Despite her embarrassment Jenna smiled

'Look at her the hussy,' Minnie Drago sneered, her arms resting on her amble bosom. 'She's pretending not to enjoy every moment of the attention.'

Stung by Minnie's harsh words, Jenna dropped the smile, until Lizzy Pike from the dairy jumped to her defence.

'Oh, shut your claptrap, Minnie - you miserable old busy body,' Lizzy scolded. 'You know full well that Jenna is no hussy.'

Minnie lifted her chin. 'How dare you call me that? Your mother will hear of this.'

'My mother would agree,' Lizzy retorted, and the crowd laughed.

'Well said, Lizzy.' Charlie Williams crinkled his eyes at her.

Minnie Drago scowled darkly, and the laughter abated and silence fell as the third lad shuffled on his knees closer to Jenna.

'Jenna my sweet, you don't want him, he has a face like a pie crust. A beautiful girl like you needs a handsome man like me.' He winked cheekily.

'And he's modest with it as well, Jenna,' Charlie Williams shouted, causing a ripple of mirth.

Finally, the fourth lad produced a bunch of daisies. 'Jenna, forget the others. I believe you need a strong man like me to care for you.' He flexed his arm muscles for all to see. 'What do you say, Jenna, will you marry me?' He asked earnestly.

Jenna, flushing now to the roots of her hair, hid behind her posy of flowers.

'Come on maid, who's it going to be?' someone shouted.

Seeing her neighbour Amelia Pascoe in the crowd, Jenna shot her a 'help me' look.

Clapping to get everyone's attention, Amelia pushed through the crowd. 'All right, get off your knees lads and leave the maid be. If Jory Trevone sees you, he'll scat the lot of you.'

Amid a collective groan the lads reluctantly stood up.

'Go on, be off with you all.' Amelia shooed them away.

The lads bowed graciously to Jenna, retreating with a chortle of laughter towards The Black Swan.

With the entertainment over, the crowd dispersed. Amelia regarded Jenna with affection. 'You are your mother's daughter, Jenna - god rest her soul. She too was a beauty and the men swarmed around her like bees to a honey pot. The other girls didn't have a chance until your mother set her sights on Jory.'

Jenna nodded sadly. 'It seems father only had eyes for her too. I don't believe he ever got over her death.'

'Well, thank goodness he had you!' Amelia regarded her thoughtfully. 'However, you're at an age where it's time to make your own life. Have any of the lads caught your eye?'

Jenna bit her lip pensively. 'They're all very sweet, but no, I have yet to meet the man who catches my eye.'

'Well, god help him whoever he is,' Amelia said with a sigh, 'for he'll have the envy of every young man in this village to deal with.'

*

Finding her father absent from the cottage, Jenna put Kate's posy in a jar, grabbed her drawing book, and still in her Sunday best clothes, walked up to the top meadow which was situated behind their cottage. As she skimmed the edge of the field, a thicket of brambles choked the wild flowers in the hedgerows, and though there was a promise of another two months of summer in Cornwall, posies of un-ripened blackberries hinted that autumn was just around the corner.

The long, sweet-smelling grass was thick enough for her to hide in for a few precious minutes. The air was hot, and her thin dress clung uncomfortably to her damp skin. Laying her shawl on the ground, she knelt down to enjoy the shade and solitude.

In the distance, a man worked relentlessly on the hedge he was laying. Jenna turned onto her stomach and from her vantage point, watched him at work, weaving and laying branches to resemble woven cloth. Unable to define his features, other than he was tall, matched against the height of the hedge, Jenna wondered if his hair was really burnished copper or was it just the reflection of sunshine on it.

The heat made him punctuate his hand movements with swift wipes across his forehead with the sleeve of his shirt. After watching him for a few moments more, Jenna turned over and began to draw - as she did for a few stolen moments most afternoons. Eventually, the gentle hack hacking sound from the hedger, the still heat, the bees buzzing lazily overhead, and all other sounds of the countryside blurred, and Jenna was lulled into a slumber.

'Excuse me, Miss?'

Jenna woke with a start. Easing herself onto her elbows, she blinked furiously into the brightness to find a figure looming over her.

'Begging your pardon, Miss, I didn't mean to startle you. It's just that someone is shouting for someone called Jenna down in the valley. I thought perhaps they might be looking for you.'

Instantly recognising the figure before her as the hedger she'd been watching, Jenna was mesmerised for a moment. He was tall and young, his skin glistened from the heat of the day, and as predicted, his hair shone with golden autumnal colours, wisps of which stuck to his damp temples.

'Oh, goodness! What time is it?'

'It's a quarter to five,' he answered, reading the fob watch from his waistcoat pocket. 'May I?' He held his hand out to help her up.

Taking it gratefully, she felt his large fingers curl around her soft hand squeezing gently as he pulled her to her feet. She could still feel the warm dryness of his skin on hers after he released her.

He bent down to pick up her drawing book as she brushed the grass from her best dress. She took the book from his hand, meeting his gaze. The look they exchanged caught her breath. He had a strong jawbone, slightly darkened with the makings of a beard, but it was his generous smile which set a tingle in Jenna's heart.

'Thank you, sir.'

'You're very welcome,' he said graciously. He bowed his head slightly. 'Lyndon FitzSimmons, at your service.'

She grinned at his gallantry. 'Jenna Trevone,' she answered, dropping a small curtsy.

'*Jenna!*' A shout rang out from down in the valley. '*Where the devil are you, girl?*'

Jenna pulled a face. 'That'll be father, wanting his tea. I'd better go. It was nice meeting you Mr FitzSimmons.'

'Likewise, Miss Trevone.'

*

Lyndon watched her run down the field, her golden hair glinting in the soft afternoon light. At the gate, she turned and waved and then she was gone. His eyes moved to the flattened grass where she'd lain. In his mind's eye he conjured her image as he had found her a few moments before, remembering the unexpected flutter in his stomach at the initial sight of her. With her being totally unaware of his presence, he had the liberty to observe her secretly for a few moments, to marvel at her creamy complexion, tinged pink at her nose and cheeks from the sun. Her full rosy lips, slightly open as she slept, made him moisten his own parched lips. He returned to his work - unable to keep the smile from his face that afternoon.

*

When Jenna entered the cottage, her father said nothing, but glanced at the clock with a withering look. Slicing some cold ham onto bread, she slathered it with mustard and cut it into squares. A small cut tomato sat alongside the plate, though she knew her father would leave it uneaten. When the kettle on the stove boiled, she mashed some tea, placed the plate in front of him and sat down opposite. There was rarely any conversation between them. Jenna had promised her dying mother that she'd look after her father, so she continued to keep house for him, though her efforts went largely unacknowledged. Her father said little to anyone nowadays, though he took himself off to The Black Swan every evening with George Blewett.

Jenna thought Blewett was a strange drinking companion. Blewett was a bad tempered, hard drinking man, quite unlike her father's own gentle temperament, but their strange friendship, if that's what you could call it, had been constant since her mother had passed away ten years ago. Jenna didn't begrudge her father the company, though she herself felt uncomfortable in Blewett's presence. From an early age, she'd been constantly aware of his lustful gaze, often wondering why her father didn't check him for it, but then again, he seemed not to notice anything. So, Jenna learned to keep her eyes averted from Blewett's - otherwise her skin would crawl under his gaze.

*

After tea, Jory sat behind the newspaper, though he read not a word, his thoughts were on his daughter. Surreptitiously watching Jenna as she moved around the kitchen, it frightened him to see his little girl blossom into a beautiful young woman. Every time he looked at her, it conjured up the image of his darling wife, Elizabeth, god rest her soul - the memory stung his heart. Watching Jenna's delicate fingers tie a green ribbon in her long flaxen hair to keep it from falling forward, Jory wished with all his heart she would cover it completely. It was her crowning glory, and he knew she was much admired by the boys in the village. That fact worried him immensely. The thought brought on a griping pain in his stomach - though he knew she was a good girl. She kept the house well and did her chores, but whenever she ran off in the afternoon, oh, my goodness, how he worried about who she might meet. More often than not, he knew she was just going to draw, as was her girlish fancy. But in truth, the time was drawing near for her to be wed. She'd be eighteen next month. He trembled again knowing he couldn't ward off the dreadful day much longer. Slowly he laid down the newspaper to steady his hands and closed his eyes to blank out the future.

*

Later, in her tiny box bedroom, Jenna lay sleepless atop her bed. The night was uncomfortably hot, even the window pushed wide open gave no relief to the airless room. Eventually conceding to wakefulness, Jenna sighed and placed her arms behind her head. A broad smile formed on her lips as she thought of Mr FitzSimmons - his strong jaw line, his kind eyes, green, as were hers, and that smile, oh that smile had melted her heart. Though she'd spent no more than a couple of minutes in his company, the way he'd looked at her and the touch of his hand in hers had stirred something deep inside her. It was a warm feeling and not at all unpleasant.

*

Lyndon settled himself down next to his wagon. On hot nights like these he would rather sleep under the stars, than the back of his stuffy wagon. His horse, Bramble was hobbled nearby, snuffling happily to itself. The grass beneath Lyndon was soft with moss, and scuffles in the hedgerows told him he would not be alone. All was well with the world. As a master hedger, Lyndon's services were much sought after, and he spent many nights on the road. His job often took him from his home on the beautiful Trevarno Estate near Helston, where his father was head gardener. The estate was owned by local gentry Andrew and Eleanor Bickford. Growing up there, Lyndon had often played together with their son Matthew. The two had become great friends and it was due to Matthew that Lyndon secured much of his work in and around the other grand estates in Cornwall. For that he was truly grateful.

As he lay quietly, he caught sight of a fox in the moonlight as it fought its way through the nearby hedge. The creature paused, sniffed the air, and realising someone was nearby, darted off down the wheat field. Accustomed to spending his nights in the company of wild animals, Lyndon would often wake to find some small, damp nose quizzically snuffling at his body. With the moon three-quarters full tonight, it would not go truly dark - maybe he wouldn't have too many nocturnal visitors.

Yawning noisily, tired with the heat and physical work of the day, he closed his eyes as the image of Jenna danced back into his mind. Was she sleeping? Was her lovely hair spread across a down pillow? He sighed, remembering her soft lips parted slightly as she slept. She looked beautifully peaceful in her nest of grass under the warmth of the sun. 'Goodnight lovely, Jenna,' he whispered into the night.

2

The humidity from the night formed ribbons of early morning mist over Gweek making the air thankfully cooler.

Jenna, up early as always, emerged from the Corn Mill, situated at the south side of the village, with a stone of freshly ground flour carried in the skirt of her apron.

'Good morning to you, Jenna,' Matthew Bickford called out, as he rode his horse down Gweek Drive. He drew to a halt and dismounted.

Matthew was gentry, but there had never been any airs and graces between these two young people, though it didn't stop Jenna from dropping a cheeky curtsy.

'Good morning to you, Matthew. I take it you're staying with the Vyvyan's at Trelowarren?'

'I am,' he said, falling into step beside her. 'I'm here for the shooting.' He glanced at the load in her apron she was taking care not to drop. 'Can I assist you, my dear?'

'No, I'm fine thank you. I'm just heading home to make my bread.'

With a gentle clop of the horse's hooves, they approached the first rise after the bridge. Matthew grinned mischievously. 'I've no doubt you know where I'm heading this fine morning.'

'Well now, let me guess.' Jenna twisted her mouth. 'Dr Eddy's house for breakfast perhaps?'

Matthew laughed. 'Am I really so predictable?'

'Do they not feed you at Trelowarren?'

'They do indeed, and very heartily I must say, but there is nothing to match Mrs Tankard's breakfast. The good doctor has a fine cook there. It'll set me up for the ride back to Trevarno later today.'

Jenna grinned, as they parted at the gates of Dr Eddy's house. 'Enjoy your breakfast, Matthew.'

'Almost certainly, I will. Good day to you Jenna.'

Back home, Jenna busied herself baking bread. Once

the loaves were cooling, she set about scrubbing the kitchen floor, faster than normal. With her father out fishing until the evening tide brought him back, Jenna was keen to complete her chores, then the day would be her own. A flutter of excitement ensued - she knew exactly where she intended to spend her day.

Grabbing her hat and drawing equipment, she gave the kitchen a once over glance before stepping out into the dazzling sunshine. Hopeful of another encounter with Mr FitzSimmons, she felt a pang of disappointment when he was nowhere to be seen. Sighing audibly, she sat in the long grass, grabbed her drawing book and held her pencil poised and ready. Glancing at the hedge where Lyndon had been working, she sighed again, put her book and pencil to one side and walked to the very spot. Slowly following the beautifully weaved hedge along, she marvelled at the intricacy of the work. Careful not to snag her fingers on any thorns, she traced the woven branches Lyndon's hands had so painstakingly placed. So intent on her task, she was unaware of the person standing on the other side of the hedge.

'You approve of my workmanship then?'

Startled at the sound of his voice, she took a step back. A moment later he appeared by the stile further up the field. At the sight of him, Jenna felt aware of a sudden sensitivity never experienced before. She watched as Lyndon pulled the wide brimmed leather hat from his head, letting his auburn hair fall loose at his neck. He adjusted his neckerchief as though to tidy himself, and from the smile on his face he looked as happy to see her as she him.

'We meet again, Miss Trevone.'

Momentarily lost for words, Jenna nodded, smiling brilliantly.

'Forgive me. I seemed to be always startling you.'

Lyndon's easy manner made her relax slightly. 'I was engrossed in admiring your work.'

'So I see. I came back to check on it myself. I'm working at the top of the next field at the moment, but I often return to my last job, to make sure nothing has come out of place.'

'I see,' she breathed, mesmerised at how his eyes twinkled as he spoke. She didn't realise for a moment that he'd spoken to her again.

'Miss Trevone?'

'Sorry,' she said, shaking herself from her reverie.

'I was just saying that I notice you like to sketch. Do you ever come to the upper field to draw?'

Delighted to find someone interested in her drawings, she answered, 'I do yes, but the wheat is high and almost ready to harvest. I don't like to trample on the crops. Hence, I'm relegated to the hay meadow for the time being.' She swept her hand towards the long grass.

He nodded. 'It's just that there is such a lovely view of the river from where I'm working - I wondered if you'd ever captured it?'

With a frisson of excitement, she answered, 'I have indeed. I've often thought the village is best viewed from the hills surrounding it. You get a fine prospect of the great oak forests flanking the river, and of course peace prevails away from the bustle of industry down there. I've done several sketches,' she paused for a moment before asking, 'would you like to see them?'

'I'd be honoured,' he said gratefully.

Following her to where she'd left her bag, Lyndon was entranced by the gentle sway of her long golden blonde hair tumbled down her back from under her hat. He watched her slender fingers flip through the pages before she offered the book to him. As he took it from her, he felt a strange sensation as their fingers brushed gently against each other.

The pages of her book were divided into quarters, so each sketch was quite small, but intricately drawn. 'You have a good eye Miss Trevone,' he said appreciatively, 'may I look at some more?'

Jenna was thrilled, she'd never shown her drawings to anyone before and felt delight at Lyndon's reaction to them.

Sitting down near her rug, he flipped through the pages. Presently she too sat down beckoning him to share the rug with her as she pointed out all the places she'd drawn.

The sketches were a perfect representation of the fields, views, bridges, stiles and Cornish hedges he was so familiar with around Gweek.

'Forgive me for asking but why do you divide all your pages into four? Your drawings would look wonderful on a larger scale.'

'Paper is a rare commodity,' Jenna answered wistfully, 'so when I am lucky enough to have some, I have to make it last. My drawing book was a birthday gift from my neighbour, Amelia Pascoe. She very kindly buys me one each year. I've learnt to draw with care, so I'm able to use both sides of the paper.'

Lyndon smiled gently. 'You must be thankful for having such a nice neighbour.'

'I am, but Amelia is more than a neighbour. She's been like a mother to me since my own died ten years ago.' As she spoke a frown formed on Lyndon's forehead and she instantly wished she hadn't spoken about her sadness.

Presently he turned towards her, his eyes were gentle and so was his tone. 'I'm sorry to learn about your mother. It's a great loss to any child, especially one as young as you were. I too lost my mother, though mine was more recent. It's a heart-breaking time, isn't it?'

It seemed quite a natural gesture to lay her hand on his in comfort. Gently he cupped his over hers and they smiled together amiably before pulling away from each other.

The day was still and hot. A Woodpecker arduously hammered a tree trunk in the nearby woods. Both seemed quite content to sit in the meadow knee-high with wild flowers and while away the time. Lyndon cradled his legs with his arms and looked out towards the river. 'Do you have to rush off?' he asked.

'No, not today,' she answered shyly.

'Then I have a mind to go and fetch some bread and barley water from the wagon, if you'd like to share it with me. My work can wait a while.' He grinned.

As they shared the simple fare, Jenna, when prompted, told Lyndon about her beautiful, talented mother.

'Our cottage was always full of love and laughter,' Jenna said, her heart lifting at the memory. 'She'd sing as she taught me to cook and sew, and when all chores were done, we would sit in these meadows, and she'd teach me to draw.'

'She's left you a great legacy then.'

'Yes.' Jenna smiled brilliantly.

'How did she die?'

Even now, the memory of that day clouded Jenna's eyes. 'She fell and banged her leg in the chicken coop one evening. I remember there was little to see except a slight swelling. She went to bed but felt quite ill the next morning. Amelia and the doctor were called, and she died quite unexpectedly later that day.'

Lyndon took a moment before he spoke. 'I am sorry for you Jenna. Tell me, do you ever draw your mother from memory?'

Jenna shook her head.

'It may help. I think about my mother as I am weaving my hedges. I feel I'm integrating her memory into the countryside I know she loved so much.'

'Oh!' Jenna put her hand to her heart. 'What a nice thing to do for her.'

The afternoon sun bathed the village in warm amber light. Eventually, the cry of gulls overhead warned Jenna that the tide would soon bring her father home. Reluctantly they had to part.

'I shall be at the top of the wheat field for the next few days. Maybe you would like to come and draw another picture of the view. There is a two-yard path right around the field, so you could sit there without damaging any of the crops. I should very much like to see you again.' He smiled hopefully as he got up off the rug.

'I'd like that too,' she said sincerely, as she took his offer of a helping hand up.

When they reached the stile, the intimacy of the afternoon fell away and suddenly everything felt very formal again.

'Goodbye, Mr FitzSimmons, I've had a lovely afternoon.' Jenna tentatively held out her hand for him to shake it.

He took her hand in his and just held it. 'I'd rather you called me Lyndon… now that we're friends.'

Jenna lowered her eyes. 'Then you must call me Jenna.'

'Jenna is such a lovely name,' he said still holding her hand, 'I do believe the name is a shortened version of Genevieve. It means 'fair lady'. A rather apt name for you I think.'

Jenna felt her cheeks pink.

'Until tomorrow then Jenna, my fair lady,' he said happily.

'Yes, until tomorrow,' she answered. Hardly able to contain her joy, Jenna set off down the lane, only to be called back a moment later.

'If by chance I'm called away to another job, as sometimes happens, I'll leave you a note in here.' Lyndon removed a loose stone in the wall. 'I found this hidey-hole yesterday,' he said. 'It's a perfect place to leave notes, don't you think? I wouldn't want you to come all the way up to the wheat field to find I'm not there.'

'No, Lyndon, neither would I,' she answered softly.

3

The next day, en route to the wheat field, Jenna stopped and checked the hidey hole, fearful of a note to tell her Lyndon would not be there. Her heart fell. There was a note, but as her fingers reached in they also found a posy of wild flowers. The gesture caught her breath. She unfolded the letter slowly and smiled.

Looking forward to seeing you again today. L

With joy in her heart, she tucked the posy into her belt and set off up Chapel Hill as fast as her legs could carry her. At the stile to the field, she stood with her hands resting on her thighs trying to regain her breath before climbing over.

'Let me help you.'

Lyndon had appeared at the other side of the granite stile. The curve of his mouth twitched slightly before he broke into a smile as he reached out to her. Jenna felt her pulse race, as she slipped her hand in his, wondering if he too could feel the tingle running through her body as he helped her over the stile. Her feet landed on the soft grass, intimately close to Lyndon, but he did not step back. His eyes crinkled, as he gazed at her, making her lower her eyes shyly.

Slightly flustered, Jenna walked over to pat Lyndon's horse. 'She's lovely, Lyndon.' Saying his name felt strange though she had spoken it to herself over and over again during the morning.

Glancing up from where he'd resumed his work he said, 'Her name is Bramble and she's a big softy. She'll stand and let you stroke her all day if you've a mind.'

Jenna gave Bramble a rub on her nose and then settled down to draw. The view was indeed fine from this vantage point, but Jenna's artistic eye was firmly on Lyndon's strongly built body. The muscles in his arms, bare from wrist to elbow, flexed and tightened as he wielded his bill hook. Jenna sketched him quickly before he caught her watching. Eventually she turned her attention to Bramble and the wagon, and by the time he stopped for refreshment had something she felt she could give Lyndon. Unprecedented, she'd filled a whole page with her drawing and as she was about to leave, tore it out to offer it up as a gift to him in thanks for the posy.

'Jenna, this is wonderful, thank you. You will come again tomorrow?' Lyndon asked, as he helped her back over the stile.

'Yes, but the day after, father isn't able to go fishing as the tides are too late. He'll work an early shift at the wood yard until the tide is right again, so I'll not be able to get away as easily.'

'That's a shame. We'll make tomorrow memorable then. For I too have to go away the week after next. I have work on the Trelowarren Estate, but I will be back at the end of August.' There was a hint of sadness in his voice at the thought of their parting.

*

On the thirty-first of August, the weather changed. Jenna stood at her open bedroom window. The stillness of the evening felt oppressive, but it was clear a storm was brewing. Though it was dark, she recognised the shape of her father as he staggered out of The Black Swan. Once a tall proud man, Jory Trevone's shoulders stooped as though he held the worries of the world on them. He drank too much, and this showed in his once handsome face. Puffy skin and purple nosed, Jenna worried for his health, and how he afforded to drink to such extent every day. The Trevones were living on the breadline. The money Jory made from his fishing trips barely covered the daily needs of the household. Jenna herself made a little money, selling preserves and eggs, but their joint income could not afford Jenna anything for herself. The clothes she wore were her mother's, altered and fashioned by Jenna's nimble fingers.

Downstairs the front door of the cottage slammed, and

she heard Jory trip and curse - thankfully he wasn't an aggressive drunk, just a sleepy one. Quietness fell on the cottage and Jenna shivered briefly as the cold front preceding the storm gave a welcome breeze. The unbearable heat over the last few weeks had begun to make even the good-natured people of Gweek edgy and irritable, but the break in the weather was not welcomed by all.

*

Farmer Jack Ferris stood with folded arms in the back yard of Barleyfield Farm, listening to the low rumble of thunder in the far distance. He feared and welcomed a storm in equal measure. A downpour would quench the dry parched earth, but if this heralded the end of summer, sustained rain from now until harvest would be disastrous.

*

Lyndon was asleep in his wagon on the Trelowarren Estate when the storm broke. He'd been working there these last five days - tomorrow he would return to Gweek and hopefully see the lovely Jenna again. Due to her father's working shifts, Jenna was unable to slip away to meet him before he'd left for Trelowarren, so they'd been apart for two long weeks. En route, he'd left Jenna a present in the hidey hole of another drawing book– he hoped that she had found it. He smiled inwardly - when he'd placed the book there, he'd found a pot of Jenna's homemade strawberry jam waiting for him. The flavour of the preserve was like tasting a summer day.

A flash of lightning preceded an immediate crack of thunder. The storm was directly overhead. Feeling the sound resonate through his body, Lyndon got up, and dressed only in his shirttail, scrambled out of the wagon and ran to where Bramble was hobbled. As expected, Bramble was wide-eyed and agitated, and her withers shivered as he laid his soothing hands on her. Ever since they'd acquired her, Bramble disliked stormy weather and would make for the nearest shelter at the first rumble.

Unfortunately, they were nowhere near a building to shelter in, so Lyndon un-hobbled her and led her to the back of the wagon, re-hobbled her and unfastened her leather and metal bridle. He slipped a webbing bridle over her nose and pulled her head and neck into the back of the wagon with him. For the duration of the storm, he sat and cradled her head, stroking her mane, softly singing a soothing song.

*

The storm raged for over two hours. It was as though it was stuck in the valley unable to make its way out of the undulating hills. Eventually calmness settled over Gweek allowing people to sleep. When the dawn came, the village steamed as the sun rose, warming the sodden ground. Ribbons of mist curled around the moored boats on the river and a fresh clean earthy smell filled the air.

The windows of Trevone cottage faced east, so the golden morning sun flooded in as Jenna busied herself with her general chores. With bread made, eggs collected and displayed on her selling shelf outside, she was busy making an early batch of bramble jam, when the postman arrived with a letter for her from Kate.

My dearest friend,

We have settled into our new life nicely, though the cottage is small, one up one down. Stephen truly believes it was built for a pygmy, as he bashes his head every time he comes through the door. Still, it looks out onto the harbour and is clean now, and ours for the time being. Stephen has been lucky with work and has found constant employment with the local boat builder. Married life is all I thought it would be. It is so lovely to be mistress of your own home. I hope you find your special someone soon so you too can be mistress of your own house. It goes without saying that I miss you terribly, though my neighbours are lovely - so I am not without people to speak to.

Please write soon with all the news from Gweek.
Love Kate

Jenna smiled. She'd write back that evening and tell

Kate about Lyndon. It was then she heard a horse and wagon trundle into the village. Her heart lifted as Bramble came into view. The wagon passed Trevone cottage and began its ascent up Chapel Hill. Lyndon smiled when he saw her and doffed his hat. He was back! Her heart filled with joy as she glanced at her new drawing book. Inside was a note from Lyndon *'Not to be used sparingly.'* She could hardly wait to show him her first full size drawings.

*

By the end of the second week in September, the crops in the field were ready to harvest. But for the recent storm, the summer had been especially dry and sunny, bringing everything to fruition a little sooner than normal.

Lyndon was in the field above the Corn Mill, hacking at a particularly thorny branch. He carefully eased the branch, which in hedging terms was referred to as a 'pleach', down into position, weaving it skilfully into the adjoining growth. It was incredibly warm again today. Trickles of sweat ran down his neck, dampening the ends of his hair. He straightened his back and ran his handkerchief swiftly over the back of his neck. As he pocketed his handkerchief, he saw Jenna walking up the meadow with some conviction. They had met several times since his return, but still the sight of her sent a happy shiver down his spine. Removing his hat as he always did to greet her, he noted her face was pink with exertion as she approached.

'Hello, Lyndon,' she said a little breathlessly, pulling a stray wisp of hair away from her face.

'Hello, Jenna.' Carrying neither hat nor drawing bag, he asked, 'Are you not drawing today?'

Holding her hands to her sides to gather her breath she shook her head. 'I've no time today. I've lots to do in the house as I'll be so busy with harvest from tomorrow, but I wanted to ask if you'll be helping with the harvest. Farmer Ferris needs all the hands he can get at Barleyfield Farm.'

'I will indeed. I offered my services to him only yesterday.' Reaching for her hand, he pulled her gently towards him. 'And I'll be asking you for the first dance at the harvest supper afterwards.'

Jenna grinned. 'If the weather stays fine, the harvest should be done in seven days' time, so the harvest supper will fall on my birthday. Dancing with you will be my birthday treat.'

Lyndon's eyes crinkled as he squeezed her fingers gently.

Whenever his hand, though dry and calloused touched her, Jenna felt a tingle of anticipation. Gently turning it over, she inspected his work-worn palm, dotted with splinters. 'Do the splinters not infect your hand?'

Lyndon shrugged. 'Sometimes, if I can't pincer them out with my teeth.' He laughed softly. 'It's an occupational hazard I'm afraid. I'm sorry if they scratched you.'

She gently stroked the palm of his hand and shook her head. 'You didn't.'

Later that day, she left a pot of lanolin in the hidey hole, along with a note:

'Apply liberally. You'll need soft hands to hold me during the dance.'

*

Summer was slipping away. It was almost dawn on the last day of the harvest and the weather had thankfully stayed dry. Everyone gathered that day in a happy mood. The previous six days of fatigue and aching bones were pushed to the very back of everyone's thoughts. Tonight, there would be celebrations at Barleyfield Farm.

For Farmer Ferris and his many helpers, it had been a week of time-consuming activity and sheer hard work. The wheat had been cut by hand with a grain cradle, a type of scythe with long fingers attached on one side. It was a long, laborious task for both cutter and the people who followed them. They'd tie the cut wheat into bundles and then pile them into shocks to dry in the field. After a few days in the sunshine, the bundles had dried enough to be stored in Farmer Ferris's barn until threshing time.

A team of workers in the far top field were finishing off cutting the hay. Jenna was working lower down in the field nearest the farm. She'd seen only glimpses of Lyndon over the week. Everyone felt too tired at the end of each long day for any form of socialising, and most had fallen into a dead sleep at night.

The church bells at Mawgan rang out each day of the harvest, and because Gweek was in a valley, the sound travelled on the still air.

As the dawn broke on the last day, everyone was ready. A team of horses and wagons stood waiting in place as the men took up their positions. Lyndon stood amongst the men of the village and raised a hand to wave at Jenna, and then with a metal husking hook strapped over a leather glove, they all bent in unison and began their work. With smooth, swift movements, each person cut an ear of corn from the stalk, removed the husk and tossed it into the waiting wagon, pulled by a team of horses. To stop any stray ears from missing the wagon, a bang board was attached to the top far side of it. Any that missed the board were retrieved by excited children excused from school to work in the fields. As Jack Ferris walked up and down the rows of corn, his team of horses pulling the wagon moved alongside him. It took all of the morning to fill, but when it was done, everyone rested as the wagonload of corn trundled down to Barleyfield Farm to be put in a corncrib – a large building with slatted sides to dry. The corn would be used to feed livestock on the farm and burned for heat in the kitchen stove, but any extra corn was sold directly to the Corn Mill.

During the rest break, Jenna brought her basket of bread and cheese to sit with Lyndon and they shared their fare with each other. Ale and water were brought to the workers by children, a welcome beverage to whet their dry, parched throats.

As the harvest happened, Jack Ferris would check for seed corn for spring planting. His wily eye could always pick out the very best examples to save, putting them in a special box, attached to the wagon.

When the very last wagon returned to the field for refilling, it was decorated with garlands of flowers and colourful ribbons. And though there were still a few hours of harvesting left, the sight of it lifted everyone's hearts.

As the workers in the field toiled in the heat, the children were busy making corn dollies for the harvest table. The older women of the village had gathered in old Ma Ferris's kitchen to cook for the harvest dinner. Long trestle tables were set out at the front of Barleyfield Farm, draped with white linen bed sheets, and jugs of mead, ale, and barley water stood waiting in the cold pantry. The fire under the hog roast now produced a deep luxurious smell of hot crackling, which wafted temptingly into the fields beyond.

At eight-fifteen, the time came for Jack Ferris to cut the last handful of standing corn. Everyone stood and watched as they waited for the 'Crying of the Neck'. Lifting the bunch high above his head he called out in a loud voice,

'I 'ave 'un! I 'ave 'un! I 'ave 'un!'

Everyone smiled at each other as the rest of the workers shouted, *'What 'ave 'ee? What 'ave 'ee? What 'ave 'ee?'*

'A neck! A neck! A neck!' Jack Ferris called.

Again, everyone joined in shouting, *'Hurrah! Hurrah for the neck! Hurrah for Farmer Ferris!'*

The neck of corn was tossed into the waiting decorated wagon, and everyone gathered their belongings and followed it happily down into the farmyard. Lyndon caught up with Jenna, his hot damp sleeve brushing slightly against hers.

'I should think I'll sleep for a week after today.' He smiled down at her.

'Not before you have danced with me, I hope,' she answered with a twinkle in her eyes.

A small group of players were blasting out a jolly tune on their instruments as everyone approached the front of the farm house. Some, though thoroughly tired, looked for partners to dance with. Lyndon closed his hand over Jenna's, apologising for the roughness of it, and began to whirl her around to the beat of the music. Jenna revelled in his arms - his strong body held firm against her own softness. She gazed into his eyes, lost in the moment. Suddenly there was no-one else in the world except two people who had fallen deeply in love. As the music stopped and they fell out of the dance, the magic of the moment lifted and they laughed joyously.

'Come, let's find a seat so we can eat - I'm famished.' He sat her down and poured a glass of ale for her before moving to the hog roast to fill a plate of steaming pork. He forked half onto Jenna's plate and pulled a hunk of bread from the nearby loaf to pass to her. Lyndon was bone-tired but had never felt happier. The smell of jasmine oil which Jenna often ran through her hair, and the sprig of lavender she wore pinned to her blouse, infused the night with a heady perfume. With a mug of ale in one hand and a plate of pork in the other, he raised a toast to her. 'To you my lovely, Jenna, I shall never forget this wonderful summer.'

When they had eaten their fill, they sat together, joining in with the chatter and listening to the band playing. The benches were full to capacity and Jenna could feel Lyndon's thigh adjacent to hers. From the smile on his face, she knew he too was enjoying the closeness. With a tingle of exhilaration, she felt his hand close over hers, and with a gentle squeeze, their fingers entwined. Jenna realised she should not be so free with him in public, but she was totally and utterly enamoured with him. Nothing could ever take this feeling of happiness away from her.

As the harvest moon rose in the night sky, Jenna noticed the furtive glances from a couple of young men around the trestle table. Remembering them falling to their knees in front of her, she felt a sudden pang of guilt. *What would they think of an outsider like Lyndon stealing her heart away from them?*

'People are watching us Lyndon,' Jenna whispered.

He smiled gently. 'Then they will see that Lyndon FitzSimmons has fallen very much in love with Jenna Trevone.' His expression gave way to purpose. 'Because I have Jenna, I've fallen hopelessly in love with you. You make my life complete.'

Flushed with delight, Jenna tightened her hand around his. 'I love you too, Lyndon.'

'Then would you do me the honour of becoming my wife?'

Everything suddenly became very still, as tears welled in her eyes. 'Oh, Lyndon, the honour would be mine.'

Lifting her hand, he kissed it lightly. 'I'm just so sorry I have to go away in the morning, my love. It breaks my heart to have to leave you, but as you know I'm committed to a job first at Bochym Manor and then on the Tehidy Estate near Camborne. I shall be away initially until the end of November, but when I return, I'll speak to your father. If it pleases you, we'll marry in the spring, when the daffodils are in bloom.'

Jenna nodded through happy tears.

'In the meantime, take a look in our hidey hole. I've left you a birthday gift to help to pass the time.'

Later that night, Jenna found a box of watercolour paints waiting for her. The note attached read: *To colour your world as you have coloured mine.*

4

Sunday December 8th dawned cold but sunny. With growing excitement of seeing Lyndon again, Jenna hardly slept that night. She'd expected him a week ago, checking the hidey-hole every day in anticipation of a note. Yesterday it was there, with his apologies and arrangements to meet.

Always an early riser, Jenna had already polished the furniture, washed the windows and set a great pot of stew on the stove to cook slowly through the day. Hopefully Lyndon would stay for a bite to eat after he'd spoken to her father. After completing her outside chores, she picked the last remaining roses from her mother's garden. There was a particular rose bush that always gave an abundance of blooms. Starting in late June, the fragrant red rose her mother had planted some twenty-years ago had been known to flower at Christmas.

Selecting an empty Dundee marmalade jar from the cupboard, she arranged the blooms in the centre of the kitchen table. They would probably wilt quite quickly in the heat of the room, but hopefully fill the house with fragrance before the petals fell.

Her father glanced at the newly polished room but said nothing as he put his hat on ready for church. 'Are you ready?' he asked Jenna. 'The wagon is here.'

The day was warmer than yesterday and thankfully dry during the mile and half journey to Constantine. The church felt chillier inside than it was outside, and the sermon as usual was slightly too long, making everyone restless to be back in the warmth of their homes.

After dinner, Jory sat by his fireside with his feet on the foot-stool snoring loudly.

Sunday afternoon was always a time for rest, but without fail Jenna took the opportunity to spend these precious hours outside, no matter what the weather. She'd washed her hair the night before and added a few drops of jasmine oil to the water giving it a subtle smell of summer. Changing from her Sunday best into the prettiest outdoor dress she owned, she checked her appearance in the mirror and smiled a secret smile. She was ready.

*

Jenna was a little early arriving in the copse just above Barleyfield Farm. The winter sun dappled the ground as it sparkled through the bare trees. As she picked her way through the peaceful glade in the middle of the copse, the ground felt thick and spongy underfoot with fallen leaves. A robin bobbed from one branch to another singing noisily. Autumn and winter were not Jenna's favourite seasons. She was always sad to see the end of summer, when cool winds and misty mornings swallowed up the heat of the sun. It all had to end though, so it could be reborn in the spring. Fortunately, spring came early in Cornwall, and with the spring would come her wedding to Lyndon. "We will marry when the daffodils are in bloom," he'd told her. She closed her eyes and smiled - she could not wait.

A pair of arms slid around her tiny waist and Jenna sighed and leant back into Lyndon's embrace.

'Hello, my darling girl,' Lyndon whispered into her hair.

Turning slowly to meet his eyes, she smiled joyfully at him.

'I know I should not yet, but I need to kiss you so desperately. Can I kiss you, Jenna?'

Closing her eyes, she lifted her chin and met his lips with hers. His kiss felt soft, and his face was clean shaven, though an odd stray bristle of beard that his blade had missed scratched her slightly, but she didn't mind. His hair, infused with wood smoke from his camp fire, fell forward and tickled her face as Jenna melted into his arms. So lost in the moment was she, her knees buckled slightly when they broke free. Flushed and breathless, Jenna lowered her eyes from his gaze.

'I've missed you so much, Jenna,' Lyndon said softly.

'Every minute of every hour of every day, I've thought of nothing but you. I'm so sorry I was delayed.' He touched the back of her neck and very gently she raised her hand to his.

'You're here now,' she whispered, 'I've missed you too.' She kissed him passionately. Pulling his hand from where it had settled in her hair and kissed his palm. 'Your hands are softer!'

'All thanks to the liberal dollop of lanolin applied last night before bed - as prescribed.' He laughed, gathering her into his arms.

'I've spoken to my father,' Lyndon told her. 'He's happy to welcome you to our home in the spring. Though I'm not sure I can wait that long to take you home. I've also spoken to the Trevarno estate manager, Matthew Bickford, whom I believe is a mutual friend?'

Jenna smiled brilliantly. 'He is, yes.'

'Well, he's delighted to hear our news and said we'll have our own cottage on the estate as soon as one comes up. I do hope your own father won't mind you being so far away. Trevarno is a good nine miles from here! Have you told him about us yet?'

'I'm afraid I haven't yet. He's been in such a strange frame of mind these last few weeks. I really don't know what is wrong with him!' Biting her lip anxiously, she added, 'Lyndon, don't expect too much from my father when you ask him, he's a quiet man of few words, but when he sees how happy we are together, I can see no objection from him.'

'Well let's hope not!'

Leading her to the wall at the end of the copse, they sat and passed a glorious couple of hours, holding hands, exchanging stories and making plans.

*

It was late afternoon. The sun setting in the western sky, bathed the village in a golden hue. The glory of autumn stayed late in Cornwall but with little warmth in the sun now December had arrived, winter was nipping subtly at its heels.

Farmer Jack Ferris was in a reflective mood as he walked through the village to The Black Swan. The harvest was in for the year, threshing finished, and half the swedes lifted. It had been a good year all round, except for the bloody badgers. They had completely destroyed another wall and brought the hedge down above it. He ordered a pint and asked, 'Anyone seen FitzSimmons the hedger these last few weeks? I could do with him to build a hedge up.'

'Badgers again?' Charlie Williams asked.

'Yes. I know they must live somewhere, but the buggers can be so destructive. They actually pulled down the wall itself! There must have been a few of them to do so much damage. I've a great big gaping hole in the top meadow damn it.'

'I'll give you a hand to build the wall up, Jack?' Charlie Williams offered.

'Thank ee, Charlie. Let me get you a drink.'

'Well, you'll be pleased to know FitzSimmons is back and working up at Ted Bolitho's. I saw him earlier today,' Charlie said, handing his glass over for a refill.

'He'll be back to renew his attentions to the Trevone girl as well I'll wager. Lucky bugger,' Jack said with a wink. 'I thought a marriage announcement would come at the end of harvest time. They looked smitten with each other then. I know I wouldn't have waited another ten weeks. I'd have snapped her up straight away.'

George Blewett had heard enough, he slammed his empty glass on the bar, pushed the stool from under him and stormed out of the pub.

A hush came over the crowd at the bar as everyone turned to look at the door George had just exited.

'What's got into him?' Jack asked.

Mary the barmaid thumped her hands into her hips. 'I don't know, but he damn near wrenched the door off its hinges.'

'Ignore him. He's a bad-tempered bugger at the best of times,' Charlie said returning to his pint.

*

The knock on Trevone's cottage door, reverberated enough to make Jory jump out of his slumber. He blinked, checked his watch and looked about the room to see if Jenna was going to answer the door. The knock came again, this time harder. 'All right, all right, don't be breaking my door down,' Jory grumbled, as he tried to make enough saliva to wet his dry stale mouth. As he opened the door, the large figure of George Blewett glowered at him, before pushing him violently back into his own kitchen so that he landed heavily on one of the kitchen chairs.

*

As the afternoon drew to a close, Jenna and Lyndon enjoyed the last few minutes of tenderness.

'Well, my darling girl, I think it's time I went to see your father.' He held his hand out and she took it willingly.

As they walked down Chapel Hill towards the cottage, Jenna released her hand from his. 'Perhaps you'd better not hold my hand as we walk into the village.'

'Well then will you permit me another kiss before we enter civilisation?' He bent towards her, and she responded passionately.

As they approached her cottage, Jory stepped out of the doorway and stopped them in their tracks.

Jenna left Lyndon's side and ran towards him.

'Father, this is Lyndon FitzSimmons, he wishes to speak with you.' She grinned with excitement, but seeing her father's unfriendly demeanour, shrank back from him. 'Father, whatever is the matter?'

Jory glared at Lyndon, his mouth, pinched white and tight twitched angrily.

Sensing Trevone's hostile mood, Lyndon stepped forward to introduce himself. 'Good day to you Mr

Trevone. Forgive this intrusion without forewarning, but I wish to make myself known to you, so I can ask for your daughter's hand in marriage. I....'

'So, it's you who has been so free with my daughter, is it?' he growled.

Lyndon faltered. 'I can assure you, sir, my intentions are honourable.'

'Honourable?' Jory spat the word back at him. 'I've just been told the whole village is talking about you and my daughter, and she is promised to someone else.'

Aghast, Jenna's mouth fell open. 'I am *not* promised to anyone else, Father,' she declared. 'Why do you say such a thing?'

Jory turned on her. 'Get inside now. You should be ashamed of yourself, carrying on with this man behind my back.'

Panic rose in Jenna's throat as she glanced wildly between her father and Lyndon. 'But Father.'

'Get inside, you deceitful girl,' he growled, pushing her forcefully into the cottage, closing the door to keep her there.

'Mr Trevone,' Lyndon stepped forward. 'You're making a mistake. *I* want to marry your daughter.'

Jory grabbed a stick and waved it threateningly. 'You will leave my daughter alone. Do you hear me? She'll be married in the New Year, and *you* shall not soil her reputation again.' He threw the stick down, marched into his cottage, slammed the door and bolted it behind him.

Lyndon stood in disbelief, as Jenna's tragic face appeared at the window. As Lyndon moved towards her, Jory pulled her away from his sight, rudely gesturing him to leave. Scraping his fingers through his hair, Lyndon glanced helplessly around the deserted village. At a loss for what else to do, he walked despondently back up Chapel Hill to his waiting wagon.

*

Jenna wiped her tears with the back of her hand, as Jory

dragged her as far as he could away from the window so that she could not look out.

'I don't understand.' Her voice cracked with emotion shuddering at her father's chilling stare and silence. Reaching out to steady herself against the table, she noted the pool of water next to the jar of battered roses. Every nerve in her body prickled with warning. 'Father, please speak to me. I don't understand why you told Lyndon I was promised to someone else.'

'I will not have you mention that man's name in this house again!' Jory slammed his fist on the table.

Trembling at his unprecedented hostility, she began to cry pitifully. 'But he wants to marry me, Father.'

'You're promised to George Blewett and that's *final!*'

Jenna gasped as she felt her world suddenly tip on its axis. 'George Blewett!' Feeling her chest constrict, she grabbed her father's sleeve. 'No, Father, this can't be true. Tell me it's not true? Please, Father?'

'Enough,' Jory retorted. 'The marriage is arranged and will not be undone.'

Jenna felt feverish. 'How could you?' she hissed, through the narrow aperture of her lips. 'How could you arrange such a thing with a man like him? Have I not been a good daughter to you? Do you not want me to be happy in my marriage like you and mother were? Because marriage to that despicable man will bring me nothing but unhappiness, and *you* know it!' Vomit rose into her throat at the thought of George Blewett's fat lipped mouth and ever lustful eyes. Her hand shot unconsciously to her bosom as though to protect herself. 'Don't do this to me, Father, please don't do this.' She flinched as Jory grabbed her by the arms and shook her violently.

'You stop this nonsense now, you hear me, stop it! George has a good business with the forge, wealth, property, you'll want for nothing.'

'I want Lyndon!'

'Enough.' He pushed her away as though she was

contaminated. 'The banns will be read at Constantine Church over the next three weeks. You'll be married on the 1st of January and *that's* the end of it. You'll not, I repeat *not,* be seeing that hedger again. Do you hear me? I've just heard you've been carrying on with him all summer. George is furious and so am I! You will not go out unaccompanied now until after the wedding. We'll be watching you like a hawk.'

Jenna shuddered with indescribable grief. Eventually she raised her chin in defiance and used the only ammunition on her father that would hurt him deeply. 'Mother would turn in her grave if she knew what you'd done.'

For the first and only time in Jory Trevone's life, he struck his daughter. The force of his hand on the side of her face sent her reeling across the kitchen floor.

Scrambling to her feet, Jenna ran sobbing to her bedroom as Jory sat with his head in his hands. Appalled and sick to the heart at his actions, there was nothing he could do about it. *What's done is done.*

*

The next morning Jenna woke early to someone hammering on the door. Forcing her tear-swollen eyes open she saw from her bedroom window Lyndon standing below. Her heart leapt.

With his jaw set in firm determination Lyndon hammered on the door again. He would not give up without a fight.

'Mr Trevone, please open this door.'

'Be off with you or I'll call the constable,' Jory shouted from within the cottage.

'I need to see Jenna.'

'You've seen enough of her already to ruin her reputation. Now get away from my door.'

'Mr Trevone, I can assure you that your daughter's virtue is intact. My intentions towards her are honourable.'

'Well do the honourable thing and leave her be. She is

promised to another.'

Lyndon stepped back and looked up at the bedroom window to see Jenna's distraught face pressed against the window pane, her cries of despair clearly audible.

5

The news of Jenna's forthcoming wedding began to circulate after the first banns were read the next Sunday. An astonished congregation looked over at Jenna, who sat in bleak desolation with her father.

The general consensus was that she must have fallen pregnant by Blewett - though none could believe she would have gone near him, never mind lay with him!

'I don't believe it for a second,' Amelia bristled, when the news was bantered around The Black Swan later that day.

'Well, why else would she marry the man?' the landlord asked.

Amelia prickled with indignation.

'The notion is ridiculous, and you all know it. Everyone could see Jenna had set her cap at Lyndon FitzSimmons. Something's amiss here, and I'm going to get to the bottom of it.'

After making a few enquiries, Amelia found Lyndon working at the top of Jack Ferris's field.

Lyndon's face was pinched with grief as they sat in the back of his wagon with a mug of tea.

'I've tried to reason with the man. I've been back to the cottage, but he won't let me near her.' He rubbed his face in despair. 'He won't even open the door to me! He just keeps shouting through the door that she's promised to another.' He gave Amelia an anguished look. 'Jenna's distraught - I know she is. I can hear her crying inside the cottage.'

Amelia handed him her empty mug. 'Leave it to me, Lyndon. I'll speak to Jory.'

Lyndon gave a rather gloomy smile - he didn't hold out much hope.

A quarter of an hour later, Amelia hammered on Jory's door.

'What the devil do *you* want woman?' Jory snarled, as he

opened the door to her.

'I want to know what's going on, Jory. What is this nonsense about Jenna marrying Blewett?'

'It's no business of yours, Amelia Pascoe. The maid is promised to George Blewett, and she'll marry him on New Year's Day and that's the end of it!'

He started to close the door on her, but she put her foot in it.

'Where's Jenna, I need to speak with her,' Amelia said, trying to look past Jory.

'Be off with you woman, this is none of your business.'

Amelia stood her ground. 'I'm making it my business Jory Trevone. Elizabeth would never agree to her daughter marrying that brute. As Elizabeth is no longer with us to look out for the maid, I'm doing it for her. Now let me see Jenna.'

Jenna sat at the kitchen table with bated breath.

'She's my daughter and she'll marry who I say,' Jory said, stamping hard on Amelia's foot.

Amelia squealed and jumped back as Jory slammed the door in her face.

He thumped the back of the door. 'Bloody, interfering busybody.' He turned scornfully at Jenna. 'Have you no chores to do?'

Jenna's heart chilled. It was clear now that no-one could help her.

*

Lyndon raked his fingers through his hair, as Amelia told him what had happened. 'Oh god! I have to leave today for another job. I'm expected back at Tehidy tomorrow.'

Amelia pulled a face. 'So, when will you be back?'

'It'll be Christmas week I'm afraid.'

Amelia pondered for a moment, tapping her nails on her teeth. 'We need to get her out of that house somehow. If I put the word out that you've gone, Jory may relax his hold on Jenna. I know he hasn't even been to The Black Swan these past few days, but I do know that Jory Trevone never misses going out on New Year's Eve. If we are going to get her out, then that will be the night to do it.'

Lyndon frowned. 'Isn't that cutting it a bit fine? The wedding is meant to be the day after.'

'I know, but I've never known Jory to miss a New Year's Eve celebration. He's bound to leave her that night. Now listen, I go to my sister's house at Christmas and stay until the New Year, so it'll be down to you to get her away. I suggest you get a special wedding licence and marry the girl as soon as possible afterwards.'

'That's all very well, but how will Jenna get out? He is bound to lock her in. I can hardly break his door down without alerting anyone.'

Amelia smiled knowingly. 'I've seen that girl climb out of her bedroom window and scurry down the wisteria many times after Jory Trevone locked her in, and she got back in without him ever knowing. If Jenna knows you're waiting for her, she'll get out, you mark my words.'

Lyndon allowed himself a small smile at the image. 'But how will you get word to her if her father won't allow you to see her?'

'Jenna feeds the hens every day. I'll leave her a note in the hen-coop. Now, let's sort out where and when you'll meet her!'

*

Amelia watched Trevone Cottage for a few days, noting the movements of the household. The daily routine was that Jenna came out to feed the hens, gather the eggs, and then sweep the front path. All the while Jory stood on guard making sure she interacted with no-one. Over the next couple of weeks Amelia tried several times to place a note for Jenna in the hen-coop, only to be thwarted by somebody passing by. The opportunity arose on Christmas Eve. Amelia thanked the lord, because this was her last chance - she was about to leave to spend Christmas with her sister, and Charlie William's wagon would be here shortly to take her. For once, everyone seemed busy with

Christmas preparations and the village was thankfully deserted. With stealth, she sneaked into Trevone's hen-coop, and left the cryptic instructions Lyndon had written for Jenna.

Minnie Drago in West Wind Cottage, a few doors down from The Black Swan, watched Amelia Pascoe with interest and wondered if she was stealing Jory's eggs. Minnie, a small unpleasant old spinster, with thin white hair and a row of crooked bad teeth was the village busybody. Not a day passed when she did not moan about something or somebody. If she could do someone an ill turn, she would, and everyone kept a healthy distance from her.

She'd taken the news of Jenna Trevone's upcoming nuptials to George Blewett with satisfied pleasure. That should bring the flighty little maid down a peg or two she thought. Having heard that Jory was keeping a watchful eye on his wayward daughter, Minnie also took it on herself to keep watch. There was definitely something shifty about Amelia Pascoe's movements that afternoon though, so Minnie stood behind her curtains for another half an hour. She watched as Charlie Williams stopped his wagon outside Amelia's cottage for Amelia to board it before setting off out of the village. Minnie, unable to contain her curiosity, rushed to get her hat and coat and scurried across the bridge towards Jory's cottage. Her eyes scanned the village to make sure no-one was watching, before she peeked inside the hen-coop. Squinting in the dim light, her eyes caught a flash of white paper in the far corner of the coop. With a satisfied grin, Minnie knocked on Jory's door.

When Jory saw Minnie standing at his door, he began to close it again. She quickly put her hand to the door and hissed at him to step outside.

'What do you want, woman?' he snapped.

Flashing a row of rotten teeth at him, she whispered, 'I thought you'd like to know that Amelia Pascoe has just left a note in your hen-coop.'

'What the devil is she up to now?' Jory pushed Minnie aside as he went to investigate.

Minnie followed, watching with deep satisfaction as he snatched the note from where it was pinned. Stuffing the note in his pocket, he pushed past Minnie and stormed back into the cottage, slamming the door behind him.

By the light of the fire, he read and tried to decipher the cryptic note: NYE6PMCHAPELHILLBAGL. Eventually the first part made sense, New Year's Eve six p.m. Jory's mouth twisted - so, there was a plan afoot, was there?

Jenna gathered the scraps together for the hens and walked to the door. Jory as always was by her side. With an irritated sigh she stepped out into the cold evening, opened the hen-coop, emptied her bowl into the hen's dishes, and then shooed the hens into their home for the night. As she slid the door closed, she saw a folded note, partially hidden in the straw. Quickly grabbing it, she pushed it down the front of her bodice.

Leaving nothing to chance, Amelia had placed two notes, just in case the hens ate one of them.

Trying to calm herself, Jenna walked past her father and back into the warm kitchen. As she began to wash the scrap bowl out, her heart soared - the note must be from Lyndon. Later that evening she read the cryptic note and smiled. It told her that she was to meet Lyndon one week from now at six p.m. on New Year's Eve on Chapel Hill and she was to bring her bag. Jenna could hardly contain her joy.

*

The thirty-first of December dawned cold. A thick ground frost laced the grass verges as Jenna and her father collected the flour from the Mill. With her bread baking, and a pot of stew simmering, she now glanced around the bedroom she'd occupied for the last eighteen-years - everything was ready. Placing only the essentials into her cloth bag she pushed it to the very darkest recesses of her cupboard. This time tomorrow, god-willing, she would be gone from here.

Jenna surmised that someone must have told Lyndon that her father was never one to miss a New Year's Eve celebration at the local hostelry, otherwise how would he have known she'd be left alone this night? Jenna knew she would be locked in her bedroom when he went out tonight, but she would do as she had done when she was younger and make her escape out of the bedroom window. It had been her plan to do so even before Lyndon had left his note and was grateful now that Lyndon would be there to help her. Thankfully she was still lithe and slight in build, even more so now - the upset of the last three weeks had diminished her appetite and she'd lost a deal of weight since learning her fate.

Acting as normal as possible, Jenna went downstairs to make her father's breakfast. Afterwards she let the hens out and started her regular chores in the kitchen. When the clock struck midday, her father came down the stairs and placed the box he was holding on the kitchen table.

Jenna looked quizzically at him but said nothing – they'd barely exchanged a word these last three weeks.

'Open it,' he demanded.

As she pulled the lid off, a great cloud of dust made her sneeze violently. The box contained an ivory lace dress. Jenna stepped back as though it was contaminated. She'd given no thought as to what she would wear for her marriage to Blewett, firstly because it made her physically sick to think of it, and secondly, she always planned to escape so it wouldn't happen.

'It's your mother's wedding dress,' her father said quietly. 'Put it on.'

'But the wedding isn't until tomorrow!'

'I said *put* it on. I want to see it on you.'

Reluctantly she picked up the box and took it to her room. Jenna knew of the dress but had never seen it before. Her mother had told her about it when she was a small child and had wanted Jenna to wear it on her own wedding day. Pulling the dress from the box, she held it against herself. Fingering the delicate lace, she wondered how her father expected her to wear something so beautiful to marry someone so awful.

'Have you got it on yet?' Jory growled from the bottom of the stairs.

Very reluctantly she took off her work dress and stepped into the froth of Victorian lace. It had a fitted bodice with tiny buttons down the front, a high neck and long tapered sleeves. The skirt was panelled and overlaid with lace and fit her beautifully. She wondered quite irrationally if she could squeeze the dress into the cloth bag ready for her escape tonight. It would be the perfect dress to marry Lyndon in.

'Jenna!' Jory shouted angrily.

'I'm coming,' she answered, picking up the skirts so as not to drag them on the stone steps.

He barely looked at her when she appeared in the kitchen but grabbed her by the arm and dragged her to the door.

'What are you doing?' she shrieked.

Jory said nothing but kept hold of her arm until they were outside to where a hired horse and cart was waiting. Without ceremony, he pushed Jenna up into the back of the cart and threw her cloak after her. After a couple of attempts, Jory hauled himself aboard beside her, ordering the driver to set off.

Jenna's face paled when she realised what was happening. She quickly gathered the skirts of her dress into her arms in readiness to jump off the wagon.

'Oh, no you don't my girl.' Jory restrained her.

Jenna flashed him a look of contempt as she struggled to pull her arm free.

'The wedding has been brought forward by one day – for the good of everyone,' he said firmly.

'No, Father!' she shrieked, pulling her arm from his grasp.

The driver turned on hearing the commotion. 'Is something amiss in the back there?' he shouted over his shoulder.

'No, nothing amiss, keep going,' Jory answered, as he yanked Jenna back into a seated position. 'Now stop this nonsense. I knew what you were planning tonight, my girl. I don't know what you were thinking, shirking your obligation like that. You could have had me thrown into prison. What sort of daughter would do that to her father?'

A quiver ran through her stomach, and she stopped struggling. 'What do you mean prison?'

'I owe him money,' Jory said irritably.

'Who?'

'George Blewett! I owe him money - a thousand pounds,' he said stiffly.

'A thousand pounds!' Jenna gasped.

'Your marriage to George Blewett will settle my debt - otherwise I'll go to prison on a charge to taking it without intension of paying it back.'

! You might want to think on that in case you get any more ideas of escaping this marriage.'

Jenna felt as though she'd been punched in the stomach. 'Oh, Father! How did you ever run up a debt such as that?'

For the first time in a month, Jory face crumpled, and tears ran down his face. 'I'm sorry, Jenna, I didn't know how to tell you all this.' He took a deep breath. 'When your dear mother died, you were but eight-years-old - somebody had to care for you. Fishing was all I knew then, but to fish from Gweek meant catching the tide, which meant I'd be gone for six hours at a time, sometimes during the night. I had no-one to look after you so I couldn't work. Very occasionally, Amelia looked after you, but more often than not, she was busy elsewhere. I found a little work sorting the fish on the river bank when the catch came in – but it only brought in a pittance.' He paused for a moment and lowered his eyes 'Eventually I fell behind with the rent. It had only been a small loan to begin with. George Blewett by Gweek standards was a wealthy man. Everyone needed a Blacksmith and he was never without money. When I asked for help, George didn't hesitate. I remember he slapped the money on my table and said jovially, "Pay me back when you can, but if you can't, I'll take your daughter as my bride when she comes of age." Jory hung his head shamefully and murmured, 'I recalled he'd winked and laughed as he said it, and like the fool that I was, I laughed too.'

'But you didn't pay him back?' Jenna asked quietly.

Jory shook his head mournfully. 'I did try. As the years passed, and you began to develop into a beautiful young girl like your mother had been, I began to feel very afraid for your future. Not being a man of numbers, I surmised I'd probably borrowed and owed George somewhere in the region of a couple of hundred pounds. You were twelve-years-old by then and able to look after yourself after school, so I stopped borrowing and drinking and set about trying to earn enough money to pay George back. Morning and night I laboured, doing anything and everything I could lay my hands on to bring some money in. By the time you were fourteen I'd managed to save over a hundred pounds.'

Jenna pulled the shawl around her thin dress. 'But?'

Jory squeezed his eyes shut. 'But, when I presented the money to George, he snatched the money and laughed in my face. He said that it wasn't a hundred pounds I owed - it was a thousand. I questioned it of course, but then he said, "what fool would lend money without interest?" From that moment on Jenna, your fate was sealed. He wanted you or I would go to debtor's prison and like the weak and foolish man I am, I agreed. Drink has been my only salvation.'

Jenna closed her eyes, feeling a shiver run down her spine. *There would be no salvation for her.*

'I'll die in prison if you don't do this Jenna.' Jory said desperately.

Remembering her mother's words to her, "look after your father" Jenna nodded, hung her head and wept for the duration of the journey.

When the horse came to a halt at Constantine Church, Jenna had neither the will nor inclination to raise herself from where she sat. All hope had left her. She knew she could not let her father go to prison and as her father said, her fate was sealed.

Jory beckoned her to get down, but when her limbs would not move, someone, vaguely resembling George Blewett, climbed aboard and pulled her from the wagon. In her haze of misery, she was escorted roughly up the church steps.

At the church door, Jory thrust a handkerchief into her hand to wipe her face and smiled at her thankfully. The church was empty, but for the vicar, George Blewett and Blewett's brother, Sam - the man who'd manhandled her from the cart. As Jory and Jenna walked tentatively down the aisle, Blewett turned and laid his lustful eyes on his young bride.

6

After dropping the wedding party off at the forge, the wagon driver tethered his horse to take libation at The Black Swan.

Taking the mug of ale from the landlord, the driver said, 'Well I can safely say I've never seen a more miserable bride in my life, than the one I took to church today. It's fair unsettled me it has. The poor maid sobbed broken-heartedly all the way to Constantine.'

The landlord folded his arms and asked, 'Who was that then?'

'Blewett's bride.' He nodded towards the forge.

The six people in the bar turned to look out of the window.

'It's gone ahead then?' Jack Ferris said in amazement. 'If she's not with child, and they say she isn't, I'm at a loss why she's agreed to the match.'

Wiping the froth from his upper lip, the driver proceeded to tell them what he'd overheard Jory tell his daughter.

Charlie Williams nearly choked on his drink. 'Please tell me you're jesting?'

'It's as true as I'm stood here. I heard it all, as I took them to church.'

They all looked at the forge again in stunned silence.

*

The pot of stew and loaf of bread that Jenna had made that morning was brought from Trevone Cottage and served as their wedding breakfast. With no appetite of her own, Jenna slowly doled out the food.

As Jory took his share, he announced proudly, 'You'll find that Jenna's a fine cook, George. A good housekeeper too - you'll want for no better.'

George nodded, eyeing Jenna appreciatively.

'Good, I've had no time for housekeeping myself. I reckon you're right Jory, I've chosen a good wife. Nothing beats a woman's touch.'

The inference did not go unnoticed by Jenna. She glanced anxiously at her father as she sat down to the plate of food she had no stomach for. Tears began to well - the thought of life with Blewett caused an uncontrollable shudder, which didn't go unobserved.

'What's the matter maid, are you cold?' Blewett asked. 'Sam, throw another log on the fire. The poor girl looks frozen to death.'

Sam grinned. 'The maid's shivering in anticipation of her wedding night, that's all.'

Glancing fearfully towards her father, Jenna saw his hackles rise.

'Hey,' Jory snapped, 'I'll not have that sort of talk!'

'Aye, shut up, Sam,' Blewett growled. 'Have some decorum in front of the maid's father. Here girl,' he said, pulling a woollen blanket from where he sat. 'Let me put this around you.'

Jenna flinched as Blewett moved towards her. The blanket stank of years of filth as he draped it around her shoulders. His breathing was hard and purposeful. Jenna's unease heightened as he held the corners for a moment beneath her chin before crossing the material tightly across her chest, deliberately stroking her breasts during the act. A tiny, terrified cry emitted from her throat.

'There, that's better, isn't it?' he said, enjoying her apprehension.

Jenna felt bile rise in her throat. *How would she ever endure this?* She watched her father smiling happily at Blewett's apparent show of affection towards her, and a knot of sickness grew in the pit of her stomach. She was under no illusions that Blewett's concern was purely pretence - she was already nursing a sore wrist, from trying to deflect his advances during their return from church.

With the meal finished, Blewett pushed a couple of jugs into Jory's hands. 'Go and get some more ale from the Swan, while I relieve myself.'

Jory frowned. 'Are we not going over there, George? We normally do on New Year's Eve!'

'Maybe later, but for now, I'm enjoying celebrating my nuptials here.' He grinned lustfully at Jenna.

Jenna's heart constricted at the thought of being left alone with the Blewett brothers, but Jory, armed with the jugs, gave his daughter a reassuring nod before he left.

Once George was out of the room, Sam dragged his chair closer to Jenna and fingered the lace of her sleeve.

'Hello pretty sister-in-law.' He slowly undressed her with his eyes. 'Isn't our Georgie the lucky one, eh?'

Jenna tried to disengage herself from his touch.

'It seems to me that our Georgie has everything a man could want - the family business – you! What have I got, eh? Nothing!' he growled. 'That's the curse of the second son. It'll be mine when Georgie dies though. Maybe jumping a feisty little filly like you will bring on a heart attack.'

Jenna sincerely hoped it would too.

A loud belch preceded Blewett's return to the kitchen.

'Hey.' He grasped Sam by his shirt collar and pulled him and his chair away from Jenna. 'What are you doing making eyes at my bride?'

Horrified, expecting a fist-fight any moment, Jenna manoeuvred away from the fracas.

'You come within an inch of my wife again, Sam and you'll feel this fist in your face.'

Terrified, Jenna shrank back into the shadows as the brothers snarled and bickered with hostility for the next few minutes.

When Jory returned with the ale, the atmosphere was thick with angry emotion. 'What's amiss here then?' He glanced between them.

'Nothing now.' Blewett snatched the jugs from him. 'What's amiss with you though? You're deathly white, as though you've had a shock.'

Jory dismissed him but sat down heavily. Wiping his

hands nervously across his face, his mind ran through what had just happened at The Black Swan. For forty-three-years he'd been a well-respected member of the Gweek community, but when he'd entered the bar a few minutes ago, everyone who knew him had turned their backs on him. He'd found himself well and truly ostracised.

As the ale was shared and drunk, Jenna fidgeted constantly. She was stiff from sitting so long - the only time she'd moved was when she needed to relieve herself. That alone had been singularly disgusting - the chamber pot had not been emptied for some considerable time. Pulling the smelly blanket closer for warmth, the old walnut clock in the kitchen struck six-thirty p.m. Her lip trembled unhappily - Lyndon would be waiting for her, unaware that the wedding had been brought forward by a day. She glanced at her father, who too was noting the time. He gave her a warning look, and then stood and excused himself for a few minutes. Jenna lowered her eyes and suppressed a heart-breaking sob, knowing Jory was about to deliver the news to Lyndon that would shatter his hopes and dreams of their shared future.

*

Lyndon checked his fob watch - it was nigh on six-forty. His knees were stiff from crouching in the undergrowth and stood to stretch his legs a little. Twice an errant owl swooped at him, making him stumble. His plan was, once Jenna was with him, that they would travel all night until they arrived at the Trevarno Estate. In his pocket was a special licence. They would be married as soon as possible, and Jenna would be safe.

As footsteps approached, Lyndon's heart thumped with excitement.

'Jenna?' he spoke softly, stepping from the shadows. He stopped short when Jory Trevone stood before him.

'Be off with you, FitzSimmons,' Jory growled. 'The maid's been wed these last five hours to George Blewett. There is nothing here for you now, so be off, or I'll tell

Blewett that you're pestering his new wife.'

A sudden coldness hit Lyndon's core. 'How could you marry your own daughter to that brute?' His voice was low and filled with the bitterest contempt.

'Hold your tongue,' Jory snapped. 'It's none of your business.'

Lyndon rounded on him. 'For sure it is my business. You know she loved and wanted to marry me.'

'Well, she loves George Blewett now, she married him happily today.'

So overcome with anger, Lyndon shouted, 'I don't believe that! If you forced Jenna to marry that bastard today, and I believe you did, you need to start praying that god will have mercy on your soul, for you have done a wicked, wicked thing.'

Jory, a god-fearing man, shuddered. 'What right have you to question my judgment?'

'I have every right because I love Jenna, whereas *you* so obviously do not. You're a despicable man, Jory Trevone.'

Both men squared up to each other, but Jory losing his nerve, backed down and walked swiftly away without another word.

'God help you, Jory Trevone,' Lyndon shouted before dropping to his knees in utter despair.

*

Miserable and terrified in equal measure, Jenna watched the hours tick by. For some extraordinary reason her father seemed reluctant to leave the forge to spend the New Year at The Black Swan. After some considerable debate, Sam was sent for more ale, and Jenna found herself confined to her uncomfortable chair for the rest of the evening.

At eleven-fifty-five, a whisky was thrust into Jenna's hand to herald the start of 1913, but her throat, so constricted with fear, rendered it impossible for her to swallow the fiery liquid.

At twelve-fifteen, Sam left to sleep on the straw floor

by the forge fire and George escorted Jory to the door, with his arm around Jenna.

'Goodnight, lass,' Jory said sheepishly as he kissed Jenna tenderly on the forehead.

Jenna nodded fearfully.

Pulling his coat tighter from the night chill, Jory turned to Blewett. 'You be kind to my girl now.'

Blewett's lip curled. 'It goes without saying, Jory.' *As long as she does as she's told,* he thought to himself.

As they watched Jory walk away, Blewett's hand grasped and fondled Jenna's bottom. Every single nerve in her body stood on edge.

Back in the kitchen, Blewett bolted the door and licked his fat lips in anticipation. 'Well then, my beauty. I've waited a long time for this night. I think it's time you went upstairs and took that dress off.'

*

Standing in Blewett's filthy bedroom, Jenna felt her stomach knot with grief. Stiff with cold and terrified beyond belief, she tried in vain to stem the tremble in her body. The bed was dirty and unmade. Grease marks stained the ticking pillows, and the smell of stale sweat caught the back of her throat.

Her fear escalated as Blewett's footsteps ascended the stone steps. A small helpless cry escaped her throat as he burst into the bedroom, threw his jacket on the chair and walked slowly round her. Averting her eyes from his wanton desire, she recoiled in disgust when he licked her face. There was no escaping what was about to happen.

'I distinctly told you to take this dress off,' he hissed, grasping the front of her bodice, ripping it open to expose her breasts.

Jenna shrieked, as his rough, calloused hands grabbed her tender skin. She slapped his hands away and stumbled towards the door, but he caught her by the hair, dragged her back and slapped her hard on the mouth.

'From now on, when I tell you to do something, you

will do it,' he said, tightening the grasp on her hair.

A metallic taste filled her mouth as he moved her to the bed, pushed her face down onto the filthy pillow and ripped the back of her wedding dress from its seams. Long into the night the abuse continued, as he subjected her to the most horrific violation. Eventually her body was in such a state of shock, even her screams stopped, and the tears ceased to fall.

*

Jory Trevone sat in his cottage and sighed with relief. Everything had turned out all right, he thought, unaware that his daughter lay battered and bleeding in George Blewett's stinking bed, praying to die.

*

Lyndon drove his wagon aimlessly through the dark lanes far away from Gweek. It was only when Bramble stumbled, did Lyndon realise he'd been driving for most of the night. 'Whoa now girl.' He pulled her to a halt, jumped down and leant against the horse's neck. 'I'm sorry Bramble, I didn't realise we were still moving.' The horse snuffled softly as Lyndon stroked her soft nose. Quickly releasing her from her harness, he gave her a drink, fed her and then hobbled her near a patch of grass. The night was icy cold and moonless, but the sky was filled with thousands of stars. Lyndon sat down on the cold hard earth, ignoring the dampness seeping through the seat of his trousers. He needed to feel discomfort. He needed to feel thoroughly wretched, for he knew that his beautiful Jenna would be suffering on this dreadful, dreadful night and there was absolutely nothing he could do about it.

He buried his head in his hands. 'I'm so sorry I didn't save you in time, Jenna. I should have broken your bloody father's door down and taken you weeks ago,' he cried pitifully into his hands.

7

At four-thirty, Jenna was unceremoniously kicked out of bed, by way of Blewett's foot in the small of her back and ordered to light the fires. Landing heavily on the grimy rug, Jenna hauled herself up with the aid of the chair. She was still wearing what was left of her mother's wedding dress, as she moved painfully from the bedroom, down the stairs and out into the freezing morning.

A ground frost encrusted the grass, stinging her bare feet as she stumbled to the water trough. Gathering the tattered ribbons of her dress into her arms, she lowered herself to sit gingerly in the icy water. The shock of the cold on her nether regions barely registered above the searing pain inside her. In absolute desolation she looked towards her father's cottage for help, but his curtains remained closed.

Without strength or inclination to move, her tongue ran along the inside of her teeth to check if any were loose, then across the swelling on her lower lip. *Someone help me, please.* In her deep despair she was unaware of a presence beside her. Only when she felt a gentle touch of a hand on her shoulder, did she lift her eyes to find Dr Eddy bending over her.

'Oh, goodness gracious! Whatever has happened here?' Realising she was badly hurt Dr Eddy gently lifted her from her icy bath. 'Come, my dear. Let me get you to my surgery.' He gathered the scraps of lace hanging from her bodice to cover her exposed breasts.

Jenna's head spun alarmingly as she tried to stand, but very tentatively, with the aid of the doctor, she urged her trembling legs to move, though each step was excruciatingly painful.

As they neared Dr Eddy's house, she faltered as Blewett's voice yelled, 'Where the hell are you, woman?'

'It's all right, my dear.' Dr Eddy gave her a reassuring hug. He could see Blewett, silhouetted at the forge kitchen door. Clad in only long johns he was arduously scratching his private parts as he peered out into the darkness.

'Jenna is here with me,' Dr Eddy called out to Blewett. 'I'm taking her to the surgery.'

Blewett bristled with annoyance. He knew he'd been rough with her during the night - the last thing he needed was any rebuke from Dr Eddy. 'You bring her back here, right now,' he ordered. 'She's wifely chores to do and fires to build.'

'I suggest you build your own fires. Jenna is in need of urgent medical treatment.'

'I'm not paying for any urgent medical treatment, so bring her back.' Blewett's hands curled into fists. *Damn the woman, why couldn't she have stayed indoors away from prying eyes?*

Ignoring Blewett's rants, Dr Eddy ushered Jenna up the path to the surgery.

'Do you hear me? I'm paying nothing,' Blewett raged, shooting a glowering look towards Jory's cottage.

*

After being helped out of the remains of her wedding dress, Jenna stepped into a bath of warm, salty water and allowed the doctor's wife very gently bathe her battered body. After being dried with a soft towel, she was dressed in a clean nightdress and put to bed in a large spacious bedroom.

Curling her fingers around the clean sheets, Jenna closed her eyes as alarming tremors pulsated through her body.

'And how is my patient faring?' Dr Eddy smiled down on Jenna.

Startled at his voice, Jenna cowered into the bed.

'It's all right Jenna, you're quite safe here.' He examined her very tenderly, anointed her many wounds with a soothing balm, but each touch made Jenna's skin crawl with disgust.

'Her urine is red!' Mrs Eddy said, showing him the chamber pot.

Dr Eddy twisted his mouth in thought. 'Is it painful to pass water Jenna?'

Jenna nodded. *Painful was an understatement! It was like peeing needles.*

'I take it you don't normally suffer from this affliction?'

'No Dr Eddy,' she answered flatly.

'Then it will be purely the trauma you've undergone. I'll prescribe one full glass of water, every hour for the next eight hours. Mavis,' he addressed his wife, 'can I leave you to make sure this happens?'

Mavis Eddy nodded efficiently.

He smiled at Jenna. 'I'm afraid it will sting for a while, but the water will flush out your bladder and soon you will be comfortable again. Do you need anything else?'

Feeling her eyes fill with tears she answered, 'No thank you, Dr Eddy.'

He patted her hand gently and smiled warmly. 'Just rest now Jenna. Mrs Eddy will take good care of you. I'll see you this evening. Try to sleep a little.'

As Dr Eddy moved away, he beckoned his wife to his side. His eyes rested on the discarded wedding dress. 'I suggest you burn that.'

'That's what Jenna said too.'

They moved into the corridor to speak more secretively. Dr Eddy's mouth was pinched white in anger.

'That man is nothing short of a monster for what he's subjected Jenna to. She'll heal of course, physically I mean, but I fear for her state of mind. I'm going to see Blewett now and give him a piece of my mind.'

'Now you watch out, my dear.' Mavis fussed. 'We all know he's an unpleasant man at the best of times.'

'I'm not afraid of Blewett,' he stated firmly. 'I'll speak to Constable Treen before breakfast as well, but we all know it's hard to intervene with domestic issues like this. I'm afraid Jenna's fate is sealed. There was much talk last night about this marriage contract. If she leaves Blewett, Jory will go to prison, and you and I both know that Jenna would not let that happen to her father. I swear I'll have some strong words to say to Jory Trevone when I see him next. It beggars belief that he should agree to such a thing.'

Jenna could hear murmuring somewhere near the room, but her body was so fatigued from her ordeal, she just wanted to sleep. The fire glowed in the grate and her tired eyes flickered over the sumptuous wall coverings and drapes. She'd never seen a room so beautiful, she mused, as she drifted into slumber.

*

After a few hours rest, Lyndon harnessed Bramble and reluctantly made his way home to the Trevarno Estate, arriving just as the clock struck five a.m.

Michael and Lyndon FitzSimmons' cottage was one of six tied dwellings snuggled neatly in a wooded dell, set back and hidden from the big house. The Madrons lived next door, seven of them sleeping in a three-bedroom cottage. The widow Gina Teague and her son Tommy lived next door to them. To the right of the dell, stood Lowenna and Peter Hoskins' cottage, then Fred Saunders, alone now since his mother had died last spring, and at the very end resided old Tom Hindle, the head gardener before Michael took over the job.

His father's cottage was dark and quiet when Lyndon arrived home. Inside, the fire, banked up for the night, sparked and spat when Lyndon prodded it. He laid a log in the embers then leant forward onto the mantelpiece in despair.

'Happy New Year to you, son,' Michael FitzSimmons yawned as he emerged from the stairs, rubbing the sleep from his eyes. He was an older version of Lyndon, still handsome and strong, though at forty-nine-years-old his hair was greying substantially.

'I take it you found a hostelry to bring in the cheer.' He yawned again noisily, shivered with the cold and warmed his hands by the rejuvenated fire. 'I must admit, my days of celebrating are long gone now. I swear I was abed afore the strike of ten last night.'

As he spoke, Lyndon stood silent. Michael frowned - it was unlike Lyndon to entertain quiet moods. 'What's amiss? A sore head, is it?'

Lyndon slowly shook his head.

Michael had only once seen his son like this before, and that was three years ago when his mother had died of tuberculosis. 'Anything you want to tell your old pa?' he asked, trying to keep the concern from his voice.

Lyndon shook his head again. He feared if he spoke, he would cry.

Michael put a comforting hand on his son's shoulders. 'Well, I'm here when you're ready.'

Lyndon nodded and Michael left him where he stood to get ready for work. When Michael came back down into the kitchen, Lyndon had gone.

*

Dr Eddy could barely contain his anger as he squared up to Blewett in the forge kitchen.

'It's truly appalling what you did with the poor girl on her wedding night. Jenna is covered in bruises, and as for what you did down below, well, that just proves you're a sadist.'

Blewett matched the doctor's angry stance.

'Serves her right for struggling, she should have done her duty meekly. Anyway, who the hell do you think you are, telling me how to treat my wife,' he snarled. 'She's done what all wives are expected to do on their wedding night, that's all. It's normal to hurt the first time, everyone says so. She'll just have to bloody well get used to it.'

Dr Eddy shuddered. 'I'll argue with you no longer, you disgust me, but I reiterate this is not acceptable behaviour, not acceptable at all.'

Blewett's face darkened. 'I'll do as I please with her.'

Dr Eddy rounded on him. 'You will *not,* sir. A wife is to be loved and cherished, not treated like a dog. I'll be watching you from now on.' He pointed a warning finger at Blewett's face before stomping out of the kitchen.

'Nobody tells me what to do,' Blewett yelled, kicking the table leg in frustration.

*

Jory had the great misfortune of meeting the doctor on the bridge. Still bubbling with anger, Dr Eddy held nothing back.

'You and Blewett should be horsewhipped for what you've done to that poor girl of yours.'

Jory stood open-mouthed at his outburst.

'How could you marry Jenna off to that monster, Jory? How *could* you?'

Taken aback, he trembled. 'Why, what's happened?'

'He's abused Jenna abominably. She's in my care for the time being. You should *both* be thoroughly ashamed of yourselves.'

*

For a normally quiet and unassuming man, Jory hammered on the forge door and then lurched furiously at Blewett when he opened it.

'What the devil have you done to my daughter? Dr Eddy says she's hurt badly. I told you to be kind to her! What sort of cowardly bastard hurts a girl so that she needs medical care?'

Blewett grabbed Jory by the jaw and slammed him against the wall. 'I'll tell you this Jory Trevone. What I do with that girl is no longer any business of yours. Remember, you sold her to me. If it's anyone's fault she's been hurt, it's yours. I gave you a choice, hand your daughter over to me or go to prison. *Now* who's the cowardly bastard?'

Jory struggled to free himself from his grasp, but Blewett held tight.

'If you think that miserable scrap of a girl of yours clears your debt, you are seriously mistaken. I suggest you tell her to get back here and do her duty from now on, otherwise you might still find yourself in prison.' He released his grip. 'Now bugger off! I've had enough interference for one day and keep your nose out of my marital affairs from now on.'

Jory walked blindly back to his cottage. At his table, he sat rubbing his hands nervously across his face. The truth hurt - he *was* a coward. He dared not even venture to Dr Eddy's house to ask after Jenna, for fear of another backlash from him. A sudden cold draft ran down the back of his neck. He shivered, as though someone had walked over his grave. *You're a miserable excuse for a father, Jory Trevone.* His dead wife's voice berated him. *Be very, very ashamed.*

*

As Mavis Eddy made sure Jenna was comfortable, Matthew Bickford appeared downstairs at the kitchen door. He sniffed the air appreciably. 'Gosh, any chance of breakfast. Mrs Tankard?'

'Of course, Matthew, sit yourself down in the dining room. The doctor is already in there. I'll put a couple more eggs on and be with you shortly.'

The dining room was east facing, so the morning sun shone brightly through the windows. A roaring fire warmed the room and the smell of bacon wafted up from the kitchen.

'Ah, good morning, Matthew, I thought you might grace us with your presence soon. We heard you were staying with Lord Vyvyan at Trelowarren for the New Year. Sit down. Does Mrs Tankard know you are here?'

'She does,' Matthew said, unfolding a napkin to place on his lap. 'Forgive me for saying David, but you look as though you've been up all night!'

'I have dear boy, I have. Mrs Bolitho always seems to want to deliver her babies in the middle of the night. This will be her fifth and every single one born between two and four a.m. Lord, but I could set my watch by her.'

Matthew smiled as Mrs Tankard bustled through the door with two steaming plates of breakfast.

'I swear to god there is no finer cook than you Mrs Tankard,' Matthew said, inhaling the meal as he picked up his knife and fork.

Just as they started eating, the dining room door opened, and Mrs Eddy stood back to let Mrs Tankard from the room.

'Oh, Mrs Tankard,' she said, 'leave Jenna for a while. The poor girl is fast asleep. We'll give her a few hours then try and tempt her to eat something light. Mercy me, I've never witnessed such injuries on a woman before. That man should be horsewhipped.'

Mrs Tankard bobbed her head. 'I agree, but horsewhipping is too good for him, ma'am! I'll take her some broth at midday.'

As Mavis entered the room she halted in her tracks. 'Oh, Matthew, I didn't see you there. This is a lovely surprise.'

On hearing the conversation, Matthew's utensils were suspended over his plate. 'Did you say Jenna, Mavis?'

Mavis blanched and glanced towards her husband.

When no answer was forthcoming, Matthew narrowed his eyes curiously.

'Why is Jenna upstairs? What's happened to her?'

Mavis could hold her tongue no longer. 'She's been viciously abused by that wicked husband of hers.'

Matthew's brows knitted together. 'What husband?'

'Mavis,' Dr Eddy's voice warned.

'No, David, I'll not be silenced. It's criminal what he's done to that poor girl.'

'I agree, Mavis, but nevertheless, it's not our place to make comment. Remember, I've sworn a Hippocratic oath, not to speak about my patients.'

'Well, *you* may have done, but I haven't,' she bristled indignantly.

'Please tell me what has happened to Jenna?' Matthew asked, his appetite waning by the second.

Mavis looked askance at her husband and relayed the

whole sorry business of the marriage contract to Matthew.

Matthew's mouth dropped open.

Mavis fussed with the lace of her cap. 'Tell him, David. Tell him what he did to that poor girl on her wedding night!'

Dr Eddy regarded his wife reproachfully. 'No dear, you tell him. You seemed to be doing a good job all by yourself.'

Matthew's face paled as he listened to Mavis's account of Jenna's injuries. When she'd finished, he felt physically sick. Placing his napkin on the table, he stood up. 'I apologise, I seemed to have lost my appetite. Please excuse me.'

*

Blewett's mood was as dark as the look on his face when Matthew entered the forge. He'd just had a visit from the constable, what with that, Jory and the doctor, he did not welcome any more interference in his domestic affairs. When he saw his prestigious visitor, Blewett quickly plastered a smile on his face, tapped his forehead and said, 'Good morning, Mr Bickford. What can I do for you?'

With one quick swipe of his hand Matthew brought the horse crop down across Blewett's face. 'You can start by learning to treat your new wife properly,' he said to Blewett, now cowering in the corner of the forge.

A great welt of angry skin burned across Blewett's face, but it didn't stop him from growling back, 'What I do with my wife is no bloody business of yours.'

'Oh, you think not!' Matthew raised his crop again and swiped it across Blewett's shoulder. 'I shall tell you this just once Blewett. If you *ever* physically harm Jenna again, I shall personally horse whip you to within an inch of your life. You may have bought that poor girl, and think you own her, but by god you will treat her with the respect she deserves.' He whipped the floor angrily with his crop again, scattering straw everywhere, then turned and left.

*

Back on the Trevarno Estate, Michael FitzSimmons began to fret for his absent son when he did not return for dinner or supper. Unable to go up to bed to rest, Michael settled himself by the warmth of the fire and waited.

He sighed with relief on hearing the latch lift at nine-forty-five. A gust of icy air preceded Lyndon as he stepped into the warmth of the cottage.

'Have you eaten, son?' Michael asked from where he sat.

Lyndon took the seat opposite and sat down heavily. 'I'm not hungry, Pa.'

Michael glanced anxiously at Lyndon. He looked pale and unhappy, and his clothes were damp and dishevelled.

'Where have you been working?'

'I haven't.' His answer was almost inaudible.

'But you've been gone all day and without an overcoat!'

He gave a half shrug. 'I forgot to take it.'

Michael got up and poured a glass of brandy. 'Here son, this will warm your bones.'

Lyndon settled the glass on his lap. 'I've been thinking Pa. I might go away – abroad perhaps.'

Michael moistened his lips ready to ask the next question, for he knew it had something to do with his melancholia. 'What about your young lady?'

Lyndon's head dropped. 'She's not *my* young lady anymore. She's - someone else's wife.' He put the untouched glass of brandy on the table and got up. 'I'm sorry Pa, I need to sleep.'

Michael sat for a long time. He knew Lyndon would reveal the whole story in his own time. For now, he knew he must wait, but it grieved him deeply. These past few months, he'd never seen Lyndon so happy. Eventually when he had told him of his plans to marry the 'most beautiful girl in the world', Michael had been over the moon for him, and looked forward to welcoming his new bride into their home come spring time. He rubbed his face with both hands. What on earth could have gone wrong?

*

Michael woke at three-thirty a.m. to the sound of breaking glass. Downstairs he found Lyndon slumped at the kitchen table with a half-finished bottle of brandy by his hand and the remains of a glass shattered on the stone floor. Michael shook his head. Lyndon never could hold his drink. Two glasses of cider and he was flat on his back.

'Come on son.' He pulled one of Lyndon's arms around his own shoulder and man-handled him back up to his bed to sleep it off.

8

The second of January saw a thaw in the weather. Matthew bid his farewells to Lord and Lady Vyvyan at Trelowarren and rode back down to Gweek, en-route home to Trevarno.

Blewett scowled darkly when Matthew Bickford appeared at his forge door. His fingers touched the red welt on his cheek, which still stung from yesterday's whipping.

Unperturbed at Blewett's demeanour, Matthew tapped his whip against his boot as his eyes took in the tools and materials of the smith's trade. Presently he said, 'I understand the marriage to Jenna Trevone was to cancel a debt owed by her father.'

Blewett eyed him cautiously. 'What's it to you?'

'A sum of one thousand pounds, I've been told.'

Blewett wiped his sleeve against his forehead.

'That's an awful lot of money. How can someone such as Jory Trevone run up such a debt?'

'He's never bought a drink in the last ten years, that's how,' Blewett quipped.

Matthew gave a short laugh. 'With the best will in the world, Jory Trevone could not drink a thousand pounds worth of ale!'

'It wasn't just drink you know. I've helped them out with food and rent and there's interest as well.'

Matthew continued unfazed. 'I know that Jory can read and write, but I also know he is not a man of numbers.'

Blewett shrugged his shoulders.

'I know you keep a good and steady business here, but I do not believe you earn enough to lend anyone one thousand pounds or even half that amount.'

Blewett licked his lips nervously. 'Kept a record of it all and that record came to a thousand pounds,' he said with a nod.

'Well, I'd like to see that record.'

Blewett flushed. 'I haven't got it anymore. I burnt it when the debt was cancelled yesterday.'

Matthew laughed cynically. 'You're a liar and a cheat Blewett and you know it. Nevertheless, I put it to you that I shall cancel that debt today myself, and you will release Jenna from her marriage contract. I know a good lawyer who could arrange the divorce.'

Blewett's mouth twisted into a smile. 'So that's what you want, eh? You want my wife for yourself.' He bared his rotten teeth at him. 'Well, you're not having her. She belongs to me.'

'Come on, a thousand pounds man, this is not to be sniffed at. Shake hands now and you'll have a note of the money today.'

Blewett scratched his head. 'Well now, tell me, what would I want with all that money? I reckon I've got what I wanted. In fact,' he said with a glint in his eye, 'I've got what every man in the village wanted - a ripe young woman to keep my bed warm. If you think I've cheated Jory Trevone, you might want to think on this - he struck a deal with me when the girl was but eight-years-old. I've waited a long time to bed that wench, so be off with you and your thousand pounds. My wife is not for sale!' He grinned balefully.

Matthew could see there was no arguing with the man. He tapped the horse whip in his hand. 'Just remember Blewett, Jenna is not without friends, and they will all be watching out for her. You treat that girl with respect, or by god, I'll do for you.'

*

Jenna felt an unnatural stillness within her as she stared out of the window in the doctor's morning room. Aware of her own heartbeat, she watched expressionless at the birds flitting about on the bare branches of the forsythia bush. There was a time she would reach for her drawing equipment, but not anymore. The pretty yellow and white patterned dress she wore, retrieved by Mrs Eddy from her father's house, belonged to a girl who used to run in meadows knee-high with wild flowers, not the damaged woman she'd become. These were the garments of a girl who lived for life, drew pictures and fell in love with Lyndon FitzSimmons. A shiver ran down her spine. It was all gone, her freedom, vitality, love - all gone.

The thought of her life with Blewett made her skin crawl in repulsion. When she'd bathed that morning, Mrs Eddy had to stop her from scrubbing her skin raw as she tried to erase the feeling of his hands on her body. Every nerve in her body felt on end - even her hair hurt. Each time her heavy plait of hair moved down her back she flinched, as it pulled uncomfortably on her sensitive scalp, painful from being grabbed and dragged to do his bidding. In short, she felt utterly wretched.

A knock came at the door. 'You have a visitor, Jenna,' Mrs Eddy said.

Jenna blanched.

Mrs Eddy caught her concern. 'Oh, my dear, it's all right, it's only Matthew Bickford. Do you feel up to seeing him?'

She nodded, dropping her eyes to the floor, embarrassed that he should see her in this state.

Dropping his hat on the table Matthew approached her with his normal familiarity. 'Oh, Jenna!' he said very gently, as he reached for her hands and held them both in his. Jenna recoiled at his touch, but Matthew curled his fingers gently around her hands to quell her trembling. 'I am so sorry to find you in this predicament,' he said sorrowfully.

Jenna's eyelids fluttered.

'You could walk away from this you know?'

Jenna thought of the desperate missive she'd received from her father that morning.

I beg for your swift return to your husband Jenna, and that you learn to obey him. I fear what George will do to me if you do not.

She lifted her eyes to his. 'My father would go to prison!'

'Matthew squeezed her hands to make his point. 'Then prison he should go, for what he's done.'

Jenna's lip trembled. 'I can't...I…I can't let that happen…. I just can't. He wouldn't survive prison. I can't have that on my conscience.'

Matthew gave an exasperated sigh. 'Oh, Jenna, you are too good. I'm sorry then, I cannot save you from this marriage. If I could, I would, but what I can ensure is that there will be no more violence towards you. I've just come from the forge - Blewett knows the consequences if he ever mistreats you again. Dr Eddy and the constable will watch out for you but I'm afraid that is all we can do for you.'

Jenna nodded slowly. 'Thank you,' she whispered, her mind drifting back to the haunted place she was hiding in.

He kissed the back of her hands. 'I must go now. Be strong Jenna,' he said with a nod. 'If you feel you cannot leave, then you must dig deep and find a way to endure this, and do not hesitate to ask if you need help.'

Feeling thoroughly dejected, Jenna's expression suddenly gave way to purpose. 'There is one thing you could do for me, Matthew.'

'Name it, Jenna. If it's in my power, I will gladly do it for you.'

'I'd be grateful if you can explain to Lyndon what has happened?' She paused for a moment, reflecting on what should have been. 'We were to be married you know.' It took all her will to hold back the tears.

'I know, my dear. Of course, I'll tell him.'

'And tell him…. I'll always love….' Her voice broke and she could speak no more.

'I'll tell him Jenna, I'll tell him.'

*

Matthew had barely left before another visitor arrived. Amelia Pascoe said nothing at first but took Jenna in her arms and cradled her like a baby, thus opening the floodgates of suppressed tears. Presently Amelia held her at arm's length, shook her head and asked, 'Whatever happened? You were meant to leave on New Year's Eve with Lyndon. It was all arranged. Did you not get the notes? I hid two, just in case the hens ate the first one.'

Jenna nodded sadly. 'It seems I got one and my father must have found the other one.'

Amelia's hand flew to her mouth. 'Oh, stupid, stupid me!'

'Amelia, please don't berate yourself. Father never ventures into the hencoop normally.'

Amelia bristled. 'Then someone must have seen me do it and alerted him.'

Wiping her tired swollen eyes, Jenna sobbed, 'He gave no indication that he knew I was planning to leave. My bag was packed, everything was ready. I had no qualms at the time about leaving father, but then he tricked me, by bringing the wedding forward by a day. I swear to you Amelia I was ready to jump off the wagon en-route to the church and run, but….,' A second wave of tears rendered her unable to speak for a moment, 'then he told me of the debt he owed. You see, he left me with no option but to go ahead with the marriage.'

Amelia gathered her again to her arms. 'Jory has done a truly wicked thing, Jenna. No-one would blame you for not honouring this debt.'

'You *know* I can't do that,' Jenna said softly. 'I promised mother I'd look after him.'

'Your sentiments do you justice, my dear, but he's not exactly looking after you, is he? Has he been to see you? Has he seen what he's brought you to?'

Jenna shook her head.

Amelia's anger gave way to contempt. 'Damn the man for his insensitivity. Look Jenna, if there is anything I can help you with, just ask.'

Jenna rubbed her eyes dry. 'You can do something. In my bedroom at home, there is a trunk of clothes belonging to my mother. Please could you fetch me the darkest clothes you can find and my sewing box and,' she added, 'if you have a spare black scarf too, I should be obliged to you if you could let me have it?'

Amelia's eyes swept over Jenna's pretty dress and nodded knowingly. 'Of course, I will.'

*

At Trevarno, Lyndon's state of mind unsettled Michael, so much so, he returned to the cottage at regular intervals during the day to check on his son. It was midday before Lyndon surfaced from his drunken stupor and Michael thrust a bowl of porridge under his nose, warning him in no uncertain terms that he had to eat the lot, or else!

Thankfully when he returned from work at six, Michael found the fire blazing, dinner simmering in a pot, and though slightly green around the gills, Lyndon sat at the kitchen table sheepishly waiting for him.

Michael nodded. 'I'll wash my hands and then you can tell me the whole sorry tale.'

*

At eight-thirty that evening, a knock came at the door, halting the debate as to why Jenna had gone ahead with the marriage.

Matthew nodded to them both as he stooped to enter the cosy kitchen. Knowing this room intimately, having played together with Lyndon as children, he threw his hat on the table and ran his hands despairingly through his hair.

'Well, Lyndon,' he said wearily, 'This is a sorry mess.'

'You know then?' Lyndon answered gloomily.

'I do, I'm so sorry for you, my friend.'

Michael poured each of them a brandy and beckoned Matthew to sit.

Lyndon pushed his glass aside. 'I just can't understand why she allowed the marriage to happen - it makes no sense. When we knew what her father was planning, we made secret plans to run away, but it seems the wedding was brought forward. I simply cannot understand why she didn't just say no to the arrangement!' He wrung his hands in desperation. 'She could have said no, Matthew! *Why* did she go ahead with it?'

Matthew made to speak but Lyndon cut in.

'I swear to god I'm going back there tomorrow to get her out of that place. I don't care what the consequences are for wife stealing, but I just can't leave her with that brute. You know what he's like, Matthew - we've all had dealings with him.'

Matthew tapped gently on the table top. 'I'm afraid you can't Lyndon.'

'Why can't I?' he retorted angrily.

Matthew drew a breath a little deeper than normal. 'She was exchanged to cancel a debt owed by her father.'

Michael and Lyndon gave a collective gasp.

Lyndon leaned forward. 'How much is the debt? Is it something I could pay off instead?'

Matthew shook his head. 'It's a thousand pounds.'

Shaken to the core, Lyndon uttered despondently, 'Oh god! I have but fifty pounds to my name!'

Matthew laid his hand on Lyndon's arm. 'I've already offered the money up to Blewett. I went to see him this morning, but he won't take the payment.'

Lyndon's mouth gaped. 'You offered him a thousand pounds!'

Matthew folded his arms and sat back thoughtfully. 'I did.'

Lyndon's head thickened with emotion. 'Then there is no hope for her. Please god let him be kind to her.' Unable to contain his grief, he choked on the last word.

Matthew watched anxiously - he knew to keep his counsel about what happened on her wedding night. What good would it do to tell him such a thing? 'Lyndon, listen to me, I warned Blewett to that effect this morning. Jenna is not without friends who will look out for her. I'm afraid that's all we can do. What's done, cannot be undone. I'm so sorry Lyndon.' He drained his glass and stood up.

Lyndon nodded appreciatively.

'Jenna asked me to explain the situation to you.' He sighed heavily as he picked up his hat. 'If it's any consolation, Lyndon, and I don't suppose it is, she also asked me to tell you that she will always love you.'

Lyndon dropped his head into his hands.

Matthew put a comforting hand on Lyndon's shoulder. 'She's very special to us all. I'm just so sorry I can't do more.'

When Matthew had gone, Michael asked. 'How could a father do that to his daughter, especially if the man is as bad as you say?'

Lyndon grunted angrily. 'I don't know, Pa, but if I were Jenna, I would surely let him rot in prison.'

*

The next day Jenna was invited to breakfast with the doctor and his wife. She sat shyly at the table which was draped in the crispest white linen she had ever seen.

'Good morning to you, Jenna, I trust you slept well?' The doctor was deeply concerned by her appearance. Her skin had taken on a sallow translucency. Dark circles had formed around her eyes and her lips looked almost bloodless.

'Thank you doctor, yes,' she answered, nervously folding and unfolding her napkin.

Dr Eddy took a deep breath. 'Your father called this morning.'

She felt her shoulders droop.

Dr Eddy gave a short sigh. 'He's keen for you to return to your husband.'

Jenna felt her appetite diminishing, knowing she'd have to return to her living hell soon.

'I'm so sorry, Jenna, it pains me to say this, but as Blewett's wife, return you must at some stage. You do know that.'

She drew a deep trembling breath and nodded.

Dr Eddy reached over and placed his hand over hers.

'Jenna, Blewett received an official caution from the constable about his behaviour towards you. I believe he understands the consequences should he repeat his violence towards you. I am sorry, but this is all we can do. I'll be looking out for you, as of course will your father, and you know that we are here for you should you need us.'

'Thank you for your kindness doctor,' she said, swallowing the lump forming in her throat.

The doctor dabbed his mouth with his napkin. 'Now, I've told your father that you will return in a couple of days. So, until then, you might like to spend some time in the morning room, we have many books if you so choose to read. I fear you will have little or no time for such luxuries, once you return to the busy forge.' He got up, kissed his wife on the head and left to do his rounds.

Jenna gave Mrs Eddy a watery smile.

'Try to eat something my dear, and rest assured I will personally castrate Blewett with a rusty scalpel if he harms you again,' she said, taking a satisfying bite of toast.

9

The dreadful day arrived for Jenna to return to the forge. Though deeply apprehensive, she was heartened that a few good people would be looking out for her - unfortunately, they could not be there to stop the horrors of the marital bed.

Almost ready, Jenna secured the black scarf around her head - she was leaving nothing to chance.

Mrs Eddy knocked on the door. 'Dr Eddy is waiting - he's going to accompany you to the forge…Oh, my goodness!' Her hands flew to her mouth.

Dressed sombrely from head to foot in black, Jenna's long blond plait lay burning on the fire. Short tufts of hair stuck out awkwardly from her black scarf. This coupled with her pale, sallow skin made Jenna appear to have aged considerably overnight.

'Jenna! Whatever have you done to yourself maid? You look… You look….'

'Dreadful?' Jenna enquired hopefully.

Mrs Eddy nodded.

'Good. I'll not give that odious man anything to desire from now on.'

Dr Eddy looked equally shocked, as she walked down the stairs. Silently he held out his arm for her to take and patted her hand sympathetically.

'May we stop briefly at my cottage, Dr Eddy?'

'Of course, my dear, you'll want a word with your father. I'm sure he'll be relieved to see you well again.'

Jenna gave the doctor a wry look.

At the cottage, Jenna saw the relief in her father's face at her return. She gave him a curt nod of acknowledgment, before running up the stairs. Glancing longingly at her old bedroom, with its soft, clean bed and lace curtains, she opened the door to the linen cupboard. A moment later, she descended the stairs with her arms full of lavender scented linen and left Trevone Cottage without so much as a 'bye your leave'.

The doctor bid his farewells to Jory, before following Jenna across the bridge. The forge kitchen was cold and unwelcoming as Dr Eddy left Jenna there while he went in search of Blewett.

The air in the forge was hot and acrid with the smell of coal smoke. Blewett hammered at a tool forcefully, before a hiss of hot water on metal filled the room.

'I've just brought Jenna back,' Dr Eddy shouted.

'Have you now!' Blewett grunted.

Dr Eddy dropped his voice, 'You heed my warning Blewett, or there will be consequences.'

Blewett scowled and spat onto the straw.

When Dr Eddy returned to the kitchen, he was struck by the sheer hopelessness in Jenna's eyes. He gave her hand a comforting squeeze. 'I'll leave you now. You know where I am, should you need me. I'll call regularly.'

Jenna nodded bleakly. 'Thank you for everything doctor.'

*

Jenna grimaced at the grubby kitchen. Everything in this house was disgusting, especially its owner. She stood for a moment in silent desolation and then with a heavy heart, began to build the kindling in the fire grate. With the fire lit, she grabbed the kettle and a bucket, and began to fill from the water pump outside. If this was her lot from now on, she would make sure she would not live in a pigsty.

After first scrubbing years of grease from the kitchen table, Jenna found a lump of mutton in the larder and set it to cook in a pot on the fire with whatever scraps of vegetables she could find. Then with a pail of hot water, she began to clean the bedroom. Stripping the stinking sheets from the bed, she remade it with clean fresh linen. Picking the grubby rug up with her finger and thumb, she threw it down the stairs to be beaten outside. The curtains were taken down, shaken vigorously to rid them of years of dust. The grime was washed from the windows and the curtains re-hung. Once the floor boards had been scrubbed, she stood back in satisfaction.

By dinner time, Jenna had scrubbed and polished the forge cottage until it shone. As she emptied the last bucket of dirty water into the river, local lad, Charlie Williams, approached her. She'd known Charlie all her life. He was four years older than her and very much in love with Lizzy from the dairy. He'd always been someone she could trust, and she smiled warmly at him.

Shocked by her appearance, Charlie was unable to mask his concern. 'Are you all right, Jenna?'

Jenna nodded - what else could she do?

'I'm so sorry you've been forced into this marriage, Jenna. You deserve so much better. If there's….' he stopped mid-sentence when Blewett appeared stony-faced behind them.

Jenna turned to Blewett, who beckoned her sharply inside.

'I'm sorry, Charlie, I'll have to go,' she said.

*

Once out of sight of Charlie, Blewett grabbed her roughly by the arm and manoeuvred her into the kitchen.

'What did *he* want?'

Wincing in pain as he squeezed her arm she retaliated, 'He didn't want anything.'

'If you've been passing messages to him for that hedger FitzSimmons, you'll feel the back of my hand.'

Jenna blanched. 'I haven't, he was just asking if I was all right, that's all.'

Blewett bared his teeth. 'What the devil has my wife's welfare got to do with him?'

Jenna turned slightly to deflect his foul breath, and answered timidly, 'Charlie was just being friendly!'

'*Was* he now? You are *my* wife, and I will not tolerate you speaking or being free and friendly with other men! Understand?'

Jenna gave a reluctant nod

'Good,' he grunted, pushing her away. As she stood back, he looked her up and down in dismay. 'What the hell have you got on? You look like a dowdy old widow!'

Jenna turned towards her stove and smiled inwardly at her small triumph.

As he sat waiting impatiently to be served dinner, Blewett observed the newly scrubbed kitchen appreciably - he'd never seen it so clean. 'I'll give you this,' he said grudgingly, 'you've done a good job with this place - see that you keep it that way.'

As Jenna placed the pot of mutton stew unceremoniously in front of him, she couldn't help staring at the angry welt across his face.

Blewett's lip curled. 'Looking at this, are you?'

Jenna stepped back as he grabbed her wrist, twisting her delicate skin in his large hand.

'Wondering where I got this mark?' He stabbed his face with his chubby finger. 'Your *friend* Matthew Bickford decided I needed to be taught a lesson. That was his biggest mistake, as *you* will find out, if you continue to tell tales about me.'

Jenna drew a deep trembling breath.

'I'll have no more nonsense from you. You'll do as you're told. You'll cook, clean, and bear my children. You'll see nobody and go no further than the Corn Mill and the dairy. Do you hear me? You're to feed and keep house for your father as well, that's the deal we've made. He'll take you to market once a week to shop and make sure you don't fritter my money away.'

Jenna winced again as he dug his filthy fingernails deeper into her wrist.

'If I hear you've been telling tales to anyone about what happens here, your father *will* go to prison, and I will break that scrawny neck of yours and bury you at sea and tell everyone you've left me. Now, take your father his dinner and come straight back.'

As he released her arm, she nursed it to her trembling

heart. At the stove, she doled out a sizable portion for her father, because in truth, she'd no appetite of her own - the thought of the coming night made her sick to the pit of her stomach.

*

As Jenna placed the meal in front of her father, his hand gently reached out to touch her bruised wrist.

'I'm sorry, maid,' he said tearfully.

Jenna retracted her arm. 'So am I, Father.'

Lonely and frightened, she walked back to the forge making the conscious decision to endure her lot with silent insolence. If she didn't respond to Blewett's unpleasantness, then he could not harm her…. or that's what she believed.

*

After supper, Blewett took himself off to The Black Swan and as a precautionary measure, locked Jenna indoors. There were no logs to feed the dying fire tonight, so consequently the room soon turned chilly. Knowing that he and her father stayed at The Black Swan until nine-thirty, she tried to read a book Mrs Eddy had lent her by the light from one candle, but her fingers trembled with a mixture of anxiety and cold. Her mind drifted from the novel to memories of Lyndon. Concentrating very hard, she could feel his fingers entwine with hers and smell the wood smoke in his hair. *I love you, Lyndon.*

The sound of the key in the lock shook her from her reverie. A quick glance at the clock said it was only eight-thirty. Panic rose in her throat as the door flew open with a crash against the granite sink. With a sharp kick of his foot, Blewett slammed the door behind him.

He studied her with cool, calculating eyes, gave a loud beer belch followed by a malicious grin.

Terror seared through her veins as he approached, snatched the book from her hand, and threw it into the embers of the fire, making the flames burst into life. His great hand grabbed her bruised wrist sending a searing pain up her arm as he dragged her up the stairs.

Kicking the bedroom door open, he pushed her inside and stopped dead. 'What the bloody hell have you done in here? It smells like a whore's bedroom.'

Closing her eyes, her heart filled with dread when she felt his foul breath, hot on the back of her neck.

He ripped the scarf from her head. 'What the hell is this?' he growled angrily, trying without success to grasp what was left of her hair. 'You little bitch,' he hissed, 'get undressed.'

*

Two days later, on the twelfth night, the village of Gweek wassailed the apple trees. The evening was cold but dry. The wind had changed over the last few hours and gales were expected later that night. The living accommodation at the forge was a cold, draughty place at the best of times. Resigned that she would not be allowed to go out wassailing with the rest of the village, Jenna began stuffing sacking into the gaps of the window frames to try and keep out the worst of the cold that evening. She had not banked on Amelia Pascoe knocking on the door.

With arms folded, Amelia stood at the forge kitchen table. 'Jenna must come with us George!' she argued. 'The whole village must be there for the wassailing.'

'Damn you and your bloody wassailing,' he grumbled back.

'You'll be grumbling if we don't get a good cider harvest. Now let her pass.' She beckoned Jenna towards her.

Unsure of what to do, having been told she was not allowed to see anyone, Jenna remained passively in the background. She knew Amelia was a force to be reckoned with in the village. She drank with the men, was the local midwife, could mend a tractor and fix a leaking thatched roof. In short, she was a formidable woman. If anyone could sway Blewett to let her go, she could.

Blewett grunted angrily, he knew better than to argue

with Amelia, so reluctantly stood to the side to let Jenna pass, but jabbed a finger at her.

'I want you back here as soon as the deed is done.'

Jenna shrank from his touch.

Amelia snorted in abhorrence and beckoned Jenna out of the house. As they walked towards the apple orchard on the river bank, she put a friendly arm around Jenna's shoulders and was shocked to feel how thin she was.

'Are you not eating properly maid?'

'I've had no appetite since all this upset began, Amelia.'

'Oh, sweetheart, you must eat. You'll make yourself very ill if you don't.'

I really don't care.

Amelia pulled her to a halt. 'Has he been violent towards you again?'

Remembering Blewett's threats, Jenna shook her head.

Amelia pursed her lips.

In truth, he'd not repeated the violation endured that first night, but he was very rough with her. 'The abuse is more verbal now,' she said to appease Amelia.

Amelia gave a tight smile. 'Well, sticks and stones may break your bones, but words will never hurt you. It's a stupid rhyme, isn't it? But it's true, as long as the abuse stays verbal, we know you're safe. Ignore the ignorant pig, that is my advice, but I reiterate, you must tell us if he physically hurts you. I have no doubt that he warned you against telling us, but you must! Do not suffer in silence! I trust your father checks on you regularly?' Knowing the coward Jory was, Amelia doubted it, but thought she would put it to Jenna to hear her response. Both she and Dr Eddy had tried to reason with Jory over this contract, to no avail.

Jenna took a slow measured breath. 'I'm sure he'll intervene should I need his assistance. What father wouldn't?' *She had to hope he would anyway.*

Amelia pursed again. 'He's been ostracized by everyone. Did you know?'

Jenna took some small consolation at this news.

'Come on,' she linked arms with Jenna, 'or we shall miss the spectacle.'

As they approached the left bank of the Helford River, a crowd had already gathered around the orchard and the wassailing had started.

Lizzy Pike, this year's wassail Queen, was small and slight in stature and easy enough for the wassail King Charlie Williams, to lift her up into the boughs of the trees in order for her to offer a gift to the tree spirits. Someone held up a cup full of cider created from the previous year's harvest, and Lizzy dipped toast into the cup and hung it on the branches. Once back on the ground they all began to sing an incantation to awake the cider apple trees and scare away evil spirits, ensuring a good harvest of fruit in the autumn.

Here's to thee, old apple tree,
That blooms well, bears well.
Hats full, caps full,
Three bushel bags full,
An' all under one tree.
Hurrah! Hurrah!

The assembled crowd began to shout, bang drums and pans until they were all making a terrible racket. When they were sure the evil spirits had been shooed away, the crowd set off to the next orchard.

For a couple of glorious hours, Jenna was free of the drudgery of life. She managed to forget her woes and gloried in this age-old tradition, unaware of what the apple harvest in the autumn would bring for her.

10

A month had passed now in the forge, one whole month of living hell. "Be strong, Jenna," Matthew Bickford had urged her, "Dig deep and find a way to endure this." Jenna took a deep trembling breath. She was trying, but her ordeal wasn't getting any easier. She always believed that when the time came for her to take a husband, their nights together would, she thought, be frightening at first to the pure woman that she was, but eventually emerge to be a gentle, rather tender coupling of two people in love. Yet she found herself thrust into marriage with a man most of the people in the village avoided because of his detestable character. Her nights were full of terror as he inflicted his unpleasant attentions on her. Normally Jenna managed to suppress her distress during the act, for she knew he revelled in her pain, but tonight he was angry with her, after tripping over one of her boots and knocking his knee hard against the bedstead. Anger was his very worst trait. Jenna believed the emotion fuelled his wanton lust and braced herself for what was to follow. As feared, he grabbed her by the neck, dragged her to his side of the bed, and though she'd tried to block out the act, the pain inflicted shot through her with such intensity she let out a piercing scream which prompted him to thump her hard on her ear.

*

Outside his cottage, Jory puffed on the last remaining tobacco in his pipe. The scream from the forge shattered the stillness of the night. A shiver ran bone deep within him, making him bite the stem of his clay pipe in two. *You're a coward Jory Trevone.* The voice in his head taunted him daily. Discarding the remains in the flower bed, he shamefully and quickly retreated indoors.

*

Nine miles away on the Trevarno Estate, Lyndon woke with a start, as a fox outside gave a harrowing, almost human like scream. These days, he too slept uneasily. Only fatigue, brought by the heavy manual work he forced his body into from dawn to dusk to cancel his misery, made him fall down into a dead sleep. But always, long before dawn, his vivid dreams brought him to wakefulness, so that he lay inanimate for the next few hours. To banish his tormented thoughts, he'd conjure up Jenna's beautiful face and imagine the softness of her small hands. If he concentrated hard, he could smell her hair, rinsed in jasmine oil. During these long hours, he painfully re-enacted their days spent together just to keep her near him.

*

For the next few hours Jenna lay motionless, staring into the darkness of the room. An owl hooted, swiftly followed by an answer in the distance, and only the occasional squabble from the nearby rooks punctured the stillness of the night. She tried to keep her thoughts very still, for if she pondered on her predicament, her resolve would crumble and that would be the end of her sanity. Focusing again on the sounds of the night, she realised farmer Williams had separated the calves from their mothers earlier today. Their pitiful cries now resonated around the village. Jenna felt their pain at being torn from a loved one. Though dreadfully fatigued, Jenna would not allow herself sleep. She simply could not, and certainly would not, rest easy beside Blewett. Only when Blewett left her in the evening for a few hours, to drink his fill in The Black Swan, did she drop her guard and fall asleep.

The great sweating lump beside her snorted noisily and Jenna's body tensed and moved away to the very edge of the wool mattress. He gave two large grunts, which indicated that his deep, ale fuelled sleep was coming to an end, and his sleep pattern would become lighter. Instinct told her the time was nearing for her to rise and start the drudge of the day. Wise now to his ways, Jenna moved before he had a chance to gouge her back with his horned toenails when he pushed her unceremoniously out of the bed with his foot. Slipping out from the blankets, she wrapped herself in her shawl, lifted her clothes from the chair and stole quietly out of the room and down the stairs. Preferring to wash in her kitchen, she broke the ice on the bowl of water and performed her ablutions of the day.

*

The day was cold. A carpet of frost covered the ground surrounding the forge. Her routine rarely varied much from day to day. Starting at four-thirty, the fires was lit, bread was made, and breakfast served at six-thirty. Afterwards, she tackled the washing and cleaning, and prepared the meals for the day - in short, life was one long drudge. A bucket of water was on the fire ready to launder the bedding, but lord knows if it would dry in this cold weather. Inevitably, stiff boards of linen would melt limply around her fireside later today. She trembled knowing that would anger Blewett.

*

Later, outside, Jenna pulled her shawl around her shoulders and inhaled the fresh clean air of this beautiful river valley. It was seven a.m. and still dark. Dawn was waiting in the wings of the night to warm the day with its wintery sunshine. The weather had been set fair and cold these last five days, making the ground as hard as nails. These precious few minutes after breakfast kept her sane. Blewett was in the forge preparing for the day. Breakfast, as always, had been fraught and fearful as he snarled and complained about everything. The bread was tasteless, the preserve too sweet, the milk sour, none of which was true, but Jenna endured this barrage of insults in silence. She rarely spoke to him and hated him intensely. Never before had this emotion – hate- reared its ugly head. The only way to deal with his enduring onslaught was to keep a dumb insolence.

The grass crunched satisfyingly underfoot. At the fringe of the river, tiny icicles hung from the longer grass.

The first show of Snowdrops or Candlemas Bells as they were known had pushed up their pure, delicate white heads, battling against all odds to flower while the earth was still under the lock and key of winter. The sight of them would normally make her reach for her drawing pad, but that was in another life. However, the very first and undeniable signal that the warm days would soon return made her heart sing. The love of nature was one thing Blewett could not take from her.

The tide was high, and the stream was running freely so she could empty the night soil bucket directly into the river, wrinkling her nose in disgust as she did so. Stretching her aching back, she watched the pale-yellow sunrise begin to light the eastern sky. The beauty and spectacle almost made her forget what she was waiting for, as she placed her hand on her tummy. Since she was thirteen, her body cycle had been as regular as the moon. She could set the clock by its appearance. At seven-twenty a.m., every twenty-eight days, this unpleasant occurrence had never altered. It was always a day of pain and discomfort, sometimes the pain was so extreme she fainted. Jenna dreaded it, but today, she willed it to happen. It was the only thing that might give her any respite from the nightly molestations. As the sun rose, the minutes ticked by, and no dull pulling pain in her abdomen came. Her heart chilled, shivering in realisation that he had succeeded in planting his disgusting seed inside her. She glanced again at the river, though this time looking at it as a means to an end. As sinful as the thought was, she would gladly plunge into its icy waters and take her own life, rather than bear *his* child.

11

Lyndon would have floundered had Matthew Bickford not arranged plenty of work for him on the estate. Work kept his mind occupied, warding off the bouts of despair that washed over him like a tide. At night though, nothing could stop the hopelessness that settled over him like a thick blanket.

It was daffodil time in Cornwall. The green shoots, now punctuated with golden trumpets, broke Lyndon's heart. This should have been a time of great happiness - when he and Jenna were to be married.

Being mid-February, the days were lighter for longer, but the cold settled quickly as the winter sun lowered in the western sky. A blackbird, high in the bare branches of the ash tree, sang gloriously, altering his tune with every song. Lyndon smiled peaceably. No matter how melancholy he felt, birdsong could always lift his spirits.

A twinge in his lower back told him it was time to gather his things together. Lyndon looked around him with appreciation - gratified that he lived in such lush, beautiful surroundings. With no-one elsc abroad, he snuck through the Italian garden as a short cut.

'I see you,' Matthew's voice rang out from within the garden. Having played together as boys there was always easiness between the two men, despite their class difference. Many times, Matthew had shared a simple jam sandwich in Lyndon's mother's kitchen, rather than going home to a formal luncheon.

Without turning, Lyndon thickened his Cornish accent and touched his forehead. 'Oh, please, sir, don't 'ee be taking me up to see the Master for trespass now. I swear I'll not do it again Sir.'

He grinned and turned to share the joke, only to find Matthew was not alone. 'Oh.' Lyndon blustered, 'begging your pardon Matthew, I didn't realise you were in company.'

Matthew roared with laughter. 'Come here you villain,' he joked. 'I'd like you to meet someone.'

Leaving his work bag on the path, Lyndon regarded the stranger with Matthew with interest.

'Lyndon, I'd like you to meet James Blackwell. James, this is my good friend of many years, Lyndon FitzSimmons.'

Conscious of his filthy hands, Lyndon wiped them quickly down his jacket before shaking the hand held out to him. If James noticed the attire of a common working man, he did not show it in his face.

'Are you James Blackwell, the writer?'

James nodded courteously. 'The very same.'

'Well, I'm very pleased to meet you,' Lyndon greeted him warmly. 'I'm reading one of your novels at the moment – The Shifting Shore. It's keeping me enthralled. I must say your love of Cornwall shines through every word you write. I congratulate you - no other author has ever been able to divert me so.'

James smiled amiably. 'You flatter me, Mr err?'

'FitzSimmons, but do call me Lyndon, and flatter be damned, I speak the truth. Begging your pardon for swearing,' he added.

James grinned boyishly, 'Pardon granted. I swear like a trouper myself.'

At their insistence, Lyndon joined them on the garden bench.

'Do you live in Cornwall?' Lyndon asked.

'For a good part of the year, yes. I've had a house built near Fisherman's Cove, Gunwalloe, looking over towards Loe Bar and Porthleven. Do you know that part of the coast?'

Lyndon thought for a moment. 'I've travelled the road past Poldhu Cove to Mullion. I've also worked on the Bochym Manor Estate, but I don't believe I have ever been over to Gunwalloe.'

'Well, it's lovely. It's a treacherous stretch of beach

mind you. Fortunately, it keeps people away, so I have peace and quiet to write. I was just telling Matthew, no matter where I have travelled in the world, and I've travelled extensively to research my books, it seems to me that Cornwall inspires me most. It is the most magical place on earth. It makes you glad to be alive.'

'I agree.' Lyndon smiled, though James noted his smile didn't quite reach his eyes.

'Lyndon is a master hedge layer you know. His fingers produce a work of art. You should watch him one day James.'

'I'd love to. Would you mind if I watched you work tomorrow, Lyndon? I'm staying the night here.'

Lyndon gave a short shrug. 'You're very welcome, James. But it's a slow process producing a 'work of art.'' He gave Matthew a cheeky smile.

As twilight descended on the garden and cold shadows chilled their bones, they stood up and shook hands.

'We're going to the Crown Inn, if you'd like to join us,' Matthew asked.

Lyndon looked uneasy.

Matthew knew where his reluctance lay. 'Come on old chap. A couple of drinks and some company will do you the world of good,' he urged with a wink.

*

They passed a pleasant couple of hours in the Crown Inn that night. James was entertaining company and Lyndon seemed to relax for the first time in weeks.

Matthew, who worried constantly about Lyndon, was glad he'd persuaded him to come, though he knew it was just the first step of a very long journey.

*

Early the next morning, Trevarno Estate was shrouded in a thick blanket of fog. Lyndon, dressed warmly, with extra socks to keep the cold from seeping through his old boots, stood observing the stillness of the valley. Through the great bank of fog occasional shafts of sunlight broke through. Soon it would burn back, and the day would warm nicely.

True to his word, James joined Lyndon high up in the top meadow. Equally dressed for the weather, he brought with him a stone bottle full of hot water to keep warm and his pen and notebook. Once comfortably settled, James watched as Lyndon worked.

It seemed quite natural for Lyndon to speak as he worked, and James was an attentive listener.

'Hedge-laying is a tradition my grandfather taught me,' Lyndon said, as he hacked away. 'It fascinated me to watch him, and from the age of five I would help whenever I could, so it was natural for me to take over when he retired. My pa was more interested in gardening you see, so I became the next hedge-layer of the family. This is his billhook.' He wielded the tool at James.

James walked nearer and studied the tool intently.

'A well-managed hedgerow has to be thick and bushy - an impenetrable barrier for sheep and cattle. It's also good for wildlife. Left unmanaged though, a hedgerow will continue to grow upwards and outwards and will eventually just become a line of trees. Once a hedge has been layered, regular trimming will keep it in good order for up to fifty years. So, unless some catastrophe happens, I'll rarely have to work on the same hedge twice,' he said with a confident nod.

The fog was lifting slightly, and Lyndon stopped his narrative to look out across the valley. 'I believe it's going to be a beautiful day.'

James followed his gaze. 'You seem at one with the countryside,' he said casually. 'When I was younger, I always believed it was only artists, writers and poets who took the time to stand and stare.'

Lyndon smiled. 'It's true, many a working man would not have the time. They work from dawn till dusk, fishing or mining. I'm lucky. I'm a man of the fields and to work as I do - you have to have an affinity with nature. You have to know the seasons and work appropriately. It must be awful not to have the freedom to do that,' his voice trailed slightly as he thought of Jenna. Her heart had been so full of the love of nature.

James watched the sadness cloud Lyndon's face. Matthew had told him of Lyndon's troubles. It was something he could sympathise with, for he too was in his own quandary regarding love.

Lyndon lifted his billhook and began again to explain. 'The aim is to reduce the thickness of the upright stems of the hedgerow trees, by cutting away the wood on one side of the stem in line with the course of the hedge.' He hacked away to show what he meant. 'Each remaining stem is laid down towards the horizontal, along the length of the hedge. This stem, called a pleacher, always has a section of bark and some sapwood left - this keeps the pleacher connected to its roots, and consequently alive. My grandfather was very particular in showing me how much to leave - this is one part of the 'art' of hedge-laying.' Lyndon lifted his hand to move a spider, which had made its way down his hat and was dangling in front of his face. 'Do you want to have a go?'

James nodded eagerly, taking the billhook from Lyndon.

'Now hack the side of the pleacher but be careful not to go right through though.'

James tentatively did as he was told, managing a fairly good cut.

'Now, the angle at which the pleacher is laid at is a factor in how I build the hedge. Hedges are built to a height according to what purpose they're intended for. The height and condition of the trimmed stem is vital, as this is where the strongest new growth will come from. In time the pleacher will die, but by then a new stem should have grown from ground level, which replaces the laid pleach.'

With instruction from Lyndon, James wove the pleacher between the upright stems and stood back in satisfaction of his work.

'I use these smaller shoots branching off the pleachers to weave between the others, to add cohesiveness to the finished hedge.' Lyndon halted his demonstration momentarily as James quickly bent to pick up his notebook. He watched as James scribbled away for a couple of minutes and wondered if he was thinking of giving up writing for hedge-laying. With that in mind, Lyndon reminded him, 'This all takes years of practice you know.'

'As does any skill,' James answered, without looking up from his notebook.

Presently, James gave his undivided attention again to Lyndon so he could continue with his master class.

'At regular intervals I place upright stakes along the line of the hedge. These stakes give the finished hedge its final strength. If the hedge is a boundary to a garden, I use a fancy effect by binding the uprights with hazel, birch, ash, or willow whips - these make the visual effect more pleasing. I've done quite a lot of that sort of finish here on the estate. Am I boring you yet?'

'On the contrary, I'm fascinated. I like to learn about different things. I often put them in my books. If you're reading The Shifting Shore, I write about the Newlyn Lifeboat. I went out on a shout with them one night and I have never been so terrified or so humbled as to see what those brave men do in such dreadful conditions. Fifty percent of my book royalties go to them.'

'So, am I to be your next protagonist?' Lyndon looked askance at him.

'Why, do you have a story worth telling?'

Lyndon twisted his mouth slightly. 'If you want to write a tale of woe, yes, I have!'

James smiled gently. 'I too have known heartbreak - it makes for good writing. Tales of woe are the best stories to write.'

'They're not the best to live through.' Lyndon looked

away. 'Though, it does make for good hedge laying,' he added seriously.

'Our everyday life is a unique story. We live and grow and learn from our mistakes. Life throws terrible things at us, but we survive and live on, albeit slightly damaged from the experience. But you know, Lyndon, life is what you make it. Just as I write a story, I generate a way through every obstacle and there is always a happy ending for those who seek it. It's out there, you just have to work your way towards it.'

'I admire your positivity, and congratulate you on it, but I can see no happy ending to my troubles.'

'I do know a little of your troubles. Matthew explained to me last night, and I'm truly sorry for you and your young lady. But for what it's worth, I believe the good people win in the end. Stay positive my friend and be ready to pick up the baton when it's handed to you. Now,' he checked his watch. 'I must be going. I am to take luncheon with Matthew and his father before taking the train to London to meet with my publisher.' He held out his hand to shake Lyndon's. 'I thank you for your time, Lyndon. I do hope we meet again soon.'

12

As the purple shoots of bluebells appeared from the warmed earth, Jenna felt the weight of the world on her young shoulders. Fatigued from illness, due to her plight and pregnancy, her body continued to reject any form of nourishment. If only she could rest a while, something may settle in her stomach, but rest was an unattainable luxury. Hidden under her thick black dress, she was bone thin. Her skin hung alarmingly from her body - this in itself conjured a sick fancy that the child clinging to her womb would not survive this famine. During her morning ablutions that day, she'd pulled a large clump of hair away in her comb and her gums bled profusely when she brushed her teeth. To say she felt thoroughly wretched was an understatement.

Heaving the last of the washing from the dolly tub, it took every bit of effort she could muster to lift the laundry up to the mangle. When the pile was done, she sank to her knees. *Get up Jenna*, the voice in her head urged. If Blewett found her sitting about - he'd box her ears. The very thought urged her back onto her feet.

A good south-westerly whistled up the Helford that morning, whipping the sheets from her hands as she struggled to peg them on the washing line stretched between the forge and the chestnut tree. With the last wooden peg attached, her head swam with sickness, and she fell to her knees dragging the line of washing with her.

Scrambling about in a cloud of white linen, trying to retrieve it from settling on the muddy ground, Jenna's desperate cries caused Amelia to look up from her task of feeding the hens. Dropping the bowl of scraps, Amelia ran to assist.

'Come on, Jenna.' She grabbed her by the arm. 'Leave that for a moment. I'll see to everything here.' Amelia was shocked at how little the girl weighed. 'Good god girl! Are you still not eating anything?'

Jenna looked at Amelia in a daze, but try as she might, she could not decipher what was being said to her. A great cavernous groan erupted from her stomach, and she buckled over and retched.

'Oh, my goodness! You're pregnant, aren't you?'

Jenna nodded in hopeless despair.

Leaving her sat at the kitchen table, Amelia went in search of Blewett.

The forge was hot and stank of stale sweat and horse dung.

'George! George!' The incessant hammering continued. 'George!' she yelled.

The hammer came down with such force, red hot embers flew everywhere. Blewett turned angrily toward Amelia.

'What the devil do you want woman, can you not see I'm busy.'

His face was black with soot and his greasy hair hung down from under his cap, clinging to his sweaty forehead.

Amelia punched her fists into her hips. 'It's about Jenna.'

'Who?'

'*Your wife!*' Amelia practically spat the words at him.

'What's amiss with her now,' he said, with the hammer raised in his hand he turned back to his work.

'I'm taking Jenna home with me. She needs to rest.'

Blewett threw a threatening glare. 'You are *not*!'

Amelia pursed her lips. 'Jenna is pregnant.'

Blewett lowered the hammer slightly.

'You didn't even know, did you?' she said stiffly. 'Have you not noticed how sick she is? Do you care nothing for her welfare?'

He drew his brows together. 'Pregnancy is not an illness. It's what women do!'

'That may be so, but Jenna cannot keep her food down. She needs to rest for a few days, so her body can take on some nourishment.'

'I said *no!*' Blewett dropped his voice to a low hiss.

Refusing to be perturbed, Amelia offered, 'I'll do her daily duties. You won't miss her.'

His lip curled. 'And what about her nightly duties, are you going to keep my bed warm too?'

Amelia balked at the suggestion. *I would rather stick my darning needle in my eye, than lay with you George Blewett.* She cleared her throat. 'You'll use a warming pan, as I do,' she quipped. 'Your meals will be on the table as usual, and your laundry will be done. You can't say no.'

He raised his eyebrows. 'Oh, can't I?'

Amelia felt her blood rise. 'If Jenna doesn't get the care and rest she needs, she will *lose* your child!'

Blewett turned this over in his mind. 'Just get out of my sight woman. I need to work.' The hammering began again.

Amelia cocked her head. He hadn't said no to her this time. That was all she needed. Gathering her skirts to avoid the horse dung, she breezed back into Jenna's kitchen to find her fast asleep at the table. Her scarf had slipped, revealing a rather alarming bald patch on her scalp. Amelia emitted a pitiful sigh, quickly checked the bread cooling under the gauze, lifted the lid of the pan on the stove and tidied the washing basket into the corner of the kitchen.

'Come on, Jenna, wake up.' Amelia said, pulling her from where she sat. 'I'm taking you home with me, but I need you to walk, I can't lift you.'

Jenna lifted her head wearily. 'I can't go. He won't let me.'

'Yes, you can. It's all sorted. Now stand up.'

It was only a short walk from the forge across the bridge to River Cottage, but the effort exhausted them both. Once inside, Jenna dug deep in order to climb the stairs, where she knew she could rest at last.

*

Sleeping for a full ten hours, Jenna woke to the delicate

smell of wallflowers and fresh bed linen. It was dark outside. There was a faint sound of movement somewhere in the cottage, and then she heard footsteps on the stairs.

Amelia appeared in the doorway and smiled. 'Welcome to the waking world.' In her hand she carried a chamber pot. 'I should think you are in dire need of this.' She placed the pot by the bed. 'I'll be back in a few minutes.'

Pushing the used pot under the bed, Jenna crawled blissfully back between the sheets, just as Amelia came back with a steaming cup in her hand.

'Now, we need to get some nourishment into you. Ginger tea to start with, it should settle your tummy. You are very dehydrated, Jenna,' she said plucking the loose skin on her wrist. 'What we need to do is give you food and drink, little and often, and you must stay in bed. It's the movement that makes you vomit. So, will you try a little ginger tea now for me?'

Jenna reached out and took the cup, tentatively smelling the tea, before bringing it to her lips.

'I'll make you a thin broth - if you can keep that down.' Amelia said closing the curtains. 'Does the doctor know you are with child?'

Jenna shook her head. 'No-one knows.'

'I'm sorry, Jenna but I'm afraid George knows now.'

Jenna looked down despondently.

Straightening the quilt on the bed, Amelia smiled gently. 'I'll get the doctor to look in tomorrow.'

Jenna felt a flash of panic. 'Oh, no don't. Blewett will be so angry. He won't pay the doctor.'

With a comforting pat on her shoulder Amelia smiled. 'Do not worry yourself. I'll sort everything out. How far gone are you?'

'Almost three months, I think.' Rubbing her hand across her face, she added desperately, 'Amelia, can you....'

'Can I what?' Amelia waited with bated breath.

Jenna swallowed hard as she touched her tummy. 'Can

you do something about it?'

Taken aback by the question Amelia shook her head. 'No, Jenna, I can't.'

Desperate tears began to fall. 'Well do you know anyone who can?'

'No, Jenna, and I would not let you go through with such an extremely dangerous procedure.'

Jenna grabbed Amelia's hand. 'Surely childbirth is an extremely dangerous procedure too?'

'It is.' Amelia's expression became serious. 'But I will be with you when you give birth.'

Jenna stared down at her hands. 'I don't want this baby!'

Sitting beside her on the bed, Amelia put a comforting arm around her. 'I know you don't, darling, but what is done is done and we shall have to make the best of things. Believe me, when baby comes, I'm sure you'll fall in love with it. Look on it as something good in your life to build on. I've never had children of my own, but they say the love a mother feels for her new-born baby is the most powerful love in the world.'

Jenna's lips trembled.

'We'll get through this together Jenna. Now drink your tea and get some more rest. You'll feel so much better in the morning.'

Amelia kissed her on the forehead like her mother used to do and left her to sleep.

13

It was May, and a haze of bluebells spread as far as Lyndon could see through the woods at Trevarno. Lost in his thoughts, he weaved and plaited his branches into place, until a flash of movement caught his sight. Narrowing his eyes curiously, a roe deer stepped into his line of vision. Hardly daring to breathe, he watched as the creature nervously surveyed its surroundings, flicking its soft velvet ears at any noise. Lyndon smiled at its feral beauty. Still wearing her grey-brown winter coat, she was a sight to behold. Always at one with nature, Lyndon stayed perfectly still as the deer bent to graze, and as it did, her stiff-legged dappled coated fawn came into view. With the sound of a woodpecker in the distance, Lyndon savoured this peaceful precious moment, until a noise startled the deer. She looked up, still holding a leaf in her mouth, and emitted an alarming bark, just as a bolt whizzed through the air, piercing the animal in its neck. The deer dropped like a stone where it stood. Lyndon baulked at the sight and leapt from his vantage point in time to witness two men running towards their catch.

Fuelled by anger, Lyndon hollered, 'Hey, you there. What the hell are you doing?'

The men came to a sudden halt before turning to flee in panic.

'Stop!' Lyndon bellowed, following in hot pursuit. The man bringing up the rear held a crossbow. He turned briefly allowing Lyndon to recognise Norman Jenkins from the nearby village of Crown Town. Sure enough, if Norman was there, so too was his 'partner in crime' Harry Baker. They were both known to the constable and had several times avoided being caught for poaching. Lyndon's shouts alerted the estate's gamekeeper, John Dunnet, who quickly joined the pursuit, but the pair scattered into the dense part of the wood. Eventually they gave up the chase content in the knowledge the rogues would not escape prosecution this time. Slowly they walked back to the deer to find its fawn knelt by its mother's body. The poor thing was too young to understand the danger of human beings.

John knelt and pulled the bolt from the deer's neck. 'Evidence,' he said passing it to Lyndon. 'I've been after those two buggers for ages.' He sighed heavily as he patted the deer's neck. 'We may as well get it up to the house to butcher it.'

Lyndon nodded. 'I'll go and get some help,' he offered. 'What shall we do about the little one?'

John shrugged. 'I doubt it'll survive. Poor little mite isn't weaned yet.'

A few minutes later, Lyndon returned with his father, Tommy Teague the groom, and a wooden rack to hoist the deer onto. As they pulled their heavy load, the tiny fawn followed its mother, occasionally nudging at her teats - it was a pitiful sight.

As the cook, Mrs Drake, fussed around the carcass, John and Lyndon went in search of Mr Brown, the head butler, to report the poachers.

When Lyndon stepped back out into the yard, the fawn was still by its mother.

'What shall I do with you then?' he said softly as he bent to pick it up. It instantly settled into his arms and nuzzled into his neck. The sound of hooves clattering into the yard made it flinch slightly, but Lyndon soothed the creature, until Matthew pulled his horse to a halt.

'Matthew, just the man, can I use one of the stable boxes? We have a little orphan who needs a home.'

Matthew dismounted as Tommy Teague rushed out to take his horse. 'You're never going to rear it yourself, are you?' Matthew said, tentatively stroking the fawn's head.

Lyndon shrugged. 'What else can I do? Norman Jenkins and Harry Baker have just killed its mother.'

Matthew's eyes widened. 'You caught them in the act then?'

'I did, but it was a bitter victory, as I now have this little fellow to look after.'

Matthew cocked his head. 'I think your little fellow is a doe actually?'

'It is?' Lyndon adjusted the fawn to inspect.

'You're lucky it's a doe, they're easier than buck fawns to rear so I understand. You have to castrate the bucks as soon as possible, otherwise they'll turn on you.' He tickled the fawn behind the ears. 'I'm telling you though, if she survives, she'll be constantly under your feet.'

Lyndon pulled a face. 'Well, I don't really think I have an option, do I? She seems to like me.'

Matthew laughed heartily. 'Well, good luck then, but you're making a rod for your own back.'

For the next four weeks, Lyndon fed, nurtured and slept in the barn with the fawn. He'd called her Fern, and true to form, she followed him everywhere. Rearing Fern gave him a purpose in life. If he couldn't help Jenna, at least he could help this tiny creature.

*

The beginning of June was very wet, but Lyndon felt there was a change in the weather coming. The fields surrounding the Trevarno Estate were lush green and the work Lyndon's father had put into the gardens was paying great dividends.

Lyndon was enjoying a rare day off, so when Matthew walked down into the dell, he found him sat on the wooden bench outside his cottage sharpening his billhook.

Noting the pensive look on Matthew's face, Lyndon sat upright. Fern ran up and sniffed Matthew, but when no treats were forthcoming, she returned to kneel at Lyndon's side.

Matthew gave Lyndon a thin smile. 'I've been over at Trelowarren this weekend.'

Lyndon made no comment as Matthew sat beside him.

Clasping his hands together Matthew looked directly at Lyndon. 'I called in on Jenna while I was in Gweek.'

Lyndon met his gaze in anticipation.

'Blewett wouldn't leave us to speak alone, but according to Dr Eddy she's been quite unwell.'

Lyndon could feel alarm bells begin to ring.

'I believe she's over the worst, though she's much changed.' He took a deep breath. 'I'm sorry, my friend, but I have to tell you, she's with child.'

Lyndon trembled with anger. 'The bastard, the filthy bastard,' he hissed through the narrow aperture of his lips.

'It was inevitable, Lyndon,' Matthew said, placing a comforting hand on his shoulder.

'I know,' he snapped. He threw his newly sharpened billhook into the ground. 'But it should have been *us*!'

'I'm so sorry, my friend. I was in two minds whether to tell you or not,' Matthew answered grimly.

Lyndon shook his head wearily. 'Don't apologise. I'm glad of any news of her. But you say she's much changed?'

Matthew nodded. 'The pregnancy has taken its toll. I believe she was ill with sickness from the onset, hence she's terribly thin, almost a shadow of her former self. I barely recognised her!'

Lyndon dropped his head in his hands. 'It grieves my heart to hear this news.'

The fawn stood and nudged Lyndon's hands and he pulled her towards him for comfort.

'I'm sorry - it grieves me to tell you, but take comfort, she is under Dr Eddy's care. I'll take my leave now Lyndon. Go gently with yourself.'

*

When the sun split the morning clouds in the east, Jenna sighed with relief that the day was going to be fine. Today she could dry her washing outside. She was five months pregnant now, and though the sickness had diminished, her body felt heavy and cumbersome, which in turn made her chores even more difficult.

'Hello, Jenna,' John the postman shouted over. 'Lovely morning, is it not?' Seeing her with her arms full of washing, he added, 'Shall I leave your letters with your father as usual?'

'Why - is there a letter for me?' she asked eagerly

John re-checked his bundle and nodded.

Jenna, flushed with excitement, put her washing basket down and wiped her hands down her apron. 'How wonderful - I haven't had a letter for months!'

John frowned. 'Yes, you have! I've delivered at least three for you since January.' Noting her puzzled expression, he added, 'Did you not get them?'

Jenna shook her head.

Just as he spoke Jory dashed from his cottage, beckoning John to hand over the post.

John retracted the letter from Jory's reach. 'The letter is addressed for Jenna,' he said authoritatively.

Jory panicked, as his eyes darted towards the forge. 'You know George told you that all his letters are to be delivered to me.' Jory flicked his fingers rudely.

John raised his eyebrows. 'I work for the Royal Mail and pride myself in my job. It is my duty to see that the addressee receives the mail, and this letter belongs to Jenna,' he answered, handing it to her.

Knowing the letter could be snatched from her grasp any moment Jenna quickly ripped it open and began to read. It was from her friend Kate:

Dear friend,

I am at a loss to know why you do not respond to my letters. I've even written to your father, just in case you'd married your young man and moved address, but still no word. Maybe my letters are going astray, so this is my last attempt.

I have news you see. I was safely delivered a little girl in April. We called her Grace, and she's such a joy. Stephen is very busy with work, and we have settled very well in our new town.

I shall keep this letter short, in case this also goes astray, but I will write more should I get a reply from you.

I so look forward to hearing all your news. I should think you're happily settled now with your hedger. I so want to know all about

your wedding, I bet you looked so beautiful.
Take care, Jenna,
Love Kate, Stephen and Grace. x

Jenna's eyes filled with hopeless tears.

'Not bad news I hope?' John asked.

'No, just a friend wondering why I haven't answered any of the letters she sent me,' she answered contemptuously.

John turned a questioning eye on Jory.

Jory, guilty in his silence, shot an anxious glance towards the forge before rushing back to his cottage.

John raised his brows. 'I'll make sure I personally hand you your letters in future.'

'Thank you, but I don't think there'll be any more letters.'

'Oh?' He adjusted the heavy bag strap at his shoulders. 'Why is that then?'

'I don't have paper or a pen, and if I did, I've no money to pay the postage,' she whispered despondently, as she bent to pick up her washing basket.

'Oh, I see,' he said stiffly. 'Here, let me help you with that. You really shouldn't be lifting things in your condition.' Seeing her up close, John observed with concern the flesh that had fallen away from her face. He also noted how her beautiful green eyes, once so admired, were dull and dark circled. Placing her basket down, he reached out and touched her arm. His eyes were gentle and so was the tone of his voice. 'Can I do anything else for you?'

She smiled warmly. 'Thank you, John, but no, I'm fine now.'

John didn't think she was but knew better than to interfere with domestic issues. Aware of her nervous glances towards the forge, he nodded slowly. 'I'll bid you good day then.'

The next morning, Jenna found writing material hidden behind her mangle in the outhouse, with a simple note attached: *Leave your letters here. I'll post them for you.*

When Blewett went to The Black Swan that evening, Jenna decided to forgo her nap and write to Kate.

Dearest friend,

Firstly, congratulations on the birth of Grace, I'm truly happy for you. I deeply apologise for the lack of correspondence - it seems all your letters were intercepted. You see, I was not allowed to marry Lyndon (my hedger). My father arranged for me to marry George Blewett! Yes, you read that correctly. It's an arrangement that I was unable to refuse, otherwise it would mean my father would have gone to prison. Father borrowed a great deal of money from Blewett and was unable to pay him back. As Father took care of me when Mother died, I feel it is my duty to take care of him and keep him from prison. I am, as you can imagine, in purgatory. Blewett allows me no freedom, no letters, nor friends, though Amelia Pascoe forces Blewett to let her see me occasionally. I too am with child, but the prospect of bringing Blewett's child into the world fills me with dread. He's the most hateful, disgusting human being and the thought of producing another in his form makes my skin crawl. I'm sorry that the only letter you receive from me is this dreadful one, but I could not write to you without telling you my woes, we have been friends for a long time, and I dearly need to tell someone.

What I do want to say though is that it fills my heart with joy to know you and your little family are happy. The postman has kindly offered to pay the postage on this letter for me, though I'm not sure how long it will be before this is discovered, and when it is, Blewett will be furious.

Do not grieve for me Kate. There is nothing anyone can do. I just needed you to know.

Forever your friend, Jenna x

Hiding the letter under the jam pan for safekeeping, she'd put it in the outhouse in the morning for John to pick up. It crossed her mind to write to Lyndon as well while she had the chance, but in the end decided against it. After Matthew's recent visit, Lyndon would now know of her condition. A letter would only add to his heartbreak.

14

At the end of July, Lyndon received a request from Jack Ferris of Barleyfield Farm in Gweek, to repair a stretch of hedge which had been destroyed again by a family of badgers. The request threw up so many concerns, namely that Barleyfield Farm held painful memories of Jenna, and was in close proximity to the Forge. There was every chance he'd see Jenna, which on one hand he desperately wanted, but on the other, the thought of seeing her heavy with another man's child was inconceivable. Eventually, Lyndon sent his acknowledgement by return post; he would be there on Wednesday at one p.m.

*

Stepping out from the hot stuffy kitchen, Jenna wiped the back of her hand across her forehead but found no respite outside. The day was hot, still, and oppressive. Thunder would rumble in sometime that day that was for sure. Her thin dress clung uncomfortably to her damp body. The bulge of the growing child inside her was barely the size of a football, even though she was over six months gone.

With her bucket in hand, she fell into step with Jack Ferris as he made his way to the forge.

'Here, my dear, let me help, you look fit to drop, if you pardon the expression.' Jack filled the bucket from the water pump for her and carried it back to her kitchen, before leaving to seek out Blewett.

Blewett disliked anyone interacting with his wife and scowled angrily at Jack as he approached the forge door.

Ignoring his manner, Jack said, 'I've come for the fork you've mended for me.'

Blewett thrust the five-pronged fork into Jack's hands without ceremony.

Jack studied the repair and nodded. 'I've young Lyndon FitzSimmons coming about now. I need this to mend a Cornish wall while he puts right a hedge....'

Before Jack could finish his sentence, Blewett pushed

him aside discourteously and ran outside.

Jenna was washing the windows when she saw Blewett running towards her, his leather apron rustling loudly as he neared. She winced as he grabbed her arm, spilling the contents of her bucket.

'You, get indoors, now!'

She fell heavily against the kitchen table, banging her elbow, and then realised Blewett was locking her in. Nursing her sore arm, she puzzled as to what was going on. Hearing muffled voices through the wall adjacent to the forge, Jenna pressed one of the jam jars, waiting to be filled with preserve, against the wall to listen. All she could hear was the murmur of Jack Ferris talking to Blewett.

With the heat of the kitchen so oppressive, Jenna moved upstairs. Pulling a chair to the window, she tried to find what little movement of air she could, but as with all the windows in the house, Blewett had fettled them, so they only opened an inch – having an inordinate dislike of draughts. The sound of hooves clip clopping down Chapel Hill caught her attention. As Bramble pulled Lyndon's wagon into view, Jenna's heart leapt. *'Lyndon!'* It was as though he'd heard her because Lyndon looked straight up at her bedroom window.

She laid her hands flat to the window, her eyes sweeping longingly over his handsome face. Her breath misted the glass, but she rubbed it clear, Lyndon's gaze had moved to Jack Ferris, who had joined him with his five-pronged fork in hand.

Jack climbed aboard the wagon next to Lyndon and with a flick of the reins they set off towards Barleyfield Farm.

Seeing Lyndon give a backward glance, Jenna knew she was not forgotten. Pressing her hot cheek against the window pane, a pitiful cry escaped her throat. Her heart ached with grief as the man she loved disappeared from sigh - another little piece of her died at the loss.

Jenna was in a dreadful state of exhaustion when

Blewett finally released her from the stifling furnace of the cottage hours later. Scarfless, Jenna's hair, what was left of it, separated into dark, damp clumps, and her dress, soaked in perspiration, clung to every undulation of her body.

Insensible to her plight, Blewett curled his lip disdainfully, gave a short derisive snort, coughed and spat a ball of phlegm at the fire, which hissed as it hit the coals - narrowly missing the supper pot. Jenna balked in disgust but ignored his baleful stare, refusing him the satisfaction of hearing her complain. She knew her dumb insolence irritated him.

Blewett hated her being pregnant - he thought her body ugly, though the fullness of her breasts pleased him enormously. He slammed his fist down on the table.

'It looks like you've done nothing all day, except for messing about in this kitchen making bloody jam. Who the hell are you making bloody jam for, eh? I hate the stuff you make! You need some proper work to do.'

Jenna winced as he prodded her swollen stomach.

'The sooner that child is born, the better. That'll stop you daydreaming all day about your fancy man. I saw that bloody hedger looking this way, and by the look on your face you saw him too, don't try to deny it.'

Jenna flinched as he grabbed her by the chin and squeezed until her teeth cut into her tongue.

'Well, you can stop any fancy thoughts of him. If I see him looking this way again, he'll end up dead, strung up in one of his hedges.'

When he let go of her face, Jenna braced herself as he raised his hand threateningly. Instead, he swept his arm across the table, pushing the five jars of jam she had made that morning to the floor.

Jenna looked down silently on the sticky puddle of jellified strawberries and broken glass.

'Clear that up before supper,' Blewett ordered.

15

The summer passed in a haze of melancholia for Lyndon. It was September, harvest time on the Trevarno Estate. All hands were needed, and hard work was the only thing that could take Lyndon's mind off Jenna.

Fern was safely shut in the stable while Lyndon worked the fields. As much as she'd been a faithful companion these last few months, she was grown now and constantly pushed him over whilst working, albeit playfully. In order to introduce her back into the wild, he regularly took her to forage in the woods, sometimes camping out there so she could get used to living amongst the other animals during the night. If she could re-establish herself there, she would be ready to breed herself this time next year, though it would grieve him to see her go.

It took twice as long to bring in the harvest on the Trevarno Estate as it had done at Farmer Ferris's farm last year, but once again the weather had thankfully stayed fine. Finally, the last wagon rumbled down the dusty fields. The 'crying of the neck' sounded and everyone cheered and began to walk down to the lower meadow for supper.

Hot and tired, Lyndon slung his jacket over his shoulder and held back from the rest of the crowd. Remembering the last harvest gave him no stomach to drink and dance this year.

A hand suddenly grabbed his, jolting him from his reverie. It was Edna Madron from the next cottage to his.

'Come on Lyndon. Let's get a place at the table.'

He smiled warmly, gently extracting his hand from hers. Edna was a pretty girl, though skinny in stature. She wore a garland of field flowers around her dark hair, and her generous mouth smiled amiably.

'Everyone wants to dance with you, Lyndon.' Edna giggled, skipping lightly at his side. 'You can't deprive all the estate girls of their one chance of being in your arms.'

Lyndon knew he had a following of girls, sweet on him,

but he gave them no encouragement, which in turn made them more determined in their pursuit of his company.

He shook his head. 'I have no heart for dancing, Edna.'

'Well, a drink and a bite to eat then. Oh, come on Lyndon, please?' She touched his arm lightly.

Admittedly, he was rather thirsty. 'Well, maybe just a drink then,' he agreed, reluctantly following her to the supper table.

The dance was in full swing and barely a space could be found at the trestle table. So, Edna pulled him towards the cider barrel, leaving him to get the drinks while she collected a couple of hot pasties. Settling at a quiet spot by the wall, they ate their supper. The cider, as always, went straight to his head and he felt himself relax. With the fiddle music pulsating through his body, his foot moved rhythmically to the music. Once supper was consumed, Edna pulled him to his feet, shook out her skirt and started him on a chain of dancing with almost every girl at the party. The more he danced, the more he drank, and everyone on the estate watched with relief as Lyndon laughed like he used to…. before his troubles.

Eventually the music ended, the supper tables were cleared away and people dispersed. Lyndon sat down on the grass under the harvest moon, his head dizzy with cider. With his arms folded against his chest, he lay back thoughtfully. He'd enjoyed himself tonight, despite himself. If only he was sharing this night with……

'Lyndon,' the female voice broke into his thoughts.

'Jenna?' he whispered into the night air.

'Lyndon,' the voice came more forcefully.

His eyes snapped open but could not locate where the voice came from.

Edna stepped closer and stared down at him. 'Lyndon, it's me, Edna,' she said sharply.

'Oh.' His disappointment was palpable.

Ignoring his tone, she asked, 'Could you walk me home please? I'm not so sure I like walking in the dark.'

'Of course, I will Edna,' he said, shaking the fug of inebriation from his head. He got up, swayed a little and brushed the damp grass from his clothes.

The night was warm and still, stars burned bright, and hoots of laughter came from people making their way merrily home.

Edna said little as they walked, but occasionally bumped into his arm as she stumbled in the dark. Eventually Lyndon offered up his arm, which she took gratefully and held tighter than necessary.

They walked together in quiet contentment and as they approached the stable block, Edna said, 'I notice Fern has grown now. I thought it was a rare thing you did - adopting her.'

Lyndon patted her hand on his arm.

'I'd dearly like to stroke her, but I'm too nervous.'

He laughed lightly. 'There's no need to be nervous, she's as gentle as a lamb,' his words were slightly slurred. 'Come on, she's in the stable. I'll introduce you to her. I need to feed her anyway.'

Lyndon lit the lantern after several attempts and hooked it high on the stall gate. The stable smelt of horse dung and sweet hay as they knelt down. Fern was enjoying this unexpected attention while she munched her supper.

It was warm in the stable, and both Lyndon and Edna became aware of their close proximity. Very slowly Edna reached out and placed her hand tenderly on his arm. When he didn't pull away, she moved to kiss him. Whether it was the cider, or the elation of the dance, he did not deflect the kiss, but gave a great sigh and lay down wearily on the hay. Edna leant over him and kissed his face with feathery softness.

'Hold me, Lyndon. Just hold me for a moment.'

Lyndon hesitated slightly, and then wrapped his arms around her skinny waist.

'There's no reason for you to be alone anymore.'

Lyndon was unsure if the voice was Edna's or in his

own head.

'*I* want to be with you, Lyndon,' Edna whispered lying beside him and lifting her skirt.

Lyndon shook his head, though his body was making its own inclination known.

Edna smiled. 'Come on, Lyndon let me make you happy again.'

Could he be happy with Edna? He moved towards her and she wriggled underneath him. *Oh Jenna.* He unbuttoned his trousers, manoeuvred slightly until they were skin on skin. Close as they were to full intimacy, Lyndon knew it was unfair to make love to Edna whilst thinking of Jenna. He forced himself to look at Edna's face, dismayed to see it contort with terror. He withdrew instantly, just as she cried, 'Stop!'

He hovered, suspended over her, his heart pounding like a drum. Utterly appalled with himself that he'd almost taken her in such a casual fashion, he said shamefully, 'I'm so sorry, Edna.'

Edna looked downcast. 'No, I'm sorry I stopped you. I was just frightened it would hurt. We… can try again if you want?' she added meekly.

Lyndon shook his head and moved swiftly away. 'I don't think that's a good idea,' he said, adjusting his trousers. 'Come on.' He held out his hand to help her up. 'Let me make sure you get safely home.'

16

It was Monday October 20th. Amelia had been to Helston market with Jory, though lately he was not the best of travelling companions, hence Amelia endured the arduous journey in relative silence. Thankfully, after two days of damp misty weather, it had been warm and dry for the journey. Jenna normally accompanied them, but the journey proved impossible during her last few weeks of pregnancy.

Almost before the wagon pulled up on the bridge, screams could be heard coming from the forge.

Amelia's eyes darted towards Jory. 'It must be Jenna's time!'

Jory's eyes widened with alarm before giving a short nod and skulked away to his cottage.

Shaking her head in bewilderment at Jory's total disregard for his daughter's welfare, Amelia gathered her shopping baskets together, deposited her groceries in her kitchen, washed her hands and ran to the forge.

Blewett glowered as Amelia entered his kitchen. 'For god's sake shut her up, will you? She's giving me a sore head with her caterwauling.'

'You shut your own mouth, George Blewett.' Amelia bristled. 'Don't you realise how much pain that poor girl is in?'

Blewett pulled his braces back over his shoulders and scratched his groin. 'She's a bloody woman, isn't she? I thought they were built to breed.'

Amelia shuddered with indignation. 'Get out of my sight, you despicable man. Have you no work to do?' She pushed him sideways and made the stairs two at a time.

Dr Eddy, already in attendance, was pinched white with worry as he met Amelia by the door. 'She's very weak and two weeks overdue!' he whispered. 'There's nothing to the girl. She's as thin as a rake. I'm not certain she's going to get through this, Amelia.'

Jenna was splayed on the bed, drenched in sweat, moaning incoherently.

Moving to her side, Amelia gently stroked Jenna's forehead. Her scarf had slipped, revealing great bald patches, and what little hair she had, stuck to her scalp in damp clumps.

On seeing Amelia, Jenna grasped her arm in wide-eyed terror. 'Please, make it stop. I can't stand this pain.'

'Shhh now sweetheart, I promise it'll be all right.' Amelia squeezed her hand reassuringly. 'How long have you been having the pains?'

'Since just after midnight,' she sobbed.

Amelia turned to the doctor, who gave a short shrug. 'I've only just been called. Blewett said her pains had just started, but she was in great distress by the time I got here. If I'd known, I would have been here sooner.'

Jenna panted exhaustedly. 'He wouldn't let me send for you. He kept telling me to shut up and get on with it. Oh, my god! Her face contorted as another pain ripped through her body.

Dr Eddy took her by the hand to reassure her. 'I've just done an examination Jenna - your baby is imminent.' He shot Amelia a worried look.

Amelia bent towards Jenna. 'Listen to me. Dr Eddy and I are going to get you through this. We've delivered countless babies. It's going to feel as though someone is pulling your insides out, and there will be a lot of pain in your lower back - it's all very normal. I know this is distressing for you, but very soon your baby will come, and the pain will end. Now, we're both here to help.' Amelia looked up at Dr Eddy who nodded. 'Right, Jenna, your baby's head is almost ready to come. I need you to be brave and strong and follow everything we ask of you, all right?'

Amelia's words were drowned by an agonising scream.

Three quarters of an hour and much anguish later, Jenna was delivered of a baby boy. The baby was long, thin, wrinkled and very, very cross.

'You have a son, Jenna,' Dr Eddy said, cutting the cord before handing the child to Amelia to do her preliminary checks. He glanced around the room for the first time since he'd entered it and realised that there were no provisions ready to accept a new-born child. 'Do you have a cot ready Jenna?'

Jenna heard him but closed her eyes to shut everything from her mind. *At last, the thing was out of her.*

Amelia noted that the child hardly made a whimper, which was unusual, they normally hollered their heads off, but everything else seemed to be normal. Wrapping him in her own shawl, she walked back to the bed.

'Jenna?' Amelia hovered to place the child in her arms.

Jenna looked at Amelia with hollow desolation before turning away to face the other side of the room.

Amelia and Dr Eddy exchanged concerned glances.

'Jenna, you need to put the child to the breast as soon as possible,' Dr Eddy urged.

Their plea fell on deaf ears, leaving Amelia to cradle the baby in her own arms, while Dr Eddy set about delivering the placenta.

Once the procedure was complete, Jenna curled her legs up to her chest, pushed her face into the pillow and sobbed with misery. Fully aware of their expectations, she wished they would just take *his* child away from her.

*

The air was thick with emotion in the forge as Dr Eddy and Amelia addressed Blewett.

'You have a son, George,' Dr Eddy announced flatly.

Blewett's face brightened. 'A son!' He wiped his sweaty hands down his shirt and took the child from Amelia.

Always angry with one thing or another, it was a surprise for Dr Eddy and Amelia to see joy on Blewett's face for once.

Feeling the weight of the child in his arms his face changed. 'Scrawny little bugger though, isn't he? I need a big strong lad to run this place so, here, *she* needs to feed him up,' he said, handing the child back to Amelia.

Dr Eddy took a deep breath, for he knew Blewett would not like what he said, next. 'Well, there's the thing. We need to employ a wet nurse, George,' he added matter-of-factly.

Blewett narrowed his eyes. 'What the devil for?'

Glancing at Amelia, who jiggled the fractious baby in her arms, he said. 'Jenna's not well enough to care for the child.'

'What rubbish are you telling me now? I've never known a woman to shirk her responsibilities as she does. No, I tell you.' He growled. 'I will not employ a wet nurse!'

'George, your son will starve if we don't get some nourishment into him soon. Now Mrs Bolitho is the perfect candidate to nurse your son. She's still suckling her own child and has nursed other women's babies before…'

'I said, *no*!' George spat the words. 'If you don't make *her* feed it, I bloody well will.'

'You will *not*,' Dr Eddy retorted. 'Jenna is very weak and if you do not allow this to happen, you will lose both mother and child!'

Almost nose to nose, Blewett glowered. 'Well, I'm not paying this Mrs Bolitho!'

'Yes, you are! Mrs Bolitho will expect payment for her services. If you do not pay her, she will not do it and your son will die.'

*

Jenna lay in quiet desolation as Amelia handed the baby into Meg Bolitho's care.

She patted Jenna gently on the arm. 'Don't you worry, maid - your babe will be fine with me. Do you have a name for him?'

Jenna lowered her eyes.

Meg Bolitho wrinkled her nose. 'Can't think of one yet, eh? Did you think it would be a girl?'

Jenna remained silent and Meg glanced at Amelia, who

just shrugged.

'Do you have a change of clothes for him then?'

Jenna shook her head.

Meg knitted her brows together. 'You've gathered nothing for the child? Well, this is a rum situation!' She directed the statement at Amelia. 'Did she not know she was having a babe? Hasn't she knitted anything?' she whispered scandalously.

Amelia put a hand on Meg's arm and moved her away from Jenna's bed. 'It's all right, Meg. Jenna hasn't been very well throughout the pregnancy you see. I've been putting some things together for him though. They're in a bag downstairs.'

'Oh!' Meg Bolitho pulled a face. 'Well, I might have one or two things that mine have grown out of.' She glanced over at Jenna, but when she received no response, she hugged the child tight to her chest and bustled her way out of the bedroom. Downstairs she sorted through the hand-me-downs, tutting loudly, before taking her leave from Amelia.

Amelia returned to Jenna's bedside, fretting over this sorry affair.

'Has it gone?' Jenna asked flatly.

Amelia nodded. 'Yes, for now.'

Jenna stared at the ceiling, with eyes as empty as her heart felt for the infant she'd given birth to. 'Good,' she whispered.

Unable to lift Jenna's spirits, Amelia sat until Jenna fell asleep. With nothing more to do, she stood up, stretched the stiffness from her body and took herself back to her own cottage.

It was dark when Jenna became aware of a presence in the bedroom. She wrinkled her nose at the undeniably stale smell of Blewett. He crawled on the bed behind her, and she opened her eyes to find him looming over her.

'You're bloody unnatural,' he hissed angrily into her ear.

An uncontrollable tremble ran through her body.

He thumped the heel of his hand into her shoulder. 'Did you hear me? You're bloody unnatural. What sort of mother would let her baby starve?'

Jenna curled into a ball as he slapped her hard across the head, knowing worse would follow.

'Well, you're not going to shirk these responsibilities.'

Jenna flinched as he dragged the sheets from the bed and though her default emotion was to always remain silent - no matter what happened, a tiny uncontrollable whimper escaped her throat as Blewett crawled on top of her.

*

Dr Eddy found her the next morning, pale and sweaty, slumped at her kitchen table. There was bread baking in the oven, but her bowls and utensils were scattered unwashed across the kitchen. Pulling her quickly to her feet, she cried out in pain and cradled her lower abdomen.

'Can you walk, Jenna?'

She looked up with glazed eyes.

With her arm pulled around his shoulder Dr Eddy practically dragged Jenna across the bridge towards Amelia's cottage.

Seeing them approach, Amelia left what she was doing to greet them at the door. 'Whatever has happened?'

'I don't know, but she's in a terrible state. We have guests staying with us - could you give her a bed?'

'Of course,' Amelia said, pulling Jenna's other arm across her own shoulder.

When Jenna felt the softness of the mattress, she shrieked in horror and tried to scramble back off the bed.

'Shhh now, everything is fine. You're in my cottage. Everything is going to be fine,' Amelia said, smoothing her cool hand over Jenna's hot forehead.

A quick examination confirmed what Dr Eddy suspected.

'Damn that man,' he said, before turning on his heel

and descending the stairs. Angrier than he had ever been, Dr Eddy stormed into the forge and bellowed at Blewett, 'Are you some sort of animal?'

Holding the hammer mid-air, Blewett stared at the doctor as though he'd gone mad.

'What the devil are you talking about?'

'Your wife! That's what I'm talking about.'

With an irritated sigh Blewett resumed his work.

'What do you think you're doing - forcing yourself on her the day she gives birth? Have you no sense of decency man? Don't you know it's highly dangerous to do so?'

'Why, what's she moaning about now?' he said, pushing the tool he was forming back into the fire.

'Jenna's running a high fever because of your actions. She's being cared for at Amelia's. I am warning you George, you will refrain from any physical activities with your wife. God damn it man! Don't you know you must wait at least three weeks? Have a care in future. Otherwise, you will not have a wife to press your marital rights on.' As he spoke the last sentence, Dr Eddy felt bile rise into his throat.

When the doctor departed the forge, George threw his hammer to the floor and shouted, 'Christ, but that woman is more than useless.'

*

Two days passed before Jenna felt well enough to sit up in bed, though the infection in her uterus was still very uncomfortable. Her milk had come through that morning, soaking her nightgown with filmy, sticky dampness, all of which added to her misery.

Amelia sat on the chair beside Jenna's bed, cradling the baby in her arms while Mrs Bolitho was downstairs, enjoying a cup of tea and a freshly baked scone.

Amelia smiled softly. 'George wants to call the child Henry - what do you think of that name?'

Jenna stared blankly into space.

Undaunted by her lack of response, she added, 'Why

don't you take him for a moment? I promise you, Jenna, once you've nursed him, you'll feel so much better.'

Through her fug of despair, Jenna shook her head and shrunk down in the bed.

'He needs to suckle you, Jenna. Your breasts will get very painful if you don't feed him,' Amelia said firmly.

Crossing her arms defiantly, she whispered, 'I don't want *his* child to suckle me.'

'It's your child too, Jenna!' she answered tightly. 'You cannot deny the child's existence forever. You'll have to take responsibility for it soon.'

'I don't want *his* baby and I don't want *this* life!' Great fat tears rolled down her cheeks.

It pained Amelia to see Jenna so broken. She reached over and dabbed her wet cheek with her handkerchief.

'Jenna please, you chose to honour your father's debt to George and a baby was the inevitable outcome to that choice.'

Jenna's eyes flashed widely. 'You *know* I had no choice!'

'Nor have you a choice now. He's just a tiny baby Jenna, he needs you. It will be something to love, something to take your mind from your predicament. Please, just hold him for a moment. Do it for me?'

Meg Bolitho, having finished her tea, arrived back in the bedroom.

'Is the maid ready for a cuddle with the babe then?' Meg asked.

'Are you?' Amelia looked at Jenna hopefully.

Despite herself, Jenna reluctantly pulled her arms from under the sheets. As Amelia moved the baby towards Jenna, its body stiffened, his face turned red, and his mouth opened as though to emit a scream, but no sound came out.

Meg grinned at Jenna. ''Tis a shame he doesn't favour his mother's looks. He's the spitting image of his father.'

With this, Jenna froze and retracted her arms.

Amelia shot an irritable look at Meg, as she patted,

soothed and jiggled the child, but nothing seemed to calm him or stop his face from contorting.

Meg bent over and gently touched his face. 'He does this with me as well. He seems to get all twisted and agitated, but never a cry comes from this little mouth. I think he's probably got his father's temperament, but not his voice, eh?' She winked at Jenna. 'I'll take him now, shall I?' Meg reached down and took the baby from Amelia's arms. 'Now, now, what's amiss with this little cherub, eh?' Meg said, as she cradled him in her arms. 'Can I see you downstairs, Amelia?' Meg beckoned her to follow.

Amelia reluctantly left Jenna to rest.

Meg's words ran through Jenna's mind, repeatedly. "He's the spitting image of his father." The words made her shudder to think she'd brought another Blewett into the world. Rubbing her face with her hands, she wondered how she was ever going to deal with this nightmare scenario. There was not a single scrap of motherly instinct pulling at her heartstrings.

Downstairs, Meg voiced her concerns about the child. 'I've had six of my own and never one like this. I never had one that didn't cry!'

Amelia agreed. 'We thought it strange when he hardly cried when he was born.'

Meg Bolitho pulled a face. 'He won't suckle properly either. It's not good for a babe, you know! They need to suckle to thrive! I'm a feared for him - truly I am. He should have had his mother's first suckle. They don't thrive as good without it.'

Amelia bit her lip thoughtfully. Jenna was in such a deep state of melancholia, suckling the child would not happen for some days yet. 'Come, we'll take a walk over to Dr Eddy's to see what he thinks. It'll put your mind at rest.'

Jenna got out of bed when she heard them leave. At the window she watched furtively as Meg and Amelia walked across to the doctors. *Oh, why didn't I die in childbirth?* She hung her head in sinful self-pity.

17

Dr Eddy had just arrived back from pronouncing old Jack Simkins dead after a long battle with lung disease, and was looking forward to a hearty lunch, when a rather breathless, dirty-faced child, banged frantically on his door.

'Mother said to come quick,' he gasped, resting his hands on his thighs to regain his breath.

Not recognising the boy at first, Dr Eddy asked, 'Who's your mother, child? What's amiss?'

'Meg Bolitho,' he gasped. 'She said to come at once. The new babe has gone blue.'

It was already too late by the time Dr Eddy pushed his way through the many children playing in the doorway of Meg's none-too-tidy cottage. As feared, the child was already dead.

Meg sat clutching the child to her breast. She shook her head forlornly. 'Poor little mite, I'm surprised he lived as long as he did. He just wouldn't suckle properly - a bit here and a bit there, but not enough to nourish a growing babe. I did tell ee yesterday, doctor, I said, that child was not long for this world, I said it - do you remember?'

Dr Eddy nodded and carefully wrapped the child in a borrowed blanket.

'I thank you for all you've done for the child Meg. There was always a hope he would come brave, even though he was very weak, but it was not to be.'

Meg looked distraught. 'Well, I just wanted to help poor Mrs Blewett. The poor girl hasn't looked well since the day she was taken as a bride, though I'm not surprised, being married to that great lug. It's a wonder she gave birth to a living child at all - and that she survived!' Meg folded her arms across her ample chest. 'Blewett came round to see me this morning, you know? He came with Jory, to tell me my services were no longer needed after today. Blewett said, his wife was home, and wanted her baby back.'

'Did he now?' Dr Eddy raised his eyebrows warily.

'I feel awful now.' Meg sighed. 'To think she was ready to nurse her babe, only for it to go and die like that! Anyway, send her my regards, and tell her, tell her I'm really sorry.'

'You have nothing to be sorry for, Meg, and I know Jenna will be forever grateful that you helped her during this unhappy time.'

Meg smiled tearfully. 'Well, tell her I'll come over and see her soon.'

*

With the sad tiny bundle cradled in his arms, Dr Eddy set off towards the forge. He hesitated momentarily at the kitchen door and took a deep breath before he entered. The kitchen was warm and quiet. A pot of stew simmered on the fire, but Jenna was nowhere to be found. Despite her fragile state of mind, she'd returned home, and was expected to carry out her many daily duties, which she so obviously had done this morning. He turned to leave just as Blewett burst into the kitchen.

'What do *you* want?' he growled, glancing at the bundle as he brushed past the doctor and lifted the lid of the pan and inhaled deeply. 'I hope that's my son you've brought back. I decided this morning that it's time that useless wife of mine did her motherly duties.'

Dr Eddy moistened his lips. 'I'm afraid I've grave news regarding your son,' he said, holding the bundle towards him. 'Your son died this morning.'

A still anger built in the room as Blewett looked viciously at the bundle in his arms and then furiously into the doctor's eyes.

'The child was unwell, I told you so yesterday. It had a weak cry, pale skin and a slow heartbeat. I had hoped that I was wrong in my diagnosis but ……'

Before Dr Eddy could say more, Blewett pushed him aside with such force he fell awkwardly, landing heavily on the stone floor, sending the child skimming towards the fire. He scrambled to gather it back in his arms and sat nursing its tiny body while he regained his breath.

Jenna handed the plate of dinner to her father just as Blewett burst through the door. In shock she tipped the plate of food on her father's lap, making him stand up and curse. Backing herself against the wall in terror, Blewett grabbed her arm and hurled her against her mother's dresser, knocking the fine china to the floor. Winded momentarily, she began to pick up the broken pieces, but stopped abruptly when a searing pain shot though her ribs and then another. With each impact of his boot, Jenna felt Blewett's violence heighten - terrifying her. Red hot pain shocked her into immobility. In between short desperate gasps she screamed for him to stop but Blewett dragged her to her feet and hurled her against the white-washed wall. On impact she felt her nose burst, splattering blood down the wall as she crumpled into a heap on the floor. Cupping her hand to her face, she screamed, 'Father. Help me. Make him stop, please.'

Her pleas fell on stony ground as Jory sat in horrified silence. Fearing the consequences if he helped, he moved not a muscle to aid her.

Blewett's fists rained down as she curled into a tight ball to deflect the punches. Her jaw ached and her teeth rattled as four more blows to the head were punctuated with the words, 'You! Killed! My! Son!'

Amelia Pascoe had dropped her best teapot when she heard the screams coming from Jory's cottage. Without pulling her apron off, she dashed towards the commotion.

From where she cowered in the corner of the room, Jenna heard Amelia shouting at Blewett to cease at once. *Oh, thank god, thank god,* she prayed silently, but Blewett ignored Amelia's pleas, and continued his relentless assault on her as Amelia tried in vain to pull him away from her. Suddenly Blewett spun round, faced Amelia with blazing eyes and delivered her a swift right hook. Amelia flew out of the kitchen door into the path of Dr Eddy.

'What the devil….' Dr Eddy stepped over Amelia and burst into Jory's wrecked kitchen. Glancing first at Jory, he drew his brows together, unable to register why Jory was doing nothing to stop this brutal attack on his daughter.

Jenna screamed pitifully as more blows rained down on her.

Dr Eddy grabbed the poker from the fire and brought it down hard across Blewett's shoulders. Blewett swung round to meet his assailant, but Dr Eddy administered a second blow across his face, which broke his nose and brought him to his knees. Amelia, sporting a swollen right eye, flew instantly to Jenna's aid.

A curious crowd had formed outside the cottage, some stood at the door, and some peered through the window. They parted the way as George Blewett staggered out into the road, followed by Dr Eddy wielding his poker. When he was happy that Blewett was a safe distance away, he threw the poker to the ground and re-entered the cottage.

'Come on, sweetheart,' Amelia said as she and Dr Eddy helped Jenna to her feet and walked her over to the kitchen sink.

Shaking uncontrollably, Jenna retched and spat blood from the many cuts to her mouth.

Dr Eddy turned, fixed his eyes on Jory and grabbed him by the lapels on his jacket, lifting him from where he'd sat for the duration of the attack.

'What sort of father are you?' He shook him violently. 'How could you let this happen? Good god, man! What sort of coward are you?'

Unable to look the doctor in the eye, Jory turned his head to deflect his harsh words. Dr Eddy shook him again to gain some response, but still Jory remained silent. Losing his patience, he pushed him back into the seat in disgust and went back to tend Jenna.

Jenna jumped fearfully when the doctor touched her, but he swept her up into his arms and carried her out to the waiting crowd. There was a collective gasp at the sight of her, and the stirrings of joint animosity that could be discharged only by one means.

*

A horrified Mrs Tankard set two cups of hot sweet tea before Jenna and Amelia, while Dr Eddy checked them both for injuries. Amelia sported a swollen cheek and severe bruising to the right eye. Jenna, however, had not a single patch of skin on her face that was not battered and bruised. From her laboured breath, he was also sure she had cracked ribs. She'd also bitten her tongue and pierced her bottom lip with her teeth during the attack.

Difficult as it was for her to speak, speak she must, and Jenna's words came out in a measured painful whisper. 'The baby?' she lisped, spluttering droplets of blood.

Dr Eddy sat down beside her and took her hands gently in his. 'I'm so sorry, Jenna, I'm afraid your baby died an hour ago. Mrs Bolitho did all she could, but I think we all knew it would have been a miracle if he'd survived. He really wasn't very well. Meg sends her best wishes and sympathy.' He squeezed her hand, but Jenna's face was so disfigured he could not measure the emotion upon it.

Jenna swallowed as her head swum with nausea. 'Did it die because of me?'

'No, Jenna,' he answered adamantly. 'His tiny heart was weak. It wasn't your fault, I promise.'

Through the fug of pain, Jenna felt guilty relief that the baby had been born a weakling and died. The suffering they would have both endured at the hands of Blewett would have been insurmountable.

Every single fibre of her body cried out in pain, and she truly believed that the injuries she'd sustained today were only the first part of her punishment for her wickedness. For she knew god would surely punish her for what she was about to say next. Dropping her head shamefully, she whispered, 'I didn't want the baby, you see.' Tiny spots of blood dripped from her mouth as she spoke.

Dr Eddy pulled his handkerchief from his pocket and

pressed it into Jenna's hand for her to stem the flow. He glanced at Amelia, whose eye was blackening by the second. 'Listen to me, Jenna. You mustn't blame yourself for any of this. God knows you've been through hell and back these last few months.'

Jenna ran her split tongue across her cracked lips and drew a deep trembling breath. 'Blewett thinks it was my fault…. he said so. I truly thought he was going to kill me.'

Dr Eddy pushed his hands against his knees and stood up wearily. 'You leave Blewett to us. He won't get away with this,' he replied gently.

When the doctor left them for a few moments, Amelia took her hand in hers. 'You'll come back home with me today. Hopefully Blewett will have calmed down by tomorrow.'

Jenna's mind was in turmoil. She was terribly afraid. To think her father sat there and let Blewett do what he'd done to her, was unforgivable. Would he sit by and watch him kill her one day? For that is what Blewett would do, she had no doubt about it. Today was a turning point. For sure, her father was dead to her now, and because of that, she felt no obligation whatsoever towards him. If god was going to punish her anyway for her sins, she might as well be 'in for a penny in for a pound' and Jory Trevone could rot in hell or prison, for she knew her mother would turn in her grave is she knew what a coward he'd become. With this new state of mind, Jenna found herself with two options, to either end her own life, or… she lifted her head, though she could see nothing through her swollen eyes. 'Amelia are we alone?' she lisped.

With another squeeze of her hand, Amelia replied, 'We are, yes.'

Jenna took a deep painful breath. 'I can't stay with him any longer. I know it's a lot to ask you, but will you help me escape?'

For a moment the only noise was the ticking of the surgery clock.

Halleluiah, Amelia thought.

Jenna felt Amelia's grip tighten around her hand, and braced herself for disappointment but then Amelia whispered, 'Yes, Jenna of course I'll help you, in any way I can.'

*

There was a great deal of animosity regarding the day's events among the good people of Gweek. So much so, local dairy farmer, Charlie Williams, took great umbrage when Blewett and Jory entered The Black Swan later that day.

Administering a blow so hard with his fist, Charlie sent Blewett flying over several tables and back down the front steps of the pub, and in doing so, managed to inflict a broken right leg, left arm, collar bone, and several ribs. His fellow drinkers in the hostelry stood open-mouthed, because this strong, powerful farmer had never in their memory, raised his fist in anger before. As Blewett lay groaning in agony in the road, Charlie studied his bloody knuckles, wiped them down his overalls and quietly said, 'That's from Jenna. If you ever harm her again, I will personally kill you!'

Jory stood mouth agape, as Charlie walked towards him. 'Now what shall we do with this cowardly piece of shit?' he asked the landlord.

The landlord placed his hands on the bar in a praying mantis stance. 'Leave this to me. I shall hit him where it hurts most.'

Jory felt his bowels turn to liquid.

The landlord winked at Charlie and said, 'Jory Trevone, you are banned forthwith from these premises for as long as I am landlord here.'

*

Dr Eddy was beginning to feel this day would never end, when he was again called upon to administer first aid to yet another villager. Dr Eddy could hear the swearing almost as soon as he left his front door and was unsurprised to find the voice belonged to Blewett. He had wondered who would serve retribution to this bully, and sure enough, someone had taken it into their own hands to deal with a wife-beater. He found Blewett writhing about in agony in the road, clearly terrified that he was going to be squashed under the hooves of a horse-drawn wagon any moment. As Dr Eddy placed his bag down, Blewett was swearing profusely at the firmly closed door of The Black Swan. Jory was sat with his head in his hands on the pub steps, and when Dr Eddy pushed past him to enquire inside if anyone could help get Blewett back to his cottage, he found that no-one, not even Constable Treen, was inclined to help. In the end, he and Jory pulled Blewett to the side of the road, while Dr Eddy splinted the broken bones where he lay. With a makeshift stretcher they stumbled with their heavy load towards the forge. Blewett's screams of agony were enjoyed throughout the village. Staggering under the weight of the man, they carried him inside, pushed everything off the kitchen table and placed him on it until they could both collect their breath.

'Where's that useless wife of mine,' Blewett roared.

'She's in no fit state to help you, as well you know,' Dr Eddy snapped back at him. 'The poor girl can see through neither of her eyes, after what you did to her. You'll have to make do with Jory for now or none at all. Right, Jory,' the doctor said breathing heavily, 'let's get him upstairs.' Without consideration of Blewett's pain, they humped and bumped him up the six stone steps and placed him unceremoniously onto his bed, though not without enduring a barrage of verbal abuse from him.

Ignoring the insults, Dr Eddy adjusted and rebound the splints to his leg and arm.

'Agh!' Blewett balled his right hand into a fist, as Dr Eddy put his other arm in a sling.

Noting the threatening stance, Dr Eddy hissed a warning. 'Don't you *dare* raise that fist at me, or I shall gladly leave you in pain.'

Blewett reluctantly uncurled and flexed his fingers. 'I want to see the Constable, now,' he demanded.

'Do you?' Dr Eddy raised his eyebrows. 'Well funnily enough, he doesn't want to see you.' He made the final adjustment to the sling around his neck.

'What the devil do you mean? Ouch!' He held his ribs with his good arm.

'Perhaps he believes this is a quid pro quo,' Dr Eddy said evenly. 'Now, lay still and drink this. It should deaden a little of the pain.' He administered laudanum without any of his usual bedside manner. 'I'll return later. I'm sure Jory will see to your every need. *Won't you?*' He shot a humourless grin at Jory.

Jory stood in quiet apprehension, as he looked from the doctor to Blewett.

It wasn't long before Jory knocked on Amelia's front door to ask for help.

Amelia opened the door and just as Jory opened his mouth to speak, slammed it shut in his face.

*

Amelia sat down with Jenna at her kitchen table.

'Are you sure Lyndon will help you if I write to him?'

Jenna nodded. 'He's my only hope. I've no money. My friend Kate can't accommodate me - there are three of them squashed into a one-bedroom house as it is. My only reservation is that Lyndon knew I was with child. He may be reluctant to help me, if he thinks I have a baby…' Jenna's voice broke.

Amelia nodded. 'Then I'll tell him you've lost the child and we'll hope for the best. Give me his address and I'll set the ball rolling.'

*

In the peaceful tranquillity of the beautiful Trevarno estate, Lyndon was making a repair to part of a hedge surrounding the Italian sunken garden. Some neighbouring cattle had burst through it three weeks ago and completely trampled almost twenty feet of it. Lost as he always was whilst working, he failed to hear someone approach from behind.

'Hello, Lyndon,' Edna said boldly.

Her voice made him jump, and the billhook he was using nicked his left thumb. Hiding his injury from her, he turned to find the skinny frame of Edna standing watching him. He smiled resignedly. 'Hello Edna,' he said flatly. After the disastrous and regrettable fumble in the hay last month, Edna seemed to think a relationship could be built from the sorry affair.

'I've been thinking,' she said gaily. 'Maybe you'd like to come and have a picnic this Sunday. The weather is set to stay fair, so the barometer says in the big house.' She looked hopefully at him.

'I'm away working at the Godolphin Estate from tomorrow. I'll be away for some time,' he answered without apology.

Disappointment flooded her face. 'Well, tonight then. What say we take a jug of cider up to the top meadow?'

'I say no thank you. I'll be busy tonight.' He turned to finish the job in hand, but still she remained behind him.

'Then I'll wait and walk back with you to your house,' she said firmly.

As he worked, pushing, and chopping, weaving and cutting, he could feel her eyes boring into him, and sighed heavily without hiding his annoyance, but still she waited.

When eventually he gathered his tools and slung his jacket over his shoulder, she slipped her arm through his.

'No, Edna, you must not hold onto me. It's not proper to walk with me that way.'

She pouted. 'You weren't so shy to have me hold you last harvest night.'

Racked with guilt, he said apologetically, 'Well, I'm sorry, but that should not have happened.'

'Oh, but it did,' she parried, skipping happily at his side.

18

It was the 21st of December. For many days a thick mist had swathed the river village of Gweek. Jenna's laundry would not dry outside, so the kitchen was draped in an array of damp sheets. Physically, Jenna had almost healed, though her ribs still pained her to breathe and lift anything. Mentally, she was in turmoil, having reluctantly returned to the forge a month after the attack, but only because Blewett was so incapacitated he could not harm her. Grudgingly she administered the doctor's medicine to him, also food and drink whenever Blewett shouted for them. She served him with icy contempt, placing everything on the bed beside him, but just so she was out of reach of his grasp. Fortunately, he could just about shuffle out of bed and stand on his good leg, so she was saved the disgusting job of helping him on and off the commode.

Since returning to the forge, Jenna ignored Blewett's wrath and slept on a makeshift bed beside the kitchen fire, where she enjoyed the best night's sleep since she'd come to this god forsaken place.

Eight weeks had passed since Amelia wrote to Lyndon for help, and as yet there had been no word back. If Lyndon didn't respond soon, Jenna feared for her future. Time was running out, she knew that. Dr Eddy said Blewett's broken bones had almost healed. It was only the compound fracture that was keeping him abed. There had been a time when Dr Eddy considered amputation, but having consulted a colleague in London, he advised him to reset and splint the leg then cover the wound in lint soaked in carbolic acid. Normally infection would set in within four days, but when the lint was removed, the wound was found to be perfectly clean. Now two months later, the splint had been removed, but the leg was extremely painful to stand on.

Anxious to get back to work, Blewett's frustration grew daily. The forge lay idle, and even though his brother Sam had offered to step into the breach, Blewett was having none of it. He was also restless to resume his marital rights and enjoyed watching Jenna balk when he told her so. One way or another he was going to make her suffer for killing his son and make her pay for what Charlie Williams had done to him.

Jenna was under no illusions that her life was in danger once Blewett was back on his feet, hence, with or without Lyndon's help, she knew she must leave, adamant never to endure his molestation again. As she nursed her mug of tea, she mulled over her options - or lack of them, in her mind. Even if Lyndon did respond, it was going to be very difficult to escape. As incapacitated as Blewett was, he still made sure she was watched constantly, and had Jory lock her in at twilight. She also knew that, if she escaped, Blewett would undoubtedly come looking for her. As she rinsed her cup in the sink, she glanced at the river. If Lyndon didn't reply, there was really only one option for her.

Jenna wearily draped the last sheet over the overhead clothes rack. As she brushed her skirt out, Amelia breezed through the door. Jenna spun round in wide-eyed anticipation, but Amelia greeted her with a sorry shake of the head.

Pouring two more cups of tea from the teapot, Jenna ignored the angry complaints about the smell of damp washing drying from Blewett above.

'If I catch a chill, I'll do for you,' he bellowed.

Jenna pursed her lips. 'As you see, Amelia, even Charlie's beating has not deterred him from threatening me.' She sighed resignedly as she sat down with Amelia.

Amelia moved closer to Jenna. 'Listen, if Lyndon doesn't respond soon, and even if he does, I've been thinking of a way of getting you out of the village.'

'You have?' Jenna enquired cautiously.

Amelia cupped her hand to her mouth and whispered, 'We'll get you away on wassailing night, the 6th of January.

For all Blewett's bravado, he's a superstitious man and will not refuse to let you go out that night. There'll be such comings and goings in the village, it should be relatively easy for you to slip away, but we have to make it look like something has happened to you. You and I both know that if you leave, Blewett will not rest until he finds you and brings you back. So, this is what we'll do.'

Relief flooded through her veins as Jenna digested the plan. In whispered tones she said, 'I'll never forget your kindness, Amelia. You've been like a second mother to me. I don't think I could have managed without you!'

Amelia smiled gently. 'I just want you away from here safely and my job will be done. I'll give you what money I can, and then it's up to you to find somewhere to live.'

*

Lyndon arrived home three days before Christmas. He was heartily weary at having been away from home for so long. The job on the Godolphin Estate was bigger than he'd imagined, but it kept his mind and body busy and that was what he needed. His father's cottage felt warm and cosy. A great pot of broth simmering on the fire filled the room with a delicious aroma, and Michael hugged his son affectionately and sat him down with a jug of ale. They ate and drank, swapping news for the next hour until Lyndon yawned noisily.

'Sorry, son, you must be dog tired, you go up. It's good to have you back though.' Michael patted him on the shoulder. 'Oh, I saw young Edna today. She'll be happy about your return. I believe she's been pining while you've been away.' Michael grinned. 'I think she's set her hat at you.'

Lyndon groaned inwardly.

'No, lad, don't be like that. She's a nice young maid, you could do worse.' As Michael bent down to dampen down the fire, he remembered the letter that had come for Lyndon some weeks back.

Lyndon took the envelope and yawned again, studying

the writing as he walked wearily up the stairs to bed with it. He washed quickly, pulled his nightshirt on, and fell exhausted into bed. God, but it felt good to be in his own bed again! The wagon, though relatively comfy, soon felt damp in this Cornish winter air. Reaching out to snuff the candle, he glanced at the letter on his bedside table. Blearily he slit the envelope open. Suddenly tiredness left him, his mind alert as though a gunshot had been fired. Jumping out of bed, he pulled a blanket around his shoulders and sat at his desk, frantically searching for a piece of paper to write on.

The next morning, Lyndon took the train into Helston and sent his reply to Amelia.

Dear Mrs Pascoe,

First, I must send my deepest apologies for the delay in replying. I've been away working. I am totally at your service. Please let me know by return what you need me to do.

Yours, LF

*

Jenna almost collapsed when Amelia showed her the letter. It was Christmas Eve and that morning had been fraught with anxiety, as Dr Eddy had told Blewett he could start to move about. The thought of having to share his bed again filled Jenna with horror, sending her into a high state of panic. Jenna could hear him thumping about upstairs and shot a terrified look at Amelia.

Amelia hugged Jenna to her breast, as though she could protect the girl, but knew it was a hopeless gesture.

Suddenly Blewett began to cough violently at the exertion of moving, and Jenna prayed he would choke. When the coughing failed to cease and became quite alarming, Jenna reluctantly ventured upstairs, swiftly followed by Amelia. Blewett was slumped on the bed, puce in the face, saliva spewing from his mouth. He glared at the women but could not get his breath to speak. Amelia turned and ran down the stairs to alert the doctor, as Jenna stood by and watched him gasp for breath. Such sinful and damning thoughts entered her head it appalled her - but she could not quieten her inner voice which willed him to die.

Dr Eddy had to physically push past Jenna to get to his patient, and then there was an urgent order to bring towels and a bowl of steaming hot water. The doctor tried to push the bedroom window open to get more air in the room to help Blewett breathe, but found they only opened an inch. Jenna awarded herself a tiny smile at the irony. Dr Eddy pulled Blewett into a sitting position and wrapped a blanket around his shoulders.

'This is the third case of pneumonia this week. Thankfully my administrations have eased the symptoms of both my other patients. I hope I am just as lucky with this one.'

Jenna watched poker-faced, hoping with all her heart that he was not.

19

Lyndon replied to Amelia's next letter by return post. It was arranged that he'd arrive in the outskirts of Gweek on the evening of January 6th. Lyndon knew that many cider growers up country wassailed on the old "Old Twelvey Night", January 17th, as it would have been in the Gregorian calendar, but in Gweek it had always been the twelfth night after Christmas.

Amelia told Lyndon that a parcel of clothes would be left for Jenna in their hidey hole, and he was to wait near the Chapel for Jenna to find him.

Lyndon sat outside his father's cottage - his thick winter coat buttoned up against the chill of the day. It was January 3rd. In three days' time he would free the woman he loved from her living hell. His fingers drummed restlessly on the bench beside him as he considered their future. Worried and elated in equal measure, Lyndon harboured grave reservations about what had happened to Jenna's baby. He stopped drumming his fingers, folded his arms and sat back, wondering also what had prompted Jenna to take the decision to leave Blewett at last. It must have been something monumental, because her leaving him would surely put her father in prison. Had Blewett killed her baby? He twisted his mouth around as he thought.

'You look pensive my son,' Michael said, as he walked into the dell and approached the cottage.

Lyndon looked up, smiled but said nothing. There was so much going on inside his mind, and all of it he had kept secret from everyone, even his Pa. He was sure if he divulged anything, he would thwart Jenna's chances of escape.

Michael frowned. It was not like Lyndon to be secretive. A father's intuition told him something was afoot. He'd seen a marked difference in his son over the last couple of weeks and wondered if it had anything to do with young Edna from next door. Michael knew she was in hot pursuit of his son's favours, and many times he'd seen them walking home together after work, and so far, Lyndon had not been unkind and sent her away. So, maybe Edna was the one to heal his sorrow. He certainly hoped someone would.

*

On the evening of the 5th of January, Edna was waiting for him as he returned from making his wagon ready for his journey to Gweek. He could see from her face that she was in earnest. A frown formed between his eyes at the sight of her. This conversation would not be easy, because she was such a sweet girl, but he knew the time had come to tell her that she must look elsewhere for her partner in life.

*

The 6th of January dawned at last. It was a mild day, though the chill breeze off the river pulled at Jenna's shawl as she went about her daily chores. Blewett was still abed, the pneumonia having weakened him. He'd tried to get up the previous day, much to Jenna's dismay, but his legs had given way under him, and she had to get her father and Dr Eddy to pick him off the bedroom floor and get him back into bed. After a restless night by the fireside, unable to sleep for the thumping of her heart, Jenna rose at four-thirty to busy herself as best she could to steady her nerves. Whenever she was near Blewett she held her head low, convinced her face would betray the anticipation of her escape.

Amelia called mid-day, to tell her everything was in place. Jenna could hardly believe it was all going to happen and she would be reunited with Lyndon, and away from her nightmare.

As twilight fell, Jenna pulled her cloak over her shoulders and waited in the kitchen with nervous anticipation. She knew her father would be here soon and as instructed would lock her in for the evening.

Jory, finding himself banned from his local hostelry, sat with Blewett every night, drinking ale from a barrel bought from Helston market.

She watched with bated breath as the door opened and Amelia breezed in bringing the coldness of the night with her. A moment later Jory entered. He glanced at their outdoor attire and the pots they held and frowned. 'What's happening here?' he hissed. 'You'll have to go!' he directed the statement at Amelia, 'You know I've to lock the maid in.'

'You're locking nobody in tonight, Jory Trevone. It's wassailing night and well you know it. Jenna and I are going out to wassail the apple trees. It's bad luck if we don't do it. Now, step aside.' She pushed him away with one arm and hustled Jenna out of the door with the other.

Jory stood open-mouthed as the door closed after them.

'What's going on down there?' Blewett shouted down.

Jory swallowed the lump that had formed in his throat as he climbed the stairs to endure Blewett's wrath.

*

Amelia gave Jenna's hand a comforting squeeze as they joined a huge crowd of people gathered under the chestnut tree. With pots and pans and other implements to ward the spirits from the apple trees, they set off for their first port of call. As always it was the orchard down by Two Quays on the river bank. This was where Jenna would make her escape. There were eight apple trees in all, and the assembled crowd began the ceremony. Jenna and Amelia stood at the very back, willing for the ceremony to be over. Eventually the crowd began to sing their song:

Here's to thee, old apple tree,
That blooms well, bears well.
Hats full, caps full,
Three bushel bags full,
An' all under one tree.
Hurrah! Hurrah!

Great shouts and bangs on drums and pans rang out in the dark night. Amelia turned and gave Jenna's arms a tight squeeze. 'God speed, Jenna.'

Handing her pan to Amelia, Jenna crept off towards a row of laurel bushes to hide. She could feel her heart thumping as she watched the crowd disperse, singing and banging just in case any evil spirits were still about. Waiting a few moments to be sure she was alone - Jenna began to search for the sturdy boots and flat cap Amelia had placed there earlier that morning. Without light, she struggled to locate them, frantically padding the ground around the bush with her hands. Twice her fingers touched something slimy, making her shudder, but her fingers continued their search until they touched something hard wrapped in muslin. Under her normal clothes she wore a pair of dark breeches and a thin black jumper, which hardly kept the chill from her bones when she stripped off her dress. She pulled on the cap, and replaced her own boots with the large, clumpy ones Amelia had left for her. Lord knows where she'd got them from, but they would have to do. Shivering, she quickly gathered up her shawl, dress, petticoat, and boots, and crawled toward the river bank to leave them in an untidy heap.

With great stealth, Jenna darted from one hedge to the other along Gweek Woolas fields until she came to the centre of the village. This was going to be the trickiest part - passing through without being seen. Crouching by the water pump she surveyed the road. All seemed quiet but as she set off towards the bridge, the door to The Black Swan opened and a large gentleman emerged.

Spotting a figure crossing the road, he shouted, 'Hey you, boy, come here.'

Jenna's heart sank, she'd been caught.

'I said come here, boy.'

With the forge on one side of her and the hostelry on the other, Jenna knew if she didn't go to him, his shouts would alert everyone. With her head hung low so as not to be recognised, she reluctantly walked towards the gentleman.

'Go and fetch my horse, boy, it's the bay with a white flash on its forelock. Go on.' He shooed Jenna away to the back yard of the hostelry.

With her heart in her mouth, she sought out the horse, and led it to the front steps.

'Right, hold her steady. I said steady,' he growled angrily as the horse side-stepped. He belched loudly then heaved his great bulk onto the horse, snatched the reins from her grasp and threw some coins at her as he trotted off.

Leaving the coins scattered across the road, Jenna ran like the wind across the bridge and up Chapel Hill, tripping clumsily in the boots two sizes too big for her. Tears of panic streamed down her face, conscious that any moment someone would see her, and she'd be dragged back to her hellish life.

Not knowing how far Lyndon would be up the road, she forced her legs to keep running. They felt weak and shaky, not used to moving fast after the sedentary life she'd had in the confines of the forge. A stitch was forming in her side and the cracked ribs pained her terribly, making her gasp for breath. It was no good, she had to stop momentarily. Staggering towards the wall, her hand reached out, settling on the damp mossy surface as she steadied her breath. Though the night was cold, she was sweating profusely. All about her was still, except for some small animal rustling in the bushes nearby. Suddenly, her ears picked up footsteps running. A pitiful cry emitted from her throat - someone was coming towards her.

20

Jenna felt a hand grasp her sleeve, and every nerve in her body pricked with warning. A terrified cry escaped her throat.

'Shush, Jenna,' Lyndon's rich voice whispered in her ear.

Jenna's legs buckled. 'Oh, god, Lyndon, I thought I'd been caught.'

His fingers pressed against her lips. 'Hurry we need to get away. The wagon is down here.'

Bramble whinnied as they approached. As Jenna lifted a trembling foot to the first step of the wagon, Lyndon cupped his hand to her elbow to help. She flinched, shrinking back from his touch.

Lyndon retracted his hand as though he'd been burnt. 'Sorry, did I hurt you?'

'No Lyndon. I'm sorry, it's just...' Her fingers reached out to his face, but he stopped her hand before she could touch him.

'You need to get in quickly,' he urged.

This time she leant on his arm to lever herself up into the wagon.

'Hide under the blanket, until we're away from here,' he said gently.

She did as he bid, as he laced the back tarpaulin.

Feeling the wagon move, she closed her eyes trying to settle her mind as a confusion of mixed emotions flooded in.

*

The next hour passed in silence, albeit for the creak of the reins, the sound of the wheels turning, and every now and then Bramble snorting loudly.

Bramble was not young anymore and found pulling the wagon in the dark an ordeal, so Lyndon led her through the darkness.

Jenna was in emotional turmoil. Though her fear of

being caught began to subside, other concerns now lay heavy on her mind. In her heart she'd wrestled with a dilemma since asking Amelia to write to Lyndon for help. There was no guarantee that he'd still want her - though he must still feel something to come to her aid, but had she imagined it, or had he really held back from her when she'd tried to touch him? Sinking deeper into the bed she took a deep trembling breath – there lay another dilemma. She desperately wanted Lyndon. Throughout this last dreadful year, she'd yearned for his loving touch, but equally the thought of it made her shudder. Would it be possible for her to lay with him and not fear or be repulsed at the act of intercourse? All she knew was that she desperately needed his love, but somewhere deep inside, a niggling doubt began to form that he was holding back from her.

Eventually the wagon came to a halt. Lyndon untied the back tarpaulin laces and whispered softly, 'Forgive me, Jenna, were you sleeping?'

'No.'

'We're on the outskirts of Helston. We'll stop here for the night. I think we're far enough from Gweek to be safe. Not many people stray far abroad in the dark - especially at this time of year.'

'Can I do anything?' Jenna asked hopefully.

'No, you stay in the warmth while I hobble and feed Bramble. There's a parcel of clothes Mrs Pascoe left for you, and if you want a bite to eat, you'll find some bread and cheese in the tin box there. I'll join you in a few minutes.'

As she inspected the clothes Amelia had kindly left for her, she hoped with all her heart that her leaving hadn't implicated Amelia in any way.

*

The Black Swan Inn was packed with villagers after the wassail. Amelia sat as she always did, at the very back of the bar, away from the men drinking, praying that Jenna had got away safely. She waited pensively, because very soon Blewett would realise she was missing.

Sure enough, The Black Swan door burst open and Blewett, pale and sweaty, staggered in, supported by Jory.

'Hey, you two, out!' John Drago the landlord shouted. 'You're both banned.'

Ignoring him, Blewett pushed his way towards Amelia, grabbing her by her coat. 'Where is she? Where's my wife?'

'Hey now - what's all this about?' John rushed from behind the bar to Amelia's aid.

'Where the hell is she woman, tell me?' Blewett growled, shaking her violently. Several buttons pinged off her coat before he was manhandled away from her.

Pre-empting this assault, Amelia kept a cool head and calmly said, 'How should I know? I left her on the bridge when I came in here!'

'Well, she didn't come home!' he snarled, spittle flying from his mouth.

'I'm not bloody surprised,' a voice from behind said loudly. A ripple of laughter ran through the bar.

Still weak from his illness, Blewett steadied himself as he shot a baleful stare at everyone. 'Shut up the lot of you.' His face, flushed with anger, turned to Jory. 'You'd better find that bloody errant daughter of yours, Trevone. Otherwise, you'll be sleeping in a cell tomorrow night,' he yelled, before staggering out of the door.

Jory blanched, feeling the shock of Blewett's words pulsate through his body. 'What do you mean?' he shouted as he scuttled after him.

Charlie Williams made his way over to Amelia. 'Are you hurt?'

'No Charlie, thank you, I'm fine,' she said, inspecting her good coat.

'Pa and I will walk with you to your door when you're ready.' He bent closer and whispered, 'Do you know where she is?'

Amelia shook her head firmly, sending up a private

prayer that she would be forgiven for telling a lie.

He regarded her for a moment. 'Well, I hope she has run away. If you ask me, she should have done it long ago.'

*

Blewett was beside himself with fury as he stood in his kitchen. As weak as the pneumonia had left him, angry adrenalin pulsated through his body. Like a bull in a china shop, he swept every pot, pan and plate off their shelves, as Jory watched on in horror. Leaving the destruction behind him, he staggered up the stairs, expecting to find her few belongings gone, but everything was still there. Her clothes were still folded in the drawers and her good boots in the wardrobe. Her Sunday coat was still on the hook behind the door. If she'd gone, she'd taken nothing but the clothes on her back. Back downstairs, he grasped Jory by the collar. 'Where is she Trevone? I swear I'll leather her black and blue when I find her.'

*

After seeing to Bramble, Lyndon climbed into the wagon, lit the oil lamp and opened a large wooden box which contained a ceramic jug filled with ale, and two tin mugs. Jenna took the mug of ale gratefully and for a while they sat in silence while Lyndon ate his supper. Though the lamp light was poor, Lyndon noted Jenna had considerably aged since he'd last seen her. Her once beautiful golden hair now hung in short lank strands from beneath her cap. The beautiful face which once glowed with health, looked drawn and sallow, and the dark circles under her eyes held a depth of horror he could barely comprehend. Lyndon was in deep turmoil. There were so many things he needed to say to Jenna, but the words stuck fast in his throat. Twenty-four hours ago, he'd have gathered Jenna into his arms, healed her emotional wounds and embarked on a new life together, but the meeting with Edna the previous day put paid to that now. How could he tell Jenna that he was no longer free to love her? The poor girl had obviously been through enough. Try as he might, he just could not bring himself to break her heart with his news. So, the silence between them grew like a cancer. His throat felt raw with grief. He loved Jenna now more than he had ever done, but all he could offer her now was a safe haven. Berating himself when he suddenly realised that Jenna must have seen his regretful look, because she lowered her eyes from his gaze, he cleared his throat.

'Forgive me Jenna it's been a long night. Are you all right?'

She nodded gratefully. 'Thank you for helping me, Lyndon.'

'It's the least I can do for you, Jenna.' He felt his throat tighten again and checked his fob watch. 'It's nine o' clock. Will you have been missed by now?'

Jenna nodded. 'I doubt Blewett will venture out looking for me until morning though. He's just recovered from pneumonia so won't risk being out in the night air. By tomorrow morning my clothes will have been found on the river bank, and he'll think that I've drowned.'

'Amelia said in her letter that was your proposal - let's hope the plan works.'

'Amen to that,' Jenna whispered.

Lyndon cleared his throat again. 'Amelia also told me that you'd lost your baby. I can't imagine how terrible that must have been for you.'

Jenna's eyes flickered. 'It was a blessing really,' she murmured, 'it was very ill.'

More than anything in the world, Lyndon wanted to gather her into his arms, to give her comfort, but again his conscience held him back.

'I'm expected at Rinsey tomorrow morning to repair a hedge. We'll go on to Trevarno afterwards. You'll be safe in my father's house.'

'Thank you, Lyndon, I can't tell you how grateful I am to you.'

He smiled kindly. 'It's been a long night - I think we both need to rest now.' Lyndon picked up a spare blanket and began to climb out of the wagon.

'Please don't leave on my account,' she said anxiously.

'I won't be far away, just at the front of the wagon. You take my bed. The sheets are clean, and I think you'll find it comfortable enough.'

'But it's cold out there!' she protested.

'I'll be fine. Sleep well, Jenna, good night.'

*

Jenna sank despondently down into the blankets as tears welled and a chill formed in her heart. She knew something was amiss with Lyndon, otherwise where was the love and compatibility they'd once shared? Without a doubt he'd been kind and caring towards her, but she very much feared that he no longer loved her anymore. The chill in her heart turned to ice.

21

It was early. The pale morning light streamed into Amelia's bedroom. From her window, she watched and waited, her eyes focused down river. Several people were abroad at this early hour, but was anyone on the river bank? A strengthening breeze had got up in the last hour. With the threat of a storm brewing, none of the fishing boats had set off on the morning tide. How long would it be before someone found Jenna's clothes, she wondered? The sooner they did, and word got around that she'd drowned, the sooner Jenna would be safe.

Amelia's heart almost missed a beat when Constable Treen walked to Blewett's door, his arms full of clothes.

*

Blewett was slumped at his kitchen table, nursing an empty bottle of brandy and a sore head.

'Bugger off,' he growled through the door.

Treen hammered on the door again. 'George, this is the police, open this door, now! I have some grave news regarding your wife.'

Standing amongst the debris of broken pots, silence swelled in Blewett's kitchen as Constable Treen held out Jenna's clothes to him.

The veins in Blewett's neck grew thick with rage. Treen moved back a step as Blewett thrust his hand out, and with one great swipe knocked the clothes from his arms.

'Get out,' he snarled, forcing him back outside. With a sharp kick, the door slammed behind the constable.

He kicked the pile of clothes across the kitchen. 'You, little bitch.' His voice was filled with the bitterest contempt. As he paced the room, his fury made him wheeze painfully. 'Right, Trevone,' he hollered as though he could make Jory hear. 'You owe me, you bastard.' He wrenched open his door and marched towards Jory's cottage.

Constable Treen was in Jory's cottage, delivering the

sad news to him, when Blewett burst in. With a swift push he knocked Treen sideways and grabbed Jory by the collar. Chairs tipped and pictures fell, as Blewett pinned Jory to the wall. 'You owe me!' he said baring his teeth.

Treen picked himself up from where he fell and pulled his truncheon from his belt.

'George, calm down and stand aside at once. This is disgraceful behaviour. A poor girl has lost her life, and this is how you act.'

Jory choked as Blewett tightened his grip.

'George, stand aside now or I shall arrest you.'

'You owe me, Trevone,' he hissed again, before loosening his grip on Jory, dropping him to the ground.

*

After a fitful night, followed by a breakfast of tea and porridge, Lyndon harnessed Bramble and they set off to Rinsey. Jenna stayed hidden in the wagon while Lyndon presented himself at the Nance's farm. She smiled watching Lyndon and Jake Nance walk down towards Trewavas Head. Lyndon had a companionable way with him. He spoke to everyone as though he'd known them forever.

Lyndon's reserve played heavily on Jenna's mind - making her horribly restless. She needed to walk in the fresh air and to think hard about her future. With Amelia's old coat buttoned up to the neck and the over-large boots on her feet, Jenna took the coastal path down towards Praa Sands.

Only ever seeing the sea from a distance before, she gazed wide-eyed at its vastness. As she approached Rinsey Head, she was astonished by the glorious stretch of white sand in front of her. Almost from nowhere, a strong south-westerly wind began to blow, ruffling the large waves which crashed against the shoreline. Twice she'd stopped her cap from whipping off her head. Taking shelter in a hollow in the cliff path, Jenna sat upon a large smooth rock and dropped her face into her hands.

Something was definitely wrong between her and Lyndon, but she knew not what? He'd said little to her at breakfast and Jenna remembered his regretful look the previous night and wondered if his reserve was something to do with her appearance. She knew she looked dreadful, because she'd barely recognised herself the last time she'd seen her own reflection. *You fool Jenna, what on earth were you thinking? How could he possibly want you, now you're someone else's damaged goods?* Clasping her hands to her head, she knew this self-pity must stop, but having lived for so long without hope, helping herself was a skill that seemed to have abandoned her. Where on earth was that confident, happy girl she used to be? *Come on, Jenna, dig deep, you've made the first move to freedom. If Lyndon doesn't want you, you'll find a way on your own.* With that decided, and the damp earth seeping through her woollen skirt, she got up to make her way back to the wagon. As she stood, a gust of wind snatched the cap from her head, sending it flying out towards the sea. Her hands flew to her head, as she began to battle against the gale. Suddenly hail began to fall horizontally, stinging her face and hands. Her coat flapped about her furiously as she struggled to keep her feet planted on the ground. Turning to deflect the worst of the hailstorm, the wind suddenly blew her off her feet, leaving her crouched on all fours in the muddy ground. Scrambling to her feet, she bent her head forward and pushed against the wind. Great balls of sea foam flew up the cliff, coating the path with a slippery white carpet. Soaked through now, her ears burned, and her eyes watered with the cold. Turning her back to the wind she unfastened her coat, pulled her arms from the sleeves and shrugged the garment up so it covered her head. Once again, the wind stopped her in her tracks and she fell to the ground, knocking her knee on a rock hidden under the foam.

A shout filtered through the noise of the wind and then Jenna felt Lyndon's arms under hers as he lifted her to her feet. Her knee pained her, but with his help she limped back towards the barn, where the wagon and Bramble had been put to shelter from the storm.

Once inside the barn, Lyndon lit the oil lamps in the wagon and retrieved a blanket for Jenna, while she discarded her wet clothes.

Shivering in only her shift, Lyndon gently wrapped the blanket around her skeletal body, unable to hide his shock of seeing the mass of bald patches covering her scalp. Seeing his expression, Jenna pulled the blanket up to cover her head as they climbed back into the wagon.

Lyndon rummaged through a large leather bag, pulling out a warm woollen jacket and a pair of socks, and passed them to Jenna.

'These should keep you warm, but you'll have to wear those breeches you wore last night until your skirt dries.' He rummaged again and handed her one of his yellow and red spotted neckerchiefs to wrap around her hair. 'Sorry about the colour,' he said, smiling warmly. Gathering some dry clothes for himself, he vacated the wagon so they could both dress in privacy.

Rubbing his hair dry with a towel, he called out, 'I can't light a fire here in the barn, so I'm going to see if I can beg a can of tea from the farmhouse to warm us. I won't be long.'

Mrs Nance wanted Lyndon to stay and eat supper with them in the farm kitchen. She even offered him a room for the night, but Lyndon kindly refused, saying he would prefer to stay near his horse, as she was old, and the storm would unsettle her. So, he returned, with not only a can of tea, but a pan of stew and two more warm blankets. As the meal warmed them, they began to relax at last in each other's company.

It was a wild night, the spray from the sea lashed against the barn door. Bramble, who had been tied to the wagon, whinnied nervously.

'She doesn't like storms.' He smiled crookedly.

'I'm not too keen on them myself,' Jenna added.

'I think we're safe here.'

A warm glow passed through Jenna - for the first time in twelve months she felt safe. 'Did you manage to finish your job here?' she enquired, draining the last of her tea.

'Unfortunately, the storm put paid to that. It'll take at least another four hours. Hopefully it will blow itself out during the night so I can finish tomorrow.'

Eventually Jenna said, 'Thank you for the loan of the headscarf Lyndon.'

He nodded. Realising she wanted to talk, he asked very gently, 'I can't imagine what hell you've been through, Jenna? You're painfully thin, and your hair, forgive me for asking, but whatever happened to it?'

Uncertain she could answer without her resolve breaking, she took several deep breaths. 'Dr Eddy says I have alopecia. Apparently, people under severe duress can sometimes lose their hair. My hair was short anyway - I cut it off so Blewett couldn't drag me about with it,' her voice faltered slightly.

She heard Lyndon catch his breath, but she continued, 'Regarding my weight, well, fear of Blewett suppressed my appetite. The porridge you made me this morning was the first meal I've wanted to eat in a long time.'

Lyndon shook his head horrified. 'Good god! What sort of bastard is he?'

'A violent one - from the first moment he took me to his filthy bed.' She answered flatly, shuddering at the memory.

Lyndon, shocked to the core, blustered, 'But Matthew told me you'd be safe. He said people were watching out for you!'

Jenna gave a short shrug. 'Blewett threatened me not to say anything - so I was forced to hide a lot of what happened. The abuse was normally verbal and sexual. No-one can see those scars.'

'Oh, Jenna, I'm so sorry for you.' He could no longer

hold back from comforting her and pulled her towards him.

Flinching at first, she tentatively relaxed and let him hug her tightly. It felt so good to be held by him at last, but the strength of his arms made her wince in pain.

'What is it? Are you hurt?' he asked, relaxing his hold.

She nodded tearfully. 'I have four broken ribs, they haven't quite mended.'

Gently wiping her tears, his fingers caressed the slightly raised skin below her right eye, and then he noticed the scar on her bottom lip, where she had bitten into it two months ago. 'Oh, Jenna, what happened here?'

Her lip quivered. 'Two months ago, Blewett beat me until I was unrecognisable.' She gently touched her face. 'Dr Eddy assures me these scars will fade in time.'

'But why did he do this to you?'

'He went into a rage and blamed me for the death of his son,' she said, wrapping her own arms around her body to stop herself trembling. 'As he beat me senseless, my father watched on passively. Truly if it hadn't been for Amelia and Dr Eddy, Blewett would have maimed me for life.'

Gathering her into his arms again, though this time more gently he said, 'I swear I'll kill that man if I ever see him again.'

'Charlie Williams damn near did kill him when he found out what he'd done to me. I'm told he only punched him once, but it was enough to put him in bed for eight weeks with several broken bones.' She lifted her eyes to his. 'So, you see Lyndon, I did have people looking out for me.'

Lyndon nodded gratefully. 'He's a good man is Charlie.'

'He is, but it didn't stop Blewett from threatening me again, so I knew I'd have to leave. If you hadn't offered to help me, I would have run away anyway. As for my father…well, I know it's unchristian of me, but I care nothing for his welfare now.'

'I knew of the duty you felt towards your father and did wonder what had broken that obligation. Your father deserves all he gets.'

Jenna nodded sadly. 'It does not sit easy with me though.'

He gave her a comforting squeeze. 'Forgive me for asking, but why did Blewett think you'd killed his son?'

Jenna sat back and pulled the blanket tight around her shoulders. It was a long time before she answered, and Lyndon wondered if maybe she had.

'Please don't hate me for what I'm about to say.'

'Go on,' he said apprehensively.

Jenna visibly shrank as she began to speak, 'I…. felt nothing for the poor child you see. It had grown in my belly like a festering wound. The birth was agonising when it pushed through my flesh, and then….then I was presented with a mirror image, albeit smaller version, of the man I detested.' She glanced at Lyndon. 'I could no more suckle that child, than fly in the air. I wanted nothing to do with it,' her voice waivered. 'In truth I wanted to die, so that I wouldn't have to raise it. I didn't know the child was ill. Apparently, his heart was weak. He was given to a wet nurse and began to fail quite quickly. He died two days later. Blewett was incensed and blamed me for its demise. God forgive me, but it was a blessing.' She pressed her lips tightly together, staring at Lyndon, waiting for his response.

Lyndon unclenched his jaw which had tightened while she spoke. He opened his arms sympathetically. 'Come.'

Gratified she moved towards him.

He took her in his arms - though he knew under the circumstances he should not. He needed to make her feel safe, and even if they could never be together, he made a silent vow that from now on he would protect her in any way he could - though lord knows that was going to be difficult. 'Everything will be all right now, I promise,' he whispered.

With a trembling sigh, Jenna snuggled into the crook of his arm, as a huge weight lifted from her shoulders. Inhaling the familiar scent of wood smoke and horse from his clothes, she felt his large hands gently caress her arms to comfort her. She wasn't quite sure, but she thought she felt the touch of his lips on her head. Heavy with fatigue, she closed her eyes and fell into a deep contented sleep.

Lyndon felt the tension in her body fall away. He held onto her for a long time, his mind running over what she'd told him, until he too fell asleep, forgetting the impropriety of their sleeping arrangements.

22

Jory sat at his kitchen table in his shirt sleeves. The fire had long since collapsed into a pile of grey ash, and cold was creeping through the cottage like death. This once happy home, filled with warmth, laughter and home cooking had long since gone. The blood-stained wall behind him bore witness to his failure as a man and a father.

He swallowed hard - his throat raw with grief for what his cowardly weakness had driven his daughter to do. Trembling at the sound of every footstep outside his door, he waited to be summoned to court. He would surely die in prison, and when he did, god would punish him for his sins.

*

The day dawned clear and breezy after the storm passed through. Lyndon finished his job in Rinsey by noon. By late afternoon they arrived at the Trevarno Estate. After settling and feeding Bramble, he left Jenna in the wagon to find his father.

Michael smiled. 'Hello, son.'

Lyndon slipped his hands in his pockets and cleared his throat.

Michael cocked his head. 'All right, what's amiss?'

Lyndon relaxed slightly. His pa could always read him like a book. 'I need to ask a favour.'

Michael put down his secateurs, leant back against the bench and folded his arms.

With his fingers crossed behind his back, Lyndon cleared his throat again before he spoke. Dishonesty went against the grain, but needs must in this case. En-route to Trevarno that morning, Jenna and Lyndon realised that the Western Morning News would inevitably report the story that Mrs Jenna Blewett from Gweek was missing, presumed drowned. So, in order to disguise her real identity, Jenna chose to alter her name to Jennifer Penvean, concocting a story that she'd been made homeless from a tied cottage in Rinsey after her parents had died. This was what Lyndon now relayed to Michael.

Michael gave a sympathetic tut. 'The poor woman, of course she can stay, but where will she sleep?'

Lyndon felt the tension in his shoulders relaxed. 'She'll have my room for now. I'll be fine on the armchair until everything is settled. Maybe Matthew will employ her up at the big house.'

With Jenna safely ensconced in their cottage, Lyndon went in search of Matthew and had not returned when Michael arrived home from work.

Jenna had managed to dry her skirt in front of the fire and had washed and tidied herself. Lyndon had found her a plain green neckerchief to cover her hair, and this was more in keeping with her clothes. With the luxury of a mirror, she'd teased out some of the remaining strands of hair, so that wispy blond curls fringed the edges of the scarf, softening her thin tired face.

Always nervous whenever a door opened, Jenna's heart jumped into her mouth when Michael breezed through the front door. Her eyes widened, startled to see he was the double image of Lyndon, only older.

'Well, hello there.' Michael narrowed his eyes with curiosity. 'You must be Jennifer.' He shook her hand warmly. Shrugging off his coat, he hung it by the door. 'Lyndon has told me of your troubles, my dear. I'm very happy to welcome you into my home. Any friend of his is a friend of mine.'

Jenna smiled. 'Thank you kindly, sir.'

'I can't tell you how good it will be to have some company,' Michael said, as he washed his hands, 'and you'll be able to help with the wedding, which will be a godsend.' He sniffed the air appreciatively. Not since his dear wife died, had he come home to the glorious smell of cooking. 'Gosh, something smells good.' He walked over to the fire and tasted the contents of the pot.

Jenna smiled happily. 'I've made rabbit stew. I found

the creature hung in the larder. I hope you don't mind me using it.'

'I don't mind at all, my dear.' Michael grinned. 'It's a rare welcome change to come home to supper, I can tell you.'

Jenna took the spoon from him and tasted the stew herself. 'Who's getting married?' she asked brightly. 'You said I could help with the wedding.'

Michael laughed again heartily. 'Why, Lyndon of course! Did he not mention it to you?'

Jenna felt as though she'd been punched in the stomach.

Michael rubbed his hands in front of the fire to warm them. 'He's marrying young Edna from next door – a nice girl, a bit frivolous, but I suppose that's what young girls are like - begging your pardon Miss, I don't mean to speak out of turn.'

Jenna fought to keep the smile on her face. 'When is the wedding?' her voice wavered with emotion.

'On Saturday week.' He wrinkled his nose. 'It's just a small gathering – a few friends – a bite to eat.'

'Oh.' She smiled. 'That sounds lovely.' Everything fell into place now. This was why he'd been distant with her.

Michael gave Jenna a thoughtful look. 'Are you well my dear, you look a little flushed. Let me get you a drink. Do you take a mug of ale?'

Jenna nodded. 'It's probably the heat of the fire that's all,' she said, taking the pewter mug just as Lyndon walked in.

'Ah, there you are! Did you find Matthew?' Michael asked Lyndon casually.

'No, he's away apparently,' he answered, noting the look on Jenna's face.

'I've just been telling Jennifer about your wedding,' Michael said, raising his eyebrows.

'Oh,' he blanched, 'have you?'

Jenna stepped forward to help Lyndon off with his

coat. 'I'm very happy for you Lyndon. I always thought you would make someone a fine husband.' She smiled gently through her heartache. 'When do I get to meet... Edna is it?'

Lyndon met her eyes with sadness. 'She's meant to be coming to tea tomorrow,' he said apologetically.

'Good,' she answered, brushing down her skirt. 'I shall look forward to that.'

He touched her arm fleetingly. 'Jenna,' he whispered so his father would not hear.

'Shhh,' she answered gently.

*

If Lyndon was to marry, and for her to stay friends with him, Jenna knew she had to dig deep and welcome Edna. Unfortunately, to put it mildly, Edna was one of the rudest, self-centred girls Jenna had ever met. She was a pretty, skinny little thing - all dark hair and dark eyes, but they were her only redeeming features. Try as she might, Jenna struggled to see why Lyndon had fallen for her.

On entering Michael's kitchen, Edna eyed Jenna suspiciously and uttered, 'Who are you?'

Michael stepped in. 'Jennifer is a friend and she's staying with us.'

'For how long?' she demanded.

'Indefinitely,' Lyndon answered firmly, taking Edna's coat.

Edna pouted, unhappy about this cuckoo in the nest. She grabbed Lyndon's arm protectively. 'We're getting married next week!' she announced proudly.

Jenna smiled and nodded. 'Congratulations.'

Edna eyed her curiously and Jenna matched her gaze.

Lyndon disengaged himself from Edna's hold and held the chair out for Edna to sit.

'We're moving into old Tom Hindle's cottage,' Edna grinned. 'He's been ill for ages and finally died last week - how very convenient, eh Lyndon?' Edna mused.

Jenna noted a hint of a scowl on Lyndon's face.

Throughout the meal Edna spoke only of herself and her needs. "I'm having this for my wedding and that for the house." Her list seemed endless. It seemed to Jenna that Edna cared not a fig for what Lyndon wanted and noted with interest how Lyndon sat in silence, watching his bride-to-be with quiet indifference.

When she finally stopped talking about herself, Edna turned to Jenna and asked, 'So, where are you from? It seems my husband-to-be knows you well!' She shot Lyndon an accusing glance.

Michael glanced at his son, who was indeed watching Jenna with interest, making an uncomfortable thought pop into his head.

Jenna had her answer finely honed. 'My family are from Rinsey. I know Lyndon because he worked on the hedges at the farm near to where I lived. I too worked there, as a milkmaid. We met on several occasions as we shared a table in the farm kitchen.'

Edna pursed her lips. 'And what brings a milkmaid from Rinsey to the Trevarno Estate?'

Jenna lowered her eyes. 'My father recently died, and as the cottage was tied, I was forced to leave. My mother, god rest her soul, was taken eleven years ago and I have no siblings or family to go to. Lyndon kindly offered to find lodgings for me here.' Jenna refrained from glancing at Lyndon.

Edna grunted. 'Well, I'm sorry for your loss, but could you not have stayed at the farmhouse?'

'No, she couldn't!' Lyndon's tone was sharp.

Edna snapped her head towards Lyndon. 'Well, I only asked, I mean, what is she going to do here?'

Through gritted teeth he answered sharply, 'The farm at Rinsey had no room for anyone else to stay there. I'm confident that Jennifer can turn her hand to anything. Matthew is away at the moment, but as he runs the estate, I'm sure he can find her some work at the big house.'

Edna pursed her lips. It was clear she could not remove

this woman from the vicinity of her husband's gaze. It was plain for all to see he was fascinated by her and that worried her greatly.

When Edna reluctantly took her leave, Jenna and Lyndon began to clear the table.

Michael lit his pipe and watched them with interest. There was a definite easiness between them - which went beyond casual acquaintance. His thoughts were interrupted as a sharp knock on the door preceded Matthew entering.

'Good evening to you, Michael, I believe Lyndon has been looking for me….? *Jenna!*' He stopped dead as though his eyes deceived him.

Lyndon stepped forward. 'Yes, Matthew this is Jennifer,' he said firmly, giving him a 'don't say anything else' stare. 'Jennifer, this is Matthew Bickford. Matthew runs the Trevarno Estate.'

Jenna nodded awkwardly as Matthew stood agape.

'I'm pleased to make your acquaintance…Jennifer,' Matthew answered gingerly.

Lyndon grabbed Matthew by the sleeve and shot him a pleading look. 'If it's all right, Matthew, I'll come and see you tomorrow about her?'

Noting the tension building in the room, Matthew nodded. He bid his goodnights to Michael and Jenna before Lyndon followed him out of the cottage.

They walked a while and when well out of earshot, Matthew hissed, 'I've just come from Trelowarren. Gweek is rife with stories of Jenna drowning. What's going on? I thought I was coming here with tragic news for you!'

Lyndon ran his hands through his hair. 'It's a long story Matthew, only you and I know her true identity. I beseech you to keep our secret.'

'Well, of course, I will Lyndon you can depend on me, but…we're only nine miles from Gweek. Someone might recognise her.'

'Well, we'll cross that bridge when we come to it. If they do find out she's still alive, then we'll do everything we can to secure a legal separation from that brute. Talking of which, I don't think you've been entirely truthful to me about her plight!'

Matthew laid a hand on his arm. 'I'm sorry, my friend, I feared the truth would have driven you crazy with worry for her. I can't tell you how glad I am to find she is alive. Is she all right?'

He sighed heavily. 'Her physical wounds will heal, but…'

Matthew gave him a gentle pat on the arm. 'Give her time, my friend. I'm sure that with your tender loving care, she'll mend.'

'Humph. You forget one fundamental thing. I'm to be married to Edna next week.'

'So you are. I'm sorry for you, Lyndon. I would not want to be in your shoes at the moment. I'll see you in the morning, we'll work something out.'

When Lyndon returned, Michael was smoking his pipe outside. 'All right, would you like to tell me what the devil you're playing at?'

Lyndon swallowed hard. 'What do you mean?'

'You know damn well what I mean. That's *her*, isn't it? That's your married lady friend from Gweek inside, isn't it? Don't dare deny it to me, because Matthew gave it away and any fool can see you're in love with that girl. How could you bring her here, to flaunt her in front of your bride-to-be? What are you thinking man?' Michael shoved the palm of his hand on Lyndon's shoulder. 'Is the wedding off?'

'No! Unfortunately, it isn't.' Lyndon lowered his eyes shamefully. 'Apparently I've got Edna in the family way.'

Michael's mouth tightened. 'You bloody fool.'

'I agree wholeheartedly with you there, Pa.'

'And what of Jennifer's husband, is he going to come looking for you? Is there going to be trouble?'

'He believes Jenna…' he stopped and corrected himself. 'He believes Jennifer is dead, drowned. She's nowhere to go Pa. When I received word that she needed my help, I had no idea Edna had fallen pregnant. I was committed to helping Jenna…Jennifer by then. You can see for yourself from the state of her that she's suffered at his hands, I had to bring her somewhere safe, I just had to.'

Michael's face softened slightly. 'I take it her real name is Jenna, as you so often stumble over it?'

Lyndon nodded.

Michael knocked the remains of his pipe out onto the ground. 'Well, this is a sorry mess.'

When they returned indoors, Jenna knew she'd been found out. Michael sat down at the table and beckoned Jenna and Lyndon to do the same.

'I'm going to call you Jennifer or Jen, if that is all right? I'm not unsympathetic to your suffering, maid, and I understand Lyndon's reason for bringing you here. As you know, my son is marrying next week,' he looked at Lyndon, who nodded. 'Well, he and his new wife will move into Tom Hindle's cottage. This means I'll have a spare room. I'd like to offer you that room, for as long as you want it. You will have to sort out the rent with Matthew, as I'm a tenant and cannot sublet to you.'

Jenna's eyes glistened with tears. 'Thank you, Mr FitzSimmons, that's very kind of you.'

He laughed gently. 'Please call me Michael. Mr FitzSimmons sounds so formal. I have to admit though I'm looking forward to more of your cooking.'

'Now Pa, don't you be taking advantage of her culinary skills.'

'Now you know I won't. I am quite capable of producing an edible supper myself. We can take it in turns.' He gave her a friendly wink.

Later that evening when Michael was out at the local hostelry, Lyndon came to sit beside Jenna by the fireside.

There was a quiet few seconds before Jenna said, 'Edna's very pretty.'

Lyndon looked into the fire. 'Aye, she's pretty all right.'
'I hope you'll be very happy together.'
He laughed tightly. 'I very much doubt it.'

They both looked at each other. Jenna frowned noting the apprehension etched upon his face.

'We have to marry you see,' he said, his voice resigned to his fate. 'She's with child.'

She reached for his hand. 'Oh, Lyndon,' her voice was sympathetic, not accusing.

He sighed heavily. 'It only happened the once.'

Jenna smiled in the firelight. 'That's all it takes I'm afraid.'

Lyndon grunted. 'It was after the harvest ball. I was missing you, thinking about the year before.' He gazed at Jenna in earnest. 'I've missed you so much. It nearly killed me to think of you with that brute. Oh, god!' He rubbed his hands over his face. 'I drank too much on harvest night. I was trying to obliterate the desperate feelings I had for you, and then there she was, right in front of me, Edna, with her dark brown eyes and her fancy dress, making free with me.' He stopped speaking for a moment, lost in some sad distant memory. 'I'm not blaming her - it was my fault.' Taking a deep breath, he exhaled noisily. 'I thought it would stop the loneliness.' He looked directly at Jenna. 'I thought, if I let my feelings go with someone else, it might chase you from my memory. I took her to the barn, and,' his head fell into his hands, 'it was very wrong of me to take advantage of her.' He glanced sadly at her. 'She came to tell me she was pregnant, just as I was leaving to help you. I'm so sorry, I didn't know how to tell you.'

Jenna curled her fingers around his hand, the hand she knew so well. 'I just wish you'd told me all this sooner Lyndon. I couldn't understand why you were so distant towards me. I truly thought you were repulsed by what I'd become.'

He knelt down at her feet. 'Oh, my love, I can see you've been through a terrible ordeal, but you're still my lovely Jenna.' He kissed her hands tenderly. 'All I have ever felt for you is love, but now I've spoilt it all. How I wish I'd come back to Gweek sooner and rescued you from him. Please forgive me.'

'Shh now.' Her fingers gently stroked his copper curls. 'You know I could not leave Blewett at first - out of regard for my father. Only when I realised, he had no regard for me did I find the strength to leave. We shall just have to make the best of a bad situation Lyndon. At least we are close by each other now.'

Lyndon laid his head on her lap. 'Oh, Jenna, my Jenna, I'm so sorry.'

23

True to his word, Matthew arranged for Jenna to work at the big house and immediately gave her the job of collecting the eggs and feeding the poultry. To Jenna's delight, and Edna's displeasure, she was also assigned to Mrs Drake the cook, to help with the chopping and preparing of vegetables.

Edna's duties were in the laundry - a hot, smelly, dirty job, which she loathed. When she learnt that Jenna had been given work at the house, she secretly hoped this awful job would now be assigned to her, being the new girl. But Jenna proved herself to be indispensable in the kitchen. With quick efficiency in all things, Jenna could turn her hand to anything the cook asked her to do. After only one morning, Jenna's job was sealed when Mrs Drake called her a 'godsend'.

*

In Gweek, the ladies of the village gathered by the bridge, baskets over their arms, and coats buttoned up to the neck to keep out the chill. It was Monday, market day in Helston. As the wagon pulled up, Amelia, Meg Bolitho and Jean Jenkins climbed aboard and settled themselves ready for the arduous journey.

Jory Trevone was noticeable by his absence. It was to be expected, his daughter's death being only a few days ago. Just as the wagon began to pull away, George Blewett came out of the forge, waving a list in his hand. His eyes quickly scanned the wagon, first for Jory, then for Amelia.

'Here.' He pushed the list towards her. 'If you're going to Helston, get me these provisions, will you?'

Amelia retracted her hand as though the list would burn her. 'I will certainly not. You can get your own provisions from Helston.'

'For god's sake woman, I've work to do, and as you're going in, you could get them for me.'

'I could, but I won't, George Blewett!'

'Why the hell not?' he snarled indignantly.

Amelia folded her arms defiantly. 'That question doesn't even merit an answer!'

'Oh, for god's sake,' Blewett growled angrily, holding the list towards the other women, all of whom promptly turned their backs on him.

Amelia gave a satisfied smile. 'I suggest you get your provisions from Moyles' shop.'

'It's bloody expensive there and you know it! Now come on, one of you take this.' He waved the list again.

'No!' they shouted collectively.

Blewett flared his nostrils. 'You're all bloody hags!' he yelled, storming off.

'Horrible man!' Meg Bolitho huffed.

'I bet he rues the day he threatened Jory with prison,' Jean Jenkins said. 'Jory normally collects the provisions for both their households.'

'Do you think he'll carry out that threat?' Meg asked.

'Well,' answered Jean knowingly, 'Constable Treen said that Blewett had Jory pinned against the wall, shouting "you owe me", so your guess is as good as mine.'

'I must say I've no regard for Jory Trevone after making his daughter marry that brute, but has anyone seen him since her drowning?' Meg whispered.

'No,' Amelia admitted. 'I'm ashamed to say I haven't been near.'

'For all his faults, it must be awful to lose a daughter like that,' Jean added.

'Huh! He seemed to feel nothing for the maid when she was alive. God rest her soul,' Meg said.

Amelia glanced towards Jory's cottage as the wagon turned up Chapel Hill. There was no smoke from the chimney. Had he already been taken away to prison? She decided that despite herself, she would knock on his door when she returned from Helston.

*

Blewett stuffed the list back in his pocket as he made his

way back to the forge. He too glanced at Jory's cottage as he crossed the bridge. He'd hoped Jory would have been on the wagon this morning, but he must still be quivering in his boots, waiting for the law to come knocking. He'd let Jory stew for a few more days, and then he'd tell him, that out of the kindness of his heart he'd cancelled the debt. After all, he'd no documentation or proof that Jory owed him money, in fact he never had, therefore couldn't really call the debt in. He snorted with mirth. Jory would be more than willing to do his bidding again, if he thought he'd been let off the debt. At least he'd duped Jory into handing over his daughter to him. The miserable little wench had kept his bed warm for a year, so that was something.

Without a second thought for the demise of his errant wife, Blewett set about lighting the forge fire for the first time in over ten weeks. Once it roared with heat, he went in search of young Jim Bolitho to work the bellows for him. He was back in business.

*

It was late afternoon when the wagon pulled back into Gweek. Amelia stepped down rubbing her aching backside. The journey never got any better. Gathering her bags of shopping, she made her way home, frowning when she noticed there was still no smoke coming from Jory's chimney.

Once the shopping was deposited, she decided that, despite her feelings towards Jory, and they were very uncharitable indeed, she'd check on him before she settled down for a well-earned cuppa.

Rapping her knuckles against the front door, no answer came. She smoothed down her skirts, knocked again and entered.

'Jory, it's me, Amelia.'

The cottage felt cold, damp and eerily quiet. Amelia shivered, wrinkling her nose at the overwhelming disgusting smell in the air. Walking around the table towards the stairs, the pungent smell of what smelt like an un-emptied chamber pot, caught the back of her throat. Cupping her mouth with her hand she shouted, 'Jory, where are you?'

The source of the smell became apparent when she found a large pool of excrement and urine on the stone step half way up the stairs.

'Ugh! You horrible man, where are you and why haven't you cleaned this up? Are you abed?' she bellowed, her words faltering as her eyes were drawn to something above her. Tipping her head slowly back, her mouth dropped in shock at Jory's stockinged feet hanging limply above.

Stepping carefully over the pool of excrement, Amelia stared in disbelief at the figure hanging from the rafters. Jory's swollen tongue lolled from the mouth of his blackened face, and his protruding eyes stared out into eternal darkness.

*

When the Western Morning News landed on Matthew's breakfast table on Tuesday 13th January, he ignored it, preferring to read the Telegraph until his father appeared for breakfast. Only then did Matthew scan through the local paper. The following article caught his breath:

Police were called to an incident in Gweek on Monday 12th January, where a body was found at the residence of Mr Jory Trevone. The coroner's report stated that Trevone, aged 45, died from asphyxiation due to hanging. Constable Treen from the local constabulary, stated that the death was not suspicious, and they are not looking for anyone else to help with their enquiries. Trevone's death comes just 5 days after his daughter, Mrs Jeannie Blewett, had been reported missing presumed drowned.

Leaving his breakfast half eaten, Matthew went in search of Lyndon.

Fearing Jenna's reaction to the news would give away her identity, after much debate, the decision was made for Lyndon to show her the newspaper at supper time.

*

Later that night, Jenna's hand flew to her own throat as she read the dreadful news. She glanced at Michael and Lyndon who were watching her with bated breath, before rereading the article in disbelief. She trembled as she placed the newspaper on the table. 'Please excuse me. I… think I'll go up to bed.'

'Jenna.' Lyndon reached out to her, but she waved him away.

Closing her bedroom door, she leant heavily against it. The window, slightly ajar, penetrated the room with cold air. It was a moonless night, but something had triggered a dunnock or maybe a robin, to sing a nocturnal song. Jenna stood stock still, listening intently for the bird's sweet song to ease her heart. Had she killed her father? Had her actions done this to him? When the bird ceased its song, the night fell silent, and Jenna crawled under the eiderdown and curled into a small ball. Another sound filled her ears, though she knew not that it was she who emitted it.

Sitting by the fireside, Michael glanced at Lyndon, both chilled by the intensity of Jenna's keening above.

*

The next morning dawned cold and damp. By the time Jenna came downstairs for breakfast, a good fire burned in the grate.

Very gently, Lyndon moved towards her. 'I'm sorry for your loss, Jenna. Are you all right?' he said, softly placing his hand on her arm.

Through tired gritty eyes she nodded slowly. 'It was just a terrible shock.' Glancing again at the newspaper, she added, 'Fortunately they spelt my name wrong.'

'They did and thank heavens for small mercies. Hopefully no-one will link you to the drowning now.'

'No,' she murmured. 'Though it pains me that my good friend Kate will see this report. She will know that it's me.'

'Can you trust her?'

Jenna nodded. 'With my life.'

'Then write to her, I'll post it for you,' he said placing a bowl of porridge in front of her. 'Matthew says you need not go to work today.'

'Oh, but I must go - I need to go. If I stay home, I'll….' She lowered her eyes. 'I need to go,' she said with a determined nod.

'Well, I'm here for you, if you need me.'

*

As it happened, Jenna had precious little time alone with Lyndon during the next week, as his attentions were taken up by Edna. Every evening his betrothed knocked on the door, insisting on sitting with him, with Jenna acting as chaperone at Lyndon's insistence. Jenna noted Edna had little of worth to say, but Lyndon, bless him, had the patience of a saint as he listened to her incessant chatter about the wedding. Michael however, seemed to grow intolerant of her company. As soon as Edna arrived, he raised his eyebrows, and shot off to the Crown Inn.

Occasionally Lyndon engaged Jenna in their conversations, which clearly irritated Edna as she was deeply jealous of their friendship.

'Why do you wear that silly headscarf all the time Jennifer, are you of gypsy origin?' she suddenly asked Jenna one night.

'Edna! What a spiteful thing to say,' Lyndon scolded, banging his mug of ale on the table.

Jenna looked up in surprise from her darning but did not answer.

'Well, *are* you?' Edna reiterated.

'Edna, stop this at once. Of course, she isn't a gypsy.'

Edna pursed her lips. 'I'm just asking a simple question. I'm not saying anything out of turn - I mean, look at her! She always wears the same scarf, and she only seems to have one skirt and that doesn't fit her!'

'For goodness' sake Edna, apologise at once for those remarks,' Lyndon snapped.

Edna flared her nostrils.

Jenna put her darning on her lap. 'It's all right Lyndon.' She smiled tightly. 'I don't mind answering Edna's questions. No Edna, I'm not a gypsy. My family were very poor though and I only own this outfit. When my father died,' her voice waivered slightly, 'when he died, it was a very distressing time for me, as you can imagine. The anxiety made me lose weight, hence my skirt no longer fits, and,' with a quick tug, she pulled off her scarf, 'it also made my hair fall out.'

Edna blanched at the sight of her balding head.

Jenna re-tied her scarf to her head. 'So, you see Edna, I wear the scarf so that I don't go around scaring the children on the estate.' As she spoke, she saw Lyndon suppress a grin.

'Oh,' Edna was clearly embarrassed, 'well, I'm sorry for you. It must be awful to lose your hair. I mean, no man is going to find you attractive if you're bald, are they? Will it grow back?' she added with interest.

Jenna resumed her darning. 'I don't know Edna, maybe it will, and maybe it won't. It doesn't really matter. I've no desire to attract any man's attention.'

Edna's eyes narrowed. Bald or not, Jenna was still an attractive woman. The last thing she wanted was for her to overshadow her at the wedding.

'What a shame then that those are the only clothes you have. I'd lend you something for our wedding, but I only have one lovely dress and I'll be wearing that. It's the one I wore at harvest, Lyndon.' She turned doe-eyed at him. 'You remember it, don't you?'

'I do,' Lyndon answered flatly.

'It's very pretty, isn't it?'

'Actually,' Lyndon said, 'Jennifer will have something else to wear to the wedding. Pa has given her my mother's Sunday best dress to alter. It's very beautiful.'

'Oh!' Edna bristled. Lyndon's mother had been a seamstress and her dresses had been the envy of the other women of the village.

The clock struck nine-thirty, and as rehearsed, Jenna yawned as though she was ready for bed.

'I think it's time for you to go, Edna,' Lyndon said standing up. 'Our chaperone looks tired and needs her bed.'

'That's fine by me - let her go,' Edna answered sourly. 'I've no idea why we need chaperoning anyway. After all, I'm already having your baby!'

'Goodnight, Edna,' Lyndon said adamantly, as he held out her coat.

Scowling, she scraped the chair legs on the stone floor as she stood up. As Lyndon helped her on with her coat, she turned to kiss him on the lips, only for him to deflect her kiss to his cheek.

'Goodnight, Edna,' Jenna said, as she put her darning into her box.

'Goodnight,' Edna answered tartly, as she was ejected from the kitchen.

Lyndon closed the door and lent against it wearily. 'Oh, Lord! I have made my bed - I must lie in it.'

Jenna smiled sympathetically. 'Once you're in your own home, and you get used to each other, it may not be too bad Lyndon.'

He raised both eyebrows. 'I think you jest?'

'I don't mean to be flippant, Lyndon, but if you have to marry her, you'll have to make the most of it.'

He walked to the fire and stabbed it fiercely with the poker. 'Damn it,' he said, leaning against the mantelpiece. 'How could I have been so stupid?'

'If it's any consolation, Edna adores you.'

'Well, the feeling isn't mutual.'

'No, maybe not at the moment, but in time, when the child comes, perhaps things might change, and you'll grow to love her.'

'There's only one woman I will ever love.' He turned to meet her gaze, 'and I'm looking at her now!'

Jenna felt every nerve-ending tingle.

*

In Charleston, Jenna's friend Kate almost fainted when she saw the handwriting on the letter the postman handed her.

Dearest Kate,

You may have seen a report in the Western Morning News which alarmed you. Rest assured I am safe, well and happy now.

J x

Kate held the letter to her heart and the tears she'd shed these last few days now turned to joy.

24

There was a melancholy feel to the trio standing in their Sunday best in Michael's kitchen.

Jenna, dressed in Martha FitzSimmons' sage green and white striped empire line dress, brought a glisten of a tear to Michael's eyes. Michael, uncomfortable in his tight newly starched collar, pulled and tugged impatiently at his neck as Lyndon stood by the window, quietly resigned to his fate.

Jenna adjusted the straw hat Mrs Drake had kindly lent her. Jenna's alopecia, thanks to Edna, was common knowledge among the kitchen staff. In truth, Jenna had about as much wish to attend this wedding as did Lyndon but attend she must.

It was a small affair. The ceremony was held in the local church, followed by a wedding breakfast at the Madron's house.

Jenna watched Lyndon go through the motions of an attentive bridegroom, but it was clear he did so with quiet detachment. Draining her glass of cider, Jenna glanced around the room. The Madron's cottage was clean and well maintained, due to Edna's father, Eric Madron, being the estate's handyman. Eric looked stern but wore a self-satisfied look. Angry at first with Lyndon, until he realised, he would not walk away from his mistake, he looked as though he was silently congratulated himself on having married his daughter off to a man with a fine work ethic.

Jean Madron, pregnant with her sixth child, smiled happily at the newly married couple, while her four sons played hide and seek under the table, oblivious to their best clothes.

Needing fresh air, Jenna stepped out into their back yard. It was a cold day. The sun, which promised so much first thing, failed to materialise. Jenna's straw hat was making her head itch, and she longed to take it off. All around her were lines of billowing washing, some of which, Jenna noticed, were linen rags - twelve feminine napkins to be exact. It suddenly occurred to Jenna that if Edna's siblings were all brothers and Jean Madron was pregnant, why would there be twelve newly laundered feminine napkins on the line? A thought caught her breath. These clearly belonged to someone who'd been menstruating for several days! Had Edna lied about being pregnant to dupe Lyndon into marrying her?

Strangely aware she was being watched from the kitchen window - Jenna turned as Jean Madron stepped out into the yard in a fluster. Jean's red face shot Jenna a contemptuous look, as she swiftly pulled the offending articles from the line and bustled back inside, slamming the back door behind her.

Realising her presence might be unwelcome back in the Madron's cottage, Jenna made her way home, took off her straw hat and drummed her fingers on the kitchen table thoughtfully. She was deeply troubled. What she'd seen could not be unseen. Only time would tell now if Edna had lied to Lyndon. Having no idea what to do with her information, she donned her scarf and old clothes, and set about making supper. The wedding breakfast had consisted of cake, bread and cheese and copious amounts of ale and cider, so she suspected Michael may thank her for something more substantial on his return. As predicted Michael returned to the cottage ravenously hungry.

'Is it over?' Jenna asked.

Michael nodded. 'I reckon the Madrons will go on a while yet. But Edna's been taken ill with a bellyache, so Jean and Lyndon took her home.'

'Bellyache?' Jenna's mind was working overtime.

'Aye. I'm not surprised though, that wedding cake was indigestible. Did you try any of it?'

Jenna shook her head. 'Hopefully this will be more palatable.' She set down a beef and potato pie.

As Michael ate, he sighed audibly at his son's fate. The wedding seemed to have lowered everyone's spirits.

'It's just you and me now, girl,' he said sadly.

Jenna nodded. 'At least he's not too far away, Michael. You haven't lost a son - you've gained a daughter.'

Michael grunted.

They both turned as the door opened suddenly. Lyndon came in, his face white and pinched, and said nothing as he paced the room in an agitated state.

Michael stood up. 'What's amiss, son?'

Taking a deep audible breath he said, 'Edna started to bleed during the wedding breakfast,' he dropped his voice, 'apparently she's miscarried.'

Jenna felt her heart lurch. *So, this was her trick.* 'Has the doctor been brought?' she asked quickly.

'She doesn't want a doctor. Her mother is with her,' he said stiffly.

Michael moved towards him, but Lyndon waved him away. He walked over to the fireplace and rested his hands on the mantelpiece. For a while he stood, visibly shaking, as Jenna and Michael exchanged worried glances.

'Why?' he shouted suddenly, thumping the wall in frustration. 'Why didn't this happen yesterday? This farce of a wedding could have been stopped!'

Placing his arm around him, Michael gently spoke, 'I'm so sorry for you, son, but perhaps you need to go back home, I should think Edna will be feeling the loss keenly.'

Lyndon turned his bloodshot eyes on him. 'You don't understand - I married her for nothing.'

'You'll have other children,' Michael said, immediately realising it was the wrong thing to say.

'That Pa ....is the *last* thing in the world that I want!' he shouted, as he stormed out.

*

As Edna's mother Jean fussed about tucking Edna into bed, Edna was unable to take the self-satisfied smile from her face. Here she was, in her own cottage. No more would she have to share a room with her smelly brothers. Their plan had worked.

'Now then,' Jean said matter-of-factly, 'when Lyndon comes back, take that grin off your face and try to look pale and wan - remember, you've meant to have miscarried. I'll suggest he sleeps in the spare room for now - until you've recovered.'

'What if he finds out?'

'He won't, men don't understand the workings of a woman's body. It was only a little lie. You'll be pregnant for real soon. You've done yourself proud, Edna. You've caught a good man in Lyndon. So, stop fretting. When old Tom Hindle died, his vacant cottage was an opportunity not to be missed. Lyndon was clearly dilly dallying about you - we just moved things on a bit that's all.'

Edna blanched. 'Huh, you didn't have to tell Pa! He's not spoken two civil words to me since you made me tell him I'd lain with Lyndon. I thought he was going to brain me.'

'Don't worry about your pa. He'll come round now you're wed. I know he'll be happy to know there isn't going to be the shame of a six-month baby now.' Jean's grin widened. 'Everyone will think you married for love.'

'I did!' Edna pouted. 'Unfortunately, I don't think Lyndon loves me!'

'Then you will have to work on him. Keep his house clean, make sure his belly is full and *do* your duty in bed.'

Edna scowled.

'You'll have to do it sometime.'

Edna shuddered at the thought. 'What are we going to do about Jennifer? You said she saw my napkins on the line!'

Jean waved away her concerns. 'If anything is said, I shall tell her that I am afflicted with terrible nose bleeds.' She pulled a napkin from her pocket and tied it under her nose. 'See!' she grinned, 'they're perfect for stemming the blood.'

'Oh, Ma, thank you. You've thought of everything.'

Jean winked. 'We had to do something,' she patted her

stomach. 'Our little cottage couldn't accommodate another. Now shush, I think I've just heard Lyndon return.'

*

Jean stopped Lyndon outside the bedroom door.

'Is she all right?' Edna heard Lyndon ask.

'Aye, she'll come brave, but she'll need a few weeks to mend,' her mother answered in hushed tones. 'I've made a bed up for you in the spare room.'

Lyndon had no idea what miscarrying implied or how long it took to recover but being relegated to the spare room had deferred the wedding night for him, which he was truly grateful for.

*

Jenna spent a rather fitful night, her conscience playing heavily on her as she debated well into the night whether she should tell Lyndon what she'd discovered. She certainly didn't relish being the one to tell him Edna had made a fool of him. However, the opportunity to speak to Lyndon didn't arise. Jenna found out he'd left home the morning after the wedding to take up a commission on the Tehidy Estate.

It was a decision Lyndon made whilst lying awake in the spare room. He was sorry for Edna's loss, for it was *her* loss - she'd been as happy about this baby as he had been dismayed. He'd initially planned to spend a little time at home with Edna after the wedding, in order to get to know her better, but try as he might, he could not shrug the need to get away.

Edna had been remarkably agreeable to his suggestion when he'd told her at breakfast time. He'd been surprised to see her up and about and looking quite well when he came downstairs and was in two minds whether to broach the subject of his leaving after she placed a delicious breakfast in front of him. She'd gone to a lot of trouble.

'Are you feeling better?' he asked kindly.

'Thank you, Lyndon, yes. But it'll take time,' she

answered sadly. 'When do you leave for Tehidy? You said you would be leaving quite soon after the wedding,' she added casually.

Quite taken aback, he answered, 'Well err,' he cleared his throat, 'today, if that is all right by you.'

Edna felt a flutter of happiness. 'Of course, it is, Lyndon. You have your work to do, and Ma will be here to help me should I need it.'

*

When Jenna called on Edna later that day, she was left in no uncertain terms that she was not welcome at the cottage. She did not try again.

*

During Lyndon's absence, Jenna took on the task of walking Fern the deer down to the woods every day. She was a fully grown doe now and would come into season for the first time in the next few months and probably leave for good. Fern still slept in the stable and though she spent a good deal of the day in the woods foraging for herself, she always returned for a bucket of kitchen scraps before nightfall.

It was lonely on the estate without Lyndon to speak to, but Jenna's work kept her busy and Tommy Teague the groom was a welcome diversion for her. His blond good lucks and wide sunny smile, mixed with a quick wit and sunny temperament, could lift anyone's spirits.

*

It was early February, Candlemas, when Lyndon returned for a brief visit to the Trevarno Estate. It was late afternoon when he arrived at his cottage. He found it cosy, tidy, and warm and his new bride quite well, though still insistent that he sleep in the spare room until she recovered completely. This he gladly did – having no desire whatsoever to share Edna's bed.

Jenna found him the next morning sat outside his father's house sharpening his billhook. She settled beside him and he smiled sadly. During his absence she fretted about his state of mind.

'Hello.' She smiled. 'I've missed you.'

'I missed you too, Jenna, but I can't stay around here. I don't want to live in the same house as Edna, and if the truth were known, she doesn't want me either.' He put the billhook down. 'I feel as though I've been trapped into this marriage, I don't know why - but it's just a feeling.' He turned and looked hard at Jenna. 'Have I? Have I been made a fool of Jenna?'

Jenna heard the crack of emotion in his voice. Should she divulge her theory of Edna's fake pregnancy to Lyndon? What good would it do to add to his misery? The poor man was suffering enough. She gave a half shrug. 'I don't know, Lyndon.'

'I'm leaving again tomorrow.'

'You *will* come back?' she asked anxiously.

'Of course, I'll be back at Easter. I've secured a good amount of work on the Tehidy Estate, which could take months. It will give me time to think about what has happened.'

'I shall make a special cake for your return,' Jenna said gently.

He gazed lovingly into her eyes. 'I'll look forward to that.' He placed his hands on his thighs and stood up. 'I'll see you before I go.'

*

In Gweek, Jory Trevone's cottage had new tenants. It was now occupied by Bill and Evelyn Norton, a couple in their forties, and their daughter Miriam, who was the local school teacher.

Everything in the cottage - furniture, crockery, and curtains – had been retained by the new owners. The only things they threw out were Jory's clothes, Jenna's cloth bag, the one she'd packed over a year ago - before her plans had been thwarted, and the pretty dresses Jenna wore as a young carefree woman. Jenna had taken none of her dresses from her home when she married Blewett.

Once his wife, she wore black to match her feelings. Evelyn Norton, a deeply superstitious woman, thought making any use of dead people's clothes - no matter how pretty the dresses were, was too much to ask.

When Amelia saw the bag and pile of clothes on the road, awaiting the rag and bone man, she knocked on the door and asked if she could take them away, stating that they could be given to the poor.

Evelyn dismissed them with a wave of the hand. 'Oh, yes please - take them away.'

Jory's clothes were given to the poor, but Amelia kept the dresses, washed and dried them by her fireside and when they were pressed, packed them up along with Jenna's cloth bag and took them with her to Helston on the next market day.

The package arrived at the FitzSimmons' cottage the last week in March. Michael inspected the large parcel addressed to his son for a moment, and then picked it up to take it outside.

'Where are you taking it?' Jenna asked.

'To his cottage! Why?'

'Well, it's addressed to Lyndon, not Mr and Mrs FitzSimmons. Maybe he'd like to open it himself. I feel sure Edna would feel obliged to open it, should you give it to her.'

Michael looked at the parcel and nodded. 'Aye, perhaps you're right.' He placed the parcel back on the table and left for work.

*

Lyndon arrived back at Trevarno on Good Friday, and his first port of call was his father's cottage. Michael was out and Jenna was putting the finishing touches to the simnel cake she had made.

'Welcome home, Lyndon.' She smiled sweetly and thought he looked easier in mind than when he'd left, as though the separation had done him good.

'My god, Jenna, I wish I was coming home to you.'

Jenna poured him a cup of tea and cut him the first slice of the cake, but just as he sat down a furious knock came on the door and Edna walked in without being invited.

'Well,' she bristled indignantly, 'this is a fine state of affairs that my husband should come *here* before he comes home to his wife. I would never have known you were home if not for ma coming to tell me. You send me no word of your return. Anyone would think there is someone here you would rather see than me!' She gave Jenna a withering look.

Lyndon cast a sideways glance at Jenna as he placed his hand on Edna's shoulder. 'Edna, there is no need for this animosity. I'm sorry I didn't come home first, but I needed to see my pa on some urgent business.'

'Huh!' She shrugged.

'I'll be home shortly.' His tone of voice changed as he gently manoeuvred her back toward the door. 'Now, I suggest you return to our cottage, and I'll join you later, *after* I've seen my pa.'

Edna shot Jenna a look of contempt before flouncing out of the house.

When the door closed, Lyndon picked up his slice of cake, cupped his hand over Jenna's and savoured the first moist bite with relish.

*

Easter Sunday dawned bright and sunny. It was one of the few days the FitzSimmons went to church en masse. Jenna had aired one of Martha's dresses again for the occasion, but she longed to have some new clothes of her own. Though she had a little money now, she dared not venture into Helston to buy anything for herself. Thankfully her hair was beginning to grow back. Mrs Drake swore it was the bay rum and cantharidine mixture she gave Jenna to rub on her scalp every night, but Jenna knew it was because she was away from the fear of Blewett's clutches. She ran her fingers through the short blond wisps of hair and pondered if she could soon stop wearing her scarf. The only other people on the estate sporting short hair were the children who'd had their hair shaved to rid themselves of head lice.

On hearing Lyndon talking to his father, she hung up her dress and joined them downstairs as Lyndon was opening the package Michael had kept for him.

He smiled warmly at her when she entered the kitchen - a gesture that always filled her heart with joy. 'We're all dying to know what's in the parcel,' Jenna said excitedly.

As he resumed his unwrapping, Jenna gasped in recognition of her clothes and bag and fell on them lovingly, pulling garment after garment from the pile and holding them to her breast as she did.

The note enclosed fluttered down to the floor. It simply said:

To Lyndon, from Amelia. No reply necessary.

Jenna wore the prettiest dress to church that Sunday, and for the first time in years, felt her old self was back.

25

May 1914 had been a strange month in Cornwall. Normally one of the sunniest months of the year, the first couple of weeks started cool, rather cloudy and generally unsettled. The spring flowers in the Italian sunken garden shivered in temperatures well below the average for this time of year, and Michael worried constantly about his newly planted vegetable patch. People began to wonder if summer was ever going to start. Fortunately, by mid-month, the temperature began to rise, and when Lyndon arrived home from Tehidy during the third week of May, Cornwall was basking in a heatwave.

It was permitted for all estate dwellers to bathe in the lake during high temperatures, and that's exactly what Lyndon headed straight to do. As he walked from the lake, damp haired and refreshed, he encountered the women of the village making their way down to bathe. He saw Jenna first and his face lit, only to quickly hide his elation when he realised Edna and Jean were walking behind her.

'Morning, ladies,' he said pleasantly.

Edna painted on a smile. 'So, you're back then?'

Lyndon inclined his head. 'As you see.'

Edna stopped to speak to him, but Lyndon carried on walking.

Folding her arms angrily she hissed, 'He's been gone these last six weeks and he can't even pass the time of day with me.'

Jean gave her a hurried, 'shush.'

'I've no doubt he'll be spending time with 'you know who' before he even bothers to turn up at his own home,' Edna said within Jenna's earshot.

Again, there was a 'shush,' followed swiftly by, 'Perhaps if you let him into your bed, you might find that he'll want to come home to you.'

'Huh! I don't think he'd want that even if I offered it,

thank goodness,' Edna quipped.

At the lake side, Jenna sat down on the bank, lifted her skirts and dangled her bare legs in the cooling water. Even though she could not be with Lyndon, life seemed just that little bit better when he was home. She was used to unpleasant comments and looks from Edna and her mother, and in truth she could not blame them. Lyndon *did* spend most of his time at his father's house, when he was home.

She pulled out her drawing book, happy at being reunited with it following the return of her cloth bag and sat with pencil poised. The lake was alive with damsel flies as they skitted across the surface, their iridescent wings glinting in the sun. The water rippled as she kicked and splashed with her feet, and watched other ladies arrive to bathe. Most had husbands to get back home for, so their dip was short, but much appreciated. Jenna was in no rush to go home that night. Michael had gone into Helston and wouldn't be back until late. He would probably grab a pasty and a mug of Spingo at the Blue Anchor, so she needn't cook. She knew out of decency Lyndon would not visit her until his father had returned.

Soon everyone started for home. Edna was a good swimmer and the last to get out of the lake. Jean, being almost eight months pregnant, had only been able to dangle her feet in the lake. The afternoon was getting on. Soon Jenna too would have to move. The rest of the village men would be finishing their work and would need their privacy to bathe.

Reluctantly she pulled her feet out of the water, dried them off and slipped her shoes back on. Standing up, she stretched her back and smoothed her dress down, but her petticoat had ruffled and caught under her skirt. Whilst bending to adjust everything, she heard footsteps behind, and then a sudden bump sent her flying head first into the water. Her dress covered her head as she struggled to the surface, coughing and spluttering. In desperation she treaded water to find a foot hold, but her head went under again. She choked and panicked as water filled her mouth. She wasn't far from the edge but her fear of water, and inability to move in it, hindered her efforts to stay afloat.

Edna looked on in amusement, but Jean became alarmed. 'The maid can't swim! We need to help her.'

From the edge of despair Jenna found her voice and screamed for help.

Edna looked about to see if anyone was coming to her aid, and then realising she would be implicated in Jenna's plight, Edna too started to shout for help. It was Lyndon and Tommy who came running to their aid first, both shedding their shoes before diving in to rescue her.

Jenna almost drowned Lyndon when he reached her, but he kept her at arm's length as Tommy assisted to pull her over to the edge. Out on the lake side Jenna vomited violently, great gushes of lake water spewing from her mouth.

Gently wiping her hair from her face, a cold chill ran through Lyndon. If he hadn't heard, she could have drowned. His face was full of concern, as he whispered fearfully, 'Are you all right?'

Her eyes were bloodshot, and when she tried to speak, she began to choke up more water.

'Christ, Jen, can you not swim?'

She shook her head, sobbing uncontrollably.

'Shh now, it's all right,' he said softly. Ignoring the disapproving looks from Edna, he cradled her in his arms. 'We'll have to remedy that. You'll have lessons.'

Jenna's eyes flashed open and shook her head in horror.

'You can't live in Cornwall and not swim! We're surrounded by water! You'll be fine. Don't worry, I'll teach you.' He smiled reassuringly. 'I'm home for a while so I'll have you swimming in a week.' He looked up at Edna's scowl and stated, 'We must make sure this situation *cannot* happen again.'

Edna pursed her lips and turned to leave, quickly followed by her mother.

When Jenna had recovered, he asked, 'What happened?'

'I don't know, I just…I was.' She lowered her eyes. 'I don't know.'

He helped her to her feet, and Jenna bemoaned that her only pair of shoes were ruined as she squelched back to the cottage. Leaving her to change, Lyndon walked over to the Madron's cottage.

Edna and Jean looked up in alarm as he walked in. With his hands resting on the back of the settle, he regarded them reproachfully. 'What happened?'

Edna's face flushed scarlet at the accusation. 'We don't know, Lyndon. We just heard her screaming in the water. Didn't we Ma?'

Jean nodded in agreement.

Lyndon emitted a growling sound before he spoke directly to Jean, 'As of tomorrow, I shall be teaching Jen to swim! I'll need to borrow one of your lads to act as a chaperone.' It was a statement rather than a question. 'Make sure he's at the lake at 7p.m.' He slammed the door behind him in his wake.

*

Though Jenna protested strongly, Lyndon insisted that she come to the lake every evening during the next week for a swimming lesson. As arranged, one of Edna's brothers chaperoned them.

It actually took two whole weeks for Lyndon to teach Jenna to swim, but with his patience and help, swim she did. On the day before Lyndon left again for Tehidy, Jenna had her very last lesson.

She stood at the edge of the lake and gave him a grateful smile.

'Thank you, Lyndon,' she said, drying her hair. 'I've always feared water since I was a small girl. I fell in the river as the tide was coming in. I was using a stick to try and reach a ball I'd accidently rolled into the water. I lost my footing and fell forwards, but it was so muddy I couldn't get my arms out. The more I struggled the more I sank into the mud. I could see the tide coming in fast and began to scream until Charlie Williams came to my aid and dragged me out by the feet. I've always kept a healthy distance from water since then.'

Lyndon put a comforting hand on her arm, and then quickly removed it in case anyone saw. 'Have you never been to the sea?'

She shook her head. 'The first time I saw the sea was at Rinsey in January.'

'Really?'

'There was never time or money for days out I'm afraid.'

'That is a shame. To swim in the sea is an exhilarating experience. My favourite time is late afternoon on a sunny day when the water glitters like millions of diamonds. I love to just lose myself in the jewels of the sea.'

Jenna smiled gently. 'It sounds lovely.'

'One day Jenna, we'll swim together in the sea, I promise,' he whispered.

26

On the 15th of June, Jenna was roused from her bed by someone frantically knocking at their cottage door. Pulling her shawl around her shoulders she followed Michael downstairs to investigate.

The youngest Madron boy stood tearfully at the door.

'What is it son?' Michael said gravely.

'It's my ma, she needs someone to come and help.'

The Madron's cottage was only twenty yards away and screams were clearly audible.

Jenna glanced at Michael. 'It must be Jean's time.' Jenna bent down to address the boy, who she now remembered as the one who'd chaperoned her swimming lessons. 'It's Samuel, isn't it?' she asked gently.

The boy nodded tearfully.

'It's all right, Samuel. You go and fetch Mrs Price.'

The boy sniffed noisily. 'Mrs Price has lumbago and can't come.'

'Oh!' Mrs Price normally helped to deliver all the babies in and around the estate. 'Well, then go and get Edna.'

'She's already there, but ma needs someone else to help!'

Jenna looked at Michael who just shrugged his shoulders.

'Okay, tell your ma I'm coming, I'll just get dressed.'

For someone who had given birth five times already, Jenna thought Jean was making a terrible racket, but when she entered the cottage, she found it was Edna making most of the noise.

When Edna saw her, she stopped howling, hiccupped and scowled darkly at her.

'What are you doing here?'

'I'm told your ma needs help,' she said, looking around the bedroom.

'What do *you* know about delivering babies?' Edna said contemptuously.

'I know that hollering along with your ma isn't going to help her. Now fetch some clean towels and hot water please.'

'Who do you think *you* are ordering me about?' Edna snapped.

Jean gave Edna a shove. 'Go and do as she says.'

*

Once Edna had gone, Jean looked at Jenna.

'Edna gets panicky with anything to do with pain, either hers or anyone else's. Lord knows what she'll be like, when she falls pregnant with *another* baby!'

Another contraction took hold of her. '*Do* you know anything about delivering babies?' she asked seriously.

'Well, not a lot actually,' Jenna confessed, 'but I'm sure with your experience and my help, we'll muddle through nicely. If you get into difficulty, I shall go and ask Mrs Price for advice. Where is Mr Madron if you don't mind me asking?'

She grimaced as another pain shot through her. 'He's out lamping for rabbits with some of the other estate workers.'

'Mrs Madron - Jean, forgive me for asking, but can you afford the doctor if we send for him?'

Jean nodded. 'We can, but he was on another call when I sent Samuel for him. His housekeeper said she would send him round just as soon as possible.'

Jean watched Jenna arrange the bed ready for birth. Unsure if Jenna had told Lyndon about the feminine napkins she'd seen, this would be an ideal opportunity to leave her in no doubt as to why they were hanging the line.

'Do me a favour Jennifer. Pass me one of those napkins there.' As Jean took the napkin from Jenna's hand, she tied it under her nose. 'I'm plagued with nosebleeds you see. They've been non-stop all through this pregnancy.'

*

Jenna felt a pang of guilt. *Perhaps she'd been wrong to judge*

Edna.

For the next three hours Jenna and Jean found some common ground as they struggled with the toils of childbirth. Jenna remembered the agony she endured during her own baby's birth and sympathised with her plight.

Throughout, Edna stood glowering by her ma's head, but thankfully stayed silent.

At three-fifty that morning, much to the relief of all, Jean was delivered a healthy baby girl and the occupants of the cottage gave a collective sigh of relief.

With a length of strong cotton, Jenna tied the umbilical cord, and then severed it from the placenta with Jean's sewing scissors. It was only when all was washed and cleaned away, did the doctor arrive, slightly out of breath and extremely apologetic.

When she knew all was well, Jenna took a peek at the sleeping child in Jean's arms and bid them all a tired goodnight.

The night was warm. Jenna sat on the bench outside Michael's cottage gazing into the night sky. The great oak trees at the edge of the dell were silhouetted against the moonlit sky. Behind her, two large moths bumped against the kitchen window, which was illuminated by the light from the moon.

Having delivered the baby into the arms of a loving mother, Jenna thought back to a time when she believed she would marry Lyndon and dreamt of having his children. Ironically, Jenna always thought she'd make a good mother, but then she hadn't envisaged the unprecedented circumstances which brought about her initiation into motherhood. She dropped her head into her hands. Curiously despite the apathy she felt towards her baby, Jenna thought of him every day. Amelia had arranged for him to be buried with old Jack Simkins in Constantine Church graveyard, because that's what happened when an infant died so young. Though clearly mentally unwell after the birth, Jenna often wondered if she would have ever found love in her heart for Blewett's son, had he lived. Poor little boy, she sighed, to go to heaven without knowing even an ounce of motherly love. God would surely punish her for her neglect. Shivering at the thought, she pulled her shawl around her shoulders and took herself off to bed to try and catch a few hours' sleep before breakfast.

The next morning, Michael watched with interest at the cloud of melancholia engulfing Jenna. Over the past few months Jenna had lost that gaunt, haunted look. She'd filled out slightly, and her sallow complexion now had a rosy glow. She would often hum a soft melodic tune to herself while she worked, so Michael knew she was happy living here. He frowned, there was no tune being hummed that morning.

'I see last night brought back memories for you?' he said, pulling a chunk of bread from the loaf.

'Not good memories I'm afraid.'

'You'll be remembering your own babe perhaps?' He reached over and held her hand. 'It's a great sadness to lose a child. One day, god willing, you'll have another.'

Jenna's eyes watered, turning them vivid emerald-green. She very much doubted god would entrust her with another.

She watched Michael shrug on his coat and get up to leave for work. When he opened the door, he bent down and picked something up. Walking back to the table, he placed a jar of preserved apples in front of her with a thank you note from Jean attached to it.

27

On June 29th, 1914, the leading headline in The Times newspaper was:

'The Tragedy of Sarajevo'
With the deepest and most profound regret we record today the tragic news of the assassination of the Archduke Franz Ferdinand, Heir-Presumptive to the Austro-Hungarian Throne, and of his wife, the Duchess of Hohenberg. The Archduke, in his capacity as Inspector-General of the Forces of the Empire, had been attending military manoeuvres in the province of Bosnia.

The below stairs staff at the big house mulled over the full story, and though the Archduke and his wife were relatively unknown, everyone felt a great sadness for the two people involved. No-one around that busy kitchen table could possibly realise what these deaths would mean to them all in the future. As they sat and discussed the tragic story, a great commotion began outside, and everyone got up to watch in amusement as Matthew Bickford and Tommy Teague returned from market and began unloading the four nanny goats they'd just purchased.

Mrs Drake clapped her hands to her face. 'Oh, how marvellous, we can have goat's cheese.'

'Well, not yet a while, Mrs Drake,' Matthew answered, as he tried to manoeuvre an errant goat into the pen. 'They have to give birth before they produce milk, so we'll have to wait a month or so until they come into heat.' He shut the pen and wiped his hand across his forehead.

Mrs Drake looked into the pen and asked, 'Which one is the Billy then? I can't tell them apart.'

'They are all Nanny goats Mrs Drake. When they're ready, Mr Johns down the road will lend us his.'

'What? That vicious little bugger! Begging your pardon, sir for swearing, but it rammed its gate as I walked past last week from Church. It gave me a terrible shock.'

'Worry not Mrs Drake. We'll keep it well away from

you when it comes,' Matthew assured her.

*

Because the goats were kept for milking, the estate children were allowed to give them all names, so Dora, Dolly, Dilly and Drew became part of the Trevarno family.

They were a huge source of amusement to the children, especially as they kept escaping their pen to gorge themselves in Michael's vegetable patch.

Michael was furious when he found them there for the third time. Enough was enough. He went in search of Mr Brown the butler, to demand that Matthew be told to secure the little beasts in a better pen.

On finding him, Michael noted a solemn look upon his face. Forgetting his anger momentarily, he asked, 'What's amiss with you, Mr Brown?'

'It seems there's to be a war in Europe, Michael' he answered gravely, showing him The Times headline. 'It says here that because Archduke Franz Ferdinand was shot by someone who thought that Serbia should control Bosnia instead of Austria, Austria-Hungary has declared war on Serbia.'

Michael tutted. 'Bloody war - a damn waste of good men I say!'

'I agree. Now what's amiss with you, Michael?'

'Those bloody goats of Matthew's are eating my cabbages again.'

Mr Brown folded the newspaper. 'I'll speak to Matthew for you.'

*

Over the next few days, the staff below stairs started to take a great interest in the newspaper. As soon as the Bickford's had breakfasted, the newspaper was sent back downstairs and spread over the kitchen table. Every few days something seemed to be happening in Europe. First Russia got involved, because Russia had an alliance with Serbia. Then Germany declared war on Russia because Germany had an alliance with Austria-Hungary. On

August 3rd, Germany declared war on France. Mr Brown trembled as he ironed Andrew Bickford's newspaper the next morning. Brown was an intelligent man and knew Britain had agreements to protect both Belgium and France. For the time being he kept his concerns to himself and went about his daily routine.

It was on 5th August, when Mr Brown was ironing the master's newspaper, ready to place on the breakfast table, that he almost dropped the iron. The headline was: ***England and Germany at War.***

Never normally one to show anybody the newspaper before Andrew Bickford had seen it, he gathered everyone around the kitchen table to share the dreadful news.

'What does it mean?' Ethel the scullery maid said tearfully.

'I'm sure there is nothing for you to worry about Ethel.' Mr Brown smiled, and then addressed the rest of the staff. 'We have a fine British Army of, I believe, over seven-hundred-thousand men, including reserves, all who are trained and ready for war. Let's hope they sort the Germans out quickly.'

'But why does Britain have to go to war, Mr Brown?' Mrs Drake asked with her arms covered in flour as she made pastry.

'Because Britain has agreements to protect both Belgium and France, so we are obliged to.'

The soft melodic hum which everyone knew to be Jenna's could be heard in the larder. They all looked up as she walked into the kitchen with a bowl of cherries freshly picked from the orchard. Putting the bowl down on the table she looked at the silent watching group.

'What's the matter? Do I have cherry juice on my face or something?' she asked seriously, looking from one to the other.

Ethel started to cry. 'What does it look like out there? Can you tell we're at war? I don't want to go out collecting the eggs, Mrs Drake, not if there is a war out there!'

Jenna felt her mouth go dry as she looked at Mr Brown. 'War! Are we at war?'

'I'm afraid so Jennifer,' Mr Brown said solemnly. 'But as I've already told Ethel, it's nothing for you ladies to worry about. The outside world doesn't look any different Ethel, so you can gather the eggs without fear.'

*

The news brought Lyndon home the next day. Stopping only for a slice of Jenna's sweet cherry pie, he immediately went up to the house to see Matthew. When he returned, Jenna thought he looked pensive.

'Are you eating with us?'

He nodded. 'I'd like to, if there is enough to go around, thank you.'

'It's always a pleasure when you join us at the table,' Jenna said softly.

'The pleasure is mine, Jenna,' he answered warmly.

She smiled uncertainly.

'I miss you most of all when I am away, you know.'

She knew she should not respond but she could not help herself. 'I miss you too, Lyndon. Though I know you're not mine to miss.'

He caught hold of her and gazed lovingly at her. 'I belong to no-one but you.'

She heard the emotion in his voice and swallowed down the lump forming in her throat.

With her small hand in his, she watched as he slowly turned it palm upwards and very gently kissed between each of her fingers.

Gasping at the pleasure of his touch, she remembered the last time he had kissed her so tenderly.

'My heart will always be yours.' He lifted her hand to his cheek, releasing it just as Michael came through the door.

Jenna turned to hide her blushing face and busied herself with the cooking.

'Ah, Lyndon my boy, you've returned to us. Are you

staying for supper? Of course, you are. Sit down, my boy. Jen, do we have ale?'

Before he could finish his question, Jenna placed two pewter mugs of ale on the table with a smile.

'I swear this girl knows what a man wants before he does. You've come on the right day we have cherry pie, though if I know you, you will have already had a piece. Am I right?'

'You know me so well.' He chinked mugs with his pa.

'What about all this talk of war, eh?'

Lyndon nodded sadly. 'I've just been speaking with Matthew. He's taking up his commission in the army.'

'Whatever for?'

'I believe his father thinks it's his duty.'

'Duty! Huh!' He took a long drink and looked seriously at his son. 'I hope you're not thinking along the same lines.'

Lyndon smiled but remained silent.

'Lyndon, look at me!' He grasped him by the chin. 'Promise me you won't go.'

'I don't know if I can promise that, Pa. I don't know what to think at the moment.'

Jenna turned around from her cooking and matched Michael's look of horrified shock.

'Let's just see what happens, eh?' Lyndon said, trying to defuse the situation.

28

Thankfully, there was no more talk of going to war whenever Lyndon was in the cottage, which to Jenna's delight was almost every day.

The estate seemed to settle back into normality, and everyone went on with their everyday chores. Jenna was now in charge of the creamery, so when the cows had been milked, she took what she needed to make the cheese and clotted cream.

Her first job that morning was to start the clotted cream process. There were ample raspberries on the canes, and the Bickfords loved clotted cream with them. The process normally took three days, but she'd started it yesterday and picked up the pan of milk which had stood overnight. Carefully, she poured the milk into a wide bowl, and then lowered it into a bain-marie, which had just come under the boil. Now she had to wait forty-five minutes for it to cook. Once that was done, she began to make the soft cheese the Bickfords also enjoyed eating after dinner. Warming some more milk in a pan, she kept checking until it was a little warmer than blood heat. As soon as it was the correct temperature she added the rennet, gave it a good stir, and put it to cool on the cold slab. It was best to leave it for a good four hours before skimming the curds into a mould. With that done, she returned to her clotted cream, lifted it out of the bain-marie and put that on the cool slab to sit overnight too. She licked her lips at the thought of skimming off the cream in the morning.

It was cool in the dairy and the heat of the day hit her like a furnace when she emerged, blinking in the bright sunlight.

Tommy Teague had Matthew's horse out in the yard, brushing it until it shone. 'She's a fine beast,' Jenna said stroking the mare's nose.

'Aye she is. Oops, Matthew's coming now, and I haven't saddled her yet.' Tommy jumped into action.

'Good morning, Jen…'. He had to physically stop himself calling her Jenna. 'How's the clotted cream coming on? Father says you make the best batch of all.'

Jenna laughed softly. 'I wish I had the same touch with the butter,' she said, as Gina Teague emerged from the buttery to join them.

'And do you not?' Matthew asked as he put his foot in the stirrup.

'No, she doesn't have the touch,' Gina said jovially. 'She's tried to do it, but it simply won't turn when Jen tries to make it! Will it, maid?'

Jenna shrugged her shoulders and shook her head.

'Why is that then?' He looked down at them from the saddle.

'I think she is in love.' Gina gave Jenna a playful push. 'Butter won't turn if you're in love.'

Matthew glanced at Jenna who quickly lowered her eyes. 'Is that so?'

'True enough. I read it once in a Thomas Hardy novel.' She frowned. 'I can't remember which one it was though.'

Matthew smiled, pulled up the reins and winked at Jenna. 'I'll bid good day to you ladies.'

Gina sighed wistfully as they watched Matthew canter out of the yard. 'I wouldn't say no to a bit of love.'

Jenna touched her softly on the sleeve of her dress. Gina had lost her husband to consumption last summer.

'But then we'd have to find someone else to make the butter,' Jenna said lightly.

'Aye, true, but I'd gladly relinquish the job for one more day with my man.' She looked at Jenna. 'I shouldn't grumble. I had twenty-years with him. Some folks don't get even half that.'

*

On the 10th of August, Mr Brown addressed the staff, with a brief account of what was on the front page of the newspaper. 'It seems Lord Kitchener has introduced a voluntary enlistment to expand the British forces.'

Mrs Drake sipped her well-earned cup of tea and frowned. 'Why would he do that? I thought we had an army, of what did you say, seven-hundred-thousand men!'

'Maybe he thinks that is not enough. Apparently over a hundred men an hour has signed up to join the armed forces since war was declared.'

The collected group went back to their chores in silence, each with their own worrying thoughts on war.

On the 11th of August, much to Gina Teague and Lowella Hoskin's dismay, their sons Tommy and Jimmy, were the first to join up from the estate. Though they were both happy with their positions on the estate, as groom and junior dairyman, the general consensus was that it would all be over by Christmas 1914, so they both agreed this was one great adventure they did not want to miss. Both women were inconsolable - even though they were told that at eighteen years old, neither was eligible to go to the front line. Jenna took the time to sit with them both and sympathise over a pot of tea.

*

It was 12th August. The kitchen at the big house was a hive of activity. Cook was busy getting the day's luncheon together, the footmen were polishing the cutlery, Edna was ironing the laundry and Jenna was busy preparing the freshly picked rhubarb.

They all looked up momentarily at the clatter of hooves in the yard, then when they heard the sound of horses trotting off down the lane, they returned to the task in hand.

'That will be them off then,' said Mrs Drake, walking back from the larder with a trug of fresh vegetables.

Jenna gave Mrs Drake a questioning look.

'Lyndon's borrowed Miss Mellissa's horse and he's going to Helston with Matthew. Lyndon's going to join up today.'

The clatter of the knife as Jenna dropped the utensil made everyone look up at her. 'Are you sure?' her voice almost inaudible.

Mrs Drake nodded confidently. 'Mr Brown heard Matthew talking at breakfast, telling his father that Lyndon had decided to go.'

Jenna felt as though she'd been winded. 'Oh, no!'

Edna looked up haughtily from her ironing. 'What's it to you what my husband does? Most of the other men from the estate have signed up, so of course, Lyndon must go. Otherwise, he would be thought to be a coward.'

Mrs Drake rounded on Edna. 'That's a stupid thing to say, to call a man a coward for not joining up. War is a terrible thing. I lost my two brothers Bert and Arthur in the Boer War. It's not a game, Edna. It's not just running around with rifles. War is real and terrible and a *widow* maker.'

Edna flushed and glared at Jenna as though it was she who was berating her. 'I'm not saying they're cowards.'

'You were the one who mentioned that horrible word,' Mrs Drake said accusingly.

Edna put her iron down and punched her fists into her hips. 'I'm simply saying that they must go. It's their duty as men to fight for their country and to keep *their* women safe.'

'I'm sure those are Lyndon's sentiments too, along with Matthew's and all our other boys, so there is no need for you ever to speak of cowardice around this table again,' Mrs Drake snapped.

Edna pursed her lips, returning to her ironing with more vigour than she had ever used before.

Picking up her knife to finish prepping the rhubarb, Jenna felt suddenly very cold, though the kitchen was stiflingly hot.

Mrs Kent the housekeeper shook her head. 'With Jimmy and Tommy gone, and Fred Saunders told Matthew that he'll go into town on his next day off to sign up too, lord knows what we're going to do without all our men folk.'

'Fred's going as well, Mrs Kent?' Jenna asked, shocked.

'I'm afraid he is. Can you not hear Ethel? She's been crying in the scullery all morning.'

Jenna quickly finished the job in hand and cleared the rhubarb scrapings into the bin. Wiping her hands down her apron, she excused herself from the kitchen.

Michael was in his vegetable patch and the look on his face confirmed that it was true - Lyndon was going to war.

'I can't stop him, Jen. Lord knows I would if I could. War is a terrible thing.' His eyes glazed over as though remembering some horror in the past. 'I blame Edna!' he said coldly. 'He is clearly unhappy with her. He spends more time with us than at home with her. I think he needs to be away from her.' He squeezed his eyes shut to stop them from watering. 'Mr Brown tells me that pages and pages of the names of fallen men are printed every day in the newspapers. I don't want my boy to be one of those. If anything should happen to him…..' he stopped himself from saying more.

Jenna reached out and placed a comforting hand on his arm. 'We'll pray for him every day he is away from us.'

Placing his weathered hand atop of hers, he said, 'It's a real shame he couldn't marry you. I see the way you look at each other - it grieves me to think that he's stuck with her. If you'd been his wife, he would never have gone!' He turned back to his pruning. 'I've said too much, I know, forgive me, I'm just upset.'

Jenna moved closer and kissed him lightly on the cheek.

*

Jenna was collecting goose eggs down by the Italian sunken garden. For some reason this gaggle of geese seemed to enjoy laying eggs in the most inaccessible places of the garden. She found a nest of three down by the boundary hedge, placed them in her basket and stood to stretch her back out from all the bending. She looked up at the intricate weave of Lyndon's handiwork. He was a rare master of his craft. Running her fingers lightly across the bent branches, she remembered the first time she touched his hands in the meadow, high above her home in Gweek. Leaning her forehead against her hand, she rested against the hedge in remembrance. The sun felt hot on her back and the soft summer breeze soughed through the leaves.

'Oh Lyndon,' she cried softly into the branches.

'Jenna.'

The sound of his voice made her spine tingle. His breath felt warm on her neck, as he stood as close as possible, without actually touching her.

'You know where I've been today!'

'I do.' She dared not look at him for fear of crying.

He put his hands on her arms and turned her to face him. 'You do realise, I have to go?'

Jenna nodded unhappily. 'When do you go?'

He pulled a tight smile. 'It will be the day after tomorrow. There are five of us going from the estate - including Matthew. We'll be joining the Duke of Cornwall's Light Infantry.'

Jenna gave an unhappy sigh.

'They say it will be all over by Christmas, but you know I have to go. As they say, safety in numbers and I think I can suffer this damn war, if I know I have my friends and colleagues around me.'

'Your pa will miss you terribly.'

'I know and I shall miss him, but most of all, I'll miss you, my lovely Jenna.'

Jenna closed her eyes to hide her unhappy tears. 'Oh, Lyndon.'

'It's the truth. You and Pa are the only people in the world who I love.'

It had been a long time since she had allowed herself to gaze into his deep amber eyes. She longed to kiss him.

'We are both caught up in our ridiculous marriages Jenna, but when I return…..'

Jenna put her fingers to his lips. 'Just return, Lyndon. That is all I ask for now.'

*

Edna arrived at Michael's cottage to see Lyndon off to war. Pre-empting this scenario, Lyndon and Jenna had said their own private tender goodbyes earlier in the day. When he'd arrived in full uniform, Jenna couldn't resist touching Lyndon's head. His long auburn curls had been cut short and tamed to sit under his cap. He cut a dashing figure as he stood in his khaki uniform, but both Michael and Jenna were fighting to keep the tears under control.

Edna however, showed no signs of distress at his going. She looked him up and down and said, 'What an awful uniform.'

Lyndon glanced at Michael. He was under no illusions that Edna relished his going and said, 'Pa, keep an eye on Edna for me, will you?'

Edna blanched at this statement.

Michael smiled knowingly. 'Of course, I will son. I'll check on her every day.'

'I don't need anybody to watch out for me!' Edna said indignantly.

Michael raised his eyebrows. 'Nevertheless, I shall do as Lyndon asks.'

Michael was inconsolable as Lyndon hugged him tightly, so Jenna gently pulled Michael into her own arms, while Lyndon picked up his knapsack.

'Look after Pa for me, won't you?' he asked Jenna, hugging her.

'It goes without saying.' Jenna longed to kiss him but knew she could not.

The hug he gave Edna was more brotherly than loving and as he did, he mouthed to Jenna, 'Goodbye.'

A small crowd had gathered outside the cottage to see him off. Michael and Jenna watched through a veil of tears, as he walked down the lane and out of sight.

29

A week after the men had departed for war, the estate was given notice that all horses of a certain age must be released for the war effort. This news sent shockwaves throughout the house.

Jenna had no idea how old Bramble was, but she was sure she was too old to go to war, so she wasn't going to leave anything to chance.

Standing in Bramble's field, Jenna watched her munching on the grass for a while. Lyndon had told her Bramble had been in the family since he was a small boy, but it was debateable how old she was when she came to them. Fortunately, though very naughtily, Lyndon had ridden her before he should have. Since then, she'd always had a droop in the saddle area. This was a good sign now as this often happened in older horses. Still though, she had to make sure that the authorities didn't take her.

With a bucket of white-wash, Jenna painstakingly and carefully coated several of the hairs around Bramble's nose and eyebrows with the liquid. She added a few to her mane and tail just for effect. Standing back, she smiled at Bramble, who now looked a good deal older than she had an hour ago. Then with another bucket, she began to collect piles of her manure and mixed it with water to make them sloppy. Bramble watched with mild curiosity as she poured the mix all over the field, especially near the gate.

'You'll thank me,' she shouted over to the horse.

There was nothing else to do except take her for a long walk first thing the next morning to tire her out. She needed to fool the authorities into thinking that Bramble was an exhausted old horse.

*

Jenna met the authority men at the gate the next morning with grim determination.

'Go and get that one, Joe,' the man in charge ordered.

'Wait a moment,' Jenna stated, 'That one is twenty years old, if she's a day. She retired from farm work a couple of years ago!'

The man blew a weary sigh. 'Well, I'll need to take a look at her.'

He opened the gate and promptly slipped on a pool of manure. He looked around the field and could hardly see a patch of grass between the pats of slime.

'What the hell is all this?'

Jenna stepped forward. 'Sorry about that, her teeth aren't as good as they used to be, so she doesn't digest her food very well, hence the loose stools. Poor old soul - still, it keeps the field fertile.'

The man curled his lip in disdain and treaded carefully as he made his way down the field.

True to form, the early walk had done the trick. Bramble always managed to look worn-out after any exertion – even if she wasn't. The man gave the horse the once over and Bramble wouldn't lift her head when he whistled, just in case an acknowledgment meant that she was required to go for another long walk. The man known as Joe asked his boss, 'Shall I rope it then?'

'God no, it's a bloody nag! I can't have anything like this shitting all over the place, it's disgusting.' He looked at Jenna. 'You need to have this thing put down I reckon.'

Jenna smiled and wrinkled her nose.

She watched as they made their way cautiously up the field, cursing occasionally when they slipped on a slimy patch of manure. Moving over to Bramble, she hooked her arm around her neck and Bramble whinnied and snorted softly as Jenna kissed her dusty face. 'Come on old girl,' she said, pulling her gently by the bridle. 'I'm taking you down to the coppice for the rest of the day, just in case they change their minds on the way back.'

Jenna had saved Bramble but could do nothing for the other horses on the farm. They were all young and strong, and two of them she knew were beloved pets.

*

While Jenna was down in the coppice, there were scenes of great upset at the big house.

Andrew Bickford knew he should have warned his daughter Mellissa about the horses going but had neither the heart nor courage to tell her. He'd watched her leave early morning, dressed in her blue riding habit, cantering out of the yard on her beloved horse, Star. At least she would have one last ride, oblivious to what was about to happen.

When Mellissa cantered back into the stable yard, Andrew Bickford braced himself, as the authorities were just roping the other horses together.

Mellissa pulled Star to a halt, and on seeing Matthew's horse Bess amongst the group of tied horses, she raised her crop up at the men and shouted, 'What the devil do you think you are doing?'

Resigning himself to a scene, Andrew said sadly, 'Mellissa, get down. All the horses have been commissioned for the war effort.'

Horror swept over her face. 'No, I will not get down,' she retorted, and began to turn Star to make her escape.

'Now, now, Miss,' one of the collection men said as he grabbed her reins.

'Let go at once.' She raised her crop again. 'Daddy, tell them! Star is a pet - she can't possibly go to war! This is ridiculous. Let go I say.' She brought the crop down on the man's hand.

'*Mellissa*, stop that!' Andrew strode forward, took the reins from the man and apologised profusely to him. He looked up at his distraught daughter and said sternly, 'Get down at once, Mellissa.'

Her face crumpled as great tears rolled down her cheeks. 'No, daddy, no!'

He gave her one more look and she reluctantly slid down off the saddle.

'Take her tack off and brush her down.'

Disbelief washed over her as she slowly undid the girth straps. Sobbing pitifully, she brushed her precious horse down for the last time.

The men stood impatiently as she finished the task, before looping the rope around its neck and tying her to the others. There were six to take in all, four working horses and two thoroughbreds. As they trotted them out of the yard, Mellissa picked up her skirts and set off down the yard screaming after them.

Andrew followed and grabbed his hysterical daughter by the waist as she crumpled to the floor, wailing like a banshee.

30

The Trevarno nanny goats came into season, mid-September. Jenna noticed that they were bleating constantly for no apparent reason, when she took them their breakfast one morning. On closer inspection, she noticed a gelatinous liquid dripping from their rear ends.

With most of the men gone to war and the harvest in full swing, she had to seek out Peter Hoskins the dairyman to help.

The look on Peter's face was a picture to behold when Jenna told him they had to arrange for Mr John's Billy goat to come a visiting.

'You *are* joking? Have you seen that goat? It's a vile creature!' he said, wiping dirty hands down his shirt.

Jenna nodded. 'I encounter it every morning when I go and see to Bramble.'

Peter scratched an itch under his hat. 'I don't relish having to deal with that thing.'

Jenna smiled knowingly. 'Neither do I, but if the goats aren't serviced, there will be no kids and no milk, and Mrs Drake will be after you.'

Peter pulled a face. 'I don't know who I'm more frightened of.'

With the help of Mr John, they managed to get the bad-tempered Billy into a truck, narrowly missing a few head butts.

Once in the pen with the nanny goats, Satan, as Peter re-named the Billy goat, went straight to work. Both Jenna and Peter watched in mild disgust as he started his mating dance, which involved him peeing all over himself before he mounted the nanny goats. Jenna felt sorry for the poor little beasts, as they seemed to cooperate, albeit with a great deal of distress. Between his sexual conquests, Satan remained alarmingly aroused, constantly dribbling from its business end if one of the nanny goats didn't immediately consent to his favours. It was all quite amusing, until an overwhelming musky aroma filled the air.

'Oh, my god! What *is* that smell? It's disgusting!' Peter said, as both he and Jenna stepped back from the gate in unison. But it was too late, being in close proximity to the Billy in rut, the odour engulfed them.

They ran to the far end of the yard, hands clasped to their noses, shrieking with laughter, in between fits of coughing and choking.

Gina ran out of the dairy to see what the commotion was about.

'What's happening?' She stopped dead when she caught a whiff of them. 'Ugh! What the hell do you two smell of?'

'It's that bloody goat!' Peter spat the taste from his throat. 'I can practically taste the stink.'

Gina started to back away from them. 'For god's sake, Jen, don't come near the dairy smelling like that, you'll turn the cheese!'

'Gina's right, Peter,' Jenna said, sniffing her clothes. 'I absolutely reek. I'm going home to change.'

Two days later, neither Jenna nor Peter had managed to rid themselves of the smell. It seemed to have permeated their every single pore. Peter had been banished by his wife Lowenna to the cattle shed to sleep, and even Michael suggested that Jenna might like to sleep in the stable with the deer. Jenna was also sent into the fields to work on the harvest, having been banned from her kitchen and dairy duties until her aroma improved.

From that moment on, no-one would go near the goats while Satan was still there. When Mr John finally came to retrieve him, he sniffed the air and shot Jenna and Peter a wry smile. 'He's a smelly little bugger when he gets going, isn't he? You've got to give him a wide berth during the rut.'

Peter exchanged a 'now he tells us' look with Jenna.

*

It was the beginning of October. The men from the Trevarno Estate had been gone six weeks. Ethel, the scullery maid, had already had three letters from her young man, Fred Saunders, and from the sound of it, he was having a rough time at the front.

Gina Teague and Lowenna Hoskins both prayed daily that the war would be over before their boys were old enough to go to the front line.

Jenna longed for news of Lyndon. The only letter Michael had received was a short missive two weeks ago to say he'd arrived in France safely, with an address for where letters could be sent to.

In desperation, Jenna asked Edna if she'd had any more news of Lyndon, but her question was not well received.

'If I have, that's my business and none of yours,' she snapped.

'I just wondered if he was all right, Edna - I meant nothing by it.'

But Edna turned her back on her. Lyndon had written, but only to tell her where she could contact him, should she need anything.

Being neither wife nor relative, Jenna was in an awkward position. She desperately wanted to write to him but was aware of the impropriety of such correspondence. Knowing she must do something, she decided that after collecting the vegetables which cook needed for the evening meal at the big house, she'd go in search of Michael. He was tending the orchids in the hot house when she found him.

'Jen, what a nice surprise, look at this beauty,' he pointed to a very beautiful specimen.

'It's lovely, yes. Michael, I'm worried about Lyndon. We've had no news from him since his first letter.'

Michael put down the flower sheepishly. 'To tell you the truth, Jenna, I haven't written back to him.'

Jenna's mouth dropped open. 'But, why not?'

Michael swallowed hard. 'I'm not great with words and letters. In fact, I can't read and write,' he said bashfully. 'I don't know what to do. I'm desperate for news of him.'

'Oh, Michael, you should have told me.'

He lowered his eyes. 'I was too embarrassed to tell you that I couldn't read and write.'

She touched his arm gently. 'Don't be ashamed. Lots of people struggle with reading and writing. I'll gladly write to him for you. In fact, if you don't think it's an imposition, I'll teach you to read and write.'

'Oh, no!' he said flustered. 'I'm a bit old for that, I think.'

'Nonsense, you are never too old to learn.'

Michael nervously bit his lip. 'Well, maybe you could show me a bit.'

'We'll start tonight then.' She turned to go. 'Oh, incidentally, do you know if Edna has written to Lyndon? I've asked her, but she nearly bit my head off in response.'

He shook his head. 'She says she hasn't had time yet.'

'What? Our poor men are out there fighting this stupid war for us, and she hasn't got time to write to him!'

'Ah, well, you and I both know their marriage wasn't working. I know she's my daughter-in-law, but I get the distinct feeling she quite likes the fact that Lyndon is away. Maybe she hopes he won't come back.'

Jenna felt a chill down her spine. 'Oh, Michael, don't say that.'

*

Later that night, Jenna sat down with Michael to write his letter.

Michael's eyes watered with appreciation. 'Thank you for doing this, Jen. I'm so grateful.'

'The pleasure is mine.' With her pen poised, she said, 'So what would you like me to tell him, Michael?'

'Tell him....tell him to take care. Tell him I think about him every day....tell him....tell him I love him. I know it's soft saying I love him, but I do.'

Jenna gave him a friendly nudge. 'He loves you too, I know he does.'

That night, Jenna added her own words to the letter,

telling Lyndon all the news from the estate. She also made up a parcel which included a couple of watercolour paintings she'd done of the boathouse and the gardens. They would spoil from being folded but it would send a little bit of home to him. She pressed a few roses in a hope that the fragrance would still linger by the time it reached him, and included a copy of The Man Upstairs, a collection of short stories by P. G. Wodehouse, a tin of toffee and a packet of tea. She had no idea what he would need, but for now, this would have to do.

The next morning, she took the letter and parcel up to the house, gave the money for the postage to Mrs Kent, the housekeeper, and then went to work in the dairy with a satisfied smile on her face.

31

The weather in October went from bad to worse. Firstly, persistent rain drenched the countryside, before icy gale-force winds took over, blowing the last of the leaves from the trees on the estate. Jenna was glad of the shelter of the dairy first thing in the mornings, but her next job was to bring in some root vegetables on her way back to the kitchen.

Pulling on the heavy winter coat Lyndon had purchased for her from Helston, Jenna turned up the collar, donned a woollen hat and set out towards the vegetable patch. The wind was blowing a hoolie and the heavy sleety rain stung her face as she battled her way to the greenhouse to pick up her trug and fork. Normally Michael was there to help her dig up what she needed, but he was suffering from a chest infection that kept him to his bed. Drenched and covered in mud, Jenna deposited the vegetables in the larder, not daring to venture into Mrs Drake's clean kitchen in her muddy gumboots. Peeling off her wet coat, she stepped out of her boots and began to clean the dirt from them in the sink, keeping a furtive look out, knowing she'd be in trouble if she was caught cleaning her boots in the vegetable sink. 'Is that you in there, Jen?' Mrs Drake shouted.

'Just washing the vegetables,' she answered, giving her boots a last quick check. Tipping the vegetables in the sink, she quickly washed the dirt from them and put them back into her trug. She walked into the kitchen just as the postman arrived.

'My goodness but look at you two. You look like drowned rats.'

'I feel like one,' Jenna moaned, watching the postman hand over the letters to Mrs Kent.

'Sit down you two and I'll make you a cup of tea.'

'It isn't fitty weather for neither man nor beast out there,' the postman said sipping his steaming tea.

'I hear Michael's taken to his bed poorly, Jen?' Mrs Drake said, returning to her chores.

'He has - a day or two rest will see him right.'

'It's a wonder no-one else has gone down with a chill with this weather,' the postman said, warming his hands around the cup. 'This cold gets right into the bones.'

Jenna watched with bated breath as Mrs Kent sorted through the letters, praying there would be one for Michael in the bundle.

After doling out the letters into their respective pigeon holes, Mrs Kent studied the last envelope. She looked up and smiled. 'There is one for Michael here, Jennifer. That should make him feel better. Will you take it to him?'

Desperate to complete her chores, Jenna peeled and chopped everything ready for dinner in super-fast time. She excused herself from joining the rest of the kitchen staff for luncheon and set off home to Michael.

When she got there, she was dismayed to find Michael up and about, albeit unsteadily.

'Don't fuss maid. I'm better sat by the fireside. I cough too much lying down.'

Jenna conceded and sat down beside him. 'I have something here that'll cheer you.' She waved the letter in front of him. 'Shall I read it?'

28th October, 1914.

Dear Pa and Jenna,

I cannot say how overjoyed I was to receive your letter and parcel and thank you from the bottom of my heart. The tea, oh the tea, I had forgotten how good English tea could taste, and the toffee was gloriously sticky. You asked if I had corresponded with Edna, the answer is yes, but only to let her know how to contact me - she did not bother to reply. The least said there the better.

Jenna, your beautiful watercolours and pressed flowers make me believe I am back at Trevarno and away from this hellhole, for that's what it is, pure hell.

After leaving Cornwall, we went to Ireland to join up with the 14th Brigade of the 5th Division, then shortly afterwards we were mobilised for war and landed in Le Havre. Everything happened so quickly after that and we were embroiled in a terrible battle, where we suffered many casualties. We were chilled to the bone at what we saw and too exhausted to move when it was over. The last few weeks have been horrific. I can't tell you everything, as they censor the letters. I am with Fred Saunders, so I am not without friends out here. Matthew too is with us some of the time.

There are a great many horses here with us on the front line. I can't begin to tell you how dreadful the conditions are for the poor beasts. I heard a rumour that they rounded up all the available horses in Britain, is this true? I fear for old Bramble if it is.

Pray for us, we need all the help from up high that we can get. They said when this all started it would be over by Christmas, my god, let's hope so. Please, I beg you, write again soon.

My love to you both.

Lyndon.

The letter seemed to lift Michael's spirits and within a few days he was back in his greenhouse setting seeds for next year's plants.

*

Matthew arrived home on leave at the end of November and came at once to see Michael and Jenna to assure them that Lyndon was safe. He sat with them both, enjoying a brandy, talking about life in the army, but it was what he was not telling them that worried Jenna. Matthew looked pale - his normal sunny disposition now held a haunting sadness. Jenna wondered what horrors he was hiding from them. The visit cheered Michael up, but deeply unsettled Jenna.

She'd written again to Lyndon just before Matthew's visit and sent another parcel of things which she thought might make life easier for him. She'd made two fruit cakes for Christmas, one to keep and one to send to him. Michael had given her two woollen scarves to put in the parcel, and Jenna had wrapped four apples in them for safe keeping. They also enclosed two bars of chocolate, a tablet of toffee and more tea. Now she would just have to wait for his reply. Fortunately, with Christmas on the horizon, Jenna kept busy with duties around the estate while she waited.

The Bickfords decided to make the occasion low-key this year, but low-key to a commoner and low-key to the gentry were two very different things. Mrs Drake had relaxed slightly on hearing Christmas might be a quiet affair, and then panicked when she was told there would be a party of twenty for both Christmas Eve and Christmas Day, and a Boxing Day ball for forty guests. Lists were made, orders sent to suppliers, jars were filled with mincemeat, preserves counted, and menus were sweated over.

Lyndon's letter came the day before Christmas Eve, but with pies, jellies and syllabubs to make, Jenna had no chance to read the letter until later that night. Impatient to hear his news, Jenna paced the kitchen waiting for Michael to come home from The Crown Inn. He'd hardly taken his coat off before she ripped the envelope open and began to read:

December 15th, 1914

Dear Pa and Jenna,

Once again you have saved my sanity with your parcel and letter. As I always said, the apples from the Trevarno orchard are the best I've ever tasted. After weeks of bully beef and hard biscuits, the sweetness on my tongue was a sensation to die for, excuse the unfortunate turn of phrase. I have to admit, I shared my fare with two of my comrades and they all thank you for the gesture.

I cannot begin to tell you how relieved I was to hear that you managed to save Bramble. The poor old girl would not have lived long if they had taken her. I can't help thinking of the fate of all the other estate horses though. I understand from Matthew that Mellissa is still weeping for her Star. I have to say that Matthew too was devastated to think that his beloved Bess went with them. I swear he inspects every horse an officer rides in on, just in case it's his Bess.

Thankfully, I do see quite a lot of Matthew. His role as an officer means he is often attending meetings away from the front line, but when he is here with us, he very rarely sits in his dugout. I've seen him drag the injured away from enemy fire, move corpses to the wagons and even dig out the latrine. All in all, he's a good officer, and the men respect him, but then we always knew he was a good man.

The food is the same day after day but eat we must. I am enormously grateful for the fruit cake you sent. You seem to know just what a man needs. The scarves too were a godsend as it is so cold now. I am always grateful for whatever you send me. I would appreciate it if you could send me some more paper to write on, as you see I had to write this letter on the fly sheet of the last book you sent me.

You ask when I will get leave. I'm sorry to say we only get home leave every fifteen months, so I fear it will be some time before I see you again.

Matthew, as an officer, receives more home leave than us, but I was pleased that he saw and spoke to you. He told me you both looked well.

There doesn't look like there is any end to this war which they said would be over by Christmas, so we will just have to make the most of it.

I think about life at Trevarno, and of course both of you, constantly. Keep praying for me and my comrades. We need all the help from up high we can get.

Love to you both,
Lyndon.

32

All the time and preparation paid off, making Christmas upstairs at Trevarno a great success. As part of the immediate household staff, Jenna and Michael were invited to share Christmas dinner in the big house kitchen. Peter and Lowenna Hoskins declined, wanting to spend the day with their relatives. Edna too declined, for which Jenna was grateful for.

'I hope you have a lovely time with your family Edna,' Mrs Drake said as Edna made to leave. 'I'm sorry Lyndon isn't here to share your first Christmas together. Have you heard from your young man recently? You never say.'

'No, I haven't,' she answered forlornly.

Mrs Drake paused from doling out the potatoes. 'You mean he doesn't write to you?'

A few people glanced at Michael in astonishment.

Edna shook her head. 'Maybe he will after Christmas,' she said pulling her hat on her head and then left before any more questions were asked.

Mrs Drake carried on putting bowls of food on the table. 'Well, that's a funny state of affairs. You've heard from him, Michael, haven't you? Why has he not written to his wife?' She raised her eyebrows. 'Is all not well with the young couple?'

The gathering fell silent, waiting for Michael's response.

'He has written to her! Maybe if she could be bothered to write back, he'd reply,' Michael said, angrily, as he began to tuck into his dinner.

One or two of the gathering pulled a face, before turning their attention to the meal.

On the way home, Michael was still visibly angry about Edna. 'How dare she say that? How dare she make out that my son is neglecting her, when he is out there fighting for us all?'

Jenna linked her arm in his. 'Take no heed. Everyone knows Lyndon to be a true and honest man.'

'How dare she make out that my son is in the wrong, I'm going to give her a piece of my mind when I see her next.'

Jenna smiled inwardly. She'd sure like to be a fly on the wall when that conversation took place.

*

The first part of January 1915 was very cold. A thick penetrating frost hardened the ground for many days after the New Year, making it impossible to double dig the kitchen garden. Michael grumbled when the weather kept him in the greenhouse. He loved to be outside turning over the soil. When at last the thaw came at the end of January, the bulbs in the gardens began to burst out of their winter crust and it felt like spring was just around the corner.

Jenna was about her first job of the morning, which was to feed Fern. With the horses gone, the deer had the stables to herself. Fern had become quite attached to Jenna, now Lyndon was no longer around and affectionately nuzzled her hand as she walked her down to the woods every day. Jenna had promised Lyndon that she would try and coax the deer back into her own habitat. Being eighteen-months-old now, Fern should have come into season a couple of months back, but had shown no signs of leaving her just yet. At the edge of the wood, Jenna let Fern walk on into the deep undergrowth. Today, unusually, Fern turned around and watched Jenna for a moment, before disappearing from sight. As Jenna began the walk back up the meadow, she gloried at the snowdrops that seemed to appear from nowhere. Great bunches of them sprang up along the hedgerows and gardens making it look as though it had snowed overnight. She wished with all her heart that Lyndon could see them. Bending down, she picked two and quickly took them back to the house to press between sheets of paper. Determined that Lyndon would see them, she would send them in her next letter to him - if only they could get a reply from the last one! Piling the books on top of the pressed flowers, she set out to start her proper chores for the day.

Michael called in at the kitchen door later that evening to see if Jenna wanted to walk back with him. At the sound of his voice, Edna blushed and rushed into the back kitchen. Jenna watched with mild amusement. She had no idea what Michael had said to her the day after Christmas, but he came back with a very satisfied smile on his face.

Jenna checked with Mrs Drake if she could go, and then picked up her hat and coat to follow Michael to the door.

'I need to put Fern in the stable first, if you don't mind waiting a moment.'

Normally Fern would be waiting at the stable door at dusk, but tonight there was no sign of her. Jenna felt a pang of anxiety and mixed emotions about Fern's absence. 'I'll leave the door ajar, and pop back later. I don't like to think of her out there on her own.'

Michael laughed heartily. 'If she is staying out, mark my words, she won't be alone.'

*

Jenna fretted all that evening when it was obvious that Fern wasn't coming back, but fortunately she had something to take her mind off things. Since Jenna found out Michael could not read or write, she'd spent a great deal of time reading to him and slowly showing him how to form words on paper. He was a proud man and Jenna could see this was difficult for him, but she was determined that he should be able to write just a few lines to Lyndon. Tonight, he'd written his name for the first time ever and she'd showed him how to write the words *'with all my love, Pa.'*

'Next time I write to him, you can put that sentence at the end too.'

Michael sighed happily as he looked at what he'd written, while Jenna tidied away the paper and pen.

'Shall I read to you now?'

'That would be lovely, thank you.'

This had become an after-lesson treat, when they both sat down by the fire. Michael would stoke the fire, pour a mug of ale or a tot of brandy, and settle down with his feet resting on a stool. He would then close his eyes to wait for the story to begin. Occasionally Jenna caught him smiling, lost in the story she told. Sometimes his face would relax, making her think he'd fallen asleep, but as soon as she closed the book, he would turn his head and open one eye as though to say continue.

Tonight, she was reading a new novel called 'The Glittering Sea' by a local author, James Blackwell. It had been recommended to Michael by the owner of the new bookshop in Helston and remembering that Lyndon had met the author the previous year, Michael was keen to have it read to him. It was a wonderfully descriptive book, set in Cornwall and both reader and listener were engrossed in the prose.

When the time came for bedtime, Michael kissed her lightly on the forehead. 'I'm glad you're here, maid. I don't think I could get through all this waiting without you. Let's hope we hear from our boy soon.'

*

The letter came three days later. But Michael was away at Helston market all day and not expected home until late. When he finally came through the door, he was merry on Spingo beer and as he had already consumed a couple of pasties, no supper was needed before the letter was read.

Lighting another candle for extra light, they sat together by the fire, but when she opened his letter, a smaller piece of folded paper fluttered out onto her lap which clearly bore the name Jenna. She glanced quickly at Michael, but he'd positioned himself in his armchair, happily puffing on his pipe and fortunately had his eyes closed waiting for her to read to him. She pushed the note deep into her apron pocket and started to read the letter:

The Glittering Sea

February 1st, 1915

Dear Pa and Jenna,

I hope you managed to have a good Christmas. We made the best of a bad situation here. There seemed to be a truce to this madness on Christmas Day. No-one was fighting and everyone on both sides must have just decided that enough was enough. We could hear the Germans singing carols and laughing and we too had a jolly time.

I thank you for the second fruit cake you sent me. I'm sure you will not mind if I tell you we all had a piece. The chocolate and tea I will keep to myself. Thank you also for The Woodlanders, I really do like Thomas Hardy novels. For a few short minutes I can feel myself back home in the West Country. If you can get hold of any more of his novels, I would be really grateful. I have probably read most of them, but they are always worth a second read.

Your story of Mr John's Billy goat made me laugh. Billys really do stink, don't they? For some reason the females find the smell irresistible. Satan is a good name for the little bugger. It's butted me on more than one occasion - and very sore it was in the nether regions; I can tell you. Hopefully soon you'll have lots of kids running about, as if you are not busy enough! What news of Fern? Has she set off to find her own mate yet, or are we to be her adopted parents for evermore?

I hope you and Pa are keeping well. I am faring well. The worst thing here is being so damn cold and wet. We are often stood ankle deep in muddy water - and other substances I don't wish to mention - so our feet are constantly wet. Oh, how we long to change into dry socks and shoes. We sleep in the trench, in dugouts, high enough above the sludge to keep dry, but of course as soon as we stand, the cold seeps through until you think you no longer have a pair of feet on the end of your legs.

I think of you both all the time. I should think the estate is bursting with spring flowers now. I can't tell you how much I miss my old life.

Well, that is all I have to tell you. There is of course an awful lot going on here that I would not wish you to know about. Just pray for us.

Love to you both always,

Lyndon.

Michael stood and yawned. 'I'm bone-tired tonight maid. I think I'll go up.'

Jenna nodded with a smile. The bellyful of Spingo might have something to do with his tiredness. When he'd gone and she could hear him snoring, she pulled the folded letter from her pocket.

My darling Jenna,

Could I ask a great favour? I would dearly love a lock of your beautiful hair. I need to feel I have something of you close to me or I shall not get through this hell.

Forever yours, Lyndon.

Touching her hair gently, she pulled a lock of it forward. Her hair had grown back now, except for one small patch at the back of her head. It warmed her heart to think that he needed her, but to think of a future together was something she dare not imagine. Picking up Lyndon's main letter again, she read:

'The worst thing is being so damn cold and wet. We are often stood ankle deep in muddy water - and other substances I don't wish to mention - so our feet are constantly wet. Oh, how we long to change into dry socks and shoes.

Holding the letter to her heart, she pondered as to what she could do to help. It was eight-thirty. Jenna knew Mrs Drake would have finished her chores for the day and would be sat at her range in the kitchen, having a well-earned rest. Very quietly she slipped out of the cottage and made her way up to the big house.

The kitchen was quiet when she entered, so she shouted a cheery, 'Hello,' to alert anyone to her presence.

'Who is it,' Mrs Drake shouted.

'It's Jen, can I come in?'

'Of course, you can, my dear. I could do with the company. There should be a brew in the pot if you want one.'

Jenna smiled when she saw how Mrs Drake was

passing away the evening. There was a ball of wool and a large square of knitting on her lap. With a cup of strong tea in hand she joined Mrs Drake at her fireside.

'I was wondering….would you… could you teach me how to knit socks?'

'Socks?'

Jenna nodded. 'Yes socks, for our men at the front.'

Mrs Drake put down her own knitting. 'What a good idea. Of course, I'll teach you. I take it you know the basics?'

Jenna shook her head apologetically.

Mrs Drake raised her eyebrows. 'Well, let's get you some wool and needles and get started then.'

It was a lot harder than Jenna thought it would be, and the first few attempts were pulled back by Mrs Drake. Jenna was thoroughly downhearted when the fifth attempt was pulled back.

'Don't you worry, maid. We all have to start somewhere. Now once more before bedtime.' Mrs Drake grinned at Jenna's tongue biting determination. Finally, Jenna produced four lines of stocking knit that she was pleased with. 'That's enough for tonight, come back tomorrow and I'll show you how to knit a sock.'

When she arrived in the kitchen the next evening, she found Gina Teague, Lowenna Hoskins, Sally Dunnet, Miss Mellissa's lady's-maid Sara, and Ethel, all sat in a circle with Mrs Drake, knitting socks.

Gina looked up and smiled. 'What a good idea, Jen. I know my boy isn't at the front thank god'- she made the sign of the cross – 'but I'm sure socks are needed by others there.'

It turned out that Ethel was the fastest knitter and had produced a sock by the end of the night. Jenna had only just managed to fashion a toe.

Gina looked up and grinned. 'I asked Edna to join us, what with Lyndon being on the front line, but she just said, "He took two pairs with him, one to wash and one to wear.'" Gina pulled a face. 'I don't think she realised what she'd said or what it's like out there.'

Jenna lowered her eyes. *Oh, I think she does.*

By the end of the week, Jenna was dismayed to have only made one and a half socks.

Ethel picked up Jenna's sock and said shyly, 'Are you knitting these to go into a parcel that Michael is sending to Lyndon?'

'I was, yes,' Jenna said deflated.

'Well here, take these and I'll finish yours off as well.' She handed her two of the pairs she had knitted. 'At least he'll have three pairs to go on with.' She smiled softly. 'Lyndon was always kind to me. Will you tell Michael to tell him I knitted them? But don't tell Edna,' she added seriously.

'Thank you, Ethel, we'll make sure Lyndon knows.'

33

Jenna wrote a more intimate letter to Lyndon than she had ever done before.

My darling Lyndon,

As promised, I enclose a lock of my hair. Keep it close to your heart, so that I can be with you always during this dreadful separation. Be sure my darling of my enduring love for you. May it keep you safe and bring you home to me.

Eternally yours, Jenna x

Perfuming the letter with a drop of jasmine oil, she kissed his name, sealed the envelope, and placed it in with the regular letter. As always, the letter was sent separate from the parcel, so if one went missing Lyndon would get the other. Jenna knew how much Lyndon looked forward to his parcel. This one contained a book, tea, toffee, shortbread biscuits, clean handkerchiefs, the three pairs of socks from Ethel, and a scarf, mittens, and balaclava that Mrs Drake had knitted for him. Placing them on the post table, Jenna set out to the dairy.

Just as she was skimming the last of milk, Peter Hoskins came looking for her. 'Hey, Jen, come quick, the goats are about to give birth.'

Little was happening when Jenna got to the pen, some goats were restless, and others kept turning their heads to see what was happening behind them.

'Do we have to assist?' Jenna asked anxiously.

'No, they should get on with it on their own. In fact, us being here might just stop them from what they're doing, so I think we should get on with other things and if I need you, I'll come for you. That's if you don't mind helping?'

'I don't mind at all.' Jenna clasped her hands together. 'I'm rather excited to tell you the truth.'

By the time Jenna had finished in the dairy, three kids had been born. The fourth one though was making rather a meal of the proceedings.

'Is everything all right?' she asked Peter, who stood at

the fence watching like an expectant father.

'I think so. This one is just taking a little longer.'

A great bubble had appeared at the goat's backside, which made her walk round in circles, licking at her sides and trying to get to the bubble. Even though Jenna knew she had many more chores to do, she could not leave until she knew the kid had been delivered safely. Within a half hour, the kid slid out, but it was still in the bubble.

Peter stood pensive for a moment. 'If mum doesn't lick the kid soon, the amniotic membrane will suffocate it.'

'The what?' Jenna quizzed.

'The bubble,' he answered, as he vaulted over the gate.

Giving a quick pull with his fingers, the membrane burst, and mum began to lick her kid frantically.

Peter looked up and grinned. 'All's well that ends well, so they say.' Suddenly the smile left his face.

Jenna turned to find Lowenna behind her, weeping.

'Whatever is the matter, Lowenna?' Jenna put her arms around her, while Peter scrambled over the gate.

'What is it Wenna?' Peter said gently.

'Oh, Peter,' Lowenna sobbed, reaching out to him. 'They're sending Jimmy to the front line. He's only a baby.'

'Oh, god!' Peter said, wrapping his strong arms around her. 'I could brain that lad for signing up. Come on my luver, let's get you home.'

A week later, Gina Teague received a letter from her son Tommy, telling her that he too was going out to the front line. As with Jimmy's letter he was upbeat about the prospect and looking forward to the adventure. Both Gina and Lowenna cried in each other's arms that day.

*

During the first week of March 1915, Andrew, Eleanor and Mellissa Bickford set off to London to meet Matthew, who was on leave, so there was a general atmosphere of relaxed calm in the kitchen.

Jenna was enjoying a cup of tea with Mrs Drake when the post came. As always there was great anticipation when the postman arrived, as everyone waited anxiously for Mrs Kent to sort the mail.

'Here's one for Michael.'

Jenna's face lit up when Mrs Kent handed the letter to her. Draining her cup, she excused herself from the kitchen and rushed to the greenhouse to find Michael. While Michael cleared his work top, Jenna carefully opened the letter, just in case there was a personal message enclosed. There was! Her fingers curled around the note, and she surreptitiously pushed it into her pocket.

March 5th, 1915

Dear Pa and Jenna,

Your parcel was an absolute godsend. I thank you, Jenna, Ethel, Mrs Drake et al, from the bottom of my heart. Woollen clothing is in great demand when the weather is bad. I never favoured balaclavas before this god-awful war, but warm clothing is essential to keep our spirits up. It started to snow the night after your parcel arrived, so you can imagine how thankful I was. You would be surprised how a little parcel boosts morale.

I was thrilled to receive the novel 'The Glittering Sea' you sent me. I wondered if you chose it because of the title. I remember telling you how I love to swim whenever the sea glitters in the sunshine. Whatever the reason, I was thrilled. I actually met the author James Blackwell at Trevarno a couple of years ago. He was a really decent chap, who spent the morning watching me hedge laying. I'm intrigued to see if he wrote me into this new book of his.

I can understand your concern for Fern, but she is a wild animal and if she has managed to find a mate then we will have done a good job at bringing her up. You never know, one day perhaps we will find a whole family of deer in the stable.

Let me also put your mind at rest, I don't spend all my time at the front lines. Our unit rotates in and out of the different trenches, and then eventually we have rest in the relative luxury of the army camps. I can tell you even the hardest army camp's beds and pillows seem heavenly after the discomfort of the trenches.

You asked what it's like out here. I cannot begin to explain, except that it's truly awful. Existence at the front line is a mixture of sheer boredom and then sudden bursts of terror. No two days are the same, but we do spend a lot of time in small, dank dugouts. We can make tea, when we have some, eat whatever delights the bully beef tin supplies and we talk, mostly about home and this futile war. We also play cards a lot to pass the time.

Matthew has just gone on leave, but he tells me that Jimmy and Tommy are at the front now. God help them both, though if I know those two, they will look after each other well. I personally haven't seen them yet, but Matthew said they're faring well.

Tell me have the goats given birth yet? By my reckoning they should have done it about mid-February.

We are preparing to move soon, so I am afraid I have rushed this letter before the chaos happens. Take care of each other and thank you once again for the parcel. As always, pray for us.

Love to you both,

Lyndon.

Jenna and Michael gave each other a gratifying hug, and then returned to their respective chores.

Lyndon's note almost burnt a hole in Jenna's pocket - she was so desperate to read it, but work came first. As soon as she got a moment to herself, she walked down to the Italian garden. Even though she knew the family were away in London, she picked a stone bench in the shadiest part of the garden, out of view. The soil there was dark and moist from lack of sun, but the tips of lily of the valley were just peeping through. After glancing around to make sure she was alone, she opened to read her personal letter:

My darling Jenna,

The smell of jasmine when I opened your letter filled my heart with joy. It took me back to Farmer Ferris's fields, to the day I met you and the day I fell in love with you. It's true, I took your soft hand in mine to help you up that day, and my heart was lost to you forever. I'll keep the lock of your beautiful hair in the pocket next to my heart. It will bring me luck and hopefully future happiness for us when I finally come home to you.

You're my first thought in the morning and the last at night. Only when I'm fighting, do I hide you in my heart for safe keeping, but as soon as the battle noise dies down, I bring you to life in my mind.

I love you Jenna, I always have, and I always will.

Forever yours, Lyndon. x

Jenna kissed the letter. Could there be future happiness for them? Would they find a way? She hardly dared to dream.

34

For two long months Jenna and Michael heard nothing from Lyndon.

As each week passed without Michael receiving any correspondence from him, Edna dared to hope that Lyndon would not return. She herself had seen thousands of names printed in the newspapers every day, so the chances of him surviving were pretty slim. She knew he didn't care for her, and worried that he might leave her but, if he was killed in action, Edna, as his widow, would surely be able to keep her cottage. After all, she herself worked on the estate.

Every morning Jenna made sure she was in the kitchen when the postman arrived and would wait with sick anticipation for Mrs Kent to sort the mail. Every morning Mrs Drake gave Jenna a sympathetic smile.

'Tell Michael, no news is good news.'

Jenna had sent a parcel of handkerchiefs, more socks, tea, homemade shortbread biscuits, chocolate and toffee in March, along with another Thomas Hardy novel and several more pressed flowers from the estate's gardens. In the letter she slipped a personal note telling him that she shared his love and hoped that one day they could find a way of being together. In the main letter she wrote about the baby goats, though since she'd written, they were about to be weaned.

There had been six kids born - two does and four bucks. Jenna knew the bucks would be kept separate when they had been weaned to be reared for slaughter in a few months' time. Mrs Drake was practically salivating at the thought of roasting them.

Jenna stood with Peter watching the goats gambol around the field. 'When can we milk the nanny goats?'

'Just as soon as the kids have weaned, which should be in a couple of days. Have you ever milked a goat?' Peter asked.

The Glittering Sea

'I've never milked anything.'

'Well.' He rubbed his hands together in glee. 'You're in for a 'teat treat'. I want you to report for duty on Friday morning, nine a.m. sharp, and I'll show you how it's done.'

'Me?'

Peter nodded. 'You've a nice way with the goats, and in truth the only person, apart from the children, who takes any interest in them.'

Jenna studied them for a moment - she had more than enough chores to do, but milking the goats rather appealed to her. 'All right.' She grinned.

When Jenna arrived, Peter had rounded up Dora, Dolly, Dilly and Drew with a bucket of feed and secured them all in one of the stable stalls. In another stall he'd installed what he called a milk stand. It had a raised platform and two wooden arms sticking up, that would cross over to keep the goat's head secure whilst milking.

Stopping short on seeing the contraption, Jenna gasped. 'It looks like a torture chamber! I thought we'd be milking them in their field.'

'I doubt these little buggers will stand still long enough for you to milk them,' Peter answered wryly.

He brought in Dora, the friskiest one first, which he'd hobbled to stop her kicking. With the promise of a bucket of grain to eat, the goat stepped up onto the platform and went straight into her food, not bothering that her neck had been secured by the two wooden head gates.

Both Peter and Jenna washed their hands, and then Jenna watched as Peter cleaned Dora's udder and teats. With that done, he dried his hands thoroughly and beckoned Jenna to come closer.

'Now listen, this is very important, and you must do this every time you milk a goat.' He picked up a pewter mug and held it under a teat. 'You have to wrap your fingers and thumb around each teat, so that you trap some milk in the teat, and then squeeze one or two squirts from each teat into the mug. This removes any milk close to the surface of the teat that might be contaminated with muck. You must always throw this away?'

Jenna nodded.

'Now, once you've done this, it's important that you start to milk her straight away, otherwise she'll get agitated.' He started to gently squeeze the teats and short milky squirts sprayed into the waiting bucket. 'Never pull on the teats, you'll hurt her. Be gentle and kind to her, even if she's being naughty. This is all new to her, so we want her to feel happy.'

Jenna watched as the bucket began to get a white filmy coating. If the goat protested, Peter began to whistle softly. He turned to Jenna and beckoned her to sit on the stool. With trembling fingers, she curled them around the teat. Dora, sensing that something different was happening, tried to kick the bucket.

'That's why we hobble her,' Peter said. 'My granny taught me to milk goats when I was five. She said no matter how long you keep them or how they get used to being milked, they will always try to kick the bucket over and that's all your good work wasted.'

As he spoke, Jenna began to get into a rhythm of milking. If the goat became restless, she began to hum a soft tune.

'You seem to have a knack,' Peter said proudly.

'Well, I don't know about that, the milk seems to be stopping.'

'Let me look. When you think the udder is empty, give the bottom of the udder a little massage just to encourage her to give more. If no more comes - she's finished.'

Peter took the bucket and poured it into another. 'Now you give her teats another wipe and then we'll put her into Fern's stall. I've hung some fresh hay there for her, so she will stand and eat instead of lying down on the ground - I don't want her open teats to get dirty.'

It took them well over an hour to milk four goats that first morning. Dora, who they thought would cause more trouble than any of the others, had been the best behaved in the end. Dolly had been the worst, she kicked and stamped and made her feelings very plain. Jenna almost lost the bucket twice with her, and no amount of humming would calm her down. Dilly had promptly peed on her, right at the end of the milking, which spoilt her yield, as Jenna didn't get the bucket away fast enough. Drew was just plain frightened of the whole procedure and made it known by expelling a foul smell from her backside throughout the session. Jenna felt physically sick when she finally got out into the fresh air.

Watching them after he released them back into their field, Peter congratulated her on a job well done. 'Right, I'll see you in twelve hours.'

Jenna looked at him open-mouthed.

Peter winked. 'They're to be milked twice a day at the moment. Did I not say?'

She punched her fists into her sides. 'No, you didn't!'

He laughed heartily. 'Don't worry, after today, we'll take it in turns. You can do the morning milk and I'll do the evening, but I'll get them ready for you.'

'Oh, thanks,' she said, playfully smacking him on the arm.

As they walked back to the dairy Peter asked, 'Has Michael had word from Lyndon yet?'

'No, it's been two months now. It's making Michael ill with worry.'

Peter sighed heavily. 'I know what you mean. I swear I'll swing for our Jimmy when I see him next for putting Lowenna into such a state. His last letter was so full of the adventure he was embarking on, the little fool has no idea what he has got himself into. I wish to god it was over.'

*

The much-awaited letter from Lyndon arrived on Friday May 8th, Helston's Flora Day.

Flora Day was a celebration of the passing of winter and the arrival of spring. Most of the estate workers managed to get some time off during the day to go into the ancient market town to see at least one of the four dances that happened that day. All of the children were excused school on Flora Day so they could dance. Everyone dressed in their Sunday best to celebrate, though this year many felt a pang of regret for their boys at the front line.

Jenna had no desire to attend, knowing full well that everyone in the surrounding area would be there that day. She just couldn't chance going and being seen. Michael had left just before the post arrived and Jenna knew she would not see him again that day. He would most probably bed down in the yard of The Blue Anchor with his belly full of Spingo. Silently cursing the day, and Michael, she placed the envelope in her pocket. At least she knew that even if she couldn't open it, having a letter meant that he was safe.

Michael arrived back at eleven-thirty the next morning, stinking of stale beer. Jenna had popped back from her chores every hour to see if he'd returned. On the third visit she found him slumped on the kitchen table, groaning into his arms. Helping him off with his coat, she hooked his arm around her neck and helped him to bed to sleep it off, which he did, snoring noisily for the next nine hours!

She could barely keep the smile from her face when he appeared at suppertime. He looked as though he'd been trampled on by a herd of cows.

'Drink this. It'll clear your head.' She passed him a mug of water. 'You'll feel better when you've had something to eat.'

'Are you sure about that?' he mumbled.

'I can guarantee it. We've had a letter from Lyndon. It came yesterday.'

Michael's eyes brightened. 'Oh, I'm sorry maid. You've had to wait all this time to read it.'

'It's all right, don't fret, the very fact we got a letter sufficed. Do you want to read it now or…'

'Now,' he said firmly, taking up his seat by the unlit fire, ready to listen.

Jenna opened it carefully just in case another letter for her dropped out, but there was only one letter enclosed.

May 1st, 1915

Dear Pa and Jenna,

I know you must be fretting, because it is a few weeks since I wrote, but I am afraid to say I am in a hospital, wounded. I got hit on 11th March at Neuve Chapelle. A piece of shrapnel shell embedded itself in the upper part of my left thigh and I received a wound to my right hand, though that has healed now.

It was a terrible day - the battle was absolute carnage. I have never seen so many men suffering. I'm told that only four out of a hundred of our company survived, so I consider myself lucky getting off with wounds.

We are led to believe that the Germans too suffered great casualties that day. But the general feeling in the hospital is that they got what they deserved. Pa, Jenna, it would make your blood run cold to hear what the good people of Neuve Chapelle say of the cruel treatment that man, woman and child alike, have received at the hands of the Germans. Oh, god, I don't like all this hatred. I wish this damn war would end, but they say it could go on for at least another twelve months.

I received your letter a few weeks after you sent it, but if you sent me a parcel in the last few weeks, I was of course not there to receive it. But rest assured it will not be lost. Some of the boys will get it and it will be divided up between them. That is what we all do when the owner is away wounded, so if you did send one, thank you.

My wounds are such that I should be fit enough to return to the front very soon. I am sorry I didn't write sooner, I struggled to hold a pen and the nurses here are so busy with casualties that I couldn't possibly ask them to pen a letter for me. I will write to you when I am back there, and I look forward to hearing from you soon.

My love to you both.

Lyndon.

Michael's face paled and he shook his head at Jenna. 'My boy was hurt, and we didn't know. Why didn't someone inform us?'

Jenna re-read the letter. 'I don't know. It depends on the injuries I suppose.'

Michael's eyes glistened. 'You would think I'd have known if he was hurt, you know, with me being his father!' He hung his head in shame. 'To think I was out yesterday, making merry and getting drunk, when my boy is in hospital wounded.'

Jenna placed her hand on his. 'I should think Lyndon hoped that's what you were doing. He wouldn't want you to fret and not to live your life.'

*

On the off chance a letter would get to Lyndon, Jenna penned one that night. She knew she couldn't send a parcel, for it would be opened by the other men. This fact she did not mind - if they enjoyed the things she had sent, then all well and good - but she wanted to make sure Lyndon received the next one she sent. She would have to wait until he was back on the front line, but for now, she could rest easy that night knowing he was away from the fighting.

*

Mrs Kent breezed into the laundry room as Edna was ironing the linen.

'Good morning, Edna, I see a letter came for Michael at last. I was wondering what had delayed his letters - is Lyndon all right?'

'I have no idea,' Edna said shortly, as she carried on ironing.

'What do you mean?' Mrs Kent drew her brows together. 'Hasn't Michael shown you the letter?'

'No!'

'Why not?'

Edna looked down-crested. 'Michael and I have quarrelled.'

'Nevertheless, Michael should pass on any information; after all, you are Lyndon's wife!' She cocked her head.

'Why do you not correspond with Lyndon?'

Edna's mouth turned down.

'Oh, Edna, is all not well between you?'

With a feigned sob she answered, 'He's been absent most of our married life. We don't really know each other. When he is home, he doesn't seem to want to spend time with me. I think a letter would be fruitless.' *In truth, she had no desire to keep in touch with him.*

Mrs Kent sighed. 'Well, this is a sorry state of affairs. I'd never had thought that of Lyndon. But you should be party to his letters. It would put your mind at rest. I'm going to give Michael a piece of my mind when I see him.'

'Oh, no!' Edna panicked. 'Please don't tell Michael what I've said. Hopefully when Lyndon comes home again, we'll sort everything out between us.'

'Well, I still think Michael is wrong to hold back information you should have.'

Edna put on her finest doe-eyed face. 'It's fine really, as long as I know Michael is getting letters from him, I know he is safe and well. Please, please, don't say anything, Mrs Kent. What I've told you is in confidence - I'd be obliged if you would keep my secret.'

*

Again, it was weeks before they received a reply from Lyndon. Jenna as usual was waiting excitedly for Mrs Kent to sort the post but was shocked when she handed Michael's letter over to Edna.

'Here you go, Edna, there's a letter for Michael from Lyndon.'

'It's all right, Mrs Kent,' Jenna tried to keep the alarm from her voice. 'I'll take that to Michael.'

Mrs Kent looked askance at Jenna. 'As his wife, I think Edna should take it to Michael. That way, she can hear all her husband's news.'

Jenna's stomach turned anxiously. If Lyndon had enclosed a note for her, Edna would surely see it. Fortunately, Michael breezed into the kitchen with a trug of vegetables.

'Michael,' Jenna said sharply. 'Mrs Kent has given your letter to Edna, so that you can read it together.' Jenna realised her voice sounded a few octaves higher than usual.

Michael's face flushed angrily. 'Oh, she has, has she?' Dropping the trug he was carrying, and without ridding himself of his muddy boots, he stormed through the kitchen, leaving dirty footmarks in his wake, snatched the letter from Edna's hand and turned on Mrs Kent. 'Tell me Madam,' he asked judicially, 'what right do you have to say who reads my letters?'

Mrs Kent swelled with indignation. 'I should think a wife has a right to know how her husband is!'

'Do you? Well, let me tell you that this wife here hasn't bothered to reply to the first letter her husband sent her!' He turned and gave Edna a hard stare. 'Too busy, were your exact words, I recall.'

Edna blanched as Mrs Kent glared at her.

Michael turned back to Mrs Kent. 'I give you a warning, madam. If you ever give my mail to anyone other than Jennifer, I will personally see that Andrew Bickford hears about it.'

Mrs Kent's bottom lip quivered slightly. 'Well, there is no need to take that stand with me!'

'Oh, you think not, do you? Try me!' he answered contemptuously.

Mr Brown the butler came rushing in. 'What in heaven's name is going on here? Who is having high words with whom? I can hear you from my office.'

'Nobody is having high words now,' Michael said, storming back out of the kitchen.

Edna had turned scarlet with embarrassment as she scurried back into the laundry. Mrs Kent brushed her skirt down, as though she'd been covered in something unpleasant, and Mrs Drake raised her eyebrows.

As Jenna was in the middle of preparing the rhubarb for the pudding, she was unable to follow Michael, but prayed he wouldn't open the letter until she was with him. As soon as she was able, she rushed over to the hothouse.

Michael was still visibly angry when she found him. On seeing Jenna, he snarled, 'That bloody woman!'

Jenna's heart sank seeing the envelope was open.

'Here,' he said, 'I believe this is for you. I opened the letter because I was so angry with her, and this fell out.' He handed her the additional note without saying anything more about it. 'I'd be obliged if you could read me the main letter, I know I can do it myself now you've taught me, but you've such a soothing voice and I think I need that right now.'

Jenna nodded awkwardly and began to read:

July 1st, 1915

Dear Pa and Jenna,

Thank you for my letter. From the date on it, it must have taken a while to find me. I love to hear your stories of normal life back at Trevarno - they make me laugh and keep me going. You are very brave Jenna to be milking the goats. I wouldn't go near them with a long stick. I especially like the watercolour of the Italian garden you sent. It brings it back to me how beautiful everything looks in early summer.

You will be pleased to know my wounds have healed nicely, though I do get twinges in my hand.

Since last I wrote to you, I have returned to the front line. No sooner had I arrived, we were in a charge. It was truly awful. The whole sky was just one great red blaze of bursting shells. The noise was dreadful. We were ordered to fix bayonets and to load our rifles and ten minutes later, down came the order to charge. We lost a good few of our boys as they fell on the parapet as the Germans fired their machine guns at us, but on we went and as one fell, another man took his place - my god but it was dreadful. When it came to it, the Germans could not match us. They shelled us the whole day after we took them and they eventually sent over loads of gas, but we won that battle in the end. We are all now sat in the sun in relative peace and calm. It's all or nothing in this place.

The better weather has improved the situations in the trenches, though I do believe no amount of sun will ever dry this mud bath out.

Though it is good to feel the sun on our faces, the heat seems to stir up the lice which make their home in our clothing. We all shave our heads completely now because of the little blighters. Gone are my auburn curls, you would not recognise me now. I have to say it's the lice and the rats that give us more trouble than the Germans. The rats gorge on the bodies during conflict, that's why we are all desperate to move our fallen comrades as soon as possible and get them on the truck to be taken away to be buried out of their reach. We have to cover our faces when we sleep to stop the rats from gnawing at us. They're not too bothered that we are still alive. As for the lice, we have to put up with them until it is our turn to get out of the trenches and go back to camp. I cannot tell you the joy of having a bath and feeling clean, while our lice-infested clothing is steam-cleaned. For a few days we have sheer comfort, and then somehow the little buggers find their way back into our shirts and trousers.

Having said all that, there is a real sense of comradeship and friendship with my fellow men, and we put up with whatever life throws at us with humour, albeit dark humour. Having just read this letter back to myself I am afraid I have made things sound very dark. Please don't be worried for me, though I know you are. Your letters help enormously and if you send a parcel that too will get to me now.

All my love to you both. Pray for us.

Lyndon.

Michael sighed contentedly. 'I leave you in peace to read your letter now, Jen,' he said without reproach.

'Michael I...'

Michael held his palm up to stop her. 'If the love you clearly have for each other gives my son something to live for, then you both have my blessing.'

Jenna swallowed hard. 'Thank you.'

Michael regarded her for a moment, twisting his mouth in thought. 'When Lyndon returns from this fruitless war, you do know your affair will cause a great deal of trouble on the estate, don't you?'

Jenna nodded and lowered her eyes.

'I'll leave you to read your letter, then,' he said gently.
Finding an upturned bucket to sit on, she read:
My darling Jenna,

You are to me the sunshine and moonlight that brightens my days and nights. Without your love, I would surely flounder in this mire of hate and hellfire. Though we were never intimate with each other, I know every inch of your beautiful face and remember the touch of your soft hands on mine. It's easy to put someone on a pedestal when apart, to omit a person's flaws, but you, my darling Jenna are flawless to me and deserve that elevated position I hold you to.

I love and adore only you Jenna, never be in any doubt of that. Equally your enduring love sees me through these dark, dark days.

Forever yours Lyndon x

35

Life on the Trevarno estate couldn't be more different from the front line. It was hard to imagine on a beautiful sunny day what horrors their men at war were going through.

Jenna and Michael longed for Lyndon to come home on leave, but there was no mention of it happening in his letters.

Matthew had been home twice this year to oversee the estate. The first time, he brought Jenna a set of watercolour paints and paper. 'Lyndon asked me to get these for you. Your paintings bring him great joy. They really are beautiful.'

'Thank you, Matthew,' she said, fingering the materials lovingly.

'Tell me, Jenna. Would you consider a painting commission?'

She stared at him blankly.

'I'd dearly like four watercolours of the estate to hang in the orangery, and you would be the perfect person to paint them. I'll supply more materials of course, and I'll pay you for the paintings. What do you say?'

Jenna was delighted. 'I'd be honoured to have my paintings hanging in the orangery.'

'That's settled then. Come on, let's go and see the goats. I understand you're making a delicious creamy cheese from their milk and I'm keen to try it.'

*

The next time Matthew came home on leave, in July, the milking of the goats had eased off a little. Eventually it would stop over the next couple of months, giving Jenna a little more time to see to her other chores. As she and Matthew inspected the goats, Jenna noticed a marked difference in Matthew's behaviour. This normally vibrant person clearly held a multitude of horrors in his mind.

'Take a walk with me, Matthew,' Jenna suggested one

afternoon. They took the path to the highest point of the estate, through knee-deep meadow grass. A skylark suddenly flew up before them, making them both jump. It hovered for several seconds - the white tips of its wings clearly visible before it dived back down into the grass. After a few minutes watching its frantic display and cries, Matthew said, 'We're near its nest - let's move over there, so the poor thing can settle.'

Once seated, Jenna said quietly, 'I'm worried about you all. Tell me what it's like out there?'

Matthew shook his head. 'You really don't want to know.'

Placing her hand on his, she said, 'I need to understand what you're all going through.'

Matthew looked out into the far distance. Hesitant at first, he began to talk. 'It's hell on earth Jenna. The smell of body odour, latrines, damp, disinfectant, and rotting corpses, it gets into your sinuses and never leaves you. My rank and position get me away from the front line, but when I'm there, our nerves are constantly strung to the highest pitch, and the noise…oh, my god, the noise is deafening. I have to watch many of my men shivering and shaking, not just from the cold, but from the shock of the noise.' He paused for a moment as his mouth twisted grimly. 'Sometimes those poor men can hardly move for shaking.' He hung his head desperately. 'But they're pushed over the top to meet their doom…. terrified men sent to their death.' Matthew fell silent for a while. 'I'm frightened Jenna, I don't mind admitting it. I worry about my men and fear that ninety percent of them are not fit to fight anymore, but still, they send them out to die.' He lowered his gaze. 'Sorry I shouldn't be telling you this. Lyndon would be angry with me if he knew.'

Jenna touched his arm softly. 'I need to know, Matthew.'

He ran his hand over the softness of the grass. 'It's so damned uncomfortable all the time. I've known men to stand in the trenches waist deep in water for days on end. Their feet rot in the wet, which in turn makes them wretched. Some days we're gassed and shelled from morning to night. We have to watch our fallen comrades lying in the mud, dying from having their limbs blown off and their stomachs splattered everywhere.' He shuddered inwardly. 'There are horses too lying dead, and rats, bloody stinking rats, eating their bodies because we can't get to them to move and bury them.'

Jenna's eyes filled with helpless tears.

Matthew put his arm around her. 'As you see Jenna, it's dreadful. My words cannot describe the true horrors. I've only skimmed the surface. Promise me you won't tell Michael what I've told you?' he asked seriously.

'I promise.' Unable to stop the tears, she pulled her apron up to her eyes and sobbed.

Matthew held her until she recovered.

'I feel so helpless, Matthew, what can I do?'

'We all feel that same helplessness Jenna. My advice to you is to keep sending your letters. I know Lyndon is married to Edna, but it's you he loves and it's your love that keeps him going.'

'But what keeps you going, Matthew?'

'Hope. My family and all the good friends I have back here.'

'Is there any sign of it being over soon?' she asked hopefully.

Matthew looked out into the distant horizon and shook his head.

*

That night Jenna wrote a heartfelt letter full of love to Lyndon. In her usual parcel she also enclosed a bunch of fresh carrots, twelve pods of swollen - and she hoped juicy - peas, and a red rose from the garden. His return letter came three weeks later.

August 1915

Dear Pa and Jenna,

Thank you for your letter and parcel. I look forward to them coming so much. What a delight to find a bunch of carrots and peas in my parcel. Fresh vegetables are so rare at the moment. The crunch and the taste of them took me right back to the vegetable patch at Trevarno. You certainly brightened my day. I'm glad to hear you are both well. Thank you for the watercolour you painted of the woods Jenna. When I look at it, it feels as though I could walk into its peacefulness. I hope you have enough paints and paper. When I come home on leave, I'll buy some more for you. Tell me, did you see anything of Fern while you sat painting?

I hope the harvest goes well and the weather stays fine. I should think all hands are needed to bring in the harvest this year, what with five of us being away and unable to help. Though I remember how back-breaking the work is, I long to follow the threshing machine and gather the crops. I hope and pray that this time next year, I will be sneezing crop dust along with everyone else at Trevarno.

Tell Gina and Lowenna that their boys are fine, though at first, I was dismayed to find Jimmy and Tommy fighting by my side, but my goodness, it's good to have them with me. Matthew too is occasionally with us and when he's here he is with us one hundred percent. He told me that he'd seen and spoken with you in July. He sends his regards and hopes the paintings you're doing for him are coming along.

The boredom between the fighting is dreadful. I try to fill my mind with countryside things, remembering what it was like to weave my branches. I long for the peace and quiet. The front lines are rarely quiet, even at night. The crack of rifle and machine gun fire, the screams of the injured and explosions from artillery and trench mortar fire make it hard for soldiers to find peace and quiet. To fill our time, we play cards. Some of the men play football in the trenches, albeit with their heads down. Strange how they can be dog-tired but still find the energy to kick a ball about.

Well, that's all for now. Take care of yourselves and it goes without saying I shall do the same. Can I hint that I hope an apple or two will find its way into my next parcel? Rest assured all the Trevarno men are safe and longing to be home. Pray for our

continued safety.
All my love to you both,
Lyndon.

*

It was late summer. Jenna was up with the lark. In the first moments of daybreak, the birds had been extremely vocal in their dawn chorus. Once awake, Jenna found she could never doze off again.

Slipping out of bed, she washed and dressed and was out of the door before Michael woke. With her basket in hand, she walked towards the woods. It had rained during the night, so she knew the moist conditions would quickly trigger the fruiting process of the mushrooms she sought. Sure enough there was an abundance of fungi and she quickly filled her wicker basket. As she made her way up the lower meadow, she waved at Lowenna Hosking coming the other way.

'I see we have the same idea,' Lowenna grinned. She looked into Jenna's basket and laughed. 'Have you left any for me?'

'There is plenty, don't worry,' Jenna replied. 'You'd better hurry up though, you have company.' She gestured to Gina Teague who was running down the meadow holding her skirts up high to keep them away from the dew.

Jenna smiled. *There'll be a lot of mushrooms eaten today.*

Taking a short cut through the Italian garden, Jenna kicked off her shoes. The path was lush green and spongy underfoot and it was one of those simple pleasures in life that cost nothing but meant so much. With her feet cooling on the damp grass, she thought of Lyndon, wishing he too could experience this same feeling.

*

Jenna had taken what mushrooms she needed and decided to take the rest up to the house for Mrs Drake to make use of. Lowenna too was in the kitchen, negotiating to swap some of hers for a couple of eggs.

Everyone looked up when they heard a bicycle bell ring, realising that it must be a telegram, for it was too early in the day for the postman. A sudden feeling of dread swept through the kitchen. When the knock came on the door, they all jumped, even though they were waiting for it. Jenna glanced at all the worried faces and thought she caught a slight look of anticipation on Edna's face. On seeing Jenna looking at her, Edna pursed her lips and looked away.

'Telegram for Hosking,' the boy said grimly.

Lowenna slumped down in the nearest chair.

A cup of sweet tea was promptly placed in front of Lowenna, while she turned the dreaded telegram over and over in her hand.

'Ethel, go and fetch Peter from the milking parlour,' Mr Brown ordered, placing his hand on Lowenna's shoulder. 'Would you like me to open it for you?'

Lowenna shook her head. 'If I don't open it, it won't happen.'

Mr Brown sent word upstairs to inform them that breakfast would be delayed slightly due to the circumstances. When Mr Brown returned to the kitchen, Peter, red-faced and breathless, was with Lowenna and they sliced the telegram open with a knife.

The normally busy kitchen came to a complete standstill.

Lowenna's hand shook as she read the telegram. 'No!' she whispered, shaking her head. 'It's not true!' She laid the telegram down for all to see:

"Regret to inform you Private James Hosking killed in action France August 25th"

A great hush enveloped the kitchen.

Lowenna grabbed Peter's hand. 'It's not true, he can't have died, Peter. It's a mistake. I'd have known if he had - I'm his mother!' She glanced frantically at everyone in the room. 'Surely, I'd have known!' She glanced at the table filled with food waiting to be taken upstairs and again at the telegram. Her fingers touched it before crumpling it into her hand. 'I want to go home,' she said simply, as Peter wrapped his arm around her and led her out of the kitchen.

Mrs Drake's eyes filled with helpless tears as she tried to organise the breakfast trays, while everyone stood in quiet disbelief, all with their own fond memories of the cheeky lad called Jimmy Hosking.

Jenna stepped outside into the warm morning sunshine and looked about the yard. Everything looked the same, but everything was so different now.

36

A week after notification of Jimmy's death, a letter arrived addressed to Lowenna and Peter in Jimmy's handwriting. On seeing it Lowenna fainted. When Mrs Drake wafted the smelling salts under her nose, Lowenna's first words were, 'He's alive! He's not dead!' She waved the envelope in front of everyone as Mr Brown helped her to her feet. 'Look! He can't be dead - he's written to me!'

'Oh, Lowenna, he might have written it before he died and it's been stuck in the post a while,' Mrs Drake warned. She lifted her apron to her face, hardly able to watch as Lowenna ripped it open and began to read it out loud.

Dear Ma and Pa,

If you are reading this letter, I am almost certainly dead, and someone has been kind enough to go through my jacket to find and send it.

Lowenna let out a low moan and dropped the letter onto her lap.

Mrs Drake sat beside her with a comforting arm around her. After a few minutes Lowenna picked up the letter again and started to read it to herself.

We all write these letters, just in case something was to happen to us, though I feel as though I'm indestructible, and if I am, you will never read these words. If I'm not indestructible, I want you all to know how much I love you. I want to say sorry to you all for signing up. I was looking for adventure. I needed to find the man in me and I think I've probably done that. I know you will never forget me and I will always be somewhere near you. Please tell my sweetheart Jane that I love her too. I did hope to marry her after all this. Tell her to grieve a while for me, then to dry her lovely green eyes and flutter those eyelashes at another lucky chap and let him run his fingers through her gorgeous red hair. Tell her to live life to the full, but to always remember her Jimmy.

Lowenna sniffed back a great sob.

Life will go on and I hope everyone else gets back home safely. I love you - I know that is a soppy thing for a son to say to his family, but I do. Take great care of yourselves. From your ever loving (adventurous) son, Jimmy.

The letter fell back on Lowenna's lap, and her heart broke all over again. Her tears rendered her unable to work, so eventually Peter was brought, and she was led out of the kitchen in a daze back to their cottage.

*

Lyndon wrote to Jenna and Michael shortly after Jimmy was killed, but it was a short sad missive. He saved his words for Lowenna and Peter and penned a heartfelt letter to them about how brave their boy had been and had been cheerful up to the end.

Lyndon's letter coincided with Jimmy's uniform arriving at Lowenna's cottage. It was all that was sent home. Jimmy had been buried somewhere in France.

*

The harvest at the end of September 1915 was a busy, but non joyous occasion. Everyone as always did their bit, and the harvest was gathered without the usual banter and songs that normally accompanied their work. Even the children were subdued, knowing there was great sadness in their midst.

The crying of the neck was shouted at the end of a very long fortnight, but the response was less than boisterous. There was food and drink laid on for the hungry, thirsty workers, but the fiddle and accordion players were conspicuous by their absence. Instead, prayers were said, thanking god for a good harvest and asking him for the safe return of all the other Trevarno men. Unfortunately, the war was not in god's hands and on 12th October another telegram arrived, this time addressed to the Bickfords.

*

The general consensus among the kitchen staff was that if a telegram had arrived, Matthew must have died. Everyone waited anxiously and Jenna could hardly contain the tears threatening at the back of her eyes. It seemed an age before Mr Brown came back downstairs and everyone dropped what they were doing when he entered the kitchen.

'It appears Matthew has been seriously wounded in action. He's in a hospital in France with life threatening injuries. Mr Bickford is leaving for London now, to make arrangements for him to be brought back to England.'

'Will they bring him here?' Mrs Drake asked.

'I shouldn't think so, but the family will feel better once he is away from France.'

*

Jenna and Michael couldn't help but fret about Matthew's news. They knew he was in the same battalion as Lyndon and waited hopefully for a letter from Lyndon to tell them he was all right. It thankfully came at the end of October.

October, 1915

Dear Pa and Jenna,

I am writing the letter in haste, as we have just come out of the trenches after being in it for five days up to our waists in water. I am thoroughly exhausted, but I understand Matthew has been wounded in the latest battle. I've tried to find out if he is all right but have not heard. If you know, please write and tell me, for I am sick with worry. I do not want any more days like that one. I'm sorry this is such a short letter, but I need news of Matthew. I will write to you properly soon, but if you have news, I beseech you to let me know.

My love to you both.

Lyndon

Jenna wasted no time in writing back to him. The letter was short but concise. She too would write a longer letter, but she knew he would not settle easy until he knew Matthew lived.

*

They heard no more from Lyndon that month. Jenna had written him a longer letter and sent some warm clothing. Winter was setting in and he would need all the warmth and comfort he could get.

The woods in November were carpeted in fallen leaves.

Jenna stepped carefully through them - they could be slippery sometimes, as she had found to her cost yesterday, still feeling the bruise on her bottom. She busily gathered twigs for the fire, carefully selecting ones that were dry and brown. Her trug was almost full now, any more and she would struggle to carry them back to the cottage. A movement caught her eye and she looked up expecting to see the wily fox who had stolen one of Mrs Drake's chickens yesterday morning. Standing for a moment, she scanned the woods searching for movement and then spotted a deer.

'Fern?' she spoke softly. The deer looked up from its foraging. She'd been gone almost nine months and although Jenna was sad at her departure, she'd hoped Fern had found a mate and was fending for herself.

Fern turned its head to look at something behind it, and then back at Jenna. Her soft ears twitched slightly as she slowly moved closer to Jenna's outstretched hand. 'Oh, Fern, you clever girl,' she whispered realising there were two fawns with her.

Fern slowed, turning to check on the two fawns, tentatively following close behind. Again, she advanced, but instead of walking to Jenna's outstretched hand, she passed her by. Puzzled, Jenna turned to follow Fern, only to find Lyndon behind her in full army uniform. She felt her breath catch.

Lyndon stroked Fern's velvet ears, but all the while his smiling eyes were on Jenna. 'Well Jenna, are you not a sight for this soldier's sore eyes?'

In a heartbeat she was in his arms.

Burying his face in her hair, he inhaled her perfume and whispered, 'How I've longed for this moment, my love.'

'Oh, Lyndon, I can't believe you're here!' Her throat thick with emotion, she clung to him as though her life depended on it. 'Are you all right?' she asked with searching eyes.

He looked down at her with love shining from his face.

'A few nicks and scratches, but just about, yes. I'm better for seeing you.'

Jenna pulled him into another embrace, and every fibre in her body tingled as his hands caressed the curve of her spine.

'I love you, Jenna Trevone.'

'I love you too, Lyndon,' she whispered.

Fern moved and they both watched her and her fawns making their way down the woods.

'We seemed to have done a sterling job there. Come on,' he said, picking up her trug. 'I'm ravenous and I believe you had something delicious cooking on the stove, when I called at the cottage.'

Their fingers entwined as Jenna fell into step with Lyndon. 'Have you been to see Edna yet?'

'Briefly, but it was you I wanted to see the most.'

Jenna squeezed his hand affectionately, before releasing it as they emerged from the woods.

*

It was late by the time they had supped. Jenna and Michael told him all they knew of Matthew's condition. He was now in a hospital in Kent having sustained bullet wounds to his stomach and pelvis. He'd had two operations and Andrew Bickford had told the household that he would require four more before he could start his rehabilitation. For Matthew the war was over, but it was feared he may never walk again.

Lyndon, when asked, declined to talk about the war. Jenna noted he looked weary, and battle scarred, with his shaved head and eyes full of haunted sadness. She had to keep squeezing his arm to bring him back to them.

Eventually Lyndon left reluctantly for his own cottage. When he'd seen Edna earlier, her first words to him were, 'Oh, you're back, are you? Please don't walk your muddy boots on my clean floor.' She'd asked nothing of his welfare, only to enquire how long he was staying.

Lying that night in the spare, though extremely

comfortable bed, his thoughts were only of Jenna. He longed to hold her in his arms. The more he thought about it the more he knew he wanted to spend the rest of his life with her. Even if they could never marry, he would find a way for them to be together once this damn war was over.

Being both Jenna and Michael's day off the next day, Lyndon suggested they take the train to the seaside town of Penzance. Catching the branch line from Trevarno to Redruth, they picked up the London train and arrived at Penzance at ten-fifteen that day. Jenna had never been to Penzance before and looked on in awe at the shimmering bay as the train pulled into its final destination. She was fascinated at the magical sight that was St Michael's Mount – a huge rocky island crowned by a medieval church and castle, sitting right in the bay.

'One day, Jenna, when the tide is low, we'll take a walk over to the mount,' Lyndon said.

Jenna looked at him with alarm. 'But won't we get stuck out there and drown?'

'No,' he laughed. 'People live there. If the tide comes in, we would just have to hire a boat to get us back to the shore.'

They took tea in a café and then walked the length of the promenade. The weather was kind to them, though a slight chill breeze soughed off the water. In Market Jew Street, Michael headed off to a hostelry, while Jenna spent some of her hard-earned money on a bolt of woollen material to make herself a new skirt and jacket, a stronger pair of boots to see her through the winter and several yarns of wool. While Jenna busied herself in the haberdashery, Lyndon purchased more watercolours and paper for Jenna and writing paper for himself. Juggling with their purchases, Jenna and Lyndon made their way down to the harbour for another cup of tea and slice of cake. It was good to see Lyndon relax at last and wonderful to spend a little bit of time alone with him. Though Michael knew of their love, they still felt uncomfortable flaunting their feelings in front of him, but whenever they got a chance, their fingers found each other's and that would have to be enough for now. They were both married and the consequences of Edna finding out would be insurmountable for Jenna.

The very next day, both Michael and Jenna had chores to catch up on and Lyndon rolled up his sleeves and set about helping them.

When Sunday came, Mrs Drake had made a special tea in Lyndon's honour as the first regular soldier home on leave. There were sandwiches, cold meats, tarts and cakes in abundance. Lowenna and Peter came to say hello, but their grief was such that they felt unable to sit down with them to share the feast. Edna had been asked but sent word that she was feeling unwell and couldn't attend. This Jenna thought to be a godsend, as the scowl she'd worn since Lyndon returned, would have turned the clotted cream sour.

It was a happy time to have everyone who mattered together. Lyndon was able to put Ethel's mind at rest by assuring her that her young man Fred should soon be home on leave. Alas he had no comforting words for Gina Teague, as Lyndon couldn't explain to her why her son Tommy had failed to come home when he'd been given leave some three weeks earlier.

'All I can say, Gina is that he is as well as can be expected, but desperately grieving for his friend Jimmy.'

Lyndon listened to all the news and stories of the estate, most of which Jenna had already relayed to him in her letters. Nevertheless, the afternoon passed happily, until Ethel accidently dropped a large metal tray behind Lyndon. The noise seemed to shatter Lyndon's nerves, and both Jenna and Michael noticed he was unable to finish his last cup of tea for the violent shaking of his hands.

As the time drew nearer for Lyndon to return to the front, he became more withdrawn. Michael voiced his concerns to Jenna. 'You talk to him, Jen. I can't get him to tell me what is wrong.'

Jenna found Lyndon sitting on the wall at the edge of the wood. Though it was November, he sat in his shirt sleeves, apparently unaware of the cold. When he saw her, he smiled, but not with his eyes. Sitting beside him she curled her fingers around his hand and the touch brought his eyes back to life.

Lifting her hand to kiss it, his closed his eyes and silence ensued.

'Tell me Lyndon. Share your pain, my love.'

He shook his head slowly.

'I know I cannot begin to understand what you're living through, but Matthew told me what it was like on the battlefield. I didn't want the soft - It's not that bad - version. I made him tell me what you and all those men are going through.'

Lyndon looked up sadly. He picked at the moss growing on the wall beside him and threw it absent-mindedly.

With a deep sigh he hung his head. 'It's beyond horrific Jenna. Now with losing Matthew, it will get so much harder. He's a good officer, but they're not all like that. Most of them never get their hands dirty, but they send exhausted, frightened men to their deaths. The next you see of those poor men, they are hanging dead on barbed wire like scarecrows, blood dripping into the mud. I am not just sad Jenna, I feel broken. I've seen things no man should see, and my nerves are shattered.' He looked up and held her gaze. 'You must have seen me jump when Ethel dropped that tea tray the other day. It set my body trembling, and when it starts, I find it difficult to stop. I feel physically wrecked.'

Jenna put her arm around him, and he laid his head in the hollow of her neck. For a long time, she just held him there. Presently she asked, 'Were you with Matthew when he was shot?'

'He was nearby, I could hear his voice, but it was full

on fighting. We'd been in the trenches five days, up to our waist in water. We started away from our camp just before dawn, but it wasn't long before we encountered the enemy. They were on the opposite side of the valley. As soon as we came over the brow of the hill, they opened fire. We lost three good officers and about eighty of the men were killed or wounded in that half hour. I found out later that Matthew was included in the wounded. We're all worn-out Jenna. It's just an utter bloodbath out there. I can honestly see no end to this war, and I have no idea how we are going to carry on fighting, we're so exhausted.'

Jenna noticed the gooseflesh rise on his forearms as he spoke.

'So many good men have fallen around me, I fear that very soon *all* the young lads at home will be trained and made to take their place in the field. If they don't, we're doomed to fail.'

He squeezed her hand and held it to his chest. 'It's only the thought of you that keeps me going, Jenna. Your letters and gifts and paintings are such a joy in the bleak world I inhabit. Without them I would flounder. I'm staying alive for you.'

'Well, you make sure you continue to do that,' Jenna said seriously.

37

At the end of January 1916, the kitchen staff at Trevarno gathered round the table to read the newspaper's worrying headline. The Military Service Act of January 1916 specified that all single men between the ages of 18 and 41 were liable to be called-up for military service, unless they were widowed with children, or ministers of religion.

'Well, all our single men have already gone!' Mrs Drake huffed.

Lowenna lowered her head to hide the tears she still shed for her Jimmy, and silently thanked the lord that her husband Peter would not have to go.

'I do believe they will not stop until every able man has been killed,' Mr Brown said seriously.

Lowenna could control her tears no longer. She picked up her apron to cover her face and ran out of the kitchen door.

Mr Brown's heart sank as he uttered, 'Damn my mouth.'

*

On hearing the news, Jenna's thoughts turned to all the young men she'd grown up with in Gweek. Though her memories of the village were tainted by her unfortunate marriage, she often spared a thought for those who had been kind to her, especially Charlie Williams.

*

The news of the conscription was indeed taken hard in Gweek. Being a farming and fishing community, only a very few had wanted the adventure of signing up when war broke out, and those few had not survived. Most of the young men could not bear to think of leaving their beloved way of life.

It meant that a lot of the men drinking in The Black Swan would not be there in a few weeks.

George Blewett, being thirty-six, should have been one of them to go. Fortunately for him the bout of pneumonia he suffered two years ago had left him with a condition of the pleura, rendering him unfit for war. He wore a self-satisfied smile that Charlie Williams would have to go. He'd never forgiven Charlie for the beating he'd received from him, though inadvertently the injuries he sustained from it would save him from being killed in the war. George hoped with all his heart that there was a German bullet with Charlie Williams name on it. It would serve him right.

John Drago the landlord of The Black Swan, already troubled with heart problems, promptly died of a heart attack the day the news of the conscription was announced. Being a single man, he'd been visibly worried at the thought of being called up, though in truth, a man in poor health such as he would never have passed fit enough to fight. The news of his death shocked the regulars of The Black Swan. He'd been a likable, humorous chap, who stood for no nonsense. There was a general consensus that the poor man had died in vain. Only one person relished his demise. George Blewett had endured an outright ban from the hostelry for the mistreatment of Jenna. The moment the new landlord was appointed, George was his first customer.

By the 2nd of March the remaining five single men in Gweek eligible for conscription, two of them from the same family, had received their papers and had reluctantly set off to a war they did not want or believe in.

*

On the 25th May that same year, the act was extended to married men. On receipt of this news, Lowenna Hosking took to her bed.

'That means John Dunnet, Peter Hoskins, Robert Bolitho, Sam Kingston, Eric Madron and Eli Dorkins will all have to go,' Mr Brown said sadly,

Mrs Kent's face was full of concern. 'The only men on the estate left will be you Mr Brown, Michael FitzSimmons, Andrew Bickford and Nick Bray who has three small children to care for since his wife died last year in childbirth. How are we ever going to cope with everything?'

Mr Brown pulled his mouth into a tight line. 'We shall just have to Mrs Kent.'

*

Letters were flying back and forth from the front line to Trevarno throughout the year. Parcels were being wrapped in haste and everyone held their breath in case the dreaded telegram boy came. The postman though was greeted with joy, and everyone descended on him in hope of a letter from a loved one.

The letter Gina Teague received in September though was not the one she hoped for. She grabbed it happily from the postman and sat down at the kitchen table to read it. The shriek she emitted sent shivers down everyone's spine.

'Oh, my poor Tommy!'

'What is it, Gina?' Jenna dropped what she was doing to be at her side. 'Is Tommy hurt?'

Gina nodded tearfully. 'He's lost three fingers on his left hand and been blinded in one eye!'

'Oh, my goodness, Gina, where is he now?' Mrs Drake said, pouring her a cup of sweet tea. 'Are they sending him home?'

'I don't know, he doesn't say,' she wailed.

Jenna put her comforting arm around her. 'Gina, they won't send him back to the front with injuries like that. I'm sure he will be home soon and then he'll be safe – wounded - but safe!' she added.

*

Tommy Teague arrived home at Trevarno on the 30th of September 1916. He wanted no fuss and locked himself in his room for five solid days.

His mother Gina fretted constantly about him. He ate little and spoke nothing of his time away. Eventually he came down the stairs, kissed his mother on the cheek and said quietly, 'I'm going out.'

Gina followed him as far as the bottom of the meadow but turned back when she realised it was useless to pursue him further. Jenna was walking by her cottage when she returned.

'Oh, Jen,' Gina cried. 'I don't know what to do about my poor boy. He won't talk to me. Could you go and talk to him?'

'Me?' Jenna said, wiping her hands down her apron.

Gina nodded hopefully. 'He always liked you. You were always joking about with him when he worked in the stable. I think he might open up to you. Please Jen, please, for me.'

Tommy was in the top meadow when Jenna found him. As she approached, he threw the stone he'd been fiddling with - a throw that would have had any cricket team desperate for him on their side.

His left hand was bandaged heavily, and he wore a large patch bandage across his left eye - and a hollow look of desperation in the other.

Jenna smiled and sat down beside him.

Eventually he laughed softly but without humour. 'We thought it would be an adventure, Jimmy and me. We thought it would be over by Christmas, see? They said it would be. We never thought that we would still be there when we turned nineteen. But we weren't scared at first though.' He looked at Jenna and shook his head. 'We just thought it would be a bigger adventure.' He visibly shuddered as though someone had walked over his grave.

'If you want to tell someone about it, Tommy, tell me.'

'It's horrible,' he said bitterly.

Jenna moved closer and put her arm around his shoulder. 'Maybe it will help.'

Tommy inhaled deeply, shuddering again. 'We began to think we were invincible. All those men dying around us and still we dodged the bullets in that stinking muddy trench. We were frightened though! Every day we feared being crippled or blinded or being hit in the bollocks.' He looked sheepishly at her. 'Sorry for swearing.'

Jenna smiled. 'I've heard worse from you.'

Tommy's lips curled into the boyish smile she remembered, before he fell serious again. 'I wrote and told the Hoskins that Jimmy died from a single bullet wound. I told them it was quick, but it wasn't, you know. I lied to them. His death was awful.' He hung his head. 'If I tell you, you must promise me that you won't repeat it to Lowenna or Peter!'

'I promise Tommy.'

Tommy took a deep breath. 'I remember he'd left my side to go to the latrine. We were under heavy fire, and he didn't get back to me. Suddenly there was a surge of men, up and over the top. I had to go without him, though we vowed we'd always fight together. Bodies dropped everywhere and we managed to push the opposition back. We all dropped back into the bunker, and I heard Private Charlie Sands shout out down the line, "Tell Teguey his mate has been wounded". When I found Jimmy, I realised he hadn't gone over with us, but he'd been flung out of the latrine by a blast from a grenade.'

Tommy sat in silence for a moment, pondering whether to say the next thing. 'His….' he shook his head, 'his legs had been blown off.' The words caught in his throat. Raising his good eye to Jenna, he said, 'He'd lost his trousers and all I could see was his shattered thigh bones covered in blood. Lyndon saw me out on the top and came up to help me drag him back down into the trench. Jimmy was still alive, and he said to me, "Reach in my pocket and give me the photograph." It was a photo of him with his mum and dad. I took it out and put it in his hands, and he kissed it. Then he said there was something else, pointing again to the pocket. So, I pulled out a lock of red hair.' Tommy smiled briefly at Jenna. 'I joked with him then and said, "What are you doing with a lock of Lyndon FitzSimmons hair in your pocket?" Though I knew full well the lock came from Jane Tandy's head. Jimmy laughed at that, then he coughed horribly and choked…..I held him until he died.'

Tommy fell silent for a moment and hugged his knees. 'That night, an unbelievable loneliness washed over me, and I wished I could have died with Jimmy. Death would bring an end to the horrors.' He turned and gave Jenna a grave look. 'For as long as I live, Jen, I will never, ever, forget the horrors I've seen.'

Jenna nodded.

'Jimmy was lucky.' He laughed ironically. 'Lyndon and I managed to get his body off the field and onto a gun carriage, which had just brought up the rations. Many times, when we are being bombarded for days on end, the bodies just lay there, being eaten by rats. Only when a lull comes in the fighting, are we able to deal with them. Sometimes there are hundreds of rotting corpses, but even though we are all knackered, we know we must move them.' His mouth twisted disdainfully. 'Rotting bodies are putrid and just fall to bits in your hands when you try to pick them up, you know? I tripped once and fell head first into someone's rotting belly. It took almost a week to get the stench out of my nostrils.'

Tommy started to cry, great sobs of uncontrollable sorrow.

Jenna felt physically sick listening to his story, but still she sat there, occasionally patting him gently.

Presently he wiped the tears from his face and held the palm of his hand to his blinded eye.

'Are you in pain?'

'A little bit. I could have been killed.' He shook his head for the umpteenth time.

'Do you want to tell me how that happened?' Jenna watched as he retracted back into the depths of his memory.

'It happened because I was stupid. It was all quiet one evening - we could hear the Hun in the trench not far from us - then suddenly one of them came from nowhere, screaming at me he was. When he reached the edge of our trench I lifted my bayonet to him, but oh, god, Jen, when I saw him, he was just a young lad like me, except he just spoke different. I had to stop him though, otherwise he would have killed me, so I did, and as my bayonet stuck in his stomach, all I could think of was his family getting word that their boy had been killed in action. Stupid me, stood there too long, just looking at him, with my hand over my face in horror, that's when I got a bullet in the fingers and eye.'

'At least you came back to us though.'

'Yes, I came back,' he answered sadly. 'Don the khaki, pick up a rifle, impress the girls, they said.' He turned to Jenna. 'I'm not likely to impress the girls now with a gammy eye and a hand without fingers, am I?'

Jenna smiled brilliantly at him. 'Oh, I don't know, Thomas Teague. You're still devastatingly handsome.'

He smiled amiably. Presently he whispered, 'I've no idea where they buried Jimmy.'

'I should think his spirit is back here on Cornish soil Tommy. He'll be looking down on you, thanking god for sparing his best friend.'

Tommy gave a remorseful sigh. 'How can I live, with what is in my head?'

'How can you not? You must find a way through this. You must live your life for you and Jimmy.'

'I hear him you know.' He laughed cautiously. 'I bet you think I've gone soft in the head. But I do hear him. I hear his whistle. Do you remember his tuneless whistle?'

'I do. He couldn't sing either as I recall.'

Tommy gave a happy grunt.

The sun was setting now, and the day began to cool. He got up and held out his hand to help Jenna. When she stood, he gave her a grateful smile.

'Forgive me, Jen for burdening you with all this, but I'm glad I've told someone.'

'I understand,' she replied softly. 'I'm always here to listen. But Tommy, speak to your ma, tell her some of your feelings if things get too much for you. She's had a terrible worrying time while you've been gone. She'll help you heal and if I might suggest something else, go and see Jane Tandy. You're the last link to her sweetheart Jimmy.'

38

Christmas 1916 came and went. Without their men, the Trevarno Estate celebrations were not the same. By mid-March, it had been two months since any letter had come from Lyndon. The last time there had been such a gap was when he'd been wounded, so both Jenna and Michael had begun to worry.

*

The battle had started at the beginning of February and had raged for eight solid days. Hundreds of men had died and everyone else left in the trench began to think their time had come to meet their maker.

The smell of fear was overpowering as Lyndon stood at the top of the trench ladder along with dozens more men, ready to make another attack on the enemy. The order came, and over the top he went, gunfire narrowly missing his head. He heard the deafening ping as a sniper hit his tin hat. Suddenly dozens of shells rained down on his head burying him under a pile of bodies.

He felt himself being dragged backwards by his legs by a fellow comrade and thrown unceremoniously into the boggy water of the trench. With the adrenalin pumping furiously through his veins, Lyndon was unaware at first that he'd been hit, until the pain kicked in as he hit the floor.

'Get him up before he drowns!' someone shouted.

Disbelief swept over Lyndon. The palm of his right hand was covered in blood and the upper arm of his jacket was ripped to shreds. Drifting in and out of consciousness now, Lyndon remembered someone cleaning his wounds and then shouting that he needed to be sent down the line. The next thing he remembered was being wheeled off the battlefield in terrible agony.

Morphia was administered and then he remembered nothing, until a tired looking nurse was wiping the mud from his body. Lyndon lay silently in his cot, hardly daring to look down at his hand.

He moistened his dry lips and asked, 'My hand?'

She smiled softly. 'It's quite bad, but don't worry, we're going to get you out of here as soon as possible.'

A tag was attached to him, labelled with information about his injuries and treatments, before being lifted onto a stretcher. He was then transported for several miles via a horse-drawn ambulance - a painful journey he recalled, but the farther they travelled, the more the sound of gun fire disappeared into the distance.

At the Casualty Clearing Station, he was assessed again, and his wounds were cleaned and dressed.

'We need to get you home, soldier,' the doctor said seriously. Thus started the arduous journey by train across country to the nearest port, and then onto a ship heading to England.

He barely remembered the sea journey, his delirium thankfully saving him from the effects of the shockingly rough weather which battered the ship. He'd been in a British hospital three days before he had any notion that he was back in the real world.

'Welcome back.' A pretty nurse smiled down at him. 'You had us worried for a while.'

Lyndon tried to lift his right arm, but the nurse stopped him.

'You need to keep it still.'

'Have I lost my hand?'

'The surgeon will see you shortly.'

'Oh god! It's gone, hasn't it?' He tried again to lift his arm.

'No, shush, stay still.' She looked about her to see if anyone was listening before whispering, 'You had a ruddy great hole in your hand. The surgeons operated on it and removed shrapnel from your arm, but it's a case of 'wait and see'. Now then, I haven't told you this, all right?'

He nodded and smiled at her.

'That's what I like to see, a smile. Now, who is Jenna,

and do we need to contact her?'

Lyndon shook his head. He didn't want to worry Jenna or his pa, not just yet. Not until he knew for sure he wouldn't lose his hand.

*

It was a letter from Peter Hoskins to his wife Lowenna, which enlightened Michael about Lyndon's fate. Peter knew no details, except that Lyndon had been wounded on February 12th and taken from the front line. Peter wanted to know if he was all right. On receiving the news, Jenna almost fainted and Michael went to see if Andrew Bickford could help in locating the whereabouts of Lyndon and find out if he was still alive.

*

It was five long days before word came through about Lyndon. Andrew Bickford had contacted the war office and confirmed that Private Lyndon FitzSimmons had been wounded in combat and transferred from France to the 2nd Southern General Hospital in Bristol, and that his wounds were not life threatening. That same day a letter came from Lyndon, though not written in his own hand.

March 15th

2nd Southern General Hospital in Bristol

Dear Pa and Jenna,

A very kind nurse has offered to write this short letter to you, as my right hand is still bandaged.

I am afraid I have been wounded again, but the prognosis is good. I've suffered a wound to my right hand and arm and undergone an operation. Rest assured I am in good spirits. I will remain in Bristol for the next month, before being allowed to return home to recuperate. I am told that in due course I will make a full recovery.

Lyndon.

Michael could not settle until he had seen for himself that his son was well.

He took the train to Bristol early the very next day. Jenna dearly wanted to accompany him but knew this would raise questions amongst the kitchen staff. When he returned on the last train home that night, Michael was tired and weary but appeased that Lyndon was indeed in one piece and in high spirits.

*

Lyndon was allowed home in mid-April. He arrived by train just as the cherry blossom flowered. His arm was still in a sling and his hand bandaged, but the hospital bed-rest had put colour back into his cheeks.

He spent a great deal of the time at his father's cottage, where Jenna fussed over him like a mother hen. He spent the nights at the cottage he shared with Edna, though there was little joy for either of them there. Try as they might they could not find any common ground, which was not surprising, as Lyndon's affections were clearly with another. Edna was deeply wary of Lyndon and fretted that he would eventually demand his marital rights, which of course as her husband he was entitled to do. Inevitably whenever he stepped over the threshold in the evening, she would put down her sewing and retire to bed, quickly bolting her bedroom door, just in case. Lyndon smiled at this - he had absolutely no intention of demanding his marital rights from her.

Lyndon's days were spent outside in the fresh air. Come rain or shine he would help where he could within the capabilities of his injuries. It felt good to work in sweet smelling soil, instead of the mud contaminated with faeces in the trenches. As he buried his good hand into the soft earth, his thoughts returned to his colleagues still fighting out there. Nobody at home would ever understand the horrors those brave men were facing every day. If this war ever stopped, he was certain that everyone who'd fought at the front line would be scarred for life, whether they received physical wounds or not.

Lyndon longed to spend his time with Jenna, but for the sake of propriety he made a conscious effort to give her no more attention than any other of the women on the estate. Every morning he would visit the dairy to pass the time with both Gina and Jenna. His next call was to venture into the kitchen to see what delights Mrs Drake had in her cake cupboard. Edna made herself scarce when he came in and Mrs Kent just gave him a cursory nod. Ethel blushed profusely in his presence, but he always had a kind word for her. Only in the evening did Lyndon and Jenna catch a few stolen moments together, and that was if Michael was down at The Crown Inn. These were precious, tender times, though the most Lyndon could hope for was to hold her soft hands in his. Still after all these months, Jenna shrank back if anyone inadvertently touched her, so Lyndon, ever mindful, always waited for Jenna to reach out to him, which she inevitably did.

*

At the beginning of June, Lyndon accompanied Andrew Bickford to Kent where Matthew was recuperating in hospital. He'd already had four operations in the last eighteen months, but Lyndon found Matthew in high spirits and able to stand and walk, albeit for only a few feet.

It was an emotional reunion. The two men, joined by the horrors of combat and a belief they would never see each other again, hugged like long lost brothers. They spoke long into the afternoon and when eventually it was time to leave, there was reluctance on both parties to part.

'I can't tell you how relieved I am to find you on the mend Matthew. I'll tell everyone back at the estate how well you look.'

Matthew nodded. 'I've been very lucky. It's a miracle I'm not wheelchair bound.' He patted his legs. 'I'll always have a limp, but I've got away with my life, unlike the other poor men out there that day, eh?'

Lyndon shuddered, remembering that particular battle.

'My war is over. I wish to god it was over for you, Lyndon. I'll pray every day for you.'

Lyndon pushed his hands against his knees to stand up ready to take his leave. 'I don't think god is listening,' he said gravely.

Matthew grabbed his hand and squeezed it hard. 'Keep your faith Lyndon, that's all I can say to you now. Until we meet again and share a celebratory drink at Trevarno when this war is over, I wish you god speed, my friend.'

*

During the last few weeks of rehabilitation Lyndon walked around the estate, mentally storing memories of sunny days and warm nights. He swam every day in the lake and ate good wholesome food to build him up in readiness for the front line. Nothing though could stop the dread which crept like death into his soul.

39

When the day came for Lyndon to return to Bristol for his final health assessment, and for the inevitable return to the front line, he asked Jenna to accompany him. This posed a few problems, though none were insurmountable.

Michael, naturally uncomfortable with them travelling together as Lyndon was still married to Edna, could not deny his son this request. So, unaccustomed as he was to lying Michael reluctantly sent word to the big house that Jenna was unwell and unable to work for the next couple of days. This would give her time to travel up with Lyndon and return without anyone suspecting anything untoward.

Slipping out of the cottage early that morning ahead of Lyndon, Jenna caught the first train to Plymouth. It meant waiting around in Plymouth railway station for a good three hours, but it was a small price to pay to be able to say their goodbyes in private.

Once reunited, they continued their journey to Bristol, consciously keeping a respectable distance apart, in case anyone on the train knew them. Though occasionally, her thigh would brush against his and they'd share a secret smile.

They were both fairly certain that Lyndon would be discharged from care that day, which meant his return to his unit was imminent. Whatever happened, they planned to spend the day together in Bristol before Jenna returned to Plymouth that evening, where she'd booked into a guesthouse. She would then return by train to Cornwall the following day.

While Lyndon kept his hospital appointment, Jenna took tea in a small café a few yards from the hospital. From her window table she watched the outside world pass by. Bristol was a bustling, thriving city which made Jenna slightly nervous coming from such a small village. She looked up at the clock. Lyndon had told her he would be no more than an hour, so she paid her bill and walked back to meet him.

The 2nd Southern General Hospital was a dark, imposing building, with many stone steps up to the huge columned frontage. As Jenna walked through the hospital, she passed many wounded soldiers, some walking with frames and some being guided by nurses down the corridors. Occasionally she glanced into wards full of men and noted how the nurses looked exhausted.

Eventually Jenna found Lyndon in the hospital grounds. He was sitting on a bench, under the dappled shade of a tree, his eyes were closed, enjoying the warmth of the day.

She touched him lightly on the arm and sat beside him. 'What did the doctor say?'

Lyndon took a deep breath. 'He discharged me from his care. I'm to return to Kent to report for duty tomorrow.'

Even though it was expected, the enormity of his words hit her hard. She reached for his hand to comfort him.

He turned to smile but she noted the anxious look in his eyes. Suddenly a car backfired in the near vicinity and Lyndon visibly cowered where he sat. For several minutes he shook uncontrollably as Jenna held onto him. Eventually the trembling abated, but it left Lyndon pale and exhausted.

'Are you sure you are well enough to go back?'

'Apparently, yes.' He covered her hand with his. 'Don't worry.'

'I *do* worry.'

They sat in silence for a while, listening to a blackbird in full song.

'Occasionally we hear birdsong on the battle field, you know? I should think they are angrily twittering at us for destroying their trees. But it's such a beautiful sound to the ear after....' His words dried up and he looked away.

Jenna squeezed his hand tightly.

'Jenna?' He said in earnest. 'Forgive me for asking but, after what you went through with 'you know who,' - he knew not to mention Blewett's name - 'would it.... could it ever be possible for you to lay with a man again?'

Taking his hand in hers she kissed it gently. 'If you'd asked me that when you rescued me,' she paused, trembling slightly, 'then I'd have had to say no. It was my one concern. I wanted you so much, Lyndon, but the thought of an intimate relationship filled me with dread.' She smiled gently. 'As it happens, that wasn't to be, was it?' She kissed his hand again. 'But it's been a long time now. I believe physically I've healed, though mentally….. well, there will always be demons.'

He nodded sadly.

'In answer to your question though, yes Lyndon, I do think it's possible for me to lay with a man again.'

As she blushed slightly, Lyndon gave a ghost of a smile, before glancing back out towards the clump of trees at the bottom of the garden. 'I'll probably be back on the front line the day after tomorrow, back to my unit, and my comrades. It's hell on earth out there, Jenna! Until someone puts a stop to this mindless, senseless war, we are just going to continue shooting and blowing each other up.' He paused to shake the horrors building in his head. 'There is a very good chance it won't stop until there are no more men left to fight.' He turned his face to hers, his eyes red with unshed tears. 'I don't want to meet my maker, Jenna without ever knowing what it is like to lay with you in my arms.'

Curling her fingers around his, she leaned on his shoulder. Everything suddenly became very still. 'You have to promise me, Lyndon, if I spend the night with you, that you *will* come back …to lay with me again.'

*

They made the decision to return to Plymouth that night. Wearing a curtain ring on her finger from a nearby haberdashery, they stood hand in hand outside the guesthouse Jenna had booked.

'This is my husband, Mrs Boyd,' Jenna announced once inside. 'He'll be staying with me tonight.'

'Will he now?' Mrs Boyd looked suspiciously at Jenna. 'You never mentioned a husband before.'

Jenna smiled sweetly. 'In all honesty, Mrs Boyd, you never asked. My husband was wounded and has just been discharged to return to the front tomorrow.'

'Oh, I see, well of course. I shall have to charge you more for the room though!'

'Of course, you will,' Jenna said tightly.

It was late afternoon. The sun filled the bedroom with dust motes. They both took off their jackets and faced each other shyly. There seemed no urgency, just a gentle feeling of shared love. Lyndon held her hand and Jenna stepped forward. He led her to the bed, all the while watching her as she sat. Slowly kneeling at her feet, he began to untie the laces of her shoes. One by one he slipped them off her feet.

Jenna's heartbeat accelerated and feeling her tremble slightly at his touch, Lyndon looked up in concern. 'Are you all right, my love?'

Jenna nodded, pulling at her skirts until the garters of her stockings showed.

Untying the ribbon on each stocking, he slipped them off her legs and laid his head on her lap. 'Jenna,' he whispered. His breath felt soft as he kissed the pale skin of her thigh.

As twilight fell, they lay warm and spent, entwined in each other's arms. Sleep came softly, and the heartache of separation diminished.

Sometime in the early hours, thunder rumbled in the distance. They both stirred slightly but slept on, until a flash of lightning lit the room, followed swiftly by a crack of thunder so loud it rattled the windows. Jenna felt Lyndon leap out of bed. Another flash illuminated him scrambling about on the floor, the sound of thunder drowning the words he was shouting. Jenna jumped out of bed to find Lyndon frantically searching for something under the bed.

'My rifle, where is it? Where's my rifle?' His body shook violently as Jenna tried to pull him into her embrace. Another crack of thunder sent Lyndon flat to the floor dragging Jenna down with such force she banged her cheek.

In a blind panic Lyndon shouted, 'Oh, Christ! Where is everyone? Where's my rifle?'

'Lyndon, be still, my love. It's only thunder!' She smoothed his hair and covered his face with kisses. 'I'm here with you, my darling. Your Jenna is here.'

A pitiful cry escaped his throat as he pulled her into an embrace.

She felt the frantic thump of his heartbeat. 'It's all right now my darling,' she murmured. Eventually the thunder faded into the distance, and she felt him relax as peace prevailed.

'I'm so sorry, Jenna,' he whispered.

Gently rubbing her thumb across his cheek to wipe a tear he could not contain, Jenna kissed him gently. Very slowly and very passionately they made love again where they lay.

*

The morning light dappled through the lace curtains and they both stirred from their slumber. Lyndon looked down at Jenna, as beautiful asleep as she was awake.

Brushing his lips tenderly across hers, he whispered. 'We need to get up, my love.'

Jenna smiled sleepily at his voice. Her fingers caressed his face as she returned his kiss. Reluctantly they left each other's arms. Realising the enormity of the parting they must now undertake, they dressed in silence. Breakfasting in Mrs Boyd's front room, the emotion between them was palpable.

Stepping out of the guesthouse, the street was damp

The Glittering Sea

and fresh after the night's storm. It was a ten-minute walk to the train station, but Jenna would have walked a million miles just to keep Lyndon safe by her side.

Every few moments, Lyndon would squeeze her hand just to make sure she was still there.

The noise at the station made Lyndon jumpy. Each bang of a door reverberated through him, though he fought hard to hide it from her.

'Are you sure you're well enough to go back, Lyndon?'

He nodded. 'All mended.' He flexed his hand.

She pulled him round to face her. 'I don't mean physically.'

'I know you don't,' he answered seriously.

'But last night….'

He shrugged. 'It happens I'm afraid. We all suffer from it. I just find it difficult to deal with in civilian life. At the front line we know what to do and how to react. I can't seem to differentiate where I am sometimes.'

Jenna's face crumpled. 'Oh, god, Lyndon, let this be over soon. I fear not only for your life but for your sanity.'

He cupped her face tenderly in his hands. 'Your love will see me through this. I've everything to live for now.'

The train whistle blew.

'It's time to go.' He kissed her deeply on the mouth.

Jenna's eyes misted and everything went out of focus. 'I love you, Lyndon.'

He gathered her into his arms. 'I love you too, my darling.'

Touching her face one last time, he stepped away to board the train. Pulling the window down, he reached over, gently kissing away her tears. Still holding hands, the train pulled away gently, until they had to let go.

'Please come back to me,' she whispered as the train moved out of the station. They waved until they could see each other no more.

Dizzy with grief, Jenna truly felt that her chest had been ripped open and her heart torn from her body, so much so, she could not physically move from where she stood.

'Begging your pardon, Miss, I need to come through,' a porter said jovially.

'Oh, I'm so sorry,' Jenna stepped aside.

'No need.' He looked at Jenna's tear-stained face and gave her a wink. 'I'll pray for him too lass.'

It would be two full hours before Jenna's train back to Cornwall arrived. She sat down on a bench feeling emotionally exhausted. How long would this dreadful war go on? Would Lyndon survive and return to her? He'd been so fatalistic in accepting whatever was held in store for him. Please god, don't let last night be the only night we spend together. His gentle lovemaking had healed her wounded soul and her love in return had given him something to live for. Would their love, and the future it held, keep him safe and bring him back to her? How long would they have to wait for this damn war to end?

*

When Jenna returned, Michael knew immediately that something had happened between them. Beyond the sorrow and anxiety of his leaving, Jenna seemed to shine from within.

'So, he got off all right then?' Michael asked apprehensively.

Jenna nodded. 'He caught the ten-thirty train this morning. I should think he'll be back with his unit by now,' she answered distantly.

'This morning you say?' He twisted his mouth around. 'I take it you found somewhere comfortable to stay last night then?' It was a leading question.

Jenna flushed slightly and nodded.

Michael drew a breath a little deeper than normal, and then he too nodded.

40

As the church bells rang in 1918, Jenna found it hard to celebrate. This was the fourth year of this bloody war and still there was no sign of an end to it.

Michael however, seemed in high spirits. She'd noticed back in November a change in him. He'd been quietly thoughtful, and Jenna thought he was ailing something. By December, she noted a real brightness in his mood, and now she knew something was afoot. It was February before she found the reason.

Quite unexpectedly she'd come across Michael and Gina in the potting shed one day sharing a box of sandwiches. Hearing Gina's laughter tinkle as Michael spoke, Jenna smiled. *Could she detect a little love interest going on here?*

Trying unsuccessfully to back out of the shed without being noticed, she tripped over the watering can, and the crash alerted them to her presence. They both jumped away from each other, making Jenna regret the intrusion.

'Right, I'll err…be off then, Michael. Thank you for showing me the orchids,' Gina said, wiping the sandwich crumbs from her mouth.

'Come back and see them anytime, Gina,' Michael called out as she rushed past Jenna.

Jenna smiled inwardly. *There were no orchids in the potting shed.*

After Gina left, Michael watched the door for a good few seconds before turning to Jenna.

'Did you want something?'

'Just wondered what you wanted for tea?'

'Anything,' he answered dreamily as he turned to finish his sandwich.

'Gina's a lovely woman, isn't she?' Jenna said softly.

Michael's nod was non-committal.

'It must be terribly lonely for her since her husband passed.'

Michael looked directly at Jenna and shrugged. It was clear he wasn't going to proclaim his love for her yet.

By mid-March, Jenna worried her intrusion had halted Michael's fledgling love affair, as he was beginning to resemble a drooping flower without water. So, having set the milk to cool on the stone slab, Jenna went in search of Gina. Standing at the door of the buttery for a moment, Jenna watched Gina turning the butter. It was clear Gina looked as gloomy as Michael.

When Gina looked up at Jenna, her face brightened. 'Ah, there you are. I was just about to come and see you. Mrs Drake has requested some cream for a cream tea tomorrow in celebration of Matthew Bickford coming home from his rehabilitation.

'That is good news,' Jenna said folding her arms. 'Gina?'

Gina raised her eyebrows.

'Go and see Michael will you. I do believe he's pining for you.'

Gina laughed giddily. 'Pining for me?'

'Yes, and by the look of it you're doing much the same.' Jenna grinned.

Gina smiled shyly. 'I confess I do like him.'

'He likes you too, Gina - a lot!'

Gina blushed faintly. 'And what would you think Lyndon would say to that?'

Jenna laughed. 'I reckon he'd be very happy if he knew his pa had someone special in his life again.'

'Really?' she asked in earnest.

Jenna nodded. 'Michael's a fine handsome man, is he not?'

'That he is,' Gina answered enthusiastically, drumming her fingers on the butter churn.

'Then what are you waiting for?'

'I'm waiting for the bloody butter, but it just won't turn.'

'Mmm, maybe you're in love.' Jenna grinned.

'God help us then, neither of us will be able to churn this butter. I take it you're still in love with some secret person?'

Jenna felt herself flush.

'I thought so.' Gina nodded knowingly. 'Thank goodness it doesn't affect your cheese making.'

They laughed together.

'Why don't you and Tommy come for supper tonight?' Jenna said.

'Oh, Tommy's off courting tonight, I think he's sweet on Jane Tandy if you ask me.'

'Well, better still, you come on your own.'

'I will.' Gina hugged her warmly. 'Thank you.'

*

It was May before Matthew Bickford felt steady enough to venture out onto the estate. Though he'd passed these long months of rehabilitation reading novels and writing letters to Lyndon at the front, his confinement was driving him crazy. Eager to see if Jenna had fulfilled her commission to paint his favourite places on the estate, Michael's cottage was his first port of call. Though exhausted from the exertion, he silently congratulated himself for making it to the Dell with only the aid of a walking stick.

Jenna, clearly delighted to find him standing at her front door, beckoned him in and fussed over him like a mother hen.

Very tentatively, Jenna spread the watercolours before him. Four pictures depicting the Italian garden, the boat house, the waterfall, and the main house itself.

Two weeks later, they'd been framed and hung in the orangery and Jenna had more money in her pocket than she had ever had in her lifetime.

*

As the warmth of the summer gave way to the cooler winds of September, when she wasn't writing to Lyndon, Jenna spent every spare hour tucked away in the grounds producing watercolours to send to him. If she couldn't have him home, she would send images of home to him. Her absence from the cottage also gave Michael and Gina a little more time for each other, without sneaking about in the potting shed.

*

Come autumn, Michael's harvest was plentiful, much to the delight of Mrs Drake the cook.

'Oh, Jennifer,' Mr Brown greeted her as she arrived with her daily trug full of vegetables. 'Matthew is asking for you. He's in the orangery. Hurry along now and see what he wants - I'm due to serve tea to him in a few minutes.'

The orangery faced south and looked out onto the Italian garden. Though the day was sunny, a chill breeze rendered Matthew to sit inside, albeit by the open door.

'Ah, Jenna, do come in.' Matthew could never get used to calling her anything other than the name he'd always known her by. 'I'd like you to meet my good friend James Blackwell, the author.'

Feeling a slight flutter in her stomach, Jenna patted her hair, straightened her apron and reached out to shake the hand James had offered.

'I'm very pleased to meet you, Miss…'

'Penvean,' Jenna said, before Matthew revealed her proper name. 'The pleasure is mine, Mr Blackwell. I've thoroughly enjoyed your novels.'

'I'm happy to hear that.' He smiled gratefully. 'Do join us,' he beckoned to the vacant seat.

'James, like myself, has been discharged from the army,' Matthew said.

'Are you injured too, sir?' Jenna asked, quickly surveying visible signs.

'Nothing noticeable, I was caught in a gas attack which caused irrevocable lung damage.'

'Oh, I'm so sorry.'

'Well, I'm luckier than most, and thankfully I got out alive. This war has claimed too many lives.

The Glittering Sea

'Yes,' Jenna answered sadly.

Mr Brown arrived with a tray of tea and frowned when he saw Jenna sitting alongside Matthew and his guest.

'Thank you, Brown, could you possibly bring another cup? Miss Penvean will be taking tea with us.'

Mr Brown nodded curtly and shot Jenna a dour look.

Matthew smiled gently. 'James has been admiring your watercolours, Jenna.'

'Oh!' Jenna flushed slightly as she sipped the best tea she had ever tasted.

'More than admiring actually, I'm greatly impressed by the intricacy of your work, Miss Penvean. You have a rare talent.'

Jenna felt a frisson of excitement. 'Thank you, it's something I really enjoy doing.'

James nodded. 'Are you professionally trained?'

'No, sir.' Jenna tried to suppress the tinkle of laughter in her voice. 'My mother taught me.'

Again, he nodded. 'I have many contacts in London associated with the art world, Miss Penvean, I'd be more than happy to introduce you to some of them, should you wish.'

'London!' Jenna glanced frantically at Matthew who in turn gave her a curious look. *She couldn't go to London. What if the war ended and Lyndon came home? She had to be here for his return!*

Seeing Jenna's unease, James added, 'You don't have to make a decision now. But it's maybe something to think about for the future.'

'Don't dismiss it for any loyalty you have to me or the estate Jenna,' Matthew added. 'I'd be very happy for you to have this opportunity.'

'Think about it, Miss Penvean.' James smiled warmly. 'I'll leave my card with you. In the meantime, I have another proposal. I have a house on the cliff at Gunwalloe. I would very much like to commission you to paint it. You will be paid well for your work.'

'Oh!' Jenna felt a bubble of excitement. 'But ….'

'Don't worry, Jenna, I'll arrange you some leave of work,' Matthew said.

'So, you would consider it?' James asked hopefully.

'Well, yes, thank you, if it's all right with Matthew,' she laughed gently.

'Matthew has kindly offered the use of his car and driver to take you to Gunwalloe whenever it's convenient to you. Hopefully the weather will be kind enough for you to paint, even though it's September. I'm afraid I shall be away from home until Christmas, and unable to offer you hospitality. But when I return, you must come for tea. You can bring the painting with you.'

Overwhelmed at this turn of events, Jenna thanked them both profusely before returning to her chores with joy in her heart.

*

So as not to draw attention to herself, Jenna arranged for Matthew's car to take her to Gunwalloe on her days off, rather than taking time off work. The weather had been kind, albeit a little chilly on both occasions. Now October, Jenna sat in the warmth of Michael's kitchen, putting the finishing touches to the painting.

'That's a rare painting you've done there, Jen,' Michael said, 'Have you considered taking up that author's offer in London?'

Jenna looked up from her work. 'How can I leave? I need to be here when Lyndon comes home. Money and fame pale into insignificance when all I want in life is Lyndon.'

Michael raised his eyebrows. 'That may be more difficult than you think. He *is* still married you know?'

'I know Michael, but Lyndon seems to think the difficulty is not insurmountable. I don't know what his plans are, except that he's adamant we will be together.'

*

Lyndon shivered in the chilly October morning. It had

been a cold night, but the day was warming, and as it did, the tension began to build in the trench. The stench of fear hung in the surrounding mud. Lyndon slid down to a sitting position, ignoring the rats which scurried across his feet. He was bone weary, filthy and hadn't been able to feel his feet for days. It crossed his mind that maybe if he took off his socks, his toes would tumble out onto the wooden boards. He unfolded the paper from the already addressed envelope and began to write the letter he'd been putting off for so long.

October 1918

My darling Jenna,

I have no idea how to start this letter. This is like no other letter I have written before - though I am not to post it. It is to stay in my pocket. If anything happens to me someone will perhaps post it. Every time we go over the top now, we wonder if it will be our last. We are all in god's hands.

My deepest regret is that I leave you. If I must die, I will go to my maker with only your beautiful face in my mind. You are an extraordinary woman, and you know I love you with all my heart.

As I sit here waiting, I think about that one beautiful night you granted me. I had hoped for a lifetime with you, but if those few hours are the only memories I can have, then they will have to suffice, for they were blissful.

The tension here is palpable, we may move at any minute. When this letter reaches you, there will be no more war for me, only eternal peace. We shall meet again, my darling, in another time, another place, when there will be no more parting. I am to write no more now, the time has come.

Goodbye, my beloved Jenna. Take care of Pa for me and tell him I love him. God bless and watch over you both.

Forever yours, Lyndon x

He folded the letter up and put it safely in his pocket.

41

It was the beginning of November. Every morning, thousands of war-weary men rose to fight another day, all wondering if this would be their last. The fighting was as fierce as ever as the British troops continued pushing back the retreating German forces.

'Come on, keep it going men, we'll get the buggers back towards their own bloody border sooner or later,' the CO shouted.

'Yes, but when?' someone grumbled.

'Next bloody year probably, I swear this damn war will never end,' another soldier griped.

'I've heard rumours that the Germans are suing for peace,' someone shouted.

Lyndon glanced at Charlie Williams's mud-splattered face and said grimly, 'I'll believe that when I see it.'

'I want to believe it - I've had enough of this, and I've only been in the thick of it for a couple of years. Christ knows how you've endured it so long, Lyndon.'

'I admit, it's been more tolerable since you joined me.' Lyndon slapped Charlie warmly.

'Just think, we might be home in Cornwall soon Lyndon,' Charlie said hopefully.

'We can but hope.'

'I'm going to ask Lizzy Pike to be my wife as soon as I get home. Do you remember Lizzy, she works in our dairy?'

'I do, she's a lovely maid, I recall.'

Charlie smiled happily. 'She is that. I've wanted to marry her for some time, but her mother is ill. Lizzy tells me she doesn't have long to live - it'll be a blessing when she goes. What about you Lyndon, what are your plans?'

'I'm going to sleep until Christmas.'

'Good idea. I think I may do the same, after I propose to Lizzy. Do you have a young lady waiting at home for you? You've never said.'

Lyndon smiled secretly. 'Maybe.' *He dared not mention Jenna to Charlie knowing that he believed she'd drowned.* In truth, his marriage to Edna caused him great consternation, not only because he wanted to end it in order to be with Jenna. It was something a fellow soldier disclosed to him. The man had been disgruntled about being duped into marrying his sweetheart when she feigned a pregnancy. A seed of doubt had been planted in Lyndon's mind. *Had Edna duped him?* He was sure going to find out, if he ever got out of this bloody war.

*

Over the week, rumours of a truce continued to grow, but the general consensus was that it couldn't be true. A feeling of nervous tension swept through the trenches. No-one wanted to take a chance of being hit if this was going to be over soon.

It was November 10th. Hope of a ceasefire was fast diminishing. The war raged on and once again the men stood in line ready to go over the top when ordered.

'God save us,' Lyndon prayed silently as he stood in the trench, his bayonet fixed and rifle at the ready. The noise of the shell fire was deafening. A shudder manifested in his kneecaps and crept slowly up his body. He glanced at Charlie whose eyes matched his fear. The air crackled, filled with fumes and noise, and a moment later the order came, and he was over the top and running. A blinding light stopped him dead. His head felt as though it had exploded as his feet lifted from the ground. For a split second he viewed the battlefield in all its horror before crashing down to earth with a painful '*Oomph!*' A weight of bodies rained atop of him. The mud he hated so much engulfed his body, wrapping a protective blanket around him. Closing his eyes to the overwhelming fatigue, darkness ensued.

*

The battle raged for hours. Only when the fighting ceased, were the dead and wounded moved to the nearest field hospital. There, encrusted with mud and blood, the men lay in rows on the cold ground adjacent to the hospital. The wounded were stretchered inside - the deceased had their name tags removed to register them dead before being placed to one side for burial. For them the war was over.

*

In the cold dark stinking trench, Charlie Williams and Fred Saunders sat in stunned silence, weeping openly for their lost friend and comrade Lyndon FitzSimmons.

*

November 11th, 1918 dawned extremely cold. A thick white crust of frost covered the mud surrounding the field hospital where one by one the deceased were hoisted onto the cart with as much dignity as could be administered by the war-weary men assigned to this post. This was no end for these brave men, but they needed to be buried, and buried quickly.

As the last body was lifted, a groan of pain emitted from the hideously swollen face of one of the bodies.

'Holy mother of Jesus, this one's alive!'

'He can't be.'

'I'm telling you, he groaned when I pushed him,' the man insisted as he pulled the filthy body off the pile.

'Many of them do. It's trapped wind,' his colleague argued.

'This was definitely a groan of pain.' Once the body was on the floor, he checked for a pulse then shouted to a nearby nurse, 'Can I have some assistance here!'

*

Later that morning the men were sat in the barracks, eating an unappetising breakfast when the colonel walked in.

'Good day to you all.' He looked at his watch and then back at the men. 'Men, it is 10 a.m. I am pleased to tell you that in one hour an armistice comes into force, and you will all soon be able to return to your homes.'

The news was greeted with stunned silence. The

colonel smiled smugly, as he sat down with the men and shared their breakfast.

'Do you believe it?' Fred asked Charlie Williams.

Charles scratched his filthy face. 'I don't know. I'll tell you in an hour.' The enormity of grief at losing his friend Lyndon took any shine off any truce.

There was a slow murmuring of suppressed excitement amongst the men. Any thoughts of home and comfort were held at bay as the element of false hope hung amongst them. A soldier took out a pack of cards and began to deal. Others followed suit. It was the longest hour.

On the stroke of 11a.m the commanding officer stood and raised his hand. 'Men, the war is over.'

Everyone in that shed stood, holding rifles aloft and cheered for the day they believed would never come. Charlie and Fred cheered along with them before their faces crumpled at the injustice.

*

As news of the armistice circulated around the world, people were celebrating, dancing, and drinking.

Trevarno estate received the news by phone, and champagne was sent down to the kitchen. An invitation to a celebration was issued to every worker on the estate.

For Charlie, Fred and the other men, there were no further celebrations that day. There was again a general consensus between the soldiers that the armistice was only a temporary measure and that the war would soon go on. After years of tension, being ready to face the daily danger of combat, it was hard for the men to detach themselves from ongoing war and dodging the enemy. A few of the men had collapsed in a state of nervous exhaustion. Many cried tears of relief. Some fell into an exhausted sleep. For the first time in four years log fires were lit for the men to gather round, but that night the unearthly quietness unnerved the men. You could feel the unease as they all sat and spoke in low tones.

'I'm expecting the shelling to start again at any moment,' one soldier whispered.

'I know. I just don't trust Fritz. They could be spying on us now,' another added.

'Well, I'm going to keep my bloody head down until I'm out of here, that's for sure,' someone quipped.

Charlie gave a shuddering sigh. 'Let's just hope it really is over, eh?'

The soldier rubbed his hands across his face and nodded.

*

As the celebration at Trevarno continued, the sound of the bicycle bell heralding a telegram was no longer feared. The war was over - someone must have sent it to inform the estate.

'Telegram for FitzSimmons,' the delivery boy said, grimly aware of breaking up the celebrations.

Everyone in the room fell silent.

42

After Matthew had accompanied them home, Michael and Jenna sat in silent desolation by a fire that could not warm them. Matthew too sat in silence - his eyes dulled with his own feelings of grief. Edna had gone home to her mother, and Gina busied herself making sweet tea.

'How the hell will I ever get over this, Gina?' Michael murmured, taking the tea that he had no desire to drink.

Remembering the loss of her husband, Gina answered quietly. 'You don't, Michael. You just learn to live with it. There will always be a Lyndon shaped hole in your heart. You just have to find ways of filling it with memories of him.'

Michael's shoulders slumped, as he raked his hand through his hair in desperation. 'Just one more day!'

Jenna glanced at Michael through a veil of tears and rested her hand on his.

He turned his bloodshot eyes towards her. 'Just one day, Jenna! One more day and the bloody war would have been over,' Michael's voice broke into a sob. 'My poor boy. Why, oh why, was he not saved, just one more day?'

Jenna's breath caught in her throat as she gathered him into her arms. Closing her eyes, her own heart-aching grief engulfed her.

*

Michael took to his bed for the rest of the week, but Jenna, unable to rest, or openly grieve for her lover, filled the empty hours of despair with chores. Endless tears salted several batches of cheese. Vegetables were wrenched from the ground in angry desperation, as she was unable to tame the violent emotions bubbling within her. Sleep brought no respite, as images of Lyndon, alive and vibrant, punctured her dreams with startling ferocity. Jenna knew without doubt she'd never get over the loss of him. Lyndon had been her one true love, her rock, and her hero - her heart was truly broken.

*

Edna dressed in black - for decency's sake. She was sorry Lyndon had died, of course she was. It was a shame their marriage hadn't worked out, but it had been just as much his fault as hers. If he'd demanded his marital rights she would have submitted, and maybe everything would have been all right, but it was clear he never wanted her. Still, she thought, as she ran her hand over the kitchen table, this cottage is all mine now, and that of course was all she ever wanted. Edna shed not a tear for her dead husband that day or any other.

*

As Fred Saunders was among the first to sign up, he took priority in the first demobilisation of the troops and returned to Trevarno on November the 29th. The others, who had joined the war by conscription, had to wait a while longer. Charlie Williams would have to wait until Christmas to propose to his Lizzy.

Fred stepped off the train to a hail of cheers and applause and Ethel threw herself into his embrace - a moment later Fred knelt on one knee and proposed marriage to her.

Jenna's heart ached at this happy scene. She glanced at Michael, who smiled tightly, deeply aware of the significance.

When the cheers died down, Fred approached Michael. 'I'm so sorry about Lyndon. He was the best of men and a damn good soldier. He got me through this war, I am just so sorry I didn't get him through it.'

Michael nodded his thanks as he laid his trembling hand on Fred's shoulder.

*

Mrs Drake had lain on a fine homecoming tea. Her kitchen table groaned with every possible cake and sandwich you could think of. Everyone, both upstairs and downstairs attended. Michael and Jenna, reluctant at first to go, did so after some persuasion from Gina. As the celebration continued, Jenna watched Edna with interest. There seemed to be no deep-seated sadness in her eyes. *Had Edna grieved at all for Lyndon?* She suspected not.

*

In the base hospital in Le Touquet, France, a nurse gently bathed the face of an injured soldier. As she did, she hummed softly to herself. Through the fug of pain, Lyndon became aware of her song. No longer was he enveloped in mud, but he could smell clean sheets and feel a soft bed under his battered body. Try as he might his eyes would not open. He lifted his hand to his face, only to wince in pain as he pressed his swollen eyes.

'It's all right, don't touch,' said the female voice as she pulled his hand away. 'He's conscious now doctor.'

Aware of someone else near him, a male voice said, 'Hello, old chap. It seems you've had a lucky escape. You were almost buried alive in a pile of dead men.'

Lyndon slowed his breathing, trying to decipher what was being said to him.

The doctor checked his pulse. 'Can you hear me?"

Lyndon's mouth moved but a pitiful groan escaped his throat.

'Perhaps he's German,' the female voice whispered.

'Perhaps. Wie heißen Sie?'

Lyndon remained unresponsive.

'Perhaps he's frightened. Tell him the war is over doctor.'

'Der Krieg ist vorbei, Soldat. Wie heißt du?'

When nothing was forthcoming, the doctor lifted Lyndon's hand again. 'If you can hear me, squeeze my hand.'

Lyndon squeezed.

'He understands English. Are you English? Can you tell me your name?'

Lyndon felt a frisson of panic. He had no idea who he was!

'He seems confused, nurse. We'll assume he's English

for now. I'm afraid that until this swelling goes down I don't think even his mother would recognise him.'

*

It was mid-December. Most of the estate men had returned from the war to the bosom of their family. The daily life went on at Trevarno as it had always done, though everything was very different now for Jenna and Michael. Jenna went about her business mechanically - her chores taking her mind away from her loss. Edna's brother William, the eldest of Jean Madron's brood, had taken over the milking of the herd since Peter Hoskins had gone off to war. Peter, being one of the last to be conscripted, was expected home this very day, along with Edna's father and John Dunnet. As for the other estate men, Robert Bolitho, the farm hand, had been reported missing presumed dead in October and labourers Sam Kingston, and Eli Dorkins were still in hospital after suffering shrapnel wounds. Jenna looked forward to Peter's return very much. William was a pleasant enough lad, though a little surly first thing in the morning, but he lacked the natural wit that Peter possessed.

Jenna took the bucket of milk she needed for the cheese and bid Gina good morning in the butter shed.

'Is the butter turning?' Jenna asked, sharing an old joke.

'What do you think?' Gina answered with a wink.

Gina had been an absolute rock to Michael. Jenna believed he would not be coping as well as he was if it wasn't for her.

Once the milk for the cheese was standing and the clotted cream skimmed from her previous batch, Jenna took the cheese to the kitchen for Mrs Kent to use with the scones.

As she entered the kitchen, she could have cut the atmosphere with a knife. Edna was there, so too was Ethel, Mrs Kent, and Mrs Drake. They were all staring at her.

Placing the bowl down on the table she glanced at Mrs

Drake. 'What's the matter?'

Edna laughed. 'Look at her! Butter wouldn't melt in her mouth!'

Puzzled, Jenna shook her head. 'What?'

'I received a parcel this morning containing my husband's belongings,' Edna said, 'they sent me his disgusting uniform, books and several *letters*.' Her emphasis on the word made Jenna's stomach churn. 'And do you know what else I found?'

Jenna's mouth felt suddenly dry - she'd sent Lyndon a lock of her hair, Edna must have found that.

'I found this in his pocket!' Edna slapped a letter down on the table before her.

There was no envelope, but the letter was clearly for Jenna. *My darling Jenna* it read. Jenna trembled as she began to read the heart-wrenching letter he'd written to her - the one all soldiers wrote in case they died. Jenna felt a lump form in her throat as she put the letter back on the table.

Edna snatched the letter back. 'Would you like to explain what my husband means by this - *As I sit here waiting, I think about that one beautiful night you granted me. I had hoped for a lifetime with you, but if those few hours are the only memories I can have, then they will have to suffice, for they were blissful.*

A voice from the kitchen door answered for Jenna. Michael walked in, stood beside Jenna and said, 'It means my son was in love with her. Jenna kept him alive with the letters she sent to him. She returned his love, where you couldn't be bothered to write a single letter to him!'

'Don't you talk to me about letters, I've seen them. They're disgusting. My marriage didn't have a chance once that floozy set her sights on him!'

'Enough.' Michael grabbed the parcel and the letter from Edna's hand. 'These belong to me!' He caught Jenna by the arm and pulled her away from the table, leaving everyone in stunned silence.

*

The fracas had deeply distressed both Jenna and Michael and both knew the dire consequences it would bring.

Outside, a cheery crowd welcomed the last remaining Trevarno men home. Jenna glanced at Michael. 'I don't think I'll be attending the celebration tea today.'

They both jumped when Gina knocked and entered the cottage. 'Ah, there you both are. I've just come from the kitchen. What a to-do eh? It goes without saying I'm not of the same mind as some here.'

Michael nodded thankfully.

Gina took Jenna into her arms.

'I knew you were in love with someone. It's no wonder the butter wouldn't turn for you!' She gave her a playful squeeze to lighten the mood before hugging her tighter. 'I'm sorry everything turned out as it did. Lyndon was a good man. I always thought he deserved better than Edna Madron. This has caused a real hoo-ha though. Hopefully it will all blow over, eh?'

*

A visit from Matthew later that evening sealed Jenna's fate. He sat down heavily, pausing before he spoke.

'I'm so sorry Jenna. Mrs Kent is adamant she'll not have you working for her. The Madrons too have been to see me and called for your expulsion from the estate. Eric Madron claims he'll not work here if you remain.'

Michael tsked.

'I'm sorry Jenna.'

Jenna stared at the grain on the wooden table and nodded resignedly. *She couldn't blame them for their condemnation, but how her fragile heart would cope with this upheaval she had no idea.*

'Jenna.' Matthew reached out and held both of her hands. 'Let me make a suggestion?'

Jenna lifted her eyes hopefully.

'Maybe it's time you took up James Blackwell's offer.'

'And go to London!' The thought of travelling alone all that way filled her with dread.

'James will be back in Cornwall in a few days. If you're in agreement I could make all the necessary arrangements to move you quietly, and swiftly to his house at Gunwalloe Fishing Cove. Just give me the word and it's done.'

Jenna glanced at Michael who gave a solemn nod.

'Thank you, Matthew.'

'That's settled then.' He gave her hands one last encouraging squeeze. 'I suggest you pack your belongings and expect to move in a couple of days.'

Jenna nodded unhappily, she felt a deep sadness at leaving Michael and the sanctuary of the cottage, for that is what it had been these last five years.

*

After a heart-wrenching goodbye to Michael and Gina, Matthew accompanied Jenna on the nine-mile journey to Gunwalloe. It was late afternoon when they pulled up outside a house named Toy Cottage.

Seeing the concern on her face, Matthew patted her hand to ease her worries. 'Stay there a moment. I'm just going to speak to James's housekeeper, Celia.'

When he returned, he said, 'Come on, Celia is looking forward to meeting you. Incidentally, you two have a mutual friend, did you know?' he added.

Jenna raised an eyebrow.

'Celia is the sister of your friend Amelia Pascoe. She's a very discreet lady and knows a little of your troubles in Gweek, but not what has happened at Trevarno.' He tapped his nose. 'After I spoke to James yesterday, he sent her a telegram to expect you, so all she knows is that you're joining the household at Loe House.'

'What about James, does he know of my troubles?'

Matthew nodded. 'He knows you're in hiding from an abusive husband - I told him just before I introduced him to you. As for what has happened at Trevarno - no.'

'Oh, why, would he mind if he knew I'd caused a scandal?'

Matthew roared with laughter. 'I shouldn't think it

would bother him in the slightest. No, Jenna, I just thought it best that he thinks that you've just decided to take him up on his offer.'

Jenna felt herself relax slightly.

'Thank you for helping me, Matthew,' Jenna said softly.

'You're very welcome, Jenna. I urge you now to make a life for yourself as an artist. It's what Lyndon would have wanted you to do.'

At the mention of Lyndon, they both shared a few sad moments in his memory, before Matthew bid her farewell and set off back to Trevarno.

*

Meanwhile, in Le Touquet France, Lyndon was surrounded by walking wounded soldiers. Apart from a grossly swollen face and several broken ribs, the only thing that concerned the doctors was Lyndon's complete lack of memory. It was clear he'd forgotten almost everything, even how to shave and fasten his clothes correctly. With the aid of a very patient nurse, he began to eat and drink by himself, though it was a slow laborious task. He could see a little, now the swelling around his eyes had abated, but try as he might he could not form a single word.

43

To Jenna's relief she found a warm welcome at Toy Cottage from Celia Inman. It was a spacious cottage, used as a guest house since Celia had been widowed. Enclosed with a picket fence, the whitewashed exterior walls of the cottage were adorned by a rose which bloomed red and scrambled up to the height of the bedroom windows in the summer.

As Celia showed her around, she told her she'd bought the house off a gentleman called Compton Mackenzie. 'He was a poet and playwright you know, He lived here with his wife Faith for a couple of years…lovely couple. I'm not sure why he came down here to live. Scotland was his heartland, though to be fair, he was English through and through. There was not a burr, growl or gruff to be heard in his voice, begging your pardon, if you have any Scottish relatives.'

Jenna shook her head.

'Aye, well, I do believe he will go on to bigger things. Anyway, it's getting late, Loe House will be a little chilly, so it might be better for you to stay here for the night, and I'll get you settled in down there in the morning. You can have the room Compton slept in, if you want.' She smiled and wrinkled her nose.

'Thank you. You're very kind, Mrs Inman.'

'Not at all my dear, any friend of Amelia's is a friend of mine.'

*

Celia placed a hearty breakfast in front of Jenna the next morning.

'Eat up my dear. We'll take a walk down to Loe House when you've finished. I must say I'm glad James has finally got around to employing a housekeeper - it's too much for me you know, what with the guesthouse. You'll be absolutely perfect for the job.'

'Housekeeper?' Jenna gasped.

'That will be your official title, though you'll find James an amiable employer, and often likes to cook his own dinner, and most likely invite you to join him.' She frowned when she saw the look of consternation on Jenna's face.

'Honest, Jenna, James is a lovely chap - you'll get on like a house on fire.'

'I know. I've already met him.'

'Well then, nothing to worry about. He's away at the moment, up in London, but he'll be back very soon. He normally brings an entourage of friends down with him when he comes home at Christmas. Some stay here, some with him and others at the Halzephron Inn.'

Jenna suddenly lost her appetite. The hope of going to London to be introduced to the art world diminished. It seems she was just to be another helping hand.

*

When Jenna stepped through the door of Loe House and saw the beautiful sea view from the large windows at the front, the vista settled peaceably on her heart. The house smelt a little damp, but Celia said it was because it had been closed up for the last few months. It was clean otherwise. The drapes were sumptuous, and a deal of money had been spent on the furnishing. It seemed a larger house inside than it looked from the outside. As she looked around the outdoor space, there were two terraces set out with tables and chairs, but hardly anything in the way of a garden.

'Nothing will grow down here, it's too salty by the sea,' Celia said, when Jenna commented on this.

'So where do the vegetables grow?'

'They don't. Everything is delivered to the door from Helston. Which reminds me, the telephone will ring at ten a.m. on Monday morning, and Mr Jackson the grocer in Helston, will expect you to have ready a list of groceries that you need. They will be with you at two p.m. the same day. The wine delivery will come on Thursday. You don't need to do anything with those except put them in the cellar.'

Jenna listened in astonishment. 'You said the telephone will ring?'

'Yes, my dear. The telephone is here.' She pointed to the black contraption in the corner of the room.

Jenna bit her lip. 'I've never seen or answered a telephone before. What do I do?'

Celia laughed softly. 'It'll make you jump the first time it rings, for it nearly deafens you. You just lift this handle and speak into the mouthpiece.'

'And say what?'

Celia smiled patiently. 'You say, "Hello, Mr Blackwell's residence. How can I help?"'

Jenna looked down in horror. 'Oh, no, I couldn't - I'd be too frightened.'

Celia patted her on the arm. 'Yes, you can, it is part of the job!'

Jenna swallowed hard. 'Oh, god! and you say it will ring on Monday morning?'

'It will, and as it is Saturday today, you won't have long to wait. I take it you still want the job?'

Jenna looked around the house - what could she say? She'd nowhere else to go. 'Yes, thank you.'

'Good. You can move in today then. Choose whichever bedroom you want, except his, of course.' She grinned. 'You will know which bedroom is his when you take a proper look around.'

Jenna wrung her hands in trepidation.

'You'll be fine, Jenna. Mr Blackwell hasn't been too well recently - he was gassed in the war,' she added in a whisper. 'That's why he needs a bit of help I suspect. If you've already met him, you'll know he's a kind, extravagant, gregarious character and I think you and he will get on just fine. Get yourself settled in and pop back to me for your supper later.'

When Celia left, Jenna inspected every room. Mr

Blackwell's was beautifully furnished with dark mahogany furniture and faced west to catch the evening sun. There were five bedrooms in all. Two at the front, two facing south, and one, which Jenna chose for herself, faced east. It was the smallest of the five, though still larger than she had ever occupied before. The bedcovers in all the other rooms were clean but felt damp and smelt a little musty. The mist had lifted around noon, and a lovely breeze had started to blow, so Jenna decided to pull the covers off both her bed and that of Mr Blackwell's. She put several pans of water on the range to boil and set about laundering them. The others she would do tomorrow, ready for the expected visitors. The next thing she did was to make an inventory of the larder and cupboards, carefully making a list of everything she thought she might need to entertain lots of guests. Jenna was thrilled to find an indoor privy, bath, sink and hot and cold running water from the taps – as long as the boiler behaved – Mrs Inman informed her. The kitchen too had a sink with taps. She lit a fire in the front room and set Mr Blackwell's bedroom fireplace with kindling ready to light when he came home. Soon the front room was toasty warm. Just before supper she brought in her clean laundry, draped it over the clothes horse she found in the outhouse, and left it to air in the warm living room, before setting off back to Toy Cottage for supper.

When she stepped back into Loe House later that night, the damp smell had diminished. Jenna felt as though she'd come home.

After a fitful night, pondering her prospects, or lack of them now, she was up with the lark the next day to launder the rest of the bedding. She tidied Mr Blackwell's clothes into the wardrobe, dusted his furniture and remade his bed. She would have normally made bread first thing in the morning, but until she received her groceries the next day, that chore would have to wait. The thought of the phone ringing tomorrow morning filled her with dread, but she pushed it to the back of her mind and carried on working.

When Monday dawned, she was up again bright and early to iron the rest of the linen. All the while she kept an eye on the telephone. She had no real idea when it would ring as all the clocks told a different time in the house.

When the phone did ring, Jenna was gazing out to sea from the front room window. The sudden shrill of the bell made her spill the cup of tea she was holding. With a shaking hand she tentatively picked up the receiver.

'Yes hello,' she said, forgetting to say what Celia had told her.

'Is that the Blackwell's residence?' the voice on the other end asked, sounding doubtful.

'Oh, err, yes sorry, yes, it is,' she shouted.

'You don't need to shout, missy - I can hear you good enough. You have a list for me?'

'Oh, err, yes, yes, I do,' she shouted again.

'Right then, let's have it, and don't shout!'

Clearing her throat, Jenna reeled off her long list of groceries.

'Blimey,' he said, 'and will that be additional to everything else Mr Blackwell normally has?'

'Oh!' Jenna had no idea what to say to that. 'Erm, yes, yes, it is.'

'Right, missy, it will all be with you at two this afternoon. If you think of anything else, phone me before half eleven.'

'Oh, tha… thank you.' But by the time she had finished talking, Mr Jackson had gone.

Jenna fretted all morning about Mr Jackson's statement, "is this additional to Mr Blackwell's normal list?". Would she get into trouble for buying extra things? Then it occurred to her that she had no money to pay for the groceries when they arrived. With that, she put on her coat and ran up to Toy Cottage to speak to Celia.

'Don't you fret a thing now, maid. Everything is paid for by Mr Blackwell. He settles his account every month with Mr Jackson. If you bought something that's already on the list, then I am sure you'll find a use for it. Now, this is Mr Jackson's phone number, you just dial this if you need anything else during the week.' She smiled kindly at Jenna. The poor girl looked fraught. 'Are you settling in?'

Jenna nodded pensively.

'Good, now will you stay for a cup of tea and a slice of my cake?'

*

The house was clean and tidy, the cupboards full of groceries and the wine cellar groaned under the weight of bottles that had arrived that day. Jenna found that when she'd made her bread and baked a cake, she'd quite a lot of time to herself. This gave her the perfect opportunity to sit outside and paint.

It was colder today, so she wrapped a blanket around her shoulders, but the cold could not take away the feeling of calm that had settled upon her. If she could no longer be at Trevarno, she could find no place finer than this, though it had been a wrench to leave Michael, him being the only connection she had to Lyndon. A deep trembling sigh engulfed her. 'I'll never forget you, my darling Lyndon,' she spoke softly into the air.

44

The sound of waves pounding on the shingle beach drowned the noise of James Blackwell's car as he pulled up to Loe House. Pushing the house door open with his shoulder, James braced himself for the damp, clawing, musty smell which normally greeted his arrival home, but today, the house felt warm and homely. The fire was lit, the furniture polished and the aroma of freshly baked bread wafting from the kitchen made him salivate. He smiled appreciatively, as he dropped his suitcases and went in search of his 'new housekeeper'. He'd learnt of Celia's mistake, when he called en-route home. 'Jenna's a houseguest! Not a housekeeper,' he'd told Celia in alarm.

Celia's hand flew to her mouth. 'Oh, lord have mercy on me! I'm so sorry James, the poor girl has been washing and cleaning for days - your house shines like a new pin.'

*

Jenna was on the lower terrace, painting. James stood watching her for a moment, not really wanting to disturb her, but eager to welcome her and apologise.

He walked a little closer, but still, she did not hear him approach. Almost behind her now, he cleared his throat for her attention.

Jenna dropped her paintbrush and stood up in shock.

'Oh, I beg your pardon, Mr Blackwell. I didn't know you were due home today.' She patted her hair and tried to smooth down her skirt to make herself presentable.

James smiled kindly. 'Don't worry yourself. I should have rung before I set off, but I forgot, but let me first apologise to you. It seems Celia was under the impression that you were my housekeeper.'

Jenna felt herself visibly relax. 'And I'm not?' she asked in delight.

'Good god no, Jenna, I'm so sorry if I didn't make myself clear to you when I offered to help move your career on as an artist. I admit though, the house has never looked as clean, so you have my sincere thanks as well as my apologies.' He grinned.

Jenna smiled too. 'Don't worry. It gave me something to do while I was waiting for you to come home. Apology and thanks accepted.'

James rubbed his hands together. 'Well, I hope you've brought the painting I commissioned from you, I'd like to hang it before everyone arrives.'

Jenna flushed. 'It's in your study.'

'Brilliant, come on, collect your things, I'm dying to see it.'

More than happy with Jenna's painting, James immediately strung the back of the canvas and swapped it with the John Opie painting hanging over the fireplace, filling Jenna with a sense of pride she'd never felt before. Standing back to admire it, James sighed happily. 'It's truly beautiful, Jenna. The depiction of the glistening sea is quite outstanding, it's just as it is on sunny afternoons. I love it. I'll have it framed as soon as possible. Now let's eat. I'm absolutely starving. You cut a couple of slices of that delicious smelling bread that is making my stomach rumble so alarmingly, while I take a look at what Mr Jackson has sent. I take it he included a pressed ham?'

'It's in the covered bowl at the back of the shelf,' Jenna shouted through to the larder.

He brought out the ham and a large cheese and started to uncork a bottle of red wine. 'We'll have a bite to eat before the rabble arrives. Did Celia tell you that a few people would be joining us?'

'Yes, she did. How many are coming and have you any preference as to what you want me to make for supper…. because I don't mind cooking?'

'Oh, god no! We're not feeding them all tonight. We'll have something in the Halzephron Inn.' He handed Jenna a glass of wine.

She looked at him in astonishment.

'What's the matter? You're not part of this temperance

society, are you?

'No,' she answered seriously.

'Do you not like red? Shall I pour you a white?'

'Sorry, I've never drunk wine before. I've taken a little ale and a tot of brandy for medicinal purposes, but never wine.' She gave a small, embarrassed laugh.

'Well, we shall have to remedy that.' He pushed the glass towards her. 'Try it. If you don't like it I'll let you taste a white. My wine merchant has a fine palate, I'm sure we'll find something to your liking.'

Jenna tentatively took the glass and sipped it slowly. The taste was sharp at first before a burst of plum and raspberries exploded on her tongue.

James watched with mild amusement. 'Good?'

Jenna licked the residue of the wine from her lips and nodded. 'I must seem very provincial to you.'

'Not at all - you're absolutely charming.'

Almost as soon as they finished their snack, a beautiful waft of perfume preceded an elegant woman as she pushed through the door with her bags into the kitchen.

'There you are, darling.' She kissed James on the cheek. 'What a journey. We've just dropped Robert and Caroline off at Celia's. Glen's on his way back to the station to pick up Gerald and Jane, they decided to come by train. Oh, hello darling,' she said, spotting Jenna. 'Hillary Stanton.' She held out her hand and Jenna shook it. 'Is this your new house guest, James? She's an absolute peach. Now, where shall I put these?'

'Oh, err, Jenna, which bedroom did you pick?' James asked.

'The back one.'

'The back one! Whatever made you choose that pokey little one? No, I insist you have the front one Jenna, it has a fine prospect, and the sea will lull you to sleep. Come on, we'll move your things. Hill, you take either of the other two large ones.'

'Oh, but James,' Jenna protested, 'What about your

other guests? I really don't mind the back room.'

'Oh, don't worry about them. They'll stay at the inn and Celia's.' He set off to Jenna's bedroom. Jenna reluctantly followed him.

Opening the wardrobe doors, James stood for a moment in confused silence, and then cleared his voice. 'Are these your only clothes Jenna?'

Acutely embarrassed, Jenna nodded. Her clothes were work-worn and shabby and some well over a decade old. 'I haven't been able to shop these last five years. I believe Matthew told you that I've been in hiding….'

He smiled sympathetically. 'Oh, of course, I do apologise for my insensitivity.'

'I can make some new clothes if I have some cloth,' she added hopefully.

James's heart went out to her. 'I'm sure we can arrange something, Jenna. You take these into the other room. I just need a word with Hillary.'

Arranging her comb on the dressing table, she looked out of the large picture window. It really did have a lovely view.

A knock came on her door. 'Hello darling, just me Hillary. Silly me, I've brought so many clothes with me I can't get them all in my wardrobe, would you mind if I put a few in yours.'

Jenna laughed. 'Of course.'

Hillary opened Jenna's wardrobe and cast her eye unappreciatively over Jenna's old-fashioned dresses. 'You know darling, we seem to be about the same size, and I have far too many clothes with me. Say no if you don't like it, but I think this little number would suit you fine.' She held out the most exquisite dress in amber coloured silk.

Jenna was speechless.

'It has a rather nice jacket to go with it. It cost a fortune darling, but it never really suited my colouring, but it should look a treat on you. What's the matter? Do you not like it?'

'Oh no, it's lovely,' Jenna whispered.

'Good, it's yours darling, I don't want it back.' She looked down at Jenna's boots and raised her eyebrows. 'What size shoe are you, darling? Can you get these on?' She kicked off her own shoes and gestured for Jenna to try them.

With great embarrassment Jenna untied her boots to reveal darned grey stockings.

Hillary pretended she hadn't noticed.

Jenna slipped her foot into the shoe. They were roomy but comfortable.

'Good fit?'

'Yes,' Jenna said quietly.

'One moment, I'll bring you some shoes that will go with the outfit.' When she returned with the shoes, she exclaimed. 'Oh, why have you not got the dress on yet?'

'You want me to put it on now?'

Hillary gave a short snort. 'Why yes, we're off to the Halzephron Inn for a bite to eat with the others. The food there is to die for, and you can't possibly go out in that dreadful thing.' She pointed at Jenna's skirt. 'Sorry darling, no offence, but it looks as though you've been scrubbing the floor with it on.'

'I have!' Jenna answered seriously.

Hillary opened her mouth to say something then closed it again. She regarded Jenna for a moment. 'Darling, I think you and I need to go to Truro shopping tomorrow.' She placed a pair of silk stockings on Jenna's bed and gave her a wink. 'I'll be back in a tick.'

Jenna washed quickly, pulled on the soft fine stockings and though it felt wrong to secure them with her old ribbon garters, she had nothing else. The dress felt heavy on her body, but it slipped down her form beautifully and finished just below the knees. She gasped at the draught around her exposed calves – the dress was verging on the indecent. The shoes though were the most perfect fit. They were made from fine soft cream leather and tied with silk ribbons. Jenna walked towards the mildewed mirror and could hardly believe the reflection was her.

A knock came at her door again and Hillary walked through with a gold hair clasp in her hand. 'Well don't *you* look gorgeous? Here darling, brush your hair back and I'll roll it up and secure it with this.'

When she was ready, Hillary gave her a satisfied once over. 'Perfect.'

They met James in the hall who gave Jenna an appreciative look. 'I see Hill has worked her magic on you. You look stunning, Jenna.'

Jenna felt a blush rise. 'Thank you, James, but I fear these shoes will be ruined walking up the lane to the Halzephron!'

'*Walk*!' Hillary laughed audibly as she drained her glass. 'My god darling! James will drive us there. We're not going to *walk* anywhere!'

James picked up his car keys. 'Your carriage awaits ladies.'

'Has Glen arrived yet?' Hillary asked as she checked her appearance in the mirror.

James nodded. 'He said he'll meet us up there.'

Though very shy of her newfound friends, they all made Jenna feel very much part of the group. Jenna had ceased drinking wine after the second glass, knowing full well she would not be able to raise her head the next morning, but this did not detract from the enjoyment of the evening. James's friends were a jolly lot, and the conversation sometimes made Jenna blush. There was talk of affairs and scandals in London, new clubs, music and fashion, things that had never been discussed in Jenna's company before. She was very conscious that the only subjects she knew a great deal about were farming and domestic issues. So, she kept her counsel and enjoyed just listening.

They arrived home noisily just after ten and after a nightcap, all dispersed at eleven-thirty. When Jenna lay abed that night, she felt a pang of guilt that she'd actually enjoyed herself tonight. *It's what Lyndon wanted for you.* Remembering Matthew's words eased her troubled mind, so she sent up a prayer to Lyndon and then slept deep and peacefully.

*

The next morning, Jenna had made bread, tidied the kitchen and laid breakfast by the time James came downstairs at seven. He took a deep appreciative smell of the freshly baked bread.

'Oh, Jenna, I think I've died and gone to heaven, having you in the house. May I?' He stood poised with bread knife in hand.

Jenna nodded. 'It'll still be warm, so it won't cut properly mind.'

'I don't care, it smells delicious.' He cut a slice, dipped his knife into the butter dish then spooned a dollop of strawberry jam on top. 'Oh, heaven!' he sighed as he savoured the piece.

'I understand Hill is taking you shopping in Truro?'

'That's if you don't mind.'

He laughed heartily. 'You are your own person now Jenna, you can do as you please, when you please.' He raised his eyebrows for a response.

Jenna felt an overwhelming gratitude for this man. 'Thank you, James, you have no idea how that makes me feel.'

'Oh, I think I do.' He winked.

When Jenna returned to her bedroom, she found another dress on her bed - a navy day-dress made of fine wool. There was also a pair of low-heeled flesh-coloured shoes and a camel coat.

After a flurry of kisses and goodbyes, Jenna and Hillary left James to his writing and set off in the car to Truro.

When they returned that evening, she was in receipt of a drawer full of new lingerie, four pairs of shoes, three hats and a swimsuit! When Jenna questioned Hillary about the latter, she just replied, 'You'll see darling.' Hillary had also ordered six 'off the peg' dresses to be altered by the dressmaker, two for day and four for the evening. Hillary had also insisted that she buy a new winter coat.

'But, Hillary,' Jenna protested. 'I have a little money saved, but I don't think I will have enough to pay for all this.'

Hillary held her hand up. 'Don't you worry, James is paying.'

Jenna stood open-mouthed.

'Close your mouth darling, it detracts from your beauty. He wants you to have a full wardrobe of new clothes before we go up to London and present you to the art world. You didn't seriously think you could go up to London in your own clothes, did you? I mean, most of them came from the last decade, if I'm correct?'

Slightly embarrassed, Jenna nodded.

'Thought so. There is nothing wrong with 'last decades' clothes down here darling, but trust me on this, you need to wow them in London.' She emphasised with a flourish of hand.

*

The next week was a whirlwind of drinks parties at the house and meals at the Halzephron Inn. Jenna found herself embroiled in a world she could never have imagined before - a world of champagne, laughter and over indulgence.

On Christmas Eve, Jenna took luncheon at Toy Cottage with Celia and Amelia. She threw herself into Amelia's warm embrace. Tears of happiness flowed, on seeing her friend for the first time since her escape.

'Let me look at you, girl,' Amelia said, holding her out at arm's length whilst taking in the opulence of Jenna's attire. 'My goodness, Jenna, I barely recognise you!'

'I barely recognise myself, Amelia. James and his friends have been so kind to me. In fact, you all have, I don't know how to thank you all.'

Amelia, full of heartfelt sympathy, hugged her again. 'I'm just sorry that you lost your Lyndon in the end, Jenna. Charlie Williams brought home the tragic news only last week.'

Jenna's shoulders sank visibly. 'I miss him terribly Amelia. Not a day goes by that I don't cry for him.'

'I know how much he meant to you. Life has been cruel to you, without a doubt, but even bad luck runs out in the end, and according to Celia, James has offered you a rare opportunity to make something of your life. You'll find a way to live your life without Lyndon, because you will always carry him in your heart.'

*

Later that evening everyone gathered at Loe House at six p.m. for pre-dinner drinks, though in truth, Hillary had started drinking at lunch time.

Glen watched as Hillary helped herself to another drink, knowing he would probably carry her home later. 'For goodness' sake Hill, steady on. That gin will kill you!'

Hillary shot him a wry smile, took a sip and answered with a wink. 'No, it won't darling, I intend to live forever.' She raised her glass. 'So far so good, eh?'

Glen pursed his lips and flapped his hand in dismissal.

James patted Glen on the shoulder. 'Don't worry old boy, I'll help you carry her back later on.'

Fuelled with alcohol, Hillary was the life and soul of the evening as usual, though true to form, she faded like a wilted lily around nine p.m. and Jenna feared she would be in no fit state in the morning to celebrate Christmas. She couldn't have been more wrong. At ten a.m. the group gathered at Loe House to fulfil their annual Christmas Day activity - taking a dip in the sea. With everyone dressed in suitable bathing attire, covered by their housecoats, a buzz of excited anticipation generated around the room as they enjoyed a cup of hot chocolate, before piling into their cars to take the short drive around the headland to Church Cove.

The day was bright and cold with a steady south-westerly breeze pulling at their flimsy attire. The sand felt chilly on Jenna's feet and a feeling of apprehension rose in her throat. Lyndon had so patiently taught her to swim, but she'd never swum in the sea before. *Are you watching me Lyndon?* she sent up a private message to him. *I couldn't do this if not for you.*

'Are you all right Jenna?' James touched her gently on the arm. 'You don't have to follow this mad lot if you don't want to.'

'Oh, but I so do want to, James.'

With a gleam in his eye, he grabbed her by the hand. 'Come on then but be careful of the current.'

'Current?'

'The pull of the water,' he shouted as the wind took away his words.

They plunged into the sea together, which was shockingly icy, and within a couple of seconds, Jenna could hardly catch her breath. James was swimming strongly, but Jenna turned quickly to make her way back to the shore. As she struggled to keep upright in the surf, she heard hoots of laughter from the rest of the party.

Gerald, Glen and Robert had run into the sea stark naked, much to the amusement of the ladies of the group.

Jenna came to stand shivering beside Hillary who was just dipping her toes in the water.

'Oh, dear.' Hillary grimaced. 'Why is it that most nudists are people you really don't want to see naked? Come darling.' She pulled a shocked Jenna away. 'Avert your eyes for goodness' sake.'

Shivering all the way back to the house, James served hot toddies to them all as they stood warming beside the blazing fire. Jenna stood in a state of euphoria - her body had never felt so alive. Her heart drummed in her chest and the warmth radiating through her body gave her such a surge of exhilaration, she thought she would faint.

Gerald, Jane, Robert and Caroline took their leave back

to their respective accommodation to bathe and dress for luncheon, leaving Glen, Hillary, James and Jenna huddled by the fireside.

James had lit the cranky, unpredictable old boiler as soon as they returned from their swim and fortunately it had managed to produce some home water.

'Right,' James announced. 'As Jenna has kindly offered to cook our luncheon, I propose she takes the first of the hot water.'

Jenna smiled thankfully. The exhilaration of the swim had now waned, and her skin felt itchy and sticky with dried salt water.

Stood in the bath, only ankle deep to save water, Jenna sponged the hot clean water over her skin. The luxury over her goose pimpled skin felt delightful.

Conscious that others were waiting with salt drying uncomfortably on their skin, Jenna reluctantly cut short her toilet and dried and dressed quickly. Though she had prepared luncheon, there was still a lot to do.

The front room table was set with a crisp white linen cloth. Holly and ivy decorated the furniture tops, and candles lit the table and darkest corners of the room.

With the fire built up, the happy group sat down to a roast goose, parsnips and carrots, followed by plum pudding and mincemeat tarts. Though almost fit to burst with food, a box of fine chocolates finished off the meal before they retired to the fireside to sip brandy.

'Shall we swim again tomorrow then?' Glen asked sleepily.

'Oh, god no, I fear for Jenna's tender disposition should you expose yourself in front of her again,' Hillary slurred.

Jenna blushed slightly.

'You do realise you're all corrupting my new friend,' James said, patting Jenna on the hand.

Gerald grinned then asked, 'What *are* we doing tomorrow then?'.

'Well, darling, I don't know about you, but I'm meeting someone if you must know. In fact, could one of you give me a lift into Helston?'

'Who are you meeting?' Glen asked as he yawned.

'Just a gentleman friend,' Hillary said evasively.

'When are we going to meet him?'

'You may have already met him!' she winked. 'But I'm keeping him away from debauched lot for now.'

'I hope you know what you're doing. You remember what happened last time?' Glen said dryly.

Hillary sighed heavily. 'Yes, darling, but some mistakes are too much fun to only make once! Don't you think?'

Glen sat up and leant forwards. 'You just tell him to be nice to you. Otherwise, he will have me to deal with.'

'You are so sweet darling.' Hillary touched Glen gently on the cheek.

'I've told you, you should marry me,' Glen said, settling back into the seat.

'You just can't afford me, darling,' she laughed, with a glint in her eye.

Everyone retired early that night. Once they had all gone, Jenna began to clear away the debris of the luncheon.

'No, you don't,' James said, taking the pile of plates from her hands. 'You've done enough today. The clearing up is my job.'

He led her back to the fireside and lifted her feet up onto a soft stool. 'You relax.'

'But….'

'I insist. You've made Christmas wonderful for us all today, Jenna, and I thank you for it.' He handed her a nightcap. 'I can hardly wait to take you to London to introduce you to everyone. We'll be leaving on the 27th December. It should take us a few days to drive up. Hopefully we'll get there in time to celebrate the New Year in style.' He chinked glasses with Jenna. 'I intend to stay there until the end of January. I need to see my editor about the first draft of my new novel. You of course can stay on in my house in Bellevue Gardens if you please, but you're equally welcome to return to Loe House with me if you so choose. Frankly, when this lot isn't with me, I quite enjoy the peace to buckle down to write the story proper. You too may find you can paint more peacefully down here. I'll leave that decision entirely up to you.'

Jenna went to bed that night with excited anticipation, but she wished with all her heart she was embarking on this new life with her beloved Lyndon.

45

Though Matthew used a stick to walk with, he'd been desperate to get back in the saddle. He'd acquired a new horse as soon as the war was over. Very few horses made it back to Britain, and those that did were deeply traumatised. New bloodstock had been shipped in from the Americas, and Matthew had selected an eighteen hands black gelding, which he'd named Sultan. It was a skittish thing, but Tommy had done a rare job of settling him down, though the horse still didn't like anyone touching his legs.

'Someone's going to have one hell of a job re-shoeing this beauty, when the time comes,' Tommy said seriously to Matthew.

'I'll take him to Stan the farrier in Crown Town. He has a good way with horses. He whispers to them you know. It seems to work.'

Tommy looked uncertain. 'Are you going far today. Mr Bickford?' he said giving Matthew a leg up.

'I'm going to Trelowarren for the New Year, so you don't have to wait for me.' He patted the horse. 'It's a good long ride and should put Sultan through his paces.'

'Take care,' Tommy said, watching Matthew trot out of the yard.

*

On January the third, the thin crust of frost had made for a slippery morning ride down to Gweek from the Trelowarren Estate. Matthew was on a mission to Dr Eddy's, to see if he could sample one of his cook's wonderful breakfasts. As he cantered over the first bridge Sultan threw a shoe.

Matthew cursed and dismounted. The nearest farrier was Blewett, and he was the last person Matthew wanted to deal with. Reluctantly he led the horse over the next bridge, past Dr Eddy's and into the forge yard.

Blewett scowled, reluctantly doffing his cap at

Matthew. 'And what can I do for you, Mr Bickford?' he said sarcastically, whilst eyeing up the gelding.

'He's thrown a shoe, can you, do it?'

'Has he now? Someone must have done a poor job then!' Referring to the fact Matthew hadn't stepped into his forge for a good few years.

Refusing to be perturbed, Matthew said firmly, *'Can you, do it?'*

'Aye, I suppose I can. You'll have to leave it though. I have other work to finish.'

'How long?'

Blewett shrugged. 'An hour, hour and half.'

Matthew smoothed the gelding's dark neck. 'Very well, I'll be back in an hour. I need to warn you though he's skittish about his legs being touched.'

Blewett sighed discourteously. 'I reckon I can handle your horse. I've managed them for years. Tie him up over there. I'll see to him dreckly.'

Matthew tied the reins over the post, gave the horse a comforting pat and headed towards Dr Eddy's house.

*

Blewett waited until Matthew was out of sight, before walking over to the waiting horse. He was a fine-looking animal and no doubt about it.

'Skittish about your legs, are you? Well, we'll see who wins that battle.' He jerked the horse to come, and the gelding's eyes rolled.

Tying the horse up, Blewett began the process. With the hoof knife in hand, he lifted its foot to clean it, but the horse was all over the place, stomping his front feet and snorting furiously.

'Shut your noise, you stupid animal,' Blewett grumbled as he pared the flaky sole from the bottom of the hoof. Sultan began to twitch his ears and stomped angrily. 'Be still.' Blewett thumped him hard.

Sultan decided he was having none of it. He suddenly lowered his rear and kicked out at Blewett, catching him full on the shin.

Reeling backwards Blewett let out an agonising yowl. 'You bastard,' he said, reaching for his hammer, 'I'll teach you a bloody lesson.' He scrambled back to the horse, but Sultan seeing him approach, reared before he got there. With a vicious buck, it hit Blewett full in the chest, sending him flying into the wall of the forge fire. Blewett sat at ninety degrees against the forge, his eyes staring forward, as the heat from the coals began to burn into his back. He felt the light in the room dim, until a white mist began to swirl around his head. A ringing noise in his ears grew louder above his own breath rattling in his throat. His chin felt heavy and very slowly his head fell forward and George Blewett departed to the next life as violently as he'd lived this one.

*

It was an hour before Matthew returned. By then Blewett's back was charred black, and the smell of burnt flesh caught the back of his throat. He looked from the body to the horse, saw that Sultan was still without a shoe, and ran back to Dr Eddy's as fast as his legs could carry him.

When Constable Treen arrived, Dr Eddy had examined what was left of the body. 'He's been kicked in the chest by the look of it.'

'By this one?' Constable Treen pointed at Sultan.

Matthew nodded.

'Is he yours?'

Matthew nodded again, anxious that his horse had killed someone and the consequences that would follow.

The constable patted the horse's neck. 'Well, he's a fine beast. I suspect Blewett was being rough with him. I've heard one or two reports from people saying their horses came back with whip marks on them after being shod. I don't think any further action will be taken.'

Matthew sighed with relief.

'Have you informed the undertaker?' the constable asked Dr Eddy.

'No, I'm just waiting for my colleague to confirm the cause of death. Then we can issue a death certificate. We'll get Jim Pendeen down then with a coffin.'

'Well, as his wife is dead, I believe his only other relative is a brother in Falmouth. I'll get word to him.'

They all looked at the charred body. 'I don't think anyone will grieve for his passing,' Dr Eddy said gravely.

*

When Amelia heard the news from Dr Eddy, her eyes widened. 'Tell me you're not jesting,' she asked cautiously.

'It's the honest truth - the man is dead.'

Amelia was unable to contain the smile spreading over her face. 'Could you possibly arrange for me to have a copy of his death certificate?'

Dr Eddy raised his eyebrows. 'Why?'

Amelia cleared her throat. 'Well, it's safe to tell you now. Jenna didn't drown that day.'

Dr Eddy gasped.

'Lyndon FitzSimmons and I helped her to escape. She's been in hiding these last five years. Blewett's death certificate will be her ticket to freedom.'

'Well, I'll be. I'll tell you something for nothing, Amelia Pascoe, if I ever need a secret kept, you'll be the one to keep it safe for me.'

Amelia grimaced. 'Lord help me though, for the lies I've told in keeping it.'

'I commend you for it, and so too will the lord, I'm sure. But tell me, I heard the FitzSimmons fellow died in the war - where's Jenna now?'

'London.'

Dr Eddy's eyes widened. 'Well, it'll be my pleasure to give her the freedom she so deserves. Send her my best wishes with it.'

*

Jenna had been in London for a couple of weeks. It had been a three-day arduous journey to get there, due to various problems with both motor cars. Jenna's bottom had been tender from sitting for such long periods of time, and once installed in James's London house it had been a good eight hours before she ventured to sit down again.

London was terrifying and exciting in equal measure to Jenna. With its bustling nightlife in the West End, clubs, restaurants and dance halls, Jenna was in awe of all she was experiencing. James and his friends, though too old to be thought of as the 'Bright Young Things,' certainly made the most of life, mixing with the aristocracy and wealthier classes.

After the spectacular New Year celebrations, Jenna's days were spent either painting, shopping with Hillary or taking tea at the Ritz, and her nights were a heady round of cocktail bars, nightclubs and jazz clubs. She was amazed at the number of motorcars on the road. She'd only ever seen a couple of motorcars before, but here the roads seemed to be full of them. There were people everywhere, including beautiful, confident women passing by her on the street, some even driving motorcars! This was a very different world, but her new lifestyle did not always sit easy on Jenna's conscience. Only a few months previously the end of the war had taken its toll on millions of young men. Those who returned were damaged and haunted by what they had seen. She could not blame people who used this hedonistic lifestyle to escape from reality. They seemed to have an urgency to enjoy life to the full, maybe because so many other young lives had been lost on the battlefields. But not a day went by, that Jenna did not think of all the young men from the Trevarno Estate who fought in the war. Those that died and those who returned like Tommy Teague, maimed and haunted for life. Lyndon of course was never far from her thoughts. She remembered Gina talk about the huge hole in her heart that had opened up when her husband had died. It was true too for Jenna, there would always be a Lyndon shaped hole in her heart.

Away from his friends, James was a very quiet and private person, and Jenna noticed that although he had a great many friends, he had no one person who was 'special' in his life. Of the women who crooned over him at the parties, he pleasantly acknowledged them, but never encouraged any of them.

Jenna had read his books, which were full of intrigue and love. Wasn't it a fact that most of what a writer writes about are taken from their own experience? If so, James knew of love, but showed no outwardly sign of being in love with anyone.

At present he was busy writing his fifth novel and spent most mornings re-writing and editing in his study. He owned a large house in Bellevue Gardens and had given over the upper floor to Jenna to use as her studio, because the room had large windows overlooking the roof tops of the surrounding houses. Almost as soon as they had arrived, he'd set her up with easel, paints and canvas - 'everything an artist could need,' he'd announced with a flourish of his hand. 'As you haven't yet accumulated a portfolio, I thought it would be beneficial for you to collate a body of work over the next few months, so we have something to back up my claim of your artistic talent,' he grinned.

Overwhelmed by his generosity, Jenna said, 'Thank you, I don't know what else to say.'

'You don't have to say anything, just paint! I have every confidence that you will blow them away with your art.'

*

It was the tenth of January, and accustomed to always rising early, Jenna was the first to stir. Out of habit, and because of James's passion for her bread, Jenna's first job was to bake a loaf for breakfast. The rest of the day, if she had no other social commitments, was spent in her studio.

Over breakfast that morning the post arrived, and with it was redirected mail from Cornwall. As James sorted through the letters, he said, 'If you're not too busy, Jenna, I should like you to come to lunch with me today. I'm meeting a good friend of mine and I'd like you to meet him too.'

'Thank you, yes. I'd be happy to come.'

Taking a bite of toast, he ripped open an envelope and out dropped another letter. 'Oh, there's one here addressed to you, Jenna.'

Jenna reached and took the letter. 'It looks like it's from Amelia Pascoe.' As she began to read, she took a sharp intake of breath. 'I don't believe it!'

'What is it?' James asked, noting Jenna's hands tremble as she held the letter.

'My husband is dead! I'm free James! I'm free!' She crumpled the letter to her chest as tears of relief streamed down her face.

Fumbling for his handkerchief, he passed it over the table with a smile. 'Your news gladdens my heart, Jenna. From what Matthew told me, you suffered greatly at that brute's hands. How did he meet his demise?'

'Would you believe it? Matthew Bickford's horse kicked and killed him.'

'Well, hurrah for the horse, eh?' James said, lifting his cup in celebration. 'Bullies always get their comeuppance. So, my dear, this is truly a new start for you. As you say, you are free to live the life you deserve. It also means you can use your real name!'

Jenna nodded as she blew noisily into James's handkerchief. The feeling of relief was incredible.

46

With a lightness of heart, she hadn't experienced for a long time, Jenna made herself ready for luncheon with James and his friend. At the restaurant, Jenna and James were shown to a table where there was seated a handsome gentleman in his early forties. He was an imposing man, with kind, dark eyes and dark brown swept back hair. He was dressed from head to foot in Savil Row clothes.

'Christian, I'd like you to meet Jenna Trevone. Jenna, this is my good friend Christian Jacques.'

'Enchanted, my dear, I'm sure.' He kissed her hand gallantly. 'I've heard a great deal about you from James. Please take a seat.'

Jenna smiled. 'I'm very pleased to meet you too,' she said, noting the gentle smile Christian gave James.

'Christian is not only a good friend - but he's also my lawyer. He deals with all my financial affairs. He's one of the top lawyers in London.'

'You flatter me, James.'

James's eye sparkled with mischief. 'But it's true. I thought perhaps he could be of some assistance to you, Jenna. I believe once your work has been seen by the art establishment, you'll be a rich woman and need someone like Christian to keep your finances in order.'

Jenna shifted uneasily. 'James, you flatter me too. I've hardly started to paint. No-one will want to see what I am doing.'

'I've seen the potential in the paintings you're working on at the moment. You have to start believing in yourself, because your life is going to change, I can guarantee that.'

Jenna felt her stomach flutter.

'I'll be happy to be of service when that happens,' Christian said. 'Shall we order?' He gestured to the waiter.

As luncheon progressed, Jenna watched the body language between the men with interest. There was an easy tenderness with each other. Sharing the same humour, gaiety dominated the conversation. Jenna wondered at their relationship, scolding herself at the very notion.

'Your wife Judith and the children are well I hope?' James asked, as the first course arrived.

Jenna felt a sting of guilt at her earlier presumption.

'They are, James, thank you. Judith sends her regards.'

'Oh, you have children?' Jenna asked, trying to keep the surprise out of her voice.

'I do, Phillip is fifteen and Celine is twelve, going on eighteen.' He grinned.

Jenna laughed. 'So, how long have you two known each other?'

James and Christian exchanged furtive glances. 'About ten years, isn't it, Christian?'

'I believe so yes.'

'I take it you were both in the war?' Jenna asked.

'We were, though poor old James here came out of it the worst with him being gassed.'

Jenna nodded. She'd heard James wheezing alarmingly whenever she walked anywhere with him.

James waved his hand in dismissal. 'The Cornish air helps with that.'

'I'm surprised you spend so much time here in London, James,' Jenna said seriously. 'The air here is dreadful.'

'So it is, but London has things I need, that Cornwall can't provide.' He smiled again at Christian.

*

As the month of January progressed, Jenna made herself ready for her regular Wednesday luncheon with Hillary.

'Where are you going today then?' James asked, watching Jenna put her hat on.

'Some new restaurant Hillary's heard of, I'm not sure where. What about you? You're normally ensconced in comfy trousers and a tweed jacket, scribbling away at your next manuscript by now. It's eleven-thirty, and you're not even dressed yet!'

James was indeed still in his house coat, though freshly

shaved and smelling of cologne.

'Oh, I'm just having a late start that's all.'

Jenna smiled inwardly. Maybe there *was* a lady friend. She leant forward and kissed him on the cheek. 'Well enjoy whatever you do today.'

*

Waiting outside the restaurant, Jenna smiled as Hillary approached.

'Darling,' she said, in a flurry of arm waving. 'Forgive me, something has come up and I'm not able to join you today. You don't mind do you, darling, but I absolutely must cry off.'

'That's fine, Hillary, enjoy your day.'

They kissed warmly and parted company. It was no great disappointment that luncheon had been cancelled. In truth, Jenna would rather spend the day in her studio. After spending her life sketching and painting small watercolours, the novelty of a large canvass and oil paints had given her new vigour. For the past few weeks, she'd worked in a frenzy of colour and freedom, and though her work had a naivety, those who'd seen the few pieces she'd done in the very short time she'd been here, seemed impressed. Her fingers itched to pick up the brush and continue, so it was with relish she walked back to Bellevue Gardens.

Letting herself in, she put her handbag and hat on the stand and made her way to her bedroom to change out of her dress and into one of James's old shirts she wore to paint in. At the top of the stairs, she stopped momentarily - voices could be heard in James's bedroom across the hall. Jenna smiled warmly and wondered who he was entertaining. As she reached for her door handle, James's bedroom door began to open. Jenna swiftly slipped into her own room, but left the door slightly ajar, unable to resist a peek at his visitor.

Her heart jolted as James passed her door, swiftly followed by Christian. As they bid each other farewell at the bottom of the stairs, Jenna glanced across into James's bedroom - his bed was clearly in disarray.

Closing her door quietly, she sat on her bed to gather her thoughts. So, her initial instinct had been correct - but Christian had a wife and children! How could that be? Homosexuality was something Jenna knew of - but had never come across before, therefore unsure of how to process it in her own mind.

*

James did not go to the door with Christian, but he said his goodbyes in the hall. Watching as the door close behind Christian, his heart was full of happiness. He checked his watch and made to ascend the stairs, stopping dead on the first step when he noticed Jenna's handbag and hat on the stand. His heart chilled as his mind began working overtime. *Where was she? Had she seen or heard anything?* Looking up the stairs, he realised he'd left his bedroom door open. Taking the stairs two at a time, he ran into his room, closed the door quickly and leant against it to gather his thoughts.

*

Jenna sat with bated breath. She'd heard James run back up the stairs and close his bedroom door, and then a few moments later it opened again, and his footsteps approached her bedroom door. Jenna sat perfectly still, until she heard him move away again. This was none of her business. James had the right to love who he wished, she just felt very afraid for them both. What they were doing was a criminal offence. If anyone found out, they'd go to prison.

When Jenna heard the sound of the bath taps running, she decided it was a good time to change and steal away upstairs to her studio. He would never know that she'd been in the house, and she certainly wasn't going to tell him, but as she opened her door, James emerged from the bathroom and they both stood stock still in silence.

'You're back early?' James said weakly.

'Yes, luncheon was cancelled I'm afraid.'

James swallowed hard. *Oh god, what had she heard?*

Unsure of what else to do, Jenna moved towards him, gently placing her hands on his arms. She could feel him visibly trembling.

His eyes frantically searched her face for some clue to what she'd witnessed. 'Jenna I ……Did you….?'

'Shh.' She squeezed his arms.

'But…' His face contorted slightly.

Jenna shook her head. 'James don't say anything. It doesn't matter. I'm happy for you, truly I am. Everyone needs someone to love.'

Tears of relief tumbled down James's cheek as Jenna gathered him into her arms.

 Suddenly the front door opened. They parted in alarm as footsteps came running up the stairs.

'James, it's only me, I've left my watch by the…. bed.' Christian faltered at the top of the stairs. He glanced at James and then at Jenna. 'Oh, my god!' he whispered, wringing his hands anxiously.

'Christian.' Jenna moved toward him.

Shaken to the core, he shot an apprehensive look at James. 'Does she know?' he asked, already knowing the answer.

'Christian, listen to me.' Jenna stood between the ashen faced men. 'I've already said this to James, and I'll say it to you too. It doesn't matter what I know.'

Christian's eyes were dark with concern. 'Oh, god, the shame of it!'

'*No,* Christian, do *not* be ashamed of loving someone! I take it this is love?'

He gave a short nod.

'Neither of you have anything to worry about from me. You're both very dear to me. What happens in this house stays here. So please, both of you take a deep breath and relax.'

Christian's eyes flickered towards James then back to

Jenna. 'You must think I'm dreadful. I have a wife and family.'

'It's not my place to pass judgment on you, Christian. This is your life. You must live it in any way that makes you happy.' She smiled gently at them both. 'I'm going up to the studio, so I'll say goodbye to you both.' She moved between them and kissed both men softly on the cheek. 'I'll see you next time you visit, Christian.'

*

The studio held a heady mixture of turpentine and oil paint when James came up to see Jenna half an hour later. He handed her a steaming cup of tea and sat down on a tea chest.

'Thank you, this is just what I needed,' Jenna said, sitting on her chair to face James. She watched him for a moment then asked, 'Are you all right?'

He nodded uncertainly.

'How long?'

'Ten years. We sort of knew as soon as we met.'

'That's nice.'

James laughed darkly.

'I imagine it must be difficult for you both.'

He raised an eyebrow and regarded her seriously. '*That* is an understatement!'

'Does anyone else know? Hillary or Greg?'

'God, no!'

'How on earth have you managed all these years?'

'With great difficulty,' he said, getting up to stand by the window. He looked down on the streets below. 'This house always seems to have at least one house guest staying, so our meetings are few and far between. Of course, we can't go to Christian's for obvious reasons and a hotel would be, well, a little unsavoury to say the least.'

'You're far too accommodating to your friends James, for which of course I am truly grateful for my part.'

He laughed for the first time since he entered the studio.

'Does Christian come down to Cornwall?'

'No, he's never been,' he answered sadly.

'Does Christian's wife know?'

James paused before he spoke. 'She believes he has a mistress and is none too bothered with that fact. They live quite separate lives. It seems to suit them both.'

'James?' she said softly.

He turned to look at her.

'Now that I know, I hope that it will make it easier for you to meet more often.'

James's brows drew together questioningly.

'You won't have to wait until I'm out anymore. I'm normally up here working, so you won't be disturbed.'

James closed his eyes and sighed deeply. 'You really are heaven sent,' he said, stepping forward to hug her.

47

As the end of January approached, James was forced to postpone the journey back to Cornwall. He had unfinished business with his editor, and they'd received an invitation to a lavish ball near the end of February. The delay also gave James and Christian the opportunity to meet up for another few weeks. James looked so much happier these days, though the pollution in London had settled on his chest.

*

Hillary shrieked with delight when she heard that Jenna too was going to the ball.

'God, darling, everybody who's anybody will be there. It's the biggest society event of the calendar. Isn't it James?'

James looked up from his writing and nodded. He was sat by the fire, wrapped in a blanket, looking rather peaky, Jenna thought.

'I rather think we'd be better going back to Cornwall, James, so you can get some fresh sea air into your lungs,' Jenna said seriously.

Hillary waved the suggestion away. 'Nonsense, you'll be back down there before you know it and you can't miss this event, darling. You're lucky to have received an invitation you know. It took me almost three years before I was included on the list - but I won't hold it against you, because you're a sweetie.' She flashed her fabulous red lipstick smile. 'James, I need to take Jenna shopping for a new dress.'

'Of course, you do, put it on my account,' he said as he began to cough.

'It's really not necessary, James,' Jenna protested. 'I have so many dresses.' She poured him a fresh glass of water and handed it to him to alleviate his cough.

Hillary gave her a withering look. 'Good god, darling, you can't possibly wear one of those old things. No, we must dress you to show you off to London society. Mustn't we, James?'

'Of course.' James grinned and coughed again.

'But…'

'No buts, darling.'

*

At the ball, Jenna descended the large staircase with her heart in her mouth. She'd never seen such a gathering. Dressed in an ivory silk drop-waist dress, decorated with emerald green embroidered ferns, ivory heels and a jewelled headband, she gave off an air of quintessential refinement.

James, whose health had improved slightly, met her at the foot of the staircase. 'Jenna, you look stunning. Is this Hill's work?'

Jenna nodded. 'She spent a lot of your money I'm afraid.'

James kissed the back of her hand. 'Money well spent I'd say. Come, I'd like you to meet Francis Knight. He owns The Black Gallery in Cork Street. Where *is* Hillary anyway?'

'I saw her over there with Glen a few moments ago.'

Jenna was led towards a flamboyant, stocky gentleman, with a sizable girth, and a friendly smile.

'Francis, I'd like you to meet Jenna Trevone. The artist I told you about.'

'Enchanted, ma'am,' he said appreciably bending to kiss her hand. 'I believe I would like to see your work, if you would permit. I'm always interested to see anything James endorses. He has a keen eye. We work well together. I'm always on the lookout for something new. Come, my dear let me get you a drink.'

Jenna looked back anxiously as she was led away, but James gave her a wink and smiled confidently to himself. Once Francis Knight saw Jenna's paintings, he would take her all the way to the top of her game.

As he glanced around, his eye caught Christian, who

was here without his wife - she never did like these sorts of affairs. Christian was deep in conversation with a rather shifty looking fellow. There was a short, sharp altercation between them, and even from this distance, James could see Christian's face had paled. Something had clearly upset him. He waited for the dubious looking gentleman to move away from Christian, but when he did, Christian stormed off the floor and into one of the antechambers.

James glanced at Jenna, who too had also seen the altercation, but was still ensconced with Mr Knight, so James made his way around the periphery of the room until he came to the door Christian had gone through.

*

Hillary and Glen, armed with glasses of champagne, were entertaining themselves with the comings and goings of people in the ballroom. Everyone who was anyone was at the ball that night.

'Good god, Glen, who's that girl with Sir Harry?' Hillary said, taking a large drag on her cigarette. They both homed in on Sir Harold King, linking arms with a girl young enough to be his grandchild.

'How old do you think she is, Hill?'

'Who knows darling, few women admit their age. Few men act theirs.'

'I can't blame him though,' Glen said, sipping his champagne.

'Steady, Glen - she's heart attack material.'

'Well, there are worse ways to go.'

'Well don't try it. I've seen you eyeing up our young Jenna. You have no chance there, my darling.'

'I don't know what you mean,' he blustered.

'You practically held her hostage on Christmas Eve.'

'I was merely giving her a seasonal hug.'

She gave him a knowing smile. 'There's a fine line between hugging and holding someone down so they can't get away.'

'Get away with you. My conscience is clear on making a

pass at Jenna.'

'A clear conscience is usually the sign of a bad memory, darling.' She grinned widely. 'Come on, I need more champagne.'

'Talking of Jenna, where is she?'

'She was over there with Francis Knight.' Hillary pointed her cigarette holder in the air and scanned the room. 'Oh, she seems to have gone and so too has James. Never mind, look the waiter is coming around again.'

∗

After arranging a convenient time for Francis Knight to call, Jenna made her excuses and followed James to the door he'd gone through and entered the sumptuous room.

Heavy, burgundy, velvet drapes hung at the windows and rich, gold brocade furnished the many seats. Christian was sat by the fire, his head in his hands. James stood with one hand on the mantelpiece and the other across his mouth. Realising something serious had happened Jenna closed the door behind her. 'What is it? What's happened?' she asked.

James and Christian glanced up at her.

The music out in the ballroom played on, as Jenna moved closer to them. 'Tell me what has happened?'

'Christian has a mole in the press office. They're going to run a story tomorrow morning about….' James closed his eyes as though to rid his mind of what was to come.

'About what, James?'

Christian took a large intake of breath. 'It's about me visiting James at his house!' He made a slight gesture of shaking his head. 'Along with the assumption of why I've been going.'

Jenna's mouth went very dry. 'Do they have any hard evidence about what they believe? I mean, does anyone else know why you visit?'

They both shook their heads.

'They intend to plant the seed of doubt, so people will think 'there is no smoke without fire,' James said grimly.

Christian sighed. 'Whatever they do, it will be enough to ruin my career, my family and,' he swallowed down the lump forming in his throat, 'enough to put us both in jail.'

'But I don't understand why they are interested in you two,' Jenna asked.

James gave a short laugh. 'The press are always looking for a story, especially if you have a modicum of fame, which I have through my books. They've been pestering me, about who you are, thinking we're a couple. They've obviously been watching the house, and seen Christian coming and going, and well, they've just put two and two together.'

'But you could have been visiting for any number of reasons!' Jenna stated.

'They have a photo of Christian adjusting his tie and shirt as he was leaving the house. I'm afraid we're finished,' James said. His face suddenly drained of colour, and he began to wheeze alarmingly.

Jenna quickly cupped his face in her hands. 'James, breathe slowly, come on, slowly now. Christian, can you get me some water?' She looked around. 'There's a jug on the whisky tray there. Come on James, breathe in….. and out… in….and out. Good, here sip this.' She took the glass from Christian who was knocking back a substantial slug of whisky.

When calmness ensued, he looked up at Jenna gratefully. 'I'm not sure I'll survive prison.'

Jenna looked from one man to the other, desperate to find a solution to their predicament. Prison was inconceivable. Conscious of their growing panic, she felt the adrenalin race through her own veins. *There must be some way I can help them, but how?* Suddenly an idea jumped into her head which caught her breath. She furiously tried to rationalise her thoughts. It was true, her heart ached with the loss of Lyndon, but James had selflessly given her the chance to be an independent woman by steering her into the path of influential people. Because of him, her future was financially secure. Jenna could not and would not allow him to go to prison, that much she owed him. She closed her eyes and sent up a private prayer to Lyndon. *Forgive me Lyndon my darling for what I am about to do.* With a deep trembling breath, she allowed a sentence to bubble up into her throat which would change the course of her life once again.

'You will *not* be going to prison!'

'Homosexuality is an offence, punishable by prison, you know that!' Christian said, draining his glass. 'As James said - we're finished.'

'You *won't* be going to prison, either of you,' Jenna reiterated. 'Now, listen to me carefully. If the newspapers want a story, then this is the story we'll give them. The reason you've been visiting us, Christian, is because as a dear friend of both of us, and you've agreed to give me away…. when I marry James.'

James's mouth dropped open.

'You've been coming to the house to help us with our secret wedding arrangements these past few weeks, and to be fitted with a new suit, that explains the adjustment of your clothing.'

'W.. Wait a moment, Jenna, what do you mean when *we* marry?'

Jenna gave James a crooked smile. 'I am well aware that I would not be your first choice of a life companion, but if we were to announce our engagement tonight, in front of everyone, the newspapers would not be able to run the story they want in the morning. So, what do you say? Let's give them a story if they want one.'

James exchanged glances with Christian. 'But, Jenna, it means you *will* have to marry me!'

Jenna nodded. 'I know that.'

He took her gently by the hands. 'But Jenna, you've only just gained your freedom from a bad marriage. You should marry someone who will love and cherish you, as you deserve.'

Jenna smiled weakly as his words caught in her throat. 'I lost the only man I wanted to marry, in the war, James.'

'Oh Jenna,' James grasped her hand. 'I didn't know that. You never said.'

Her eyes filled with sorrow. 'There will never be anyone else for me - so I'm quite willing to marry you, James. I don't expect any commitment from you, but we'll act like a proper married couple to the outside world.' She paused for a moment while he digested her offer. 'So, shall we do it?'

James tapped gently on the mantelpiece. 'It could work,' he answered tentatively.

'It *will* work James!' Jenna stated.

James glanced wistfully at Christian whose face was fraught with anxiety. 'What do you think, Christian?'

Christian nodded. 'Sometimes, my friend, the hardest thing to learn in life is which bridge to cross and which to burn.'

Jenna touched Christian gently on his shoulder. 'There will be no bridges to burn. Nothing will change between you and James.'

With a trembling sigh, James squeezed Jenna's hand. 'Oh, Jenna, if you are absolutely sure, then yes. Thank you.'

Tucking Lyndon back in her heart where he would always belong, she gave James a brilliant smile. 'Come on. Let's announce our engagement to the world. I believe you're a dab hand at spinning a good yarn.'

Jenna linked arms with James as they opened the door to the ballroom and walked straight into a glittering publicity storm.

There was a frenzy of cameras flashing as the reporters gathered around the trio.

'When's the wedding, James?' A reporter asked.

'Easter.'

'Will it be a large affair?'

'Large enough.'

'In London?'

'Of course.'

'Miss Trevone. Have you decided what you'll be wearing?'

Jenna smiled sweetly. 'Why a dress, of course.'

Everyone laughed.

'A white one?'

Though totally shocked at this turn of events, Hillary quickly stepped in and took over the answering of this question. 'Of course, she won't be wearing white, you fool. It would look dreadful with her colouring.'

'Mr Blackwell is quite a catch, Miss Trevone. I would think your parents are pleased with the match.'

'Unfortunately, my parents are dead.'

'Begging your pardon, Miss, so who's to give you away then?'

Jenna pulled Christian closer and kissed him warmly on the cheek. 'My wonderful friend, Mr Christian Jacques will give me away. He's been an absolute godsend these last few weeks, helping us with all the arrangements. I'm honoured that he's agreed to stand in for my late father.'

When the excitement died down and Hillary got Jenna on her own, she said, 'Darling, congratulations, though I admit, I'm astonished at your news. I thought James was a confirmed bachelor.'

'Thank you, Hill,' Jenna said sheepishly.

'To tell you the truth, I always thought he batted for the other side - if you know what I mean.' She raised an enquiring eyebrow. 'How wrong can one be?'

Jenna suppressed a smile.

'I must say, I'm a little put out that you told the press before you told me,' Hillary pouted.

'I'm sorry, Hill. We were keeping it a secret, but the press got wind of our relationship, so we had to go public.' Jenna astonished herself how easily she lied to Hillary.

'Never mind. So, it's to be an Easter wedding then? Oh, do let me help you choose your trousseau. I have form you know.' She swept her hand down what Jenna was wearing. 'You're not… err….' She raised her eyebrows.

'I'm not, and yes, I will need your help, otherwise I shall be married in the skirt I use for scrubbing the floor.'

'What, that frightful thing? Over my dead body darling! Anyway, enough about you, I have someone I'd like you to meet,' she said excitedly. 'Stay there and I'll bring him over.'

Jenna looked up and smiled when she saw Hillary making her way back over to them.

'Now, darlings, may I present my new beau.' She pulled the gentleman from behind her. 'Matthew Bickford.'

Jenna gasped audibly as James leapt to his feet and shook Matthew's hand vigorously. 'Matthew, how good to see you. Come join our celebration. Hillary, you've kept him a secret.'

'If you can keep secrets, then so can I.' Hillary pouted.

'Touché,' James answered.

'This is Jenna, Matthew… James' fiancé,' Hillary said with a raise of the eyebrow. 'Jenna, this is Matthew Bickford from the Trevarno Estate.'

Matthew stepped forward and kissed Jenna's hand. 'We're actually acquainted, aren't we Jenna?'

'Oh, are you?' Hillary looked between the two of them.

'Yes,' Jenna said, 'I've known Matthew for some years. I lived at Trevarno for a time. It's where I met James.' She saw Matthew frown slightly as he sat down to join them.

'Gosh, what a small world we live in,' Hillary said, 'let's order more champagne and celebrate our mutual friendship.'

As James handed a glass to Matthew, he said, 'I see you're walking a little easier?'

Matthew pulled his gaze away from Jenna and nodded, 'I'll always have a limp, but it's better than the alternative. So, you're to be married?' Matthew directed the question to Jenna. He could see her shift uncomfortably under his gaze so turned to James. 'I thought you were a confirmed bachelor, James?'

'Oh, he was just waiting for the right woman, Matthew,' Hillary said, taking a large drag on her cigarette. 'Jenna is perfect for him. I knew as soon as I met her, they were destined for one another.'

'I can see the attraction,' Matthew said dryly.

Jenna truly wanted the ground to open up and swallow her.

'And what of you two,' James asked, 'will we hear wedding bells from your quarter?'

'Oh, god James, don't frighten him away. We've only been together a couple of months,' Hillary hooted. So, you know the Trevarno Estate Jenna? Matthew tells me it has some lovely grounds. He's invited me down at Whitsuntide. Maybe we could all take a visit there one day?'

Jenna smiled nervously.

'Do you dance, Jenna?' Matthew butted in.

'No, not very well,' she muttered.

'Of course, you do, Jenna.' Hillary laughed as she pushed her playfully. 'You've spent long enough practising.'

'Well then James, would you mind if I take your bride-to-be for a spin on the dance floor?'

Jenna looked anxiously at James, who smiled happily at her. 'Be my guest.'

Jenna felt rooted to her seat. 'Oh, no, I'm sure you would prefer to dance with Matthew, Hillary?'

'Oh, god no Jenna, take him. My feet are killing me with standing all night. Go on shoo.' She dismissed them with a brush of the hand.

Matthew was standing now, his hand held out as though he would not take no for an answer. Hand in hand Matthew led Jenna into the middle of the dance floor. He took her in a dance hold and there was a period of icy silence between them.

Jenna took a deep breath. 'Matthew I…'

'It's all right Jenna, you don't have to explain anything. I don't blame you for trying to carve a life out for yourself. God knows it hasn't been an easy life so far. It's just that…well… I loved Lyndon like a brother.'

'I loved him too,' Jenna retorted. 'I still love him!'

'Then have a care for his memory, Jenna and wait a while until you marry again.'

His tone was sharp, and Jenna stopped dancing abruptly, causing confusion on the dance floor.

Matthew took her back in his arms to make her move again. 'I'm sorry to be so harsh, Jenna, but it's only been four months since he died for god's sake.'

'Please, Matthew don't.' Jenna turned her emerald eyes on him.

'It's too soon, Jenna, please wait a while.' Seeing her eyes watering, his brow creased into a heavy frown. 'Do you love James?'

'Yes.'

'Why don't I believe you?'

Jenna felt her shoulders drop. 'Whether you believe me or not, Matthew, we're to be married. I'm really sorry, but there it is.'

'After all these years, I don't believe I know you at all.'

Jenna's lips trembled. *It broke her heart to think Matthew thought ill of her.*

'Michael will be devastated you know?'

'I know, I'm so sorry, Matthew, I'm sorry for everyone, but the wedding is at Easter,' Jenna said, fighting the tears which threatened to fall. 'Now, I would rather like to go and sit down if you don't mind.'

*

Jenna was glad when the night was over. She felt guilty enough over Lyndon's memory without Matthew's condemnation. A few days later, she sat at her desk and wrote to Michael.

Dearest Michael,

I do hope this letter finds you and Gina in good health. I miss you both so much. Life is very different here in London from Trevarno. You will be heartened to hear that I have found some success with my paintings, though I do so crave the fresh clean air of Cornwall.

Michael, it is with great trepidation that I write to tell you that I am to be married to James Blackwell on the 12th April. I beg you not to judge me too harshly, for I know this news will hurt you deeply. James is a good and kind man, but please be assured that Lyndon will always hold a special place in my heart. I will never forget him for as long as I live. He is and always will be my one true love.

With love always
Jenna x

*

On reading the letter, Michael crumpled it in his hand, though he did not throw it in the fire, which was his first instinct. Words could not express his hurt or sadness at Jenna's news. He knew for sure that their correspondence would cease forthwith.

48

James's health was a worry to everyone. His chest infection had returned, and he was now afflicted with an alarming cough.

Jenna eventually called for a doctor who strongly advised that he keep away from smoky nightclubs. The decision was made to drive back down to Cornwall the first week in March, to enjoy a good six weeks of clean Cornish air until they returned to London for their wedding on the 12th of April.

The journey back to Cornwall was as arduous as the journey up. The weather had not been kind, making the roads slippery with water and mud. They stayed over for three nights en-route and collapsed in exhaustion at Loe House late on the fourth day.

Jenna was pleased to see the groceries had been delivered. Celia had obviously put them away. Jenna had asked James to stop in Truro for her to buy some other essentials that she knew would not be on the normal list.

Even though the night was cold and damp, Jenna threw open the bedroom windows to air them, and then warmed some clean linen by the newly lit fire, before she remade the beds.

'You'll make someone a wonderful wife one day, Jenna,' James said ironically.

She turned and smiled.

'Are you still sure you want to go ahead with the wedding? You've been a little quiet since we announced it to the world.'

'I'm absolutely sure James. I've had a lot to think about, that's all,' she said reflectively.

'Do you want to tell me about the young man you lost? I'm happy to listen you know.'

Jenna felt a lump form in her throat but shook her head.

'Well, if ever you do,' he said sympathetically.

*

James's health improved considerably with the Cornish air. He sat wrapped in a blanket writing most days while Jenna brought him drinks of honey tea.

'Jenna, please stop fussing and take yourself off to paint for the day. I can manage quite well on my own, I always did before.' He grinned. 'You must take every opportunity to paint. Francis Knight was really impressed with your work. You have a wealth of beautiful scenery here, so go, go and paint - I absolutely insist.'

Jenna did as she was told and set her easel up on the cliff above Loe House. From here she could see James and could be back down at the house if he looked like he needed anything. She laughed inwardly - James would scold her if she knew why she'd set up here. As it turned out, Jenna lost herself in her painting, and it was James who came looking for her as twilight began to fall.

'There you are. Supper is ready.' He began to gather her things as Jenna stretched the stiffness out of her back. Taking a peek at the canvas, he exclaimed, 'Jenna, this is powerfully evocative.'

'Oh! Is it?'

He laughed heartily. 'You really don't know how good you are, do you?'

She shrugged her shoulders.

Later that night, as they sat by the fireside, James announced that he was going to teach Jack, the landlord's son from the Halzephron Inn, to drive his car. 'He can drive us to the railway station to catch the train back to London. Then when we come back, he can pick us up again. I don't really need my car in London, and the drive just takes it out of me at the moment.'

'Are you still feeling unwell?'

'I'm a little tired that's all.'

'I heard you coughing again last night.'

He nodded. 'My lungs feel so tight.'

'Can the doctors do nothing else for you?'

'Clean air, that's what they recommend,' he said resignedly. 'I can't get that in London.'

She reached over and gently touched his hand. 'Has Christian rung you today?'

James nodded with a smile.

'I'll ask Mr Jackson if he can get us some menthol. It's very good at clearing your chest if inhaled over steam. It might just help you to sleep at night.'

'Thank you, Jenna, you make a fine nurse.'

*

They spent a very pleasant few weeks, enjoying the peace and calm that only Cornwall could bring. Jenna preferred being here, to the hustle and bustle of London, but they both knew they could not put off their return much longer.

Jenna had written to both Amelia and her good friends Kate and Stephen, inviting them to the wedding, with an offer to pay all their expenses, but all wrote back thanking her, wishing her luck, but declining, as it was too far away. The wedding date was Saturday the 12th of April and they had much to plan, hastened by a frantic telephone call from Hillary at the end of March.

'Darlings you absolutely must return forthwith. We have to sort out your trousseau and I simply cannot do that until you are here. What ideas have you had about your dress darling?'

'Erm.'

'Oh, god, don't tell me you haven't given it a thought?'

Jenna's silence confirmed Hillary's worst fears. 'For goodness' sake darling, what sort of woman gives little or no thought to the dress she's to be married in?'

'I'm sorry, Hill.'

'When are you coming back? I need to know!'

'I'll get James to speak to you.' She held the telephone out to James, mouthing the words, 'Help!'

*

London was hot and stuffy when they arrived. Almost

immediately James began to cough. Jenna didn't want to leave him, but Hillary insisted that they must go and arrange everything immediately.

Before going to the couture house, Hillary and Jenna paid a visit to The Black Gallery. In the two months since she had been introduced to Francis Knight, every piece of work she'd produced had been snapped up by him for his gallery and hung with an extortionate price tag - and they actually sold! Jenna was astonished.

'Darling, this is London. People have money here,' Hillary said when Jenna was presented with her first payment. It was more money than she knew what to do with.

'But they're not worth it!' Jenna whispered. 'They only take me a few days to paint.'

'You put yourself down, darling. They really are very good and besides, art is worth what people are prepared to pay for it. Mr Knight is no fool, and people follow his lead in art. You my darling are *'the'* artist of the moment. Everybody, but everybody is talking about you.'

'Are they?'

'Of course, they are, darling' She flashed her fabulous red lipstick smile. 'Now come on, we need to sort out this wedding dress.'

In truth, Jenna's input to her trousseau hadn't been needed. When she arrived at the wedding couture house, everything was waiting for her. Hillary had worked her magic, knowing exactly what style and shade would suit Jenna's figure and colouring. 'Everything is ready, darling,' Hillary said as she helped Jenna into the most stunningly beautiful dress Jenna had ever seen. 'The venue is booked - I've gone for the Oriental Club. It's rather stylish and will appeal to James. You'll love it too. We'll take tea there after this fitting. Now what do you think?' Hillary stood back and gasped in awe. 'Oh, darling, you look divine.'

Jenna looked at her reflection in the full-length mirror

and hardly recognised the woman looking back. The dress was ivory silk and lace, tight to her body, fanning out to a fishtail train. It had a straight neck and fitted sleeves, all scalloped with fine handmade lace.

'I rather think that a halo of tiny ivory and red roses around your head and a bouquet of the same roses will set the dress off perfectly, Jenna.'

'I rather think you're right, Hillary,' Jenna said to her reflection.

*

It was April, the sun was warm and the birds singing happily in the trees above the bench where Lyndon spent most of his time. He'd been moved from the base hospital in Le Touquet, France to the Queen Alexandra's Military Hospital in London in early January 1919. Since then, there had been little improvement in his condition other than him uttering a few incoherent words. For some patients, amnesia was a temporary affliction, so after some debate as to his care, the doctors decided that instead of placing him in an asylum for the mentally unfit, he would be in the care of nurses and doctors at the hospital where amputees rehabilitated to life without limbs.

The days were long and confusing for Lyndon - he had no recollection of day, time or year. Locked in a world of mystifying trepidation, he watched with caution as a gentleman sporting an eye patch, and one trouser leg pinned up, approached him on crutches. He was cursing furiously as he wobbled precariously.

'I'll never get used to this, nurse,' he protested.

'You will, Mr Jones,' she assured him.

'Here, let me sit down a moment. I need to catch my breath.' He sat down heavily on the bench beside Lyndon.

'Damn the bloody Hun to buggery for blowing my leg off,' he grumbled. He gave Lyndon a quick once over, scanning him for visible injuries. 'Bloody hell, if it isn't FitzSimmons. Hello old chap.' He moved his crutches and held his hand out for Lyndon to shake. 'What's up mate?

Don't you remember me? It's Jonesy, Cyril Jones, we met on the train a few years ago.'

Not knowing how to deal with the gentleman's interrogation, Lyndon's pulse began to race. He made to get up.

The nurse accompanying Mr Jones put a gentle hand on Lyndon's shoulder. 'It's all right sir - don't be uneasy.' But Lyndon got up and walked quickly away.

She looked at Mr Jones. 'I'm afraid this gentleman is suffering from amnesia. You say you know him?'

'Aye I do. Well, I'm saying that I know him - we were on a train together for some hours en route to Cornwall in November 1915.'

'You called him FitzSimmons? Do you know his Christian name?'

Mr Jones blew a heavy sigh. 'It was an unusual name if I recall. It began with L I think. Linus or Lionel, I just can't remember. But he was on his way home to the Trevarno Estate in Helston if that helps.'

*

As Jenna walked up the aisle on Christian's arm, James shook his head at the sight of her as she joined him at the altar. His first thought was what a terrible waste this beautiful girl was on him.

Seeing the look in his eyes, Jenna faltered as she neared him, but his face relaxed and smiled softly at her in gratification.

'You look stunningly beautiful, Jenna,' he whispered, squeezing her hand as they prepared to take their wedding vows.

Glen stood to James's right in his role of best man. Christian stood ready to give the bride away and Hillary sat in the front pew with Matthew Bickford, admiring her handiwork, unaware of Matthew's reservations about the marriage.

After a lavish reception attended by many people Jenna had never met in her life, toasts were made and Jenna tossed her bouquet, making sure only Hillary caught it. With a flurry of kisses and goodbyes, they set off on their honeymoon to Nice on the French Riviera.

*

The morning newspaper arrived in the kitchen at Trevarno and Mrs Kent took it straight to Mr Brown's office.

'Oh, thank you, Mrs Kent, just pop it there.' He had the iron poised and ready with his free hand. When he began to smooth the front page with it, he uttered, 'Well, I'll be.'

Mrs Kent came back into the office. 'What is it?'

'Look whose photograph is on the front page! It's only Jennifer who worked here!'

There was a large wedding photograph with the heading:

'The author James Blackwell marries artist Jenna Trevone in society wedding.'

'Artist! She's no artist; I saw her scribble a few things, but I wouldn't call her an artist and look, she's changed her name!'

Mr Brown re-read the headline. 'So she has. Actually Mrs Kent, she wasn't a bad artist. Those four watercolours in the orangery were painted by her.'

'They never were! Were they?' Mrs Kent pursed her lips. 'I never did like those paintings. I always thought they were done by an amateur.'

'Well, she seems to have done all right for herself.'

'Aye, she didn't waste any time moving from our poor Lyndon to him. Who is he anyway?'

'You know, James Blackwell. He came here a few months ago to see Matthew, do you not remember? They asked to see Jennifer, and I had to serve tea to her!' Mr Brown said affronted.

'I bet she relished that. She always did think she was lady muck. I wouldn't be at all surprised if she caught this James Blackwell's eye then.' She folded her arms over her amble bosoms, 'and her making eyes at our dear departed

Lyndon at the same time – tut, tut. It's the quiet ones you have to look out for!'

When the paper returned to the kitchen after breakfast, Mrs Kent left it on the kitchen table ready for Edna to see. Edna put her heavy bowl of potatoes down with a bang and began to peel. Everyone was looking at her.

'What is it? Have I got mud on my face?' She began to rub randomly at her cheeks.

'Seen the paper, have you?' Mrs Kent asked.

'When do I have time to read the paper?'

'Well stop your work and read it now, see.' Mrs Kent prodded the front page.

Edna read the article in silence, turned the paper over and then picked up her knife and began to peel.

'What do you think of that then?' Mrs Kent pressed.

Edna looked up and said darkly, 'I hope her marriage is as unhappy as she made mine.'

*

In Gweek, Amelia Pascoe sat at her kitchen table, cutting up newspaper squares for the privy. She stopped when she saw Jenna's face on the front page. She'd known of the marriage of course, first from Celia and then from Jenna's wedding invitation. Amelia was happy and dismayed in equal measure. A broken heart took time to heal. She hoped with all her heart that Jenna wouldn't regret rushing into this marriage.

*

As breakfast was served at Trevarno a couple of days later, Andrew Bickford picked up the letter on the silver platter and frowned. The address read: *To the occupier, Trevarno Estate, Cornwall.* He ripped it open.

To whom this may concern.

It has been brought to our attention that an amnesia patient residing at *Queen Alexandra's Military Hospital, London is that of a Mr FitzSimmons of the Trevarno Estate Helston. He is approximately 5ft 11 inches, with auburn curly hair and green eyes.*

If you would be so kind as to telephone the hospital as soon as it is convenient so as to ascertain if this gentleman's name and description is indeed familiar to anyone on your estate, we would be truly grateful.

Yours truly,

Dr Anthony Shearer MRCS

Andrew Bickford gasped audibly.

Matthew looked up from his newspaper. 'What is it, father?'

'Here, I think you need to make a telephone call,' Andrew said, handing the letter over.

*

Matthew stood for a moment in stunned silence after replacing the telephone receiver. His mind was reeling. He rang for the car to be brought to him. There was no doubt about it, he must go back to London to see for himself if a miracle had really happened.

49

Matthew had been away from Trevarno for three days when Mr Brown answered a call from him, requesting that he bring Michael to the telephone immediately.

Michael was brought grumbling from his vegetable patch. 'Are you sure he wants to speak to me?'

'That's what he said.' Mr Brown led him into his office.

Never having used a telephone before, Michael picked up the receiver with great trepidation. 'Hello,' he yelled.

'Michael, sit down, I have something incredible to tell you.'

*

The news of Lyndon whipped around Trevarno like wildfire. Edna stood stock still in her tidy cottage following the revelation. Her mind whirled with mixed emotions. It was a miracle he was alive but was still angry with him for his indiscretion with Jennifer. However, it seemed that Lyndon had completely lost his memory. So maybe there was a chance that they could rebuild their marriage, especially now Jennifer was out of the way. She knew it was Lyndon's intention to leave her for Jennifer, which would have meant a divorce and the loss of her home. Yes, she would make a determined effort with him - she would even sleep with him if she had to, so that when his memory returned, she might, just might, hold on to her beloved cottage.

*

After hours of waiting patiently for Matthew to return with Lyndon, Michael fell on his son and sobbed with relief at seeing him again. He ushered him into the cottage and settled Lyndon in a chair by the fire and hugged him again awash with tears.

Lyndon's eyes darted around the room uneasily. He'd had a truly terrifying drive down to Cornwall in Matthew's car, holding on with white knuckles as the road sped past him at alarming speed. The journey, which had been punctuated with several stops in order for him to get out and vomit, made him more fearful than being taken away from his orderly life by this stranger who clearly knew him. He glanced down at the unknown man sobbing at his feet and had no idea who he was or why he'd been brought here.

'Lyndon, my boy, you are home with us at last,' Michael said and then looked up in astonishment when the front door opened and Edna burst passed Matthew and flung herself at Lyndon's feet.

'Lyndon love, you've come back to me,' she gushed.

Clutching the arms of the chair Lyndon's body tensed at the encounter.

'What the *hell* are *you* doing here?' Michael got up off his knees and glowered at Edna.

'He is my husband - I have a right to be with him!'

'The devil you have.' Grabbing her by the arm he yanked her away from Lyndon. 'If you think that because he's lost his memory, you can worm your way back into his affections, you have another think coming! Your indifference to him is the first thing I will remind him of as soon as he's better. Now, get out of my house woman!' He pushed her unceremoniously out of the door.

'*He's my husband!*' she shouted, hammering on the door as he closed it behind her.

Lyndon felt totally and utterly disorientated at the altercation. What with strangers in the room, doors slamming and constant shouting from that woman, he felt his eyes fill with desperate tears. *Oh, god! Let me out of here.* He stood up, pushed past Michael and Matthew and ran outside.

'Damn that woman,' Michael hissed as he set off after Lyndon. He found Lyndon walking aimlessly in the middle of his vegetable patch. He was caked in mud and deeply distressed. Very gently he grabbed Lyndon by his jacket sleeve and pulled him out of the mud.

'Come on, son, you're coming back home with your old

pa. I'll make sure there are no more disturbances to upset you.'

Lyndon sighed resignedly. He had no other option but to follow him.

*

The weather in Nice was incredibly hot. Jenna had found sanctuary in the shade of a small café. During the last two weeks of their honeymoon, Jenna's and James's paths hardly crossed. James was researching his next book and Jenna spent her days walking and visiting art galleries. They came together only for evening meals to share their experiences of the day. It seemed this was how their married life would be conducted. There were worst ways to spend her days, Jenna thought, remembering her life in the forge with a shudder. She missed life on Trevarno though. She missed her goats and her cheese shed, Gina and of course Michael. She hadn't received a reply to the letter she'd sent to Michael. Though not entirely surprised, it made her heart sore that she had lost his love and respect. During the long nights spent alone in bed, her heart yearned for Lyndon's touch. For over six years, and through hell and war, they had loved each other, but they'd only spent one night together. The memory of that night, his gentleness and love, she would cherish forever.

*

Lyndon fell into a routine during those first couple of weeks home. Michael, aware that any altercation with Edna would set his recovery back, kept him constantly busy beside him. Lyndon felt safe and relaxed for the first time in a long time. Matthew had paid for Lyndon to see a specialist in the field of amnesia at the Royal Cornwall Hospital, and though it was not always the case, he told them that many patients regained some or most of their memory eventually. Heartened to hear this news, Michael spent long hours filling in the gaps of Lyndon's life, hoping and praying something would spark his memory.

*

On May 1st Lyndon sat on his bed, casting his eyes around the room that seemed to trigger an odd sensation of familiarity. He got up and pulled open his drawer, to see if his mother had placed a clean shirt in there for him. He frowned. His shirts were there, but in a crumpled pile, which puzzled him. Pouring water into his pitcher, he began to shave.

Washed and dressed, Lyndon made his way down the stairs into the kitchen to where Michael, or Pa as he liked Lyndon to address him as, was making breakfast.

'Morning son, how are you feeling today?'

Different he thought, but he just smiled and nodded.

Every morning, Michael placed a bowl of porridge in front of him and then dropped a generous dollop of honey in it. Everyday he'd said the same words, 'I'll put some honey in for you because I know you like it.'

Today when the bowl of porridge was placed before him, Lyndon automatically reached for the honey jar.

Michael's mouth dropped open, watching for any other signs of normality. Nothing else seemed forthcoming until Michael, finishing his own breakfast, said, 'Come on son, time for work.'

Lyndon nodded then said in a very rasping voice. 'Has any work come in for me?'

Michael stood agog with his jacket half on. These were the first words Lyndon had uttered. 'And what sort of work would that be then?' he asked tentatively.

Lyndon frowned. 'I..I don't know,' he croaked.

Sitting back down, Michael reached for Lyndon's hand. 'Are you starting to remember things?'

Lyndon shrugged.

Later that day, Michael and Lyndon sat outside their cottage enjoying the warmth of the evening. They both looked up when Matthew rode by.

'Good evening, gentlemen.'

'Hello, Matthew,' Lyndon croaked.

Matthew shot Michael a curious look, pulled Sultan to a

halt, and dismounted. 'Do you remember me, Lyndon?'

Lyndon held his throat, which was sore and scratchy after being mute for so long. 'I think I do, yes. We used to play in those meadows over there.'

Matthew sat beside him. 'That's right we did. We've been friends for a long time.'

Lyndon nodded, but Matthew could see his eyes remained distant.

Michael stood up. 'Will you share a mug of ale with us Matthew?'

'Thank you, Michael, I will.' He turned his attention back to Lyndon. 'Lyndon, we served together in the war, do you remember? We all went, Tommy Teague, Jimmy and Peter Hoskins, do you remember them?'

'Erm ….' He gave Matthew a puzzled look. 'I think so.'

Michael produced three mugs of ale. As he handed one to Lyndon, he took the mug gratefully and said, 'Thank you, Pa.'

Michael's eyes filled up. 'Oh, son, you remember me now?'

Lyndon nodded. 'Where is Ma?'

Michael blanched. 'I'm sorry son, your ma died over seven years ago.'

Crestfallen, he nodded. 'I did wonder. I haven't seen her all day and there were no ironed shirts in my drawer this morning.' He glanced between his pa and Matthew as an enormous sadness filled his heart. He gave a quivery smile before taking a sip of ale.

'What do you know about hedge laying, Lyndon?' Matthew asked.

Lyndon shrugged. 'Nothing, why?'

'You used to be a master hedge layer.'

'Did I?'

'We'll take a walk around the estate tomorrow if you want. Maybe something will spark your memory, now a little of it is coming back.'

Lyndon jutted his jaw out and nodded.

Matthew drained his mug and patted Lyndon on the back. 'It's good to have you back my friend.'

Lyndon smiled uneasily.

Michael held the reins of Sultan and gave Matthew a leg up. 'This is splendid news.'

Michael nodded in agreement. 'What happens when he asks about Jenna though?' he whispered.

'We'll cross that bridge when we come to it. I'll be back for Lyndon in the morning.'

*

The news that Lyndon was regaining his memory reached the kitchen staff the next morning.

'That must be a great relief to Michael,' Mrs Drake said, pulling the bread dough from her bowl.

'I agree,' Mr Brown answered. 'I believe Matthew is taking him around the estate this morning, so they may pop in to see if he remembers any of us.'

Everyone in the kitchen glanced at Edna, but she kept her head down, concentrating on peeling the potatoes visibly shuddering.

Mrs Drake stopped her kneading. She'd never forgiven Edna and her family from banishing Jennifer, the best kitchen help she'd ever had, from Trevarno. She smiled wryly. 'What's the matter with you, Edna? Someone walking over your grave is there?'

Edna shot her a withering look. She knew Michael would relish telling Lyndon about her part in the banishment of Jennifer and was sure he would try to divorce her now. She wouldn't go without a fight though - after all she was the one who'd been wronged and there was no way she was going back to her mother's house with her noisy siblings.

*

Down near the woods, Matthew stood with Lyndon at the hedge he'd laid almost five years ago.

'Do you remember doing it?' Matthew asked.

Lyndon shook his head as he ran his fingers along the

pleats. Some had re-grown to make the hedge lush and bushy, but others were now brown twigs, their use over.

'Here.' Matthew handed Lyndon his billhook.

Lyndon turned the billhook in his hand.

'My grandfather had this made. I believe he gave it to me when he retired.'

'That's right.' Matthew nodded. 'Do you remember how to use it?'

'I don't know, maybe.'

'There is a gap in the hedge down here. Come and show me how it's done.'

Lyndon stood for a long while, turning over in his mind which branches to pleach and which to leave standing. He shrugged his jacket off, flexed his hands and went to work. He worked for several hours. By the time he'd finished, his soft hands, not used to working these past few months, were now cut and bruised from his day's toil, but he felt renewed for being out in the fresh air.

Back at the cottage, and before supper, Lyndon washed off the dirt and sweat of the day and reached into his drawer for a fresh shirt. As he did so, his fingers touched a small vial at the back of the drawer. He brought it out and studied it. It certainly wasn't his! Maybe it belonged to his ma? He uncorked the tiny vial and closed his eyes as the aroma of jasmine hit his senses. Suddenly he was back in another world. Locked in his sinuses, the jasmine played tricks on his mind. There was a woman, a blonde, lithe, happy woman in a meadow. He could see her from where he worked, walking slowly through the long grass, trailing her soft hand across the tops of the barley. An overwhelming sense of well-being overtook him as he held the vial to his chest.

'Jenna,' he whispered happily. Suddenly his eyes widened. 'Oh, god! Jenna where are you?' he yelled, as he thundered down the stairs and burst into the kitchen.

Michael dropped the cutlery he was holding and grabbed Lyndon by the arms.

'Where's Jenna, Pa?' he asked, frantically struggling to free himself from Michael's grip. 'Her husband hasn't found her here, has he? Oh, tell me he hasn't found her?'

Michael pushed his back against the door to bar Lyndon's way from leaving. 'Lyndon, listen to me,' Michael said firmly, 'Jenna is safe.'

'So, he hasn't found her?'

'No, son, there is nothing to worry about there. Blewett is dead. He was kicked in the chest, whilst shoeing Matthew's new horse. I assure you Jenna is safe.'

Lyndon drew a deep shuddering breath. 'Well, where is she? Why is she not here?' He searched Michael's face for answers.

Michael felt a chill in the pit of his stomach for what he was about to disclose. 'Come and sit down, son, I need to tell you something.'

Lyndon dropped heavily on the chair as Michael handed him a glass of brandy and began to explain about the letter Edna had found in his uniform pocket. 'Edna made such a fuss about your affair Jenna had no option but to leave.'

Lyndon ran his hands through his hair as his mind worked furiously. 'So where did she go?'

Michael wiped the perspiration forming on his top lip. 'I believe she's in London.'

'London!' His eyes widened in astonishment. 'What is she doing in London?'

Michael got up and walked anxiously towards the fireplace. He'd no idea how to tell his son the next fact.

Lyndon's eyes darkened with concern. 'What is it, Pa?'

'The art establishment in London have seen Jenna's potential and she's become quite successful.'

Lyndon threw his head back and laughed with joy. 'Well, that's wonderful news. Do you know where in London she is? I must go to her. I'm so happy for her, she deserves this.'

Lyndon noted Michael's face pale significantly.

'Oh, Lyndon,' he said, rubbing his face with his hands. 'Jenna has also re-married.'

Unable to decipher what was being said to him, Lyndon laughed incredulously. 'What?'

'I'm so sorry, son.'

Shaken to the core, he whispered, 'Who the hell has she married?'

Michael took a large intake of breath. 'James Blackwell, the writer. I believe we've read some of his books....' his words faded away.

Disbelief washed over him. 'No! I don't understand it. She loves me! We've loved each other for six years. Why.....why would she marry someone she hardly knew?'

'I don't know son. Jenna thought you were dead. Matthew thought perhaps... money!'

'No, I will not believe she would marry for money,' he said vehemently. 'Jenna is the most un-materialistic person I know. She wouldn't do that!' His throat felt raw with grief. 'Oh, god, was she pregnant? Did Blackwell take advantage of her?'

Michael shook his head. Matthew said they announced their intention to marry at the end of February and were married on the 12th of April.

Lyndon felt his jaw slacken. 'Matthew knew? Why the hell didn't he stop her?'

Michael moistened his dry mouth. 'He did try, but she wouldn't change her mind.'

The room fell silent but for the crackling embers of the fire. Lyndon looked into his brandy glass - it was as empty now as his heart. 'I can't have lost her again, it's just not possible!' his voice cracked with emotion. He stood up wearily, grabbed his coat and walked out into the night.

A million stars burned bright in the night sky as Lyndon walked slowly down to the bottom meadow. An owl hooted and was swiftly answered in the distance. Bramble, sensing someone at the gate, made her way to greet her visitor. She snorted softly and rubbed her soft nose against Lyndon's hand.

'She saved your life old girl, didn't she?' He patted her woolly coat. 'Oh, Bramble, what the hell am I going to do without her?' He squeezed his eyes shut and shoved the gate violently with pent up emotion. Bramble whinnied and stepped back, shook her head crossly and moved back down the field away from Lyndon.

He turned towards the night sky. 'Why, oh why, did you marry so quickly?' His voice disturbed the rooks nesting in the trees, making them squawk hideously. With his mind whirling alarmingly, he buried his head in his hands in despair. The sounds of the night dissipated, replaced by the unreal quality of a bad dream. A hot thumping feeling of dread pounded through his head as he crumpled to sit on the cold hard earth.

For several long hours he sat, until his body ached with the cold and damp. As dawn broke, he stood wearily and slowly made his way back home.

The fire in the cottage had collapsed into a pile of grey ash. His pa stirred in the chair, woken by the smell of the cold damp earth which clung to Lyndon's clothes.

Michael looked up at Lyndon, whose face was devoid of expression.

'Are you all right?'

Lyndon nodded. 'What's done is done Pa,' he said judicially, before climbing the stairs to bed.

Shedding his clothes, he lay in his bed and closed his eyes. Jenna came to him. Her lovely face, framed by jasmine perfumed hair. His eyes looked at her and she looked back and smiled. Lyndon opened his tired eyes and reached out, but she was not there.

*

Apart from a dull headache, the next couple of weeks saw Lyndon make a full recovery. It was time to speak with Edna.

Having been asked to meet him in the cottage, Edna stood in her kitchen, fists thumped into her waist, ready for battle. The moment Lyndon stepped through the threshold of their cottage, she announced, 'I know Michael's told you why Jennifer has gone, but as your wife I was well in my right to make her go!'

Lyndon threw his coat on the chair behind the door and matched her stance. 'Well, there's the thing you see Edna, I don't believe you are my wife. I'm not a fool, except for the foolish act in the stable that harvest night. I know we didn't have full intercourse that night, and I now believe you duped me into marrying you, because you were never pregnant, were you?'

'I was too!' she shouted indignantly.

'No, you weren't! You wouldn't let a doctor attend you when you supposedly miscarried. Nor did you look like you were suffering any loss the next day. So, Edna, I've arranged for the doctor to examine you today. He'll confirm my suspicions that you are still a virgin.'

'*No*!' Edna visibly shrank in front of him.

A knock came at the door and a doctor stepped through.

'Good afternoon to you, Dr Nance. I trust this examination today will be conducted with the utmost discretion.'

'It goes without saying, sir,' the doctor assured him.

'Edna, go upstairs. Doctor, I will be in the room, but I will not watch.'

Edna was distraught. 'No, Lyndon, don't do this to me please.'

Lyndon stared right through her. It was not in his nature to be cold hearted, but this must be done. 'Go upstairs, Edna,' he said flatly.

Edna sobbed throughout the examination. When the doctor had finished, she pushed down her petticoats and cried into the pillow.

Lyndon looked at the doctor as he washed his hands.

'Your wife is still a virgin, Mr FitzSimmons.'

The relief was palpable. 'Thank you, doctor, I'll see you

out.'

When the doctor left, Lyndon built up the fire in the kitchen and sat at the table. With a mug of tea in one hand, his other drummed on the table top. It was almost an hour before Edna descended the stairs.

Edna slowly looked around the home she'd made for herself before she spoke. 'So, are you leaving me?'

'No, Edna, you're the one who's leaving. As you had Jenna banished from this estate, I am banishing you from my cottage. This letter from the doctor will be used to annul our marriage.' He stood up. 'I want *you* and your things gone by this evening.'

50

On May the 5th, Matthew received word from Hillary that James and Jenna had returned to Cornwall because of his health. Due to the worried tone of her letter, Matthew decided to visit them.

The day was warm and breezy. James was walking along the shingle beach when Matthew arrived at Loe House. He found Jenna on the terrace, arms folded, deep in thought, looking out towards the beach. She was beautifully dressed from head to toe in the best of London couture - a far cry from the emaciated woman dressed in black rags, he'd encountered when she'd been Blewett's wife.

She turned towards him when he approached.

'Hello, Jenna. Hillary told me you were home,' he said stiffly.

Jenna felt the marked reserve between them keenly. 'Hello, Matthew. It's good to see you,' she replied cautiously.

He smiled briefly.

Unable to tolerate the icy silence, she said, 'Matthew, please don't be angry with me for marrying James.'

'I'm not angry with you, Jenna, I'm just sad for my friend Lyndon,' he said tartly. 'You'd better sit down. I have something to tell you.'

Jenna's head tightened and her world tilted as Matthew told her the news. She opened her mouth but was too shocked to speak.

Matthew sat down beside Jenna and cupped his hand over hers. 'None of us knew something like this would happen, but oh Jenna, I wish you'd have waited a while longer before marrying James. Lyndon has taken the news of your marriage very hard.'

Burying her face in her hands, Jenna could hardly breathe for the pain growing in her heart. 'Please don't berate me. It was something that I felt I had to do.'

Matthew blew an exasperated sigh. 'Well, I'm sorry Jenna, but I can't think of a single reason why you felt you had to do it. I'm not even sure you're in love with James. I've never once seen you be demonstrative with him.'

Jenna's distress turned to anger. 'My relationship with James is really none of your business, Matthew. If we cannot be friends anymore, and it's clear to me that we cannot, we must agree to be civil and let the matter rest there. Now please - your news has greatly distressed me.'

Abashed, Matthew reached out to her. 'Forgive me, Jenna. You're right. I've no right to question you. We've known each other a long time. I'd like us to stay friends. I'm simply trying to fight Lyndon's corner for him, you have to understand that.'

'I know, Matthew,' she said, her anger diminishing. 'I do understand your concern for Lyndon, but what is done is done.' Her eyes filled with desperate tears.

Jenna could see James, walking back up from the beach and wiped her face with the back of her hand.

'How is James?'

'Not in the best of health, I'm afraid. He normally fares better in the clean air down here, but….'

'Are you saying it's serious?'

'I don't know, maybe.'

'Jenna, is that why you…?'

'No, Matthew - It's not why I married him.'

*

It was blowy on the beach. The exertion of the walk had tired James, but it was something he forced himself to do most mornings. His chest protested, but his heart needed to experience the elements. He dodged a wave as it licked the shingle beach. Sunlight winked periodically through the scattering of white clouds, as seagulls drifted and cried gently on the breeze. At the water's edge he felt alive, but he knew his health was failing. He waved on seeing Matthew with Jenna and made his way back up the beach to Loe House.

*

They both stood to meet James as he walked down the terrace steps.

Jenna had composed herself as best she could. She smoothed down her skirt and said cheerily, 'I'll make us all some lunch, shall I?'

'Thank you, Jenna.' Seeing her tearful eyes, he asked, 'Are you unwell, my dear?'

Jenna smiled and nodded. 'A little sand in my eyes, I think.'

James watched thoughtfully then turned his attention to his guest. 'Matthew, it's so good to see you, my friend.' They shook hands vigorously. 'How are you?'

'Well, more to the point, how are you? Hillary's fretting about you.'

'Bless her. Tell her the grim reaper isn't stood behind me yet.'

Matthew raised his eyebrows. 'Are you expecting a visit from him?'

James glanced towards the house. 'I think he may be planning a trip to Loe House in the near future. I saw a doctor in London last week who confirmed my fears.'

'Oh, god, James, I'm so sorry.'

James waved away his concerns. 'Don't be. I've had a very successful, albeit shorter life than I had hoped for, but it seems that the Hun got me in the end.' He thumped his chest and gave a dry smile. 'My lungs crackle like firecrackers now.'

Matthew's face paled. 'I take it Jenna doesn't know how serious it is?'

'Not yet - please don't tell her. She'll fuss over me and neglect her paintings if she knows it's serious.' He gestured to Matthew to take a seat. 'She's become very successful in London you know?' he said proudly. 'I don't want anything to stop her creativity. Anyway, tell me Matthew, how is life at Trevarno. Do you see anything of your friend the hedger? I remember watching him work one day on the estate, and often think about him.'

Matthew faltered slightly. 'Lyndon?'

'Yes, Lyndon, that's the chap. Is he still on the estate? Did he come home from the war unscathed?'

'Not entirely unscathed no,' he answered evasively.

'He was bloody good at his trade. Nice chap, though I recall he was unlucky in love. Did he ever win his lady?'

'Um, no.'

James clicked his tongue. 'That's a shame. I can't recall what the problem was?'

Should he tell him? Matthew pondered momentarily. 'He fell in love with someone promised to another, who turned out to be a rather unsavoury violent man, who beat her.'

James frowned. 'Oh, yes, I remember now. Is she still with her violent husband?'

'No, Lyndon eventually helped her to escape and brought her to Trevarno. Unfortunately, by then Lyndon was betrothed to another.'

James nodded. 'That must have been very difficult for them both.'

'Well, most of that time Lyndon was away at war. I believe they rekindled their love during their separation via letters. They planned to go away together on his return, but Lyndon was reported dead just before the armistice. Unfortunately, a 'last letter'- you know the one we all write just in case - well that turned up in his uniform when it was returned to his wife. Unfortunately, the letter wasn't written for her, thus bringing their love affair to light. As you can imagine, this caused ructions on the estate and the girl had to leave.' He paused for a moment. 'We found out in April that Lyndon wasn't dead after all, but in hospital in London suffering from amnesia.'

James's mouth dropped. 'This is incredible Matthew. It's like a plot from a novel! So, has Lyndon regained his memory?'

'He has. It returned fully last week.'

'That's such good news. So, where's the girl now? Is

there not to be a happy ending?' James looked searchingly into Matthew's face. 'From the look on your face, I take it - no.'

'By the time his memory came back…. the girl had re-married.'

'Really? Whatever made her do that so soon?'

'I don't know,' Matthew said, directing the question in Jenna's direction, as she emerged from the house with a plate of sandwiches.

James followed his gaze, baulking in realisation.

Jenna placed the tray of sandwiches down. 'Is everything all right, James - you look a little pale?'

He nodded.

'I'll just go and get the tea tray then.' She set off back to the house.

'Oh, god.' James stiffened. 'Lyndon was in love with Jenna! Wasn't he?'

Matthew nodded slowly.

James raked his fingers through his hair. 'I knew she'd had a violent husband, but she never told me about Lyndon. You should have told me, Matthew, the day you introduced us, you should have told me then about Lyndon.'

Matthew twisted his mouth. 'Their love affair wasn't common knowledge, and to be truthful, I didn't think she'd fall in love and marry you!'

James's eyes widened. 'Oh, Matthew, Jenna and I aren't in love. She agreed to marry me to stop a scandal from breaking. I don't want to go into any details, but if she hadn't married me, a good friend and I would have gone to prison… if you know what I mean?' he said abashed. 'Truly, Jenna and I are married in name only!'

Jenna returned with a tea tray. 'You two look deep in conversation, shall I leave you to it?'

They both smiled nervously. 'No, it's nothing important,' James answered, his voice wavering slightly.

51

The month was June, but the remnants of a summer storm had left the weather cool and inclement. Unable to walk along the beach, James now sat on the terrace, wrapped warm in a tartan blanket to keep off the chill. Beside him was his writing pad, but he'd written nothing today.

Jenna tried the phone again, but the storm had brought down the line three days ago and it was still dead. Five days previous, it had become clear to Jenna that James was dying. The doctor confirmed her fears. At the window, Jenna looked out at James sitting on the terrace. In their hearts they both knew this would be his final day on this earth and sitting watching the sea in his beloved Cornwall was where he wanted to spend it.

Only one thing was needed now, but with the phone lines down, Jenna feared it would not happen. A few days ago, when it had become apparent that James was desperately ill, Jenna had phoned Christian at his office, but was told he was away on business. Careful about what she could say, she had left a short but urgent missive with his secretary: *Jenna Blackwell would not be returning to London for the foreseeable future, due to her husband being gravely ill.*

Jenna knew Christian would have phoned James on receipt of her message. Unfortunately, the storm now rendered that impossible.

*

Jenna made two cups of beef tea, though she knew James would probably not drink his, he hadn't eaten for two days now. Not even Jenna's delicious homemade jam and scones could tempt his taste buds. She stepped out onto the terrace with her tea tray, just as Jake the postman arrived.

'Good morning to you, Mrs Blackwell.' He waved a letter in the air and Jenna's heart soared. With luck this would be from Christian. Placing the tray on the table, she took the letter - the postmark and handwriting made her smile.

'How's Mr Blackwell today? I heard from Celia he'd taken a turn for the worse.'

'He's enjoying the sea air, Jake. Thank you for asking.'

'That should put him right then. There's nothing like the sea air to blow away the germs.'

Jenna smiled gently. *If only that was the case.*

'Give him my best. I'll see you both tomorrow perhaps.' He touched his cap.

Jenna smiled sadly.

James had his eyes closed but opened them as she approached.

'Beef tea?'

He smiled and gestured for her to put it on the table.

She sat beside him and passed him the letter.

His eyes brightened. The handwriting was clearly familiar to him. Glancing first at Jenna, he swiftly ripped it open.

My dearest, dearest friend, you have been, and always will be, loved. When the light goes from your life, it will also leave mine. You will stay forever in my heart, never to be forgotten. Until we meet again, another time, another place, I bid you bon voyage. C

James gave a heartfelt sob as Jenna wrapped her arms around him. If he could not have Christian near him, Jenna was the only other person who understood him totally. The letter in his hand allowed him to let go, though he would have dearly loved to have seen Christian - just once more.

The waves, gentle on the beach today, soughed against the shingle. The rhythmic sound soothed their troubled minds. James shivered involuntarily. He knew death was approaching. The light against the cliffs near Loe Bar seemed to be fading ever so slightly. He felt Jenna's arm tighten around him, trying to protect him from the inevitable, and then she released him slightly as a shadow obscured the sun. James looked up in disbelief at the figure in front of them. *Had he died?* He could still smell the salt air, and feel Jenna's arm about him, but…. 'Christian…. is it you?'

Christian knelt at James's feet and laid his head on his lap. Jenna let go of James as Christian's hands sought his. With tears in his eyes, Christian looked up at the man he loved.

'I was not allowed to walk hand in hand with you through life, James, but I should like to be with you and walk hand in hand with you towards the end of your life.'

*

A strange sense of the unreal settled on Loe House. Though Christian stayed with Jenna after James's death, every room seemed very empty, as though no-one had ever lived there. During those first few days, Jenna would stop what she was doing, imagining she could hear James coughing. She was bereft - more than she imagined she could ever be. Mealtimes were silent, sad affairs; neither she nor Christian seemed to have any appetite. As James's lawyer, Christian dealt with all the funeral arrangements and the many legal documents surrounding his death, which kept his mind from falling into despair.

When James's many friends descended on Loe House the day before his funeral, Jenna found that this crowd, normally vibrant was now quiet and sombre.

James was buried at St Winwaloe's Church, Gunwalloe, on what was a gloriously sunny day - a fitting day for someone like James. Everyone was visibly heartbroken, but Jenna felt for Christian the most.

Once the burial was over, Jenna and Christian requested that the wake should be a celebration of his life, instead of mourning his death, so everyone drank to his health from his well-stocked wine cellar.

Hillary laid her perfectly manicured hand on Jenna's arm. 'You *will* come up to London soon Jenna darling, won't you. Don't hide yourself away down here.'

'I don't know what I'm going to do just yet, Hillary.'

'Listen, darling, if life hands you lemons, open a bottle

of gin!' She winked. 'You'll be fine. James would want you to continue what you've been doing. Trust me. I've known him forever.'

Jenna gave a weak smile. 'I just don't have the heart to think of anything yet.'

'But your public awaits you, darling. Everyone who's anyone wants one of your paintings on their wall.'

'You do exaggerate, Hillary.'

'Nonsense darling, if I've told you once, I've told you a million times - I never exaggerate.' She curled her lips into a smile. 'Now, what say we all go for a dip in the sea tomorrow, in memory of James? What do you think Matthew? Glen?'

Glen frowned. 'But we can't do that Hill, it's Sunday tomorrow!'

Hillary raised an eyebrow. 'If god is watching us, the least we can do is be entertaining darling. What do you say Jenna, shall we have one last dip for James?'

'It would be a lovely idea, Hill.'

When everyone else decamped up to The Halzephron Inn, Jenna handed Christian a glass of brandy.

'What *are* your plans, Jenna?' he asked seriously.

'I don't know. Find somewhere to live I suppose. I shall miss this place though and I'll miss James very much.'

Christian gave a small laugh. 'This place belongs to you now, Jenna. You were his wife, so legally everything he owned is yours.'

Jenna dropped her head to one side. 'Everything?'

Christian nodded. 'This house, Bellevue Gardens, and all the royalties from his books, James didn't want you to want for anything ever again.'

Jenna's mouth formed a surprised O.

'James was not indifferent to the fact that you relinquished your chance of marrying someone you really loved to save us, Jenna. This is his way of saying thank you. As for myself, I can only offer any service you may need from me in the future, whatever it may be.'

'But, what about James's father, surely, he has some claim on his estate? I know from Hillary that James was estranged from him, but…'

'No, James made it perfectly clear. Everything goes to you and you alone. I've dealt with everything.'

Before everyone gathered at Loe House the next morning ready for the memorial swim, Christian bid Jenna a fond farewell and set off back to his wife and family in London.

The swim turned out to be more of a paddle, and soon everyone was back at Loe House, enjoying a nip of brandy and a hot bath before departing for their journey home.

'Well, goodbye, Jenna.' Hillary kissed her warmly.

Matthew too stepped forward, kissed her and gave a sympathetic smile.

'Goodbye to you both. Take care driving home.'

'We will. We're only going to Trevarno, then up to London next week, aren't we darling?'

Jenna's eyes flickered at the mention of the estate.

'If we don't see you before, we'll see you in August for the wedding, won't we?' Hillary asked.

Jessie smiled. 'Glen said you'd set a date. I'm sorry I meant to congratulate you sooner - I'm very happy for you both.'

'Thank you, darling.' She waggled her ring finger, which sported a fabulous diamond. 'We've kept the engagement very low key, what with James being so ill and all that. So, it's August the 10th at the Parish Church of Saint Michael's, Helston. The wedding breakfast is at Trevarno.'

Jenna glanced nervously at Matthew.

Hillary caught their furtive glances. 'What is it? What's the matter?'

'Maybe it's too soon after James's death for Jenna to attend our wedding,' Matthew said diplomatically.

Hillary's face tightened. 'I'd agree with you darling, but then we'd both be wrong. Of course, Jenna must attend. It's what James would have wanted.' She bent to kiss her again. 'Invitations will go out next week.' She took a deep breath. 'Damn James, he's going to miss my wedding.' Hillary pouted.

Jenna smiled softly. 'I'm sure he'll be there in spirit, Hill. James was never one to miss a good party.'

52

With everyone gone, Loe House was as quiet as a grave. All that could be heard was the song of the sea. Unable to muster any enthusiasm to paint, Jenna took solace in the cliff walk surrounding Gunwalloe peninsula. She had never felt so alone.

*

At Trevarno a letter had arrived for Matthew. It was presented to him on a silver platter, and he read the missive with interest.

My dear friend,

May I beg that you grant me this one last favour? Deliver this letter to Lyndon FitzSimmons.

Farewell, Matthew. Until we meet again.

James Blackwell

Matthew looked inside to find another envelope.

'Is everything all right Matthew?' his mother asked.

'Yes mother. I'm just going out. Tell Hillary, when she comes down for breakfast, that I'll be back shortly.'

Lyndon was on the bench outside Michael's cottage, sharpening his billhook when Matthew found him. He'd not informed Lyndon of James's death yet, he knew not why, he just hadn't.

They exchanged a smile as Matthew sat beside him.

'I've just been to your cottage. I thought you would be there now Edna has moved back to her father's place.'

'I've sort of being staying here with pa, until I decide what to do. Though I suspect I'm going to be in the way soon.'

Matthew raised his eyebrows.

'Pa and Gina.'

'Ah!'

'Ah, indeed.' Lyndon smiled.

'I have a letter for you Lyndon. It's from James Blackwell.'

Lyndon's shoulders visibly sank. 'What does he want I

wonder?'

'Very little I should think. I attended his funeral yesterday.'

Lyndon looked up blankly.

'He'd been ill for some time with lung disease.'

'Oh, well…I'm sorry for him…and for Jenna too,' he added. 'But why is James writing to me?'

'Well,' Matthew pushed his hands against his knees and stood up, 'I shall leave you to find out. Hillary will be wondering where I am. Oh, it looks as though you have another visitor.'

Sally Dunnet, the pretty nineteen-year-old-daughter of John Dunnet the gamekeeper, was walking towards them smiling.

Lyndon pushed the letter deep into his pocket and smiled back as Sally approached. Over the past few weeks, she'd taken a shine to Lyndon, and in turn Bramble had never been so groomed and pampered before.

'Hello, Lyndon, I'm just on my way to see Bramble,' she said shyly, smoothing down the folds of her pretty floral dress.

'Thank you, Sally, I should think Bramble will enjoy that.'

'Would you like to come with me?' she asked boldly.

'Maybe later.'

Her eyes shone in anticipation as she walked away with a dance in her step. A few steps down the road she turned to see if he was still watching her.

Lyndon sighed heavily.

'You could do worse, Lyndon,' Gina said, as she stepped out of the cottage. 'She'd be a safe pair of hands to help heal your broken heart.'

He glanced at Gina, noting her face was slightly flushed. 'Are you matchmaking?'

She laughed heartily. 'I wouldn't dare.'

'Oh, wouldn't you? I reckon it was you who got your Tommy and Jane Tandy together.'

'Well, I cannot tell a lie. They were both grieving for Jimmy. All I did was help two lonely people find each other.' She touched him on his shoulder. 'I don't like to see anyone lonely.'

'So, I see.' He gestured to his pa who had just joined them outside.

'Speaking of that, we do have some news for you, don't we Michael?'

Michael put his arm around Gina. 'We do. Lyndon my son, Gina has agreed to marry me - if that's all right with you?' He raised his brows hopefully.

'I couldn't be happier for you both,' he said hugging them.

'We're off to Helston to see the vicar. Do you want to come with us?'

'No, thank you, Pa, I've something I must do here.'

Gina gave Lyndon a knowing look.

*

Lyndon found a sunny bench to sit on in the Italian garden. Being early summer the garden beds were ablaze with colour, with an array of godetias, yellow and purple irises, pink dianthus, and a blousy purple clematis scrambled over the pagoda above him. He could never tire of the peace this garden brought him. Whenever the war came back to haunt him, as it often did, this tiny piece of Cornwall settled his nerves like nowhere else could.

He pulled the envelope from his pocket and laid it on his lap for a few moments before opening it. He read:

To Lyndon FitzSimmons
Trevarno Estate

My friend,

I feel I have done you a great injustice and I very much want to make amends. I recently learnt from your friend Matthew, that the woman I married was romantically attached to you. I swear I knew nothing of your attachment when I married her.

The circumstances of our marriage were complicated. In February, my name was linked to a very public scandal and Jenna - remarkable woman that she is, pushed her own happiness aside to help me in my hour of need. I am telling you, Lyndon that Jenna has been my wife in name only.

When I learned from Matthew that Jenna was the woman you loved, it grieved me deeply to think I'd taken her from you. To think you waited so long and patiently for her, only for me to whisk her away from under your nose. I hope you'll forgive me in time.

I admit, I should have released her from her commitment to me the moment I found out, but I thought perhaps you would grant me the luxury of keeping her until my end came. If you're reading this letter now, it will be because I have died.

I know Jenna is lonely, and someone as lovely and caring as she is, should not be alone. I plead to your good judgment and sensibilities to visit her. It is my dearest wish that now all obstacles are removed, that you take your place by her side and be together forever. It will be the last fitting love story this author can hope for.

I leave her fate in your hands.
Your obedient servant
James Blackwell

Lyndon folded the letter and put it back in the envelope. The dull ache in his heart, which he'd learned to suppress, began again in earnest. He thought of Sally Dunnet, with her, "safe pair of hands to heal his broken heart", waiting hopefully for him to join her. Putting the letter back in his pocket, he made his way to Bramble's field.

53

Jenna walked out into the hot, still, morning sunshine. Below the terrace, the sea, sleek and luminous, showed not a ruffle or ripple as it gently kissed the shingle beach. Despite her sorrow, the beautiful view sparked within her a passion to paint once more. Knowing James would approve of her renewed enthusiasm, she grabbed her straw hat and headed to the Halzephron Inn in search of Jack.

'Morning, Jenna,' the landlord greeted her with his normal familiarity.

'Morning, Richard, I wondered if Jack was around.'

'He's just bringing another barrel up. Do you want him to drive you somewhere?'

'Yes please - if he's not too busy.'

'Are you going far?'

'No, just over to Church Cove. I'd walk there, but as the day is so lovely, I feel as though I should at least try to capture the day on canvas. Unfortunately, the easel is too cumbersome to carry for that distance.'

*

Jenna set up her easel adjacent to St Winwaloe's Church, but before she did anything else she visited James's grave. There would be no headstone for at least six weeks, so she bent and placed a posy of pink thrift next to the small temporary wooden cross.

'I miss you, James. You made the world a happier place for us all.'

Returning to her easel, she looked out at the seascape before her. It was low tide, and the sandy banks were clearly visible, but the luminescent sea looked gloriously inviting, though James had always warned her not to swim at low tide. He'd been caught in a riptide once that pulled him right around the headland to the beach behind the church. A dip in the sea would have to wait until the tide turned.

She secured her hat and pulled down the sleeves of her

blouse, so as not to burn in the sun, dipped her brush in the jar of water and selected her first colour. Totally immersed in her work, her packed lunch lay forgotten in her bag. Painting occupied her mind like nothing else could. It also stopped the dreadful aching loneliness from engulfing her.

Eventually she sat down and took a drink from her flask. No one had disturbed her all day - the beach was completely deserted. Kicking off her sandals, she buried her toes into the coolness of the sand. Releasing the ribbon tie of her hat, she shook her hair free. The light breeze which gently ruffled the sea, gave cool relief to the damp nape of her neck. Cradling her knees with her arms, she watched the soft lace-edged waves licking the shoreline. A shaft of brilliant sunlight glittered like sparkling diamonds across the surface of the water.

"My favourite time is late afternoon when the water glitters in the sun like millions of diamonds. I love to just lose myself in the jewels of the sea." The memory of Lyndon's words pulled at her heartstrings.

She sat motionless under the cobalt blue sky. 'I love you Lyndon, I always have and always will,' she whispered into the breeze.

Dropping her head back she let the sun warm her face. James had left her everything she could possibly need to make a life for herself. It was perhaps time to go back to London - Cornwall held too many memories.

The heat of the day and the sound of the waves seduced her. Peeling her clothes from her hot body, she walked naked towards the water's edge. The sea dazzled her with its brilliance as she stepped into its silky coolness. Plunging into its embrace, she took Lyndon's advice to lose herself amongst the jewels of the sea. With her head back and her arms outstretched, she floated for a few minutes as though in a dream.

Something brushed her fingers, seaweed perhaps. A second touch was followed by the feeling of a hand as it curled gently around hers.

Jenna turned, shielding her eyes from the blinding sun. Her heart shifted, and her eyes misted, as she drew a deep trembling breath. There before her, droplets of water glistened on Lyndon's handsome face. He smiled gently and without speaking, he gathered her into his arms and kissed her. Nothing would ever part them again.

∽ ∾

If you enjoyed The Glittering Sea, please share the love of this book by writing a short review on Amazon. x

Printed in Great Britain
by Amazon